HYMNS OF BLUE HOLLOW

BY

Kemma Marshall

To everyone who didn't know they had a choice—

that freedom was waiting for them to claim their

life.

Content Warnings

This story contains mature themes, including sexually explicit content, nudity, profanity, depictions of violence, and sensitive topics such as underage sexual assault from the victim's perspective. Reader discretion is advised.

This book is a work of historical fiction that portrays perspectives and events from the 1940s to provide an authentic portrayal of the period. Some of the views and behaviors represented are not those of the author and are included to address themes such as racism and social attitudes of the era.

Playlist

"Girl"—SYML

"All My Tears" Ane Brun

"Savagery"—Lissom

Winter Ghosts"—Jesse Marchant

"How to Disappear Completely"—Ane Brun

"Hold My Hand"—Hugo Barriol

"Where's my Love"—SYML

"Without You"—Ursine Vulpine

"Wicked Game"—Ursine Vulpine

"Fear of the Water"—SYML

"I Waited for You"—Daniel Norgren

"An Opening"—Charlie Cunningham

"Long Way From Home"—Hugo Barriol

"Stay"—Hugo Barriol

"Reborn"—Sod Ven

"Now You Don't"—Ocie Elliott

"To Protect"—Mackintosh Braun

When It's All Over"—Raign

"Take My Leave of You"—Olafur Arnalds

Author's Note

This story is written in an emotionally textured style, with a lyrical touch, honoring the narrative traditions of writers like Alice Walker, Toni Morrison, and Delia Owens—women whose work has shaped how language can hold both beauty and sorrow in the same breath.

The pacing is often intentional, with paragraph breaks used for rhythm and silence, or to push the current forward when the moment demands. Dialogue carries the heartbeat of the characters' inner lives. I've allowed space for the sensory, the poetic, and the unspoken—trusting the reader to sit with both grace and grit as they unfold.

Thank you for stepping into the world of *Hymns of Blue Hollow* with open eyes and an open heart.

Prologue: Tennessee, 2023

In the fervent, beating heart of Appalachia, the Blue Hollow Hills stretched out like old hands beneath a canopy of timeworn trees. In its shadows, the Old Reed Estate stood in quiet dignity. The house, with its weathered charm, hinted at wealth and history—a place where stories lived in the very walls and were whispered by the winds through the cracks of the old windows.

At the end of a long-pebbled driveway, by the painted mailbox, stood Marissa, an inquisitive girl with unruly curls and a gaze bright with wonder. She lingered by the spot, feeling the breeze's soft caress as she searched the horizon.

But when nothing showed up, she shuffled her feet, frustrated. Waiting wasn't easy, but she was determined to do her very best. It wasn't often she was given such an important task.

A red ladybug on a wooden post soon caught her attention. Marissa reached out a small finger, but just as it might have crawled into her palm, it spread its wings and lifted away, leaving her hand empty.

The distant rumble of an engine quickly shifted her focus. She straightened—her disappointment gone—as her eyes locked onto the white vehicle creeping along the narrow road.

Was he finally here? She hurried back to the mailbox, her breath quickening as the wheels drew closer, knowing today was special. Today, she was waiting for something important.

Her heart soared as the postman leaned out with an amused smile, passing her a large padded envelope. The weight of it sparked Marissa's curiosity—her fingers wrapped tight around it, feeling the mystery nestled inside.

The mailman tried to hand her the rest—a handful of letters and glossy catalogs—but she was already halfway up the driveway, clutching the package to her chest.

Excitement bubbled within her as she kicked off her shoes, running across the grass. When she neared the large front door, she paused, looking up at the brass knocker—its imposing lion face gleaming in the sun.

"Grrr…" she said playfully, challenging it as she nudged it open.

The house was cool, smelling of freshly waxed floors and lavender. Newly renovated with a fresh coat of paint, it still radiated with the presence of its former self, holding the murmurs of conversations long gone.

Sunlight streamed through the windows, casting soft, dancing patterns on the floor as if the past and present were waltzing together.

Marissa tiptoed down the hall, her steps light as if not to disturb the spirits still lingering there, her eyes glancing at the old photos hanging on the wall.

When she reached her great-grandmother's office, she lingered, peeking her head into the room.

Neatly lined bookshelves cradled volumes collected over years of study and care. There, seated behind a large oak desk, Marissa's great-grandmother exuded a timeless beauty. Her caramel skin, silver hair, and graceful hands spoke of a life lived with purpose. Though in her late eighties, her eyes held a deep, unwavering wisdom that softened with affection as she looked up at her great-granddaughter.

"Grandmaw, it's here!" Marissa said, raising the large package, her grin stretching from ear to ear.

Her great-grandmother set aside her papers, a hint of amusement on her face.

"Is it now?" she said, reaching for the envelope. "Let's see what we have here."

The little girl handed it over, her eyes wide with anticipation, watching as her great-grandmother's fingers worked patiently at the edges of the package. She peeled back the layers with care, as if unwrapping something sacred.

Inside, cradled in delicate tissue paper, was a large, leather-bound book. The title, Hymns of Blue Hollow, gleamed in the light, the embossed gold letters catching the eye.

As her great-grandmother lifted the cover, she let the thick, creamy pages fall beneath her fingers like a fan. Marissa's mind wandered to the untold stories hidden inside, tucked between the pretty pictures.

There was a light in her great-grandmother's eyes, a joy Marissa had never seen before. It glowed with love for the book she cradled.

A distant murmur of voices and laughter floated through an open window, carried on the evening breeze. In the backyard, a gathering had formed, their sounds mingling with the calls of birds settling for the night, blending together in a soft, almost otherworldly song.

The little girl, unable to hold back any longer, stepped closer.

"Ya happy, Grandmaw?" she asked.

"Yes, dear," her great-grandmother said with a gentle sigh and secretive smile.

"Just need me a few minutes, honey," she added. "Then I'll come on out, and we'll look through it together."

Marissa's head dipped in a quiet nod, not a trace of disappointment on her face.

Unable to contain her excitement, the little girl danced her way out of the room, her skirt spinning in a wide arc as she twirled once, drawing a low, rich chuckle from her great-grandmother. With a final, playful bow, she slipped out, the door shutting behind her.

Left in the room's hush, the old woman eased back into the embrace of her chair, opening the book back up as if she were discovering it anew.

Nestled within the pages, a sparrow sat in its nest. Each feather so tenderly drawn it felt only a heartbeat away from taking flight, as if the wind itself might coax it free.

In the background, faint words of a hymn lingered, almost indistinguishable.

Her finger rested on the picture—the years and stories held in its fibers. The surrounding air pulsed with the world beyond, but she sat in the stillness, savoring the moment that connected her to both the past and the present.

Letting out a breath, Marissa's great-grandmother closed the book, resting it in her lap as she let her thoughts drift through the echoes of time, gone but never forgotten.

Chapter 1: Sparrow

In the early spring of 1941, the eastern mountains of Tennessee hummed with the life of a swift river, its waters weaving through thick woods, bringing with it the first breath of the season.

Esther Primm sat on a flat rock by the riverbank, her long dark hair falling in untamed waves around her freckled face, giving her the look of a girl younger than her years. Her clothes, worn thin and ragged, clung to her slender frame, a testament to the hard life she led in those hills.

The river was Esther's quiet church, a place where the earth seemed to speak only to her. When she prayed, it wasn't in words—those always failed her, sticking in her throat. Instead, she listened. The wind, she thought, might carry God's voice, tucked somewhere in its soft whistle through the trees.

The murmur of the water below whispered back, as though a distant choir hummed a slow and gentle "Amen," reminding her that maybe the Almighty spoke in the small things, too.

Most days she watched the leaves float down the current, harboring a silent longing to be one of them—carried away to anywhere.

In her lap rested an old hymn book, its pages weathered, each crease a testament to years of handling. It had become her canvas now, a surface for her artistry.

Tight between her fingers, she held what remained of a chiseled pencil. Leaning in close, her brow furrowed as the lead glided across the paper, tracing the fine, interwoven lines of a sparrow's nest, each stroke as careful as if she were tending to the fragile twigs herself.

Esther approached her work with utmost care, finding in it a sense of control she seldom experienced, a rare pleasure life allowed her.

As her drawing took shape, the river's rippling call, the rustling leaves, and the birds' chatter slipped into the background, overtaken by the rhythm of her hand. The pencil danced across the page, and with it, a quiet joy bloomed inside her, so soft and unexpected that it coaxed a smile to her lips.

Just as she was about to look up, a sharp rustling in the brush behind her shattered her peace.

She snapped the hymn book shut and tucked it into the patched pocket of her overalls.

In one smooth motion, she stood, grabbing an empty bucket beside her, hiding her reprieve under the guise of a simple task—fetching water.

Her ears strained as she waited.

When the rustling died away, she let out the breath she'd been holding. Then she leaned over to fill the tin pail before starting up the hill, water sloshing with each step.

The path up was steep and rocky, terrain that could twist an ankle if one wasn't careful. But Esther knew every inch by heart. Each stone and root was as familiar to her as the lines on her hands, which had toughened over years of hard labor.

The old still crouched on a slope, near invisible unless you knew it. Its rough-hewn structure had weathered countless seasons, blending into the land as if it had always been there.

As she neared the blackened kettle, her earlier peace gave way to the familiar knot of anxiety that always came with thoughts of her grandmother. The contraption seemed bound to the old woman, as much a part of her as bone and flesh.

The copper distillery resembled an ancient relic—oxidized, patched, yet still working. It represented both survival and the chains that kept her bound to the mountains.

Gran—Pearl Primm—was already there, her formidable frame emerging from the shadows, an apparition of haunting authority.

She carried an armful of wood with a force that defied her age, each step revealing a strength uncommon for someone so advanced in years. Without a word, she dropped the bundle beside the still, the pieces clattering to the ground, making Esther flinch.

Gran's eyes narrowed as she inspected the large pot, her expression darkening with dissatisfaction.

Even the smallest imperfection appeared to be a monumental failure under her gaze. Those once-bright eyes, now dulled by years of hardship, still held a sharpness that could cut through the toughest hides.

To Esther, Gran's approval was something she had been chasing for as long as she could remember.

"Ya swab it out good?" Gran growled.

"Yes'm, Gran. I cleaned da pot good," Esther said with a timid nod.

Not convinced, Gran leaned in closer, scrutinizing the inside of the vessel. Her warm breath, thick with the scent of tobacco and old age, puffed out in clouds that hung in the chilly morning air.

After what seemed to stretch into an eternity, she slammed the lid down with a sharp clang that echoed through the trees, startling a nearby bird into flight.

"We'll come back in a few days and stoke it up right," Gran mumbled, her words rough and ground down as she pointed a crooked finger to an old tarp.

Together, the two women moved with a rhythm that spoke of years spent in each other's company, their hands dancing through the pine boughs and dead leaves. The forest loomed as a deep and brooding presence, its silent trees bearing witness to the illegal operation concealed beneath the woodland floor.

Blanketed in foliage, the still vanished from sight, as though swallowed by the earth, leaving no trace it had ever been there.

Esther had long adapted to the grueling demands, her fingers stiff with cold and effort.

Yet, she couldn't deny there was a certain satisfaction in the task, a sense of purpose that came from knowing she was doing something necessary, something her family had done for generations.

Gran, content with their work, pointed to two brown jugs resting against the base of a tree.

"Ya get both those," she instructed.

Esther moved, cradling the heavy vessels as she followed her grandmother to the nearby wagon.

The scruffy mule hitched to the buckboard looked as worn and weary as Esther felt, its dark eyes carrying the weight of countless burdens, its coat tangled with neglect.

Placing the jugs near the front, Esther nestled them among the others as Gran drew an old tarp across the lot, stacking white oak baskets on top—a disguise plain, but practiced.

Esther stepped back from the wooden side, unable to hide the persistent pang of disappointment. The morning had whispered promises of change, hinting at something beyond the ordinary confines of her world. But as the sun climbed higher, it brought no transformation, only the same plain reality.

She remained just a girl in rags, tethered to a path she could scarcely influence.

The yearning to break free, to discover what lay beyond the Blue Hollow Hills, was a constant ache.

With each passing year, those dreams pushed further away, delicate birds flying out of reach, leaving her on the ground watching them disappear.

Her aging grandparents needed her more each day, and Pawdad's once keen eyes had dimmed to shadows of their former sharpness. With his sight failing, the burden of hunting had shifted to Esther, a task that tore at her insides and clashed with the quiet gentleness she had tried to preserve.

Gran caught a glimpse of Esther's expression, and for a fleeting moment her eyes stilled, a rare crack in the fortress of hardness she'd built.

The softness was brief, gone almost as soon as it appeared. As the familiar sternness reclaimed her features, she urged the mule forward. The wagon creaked and groaned as it trundled over the uneven ground, its wooden wheels biting into the soft earth.

After a few feet, Gran halted, pulling back hard on the reins as her gaze drifted out.

She sat there in silence for a moment as the world seemed to hold its breath. Finally, she let out a deep sigh.

"Well… come on," she said. Her words were thick with meaning, a subtle invitation wrapped in layers of unspoken expectations.

Surprise flickered in Esther's eyes. With a quick, reckless movement, she jumped up to the wagon seat beside Gran. Her heart raced with a mix of anticipation and confusion.

To Esther, it was a small victory, an inkling that perhaps, just perhaps, things could be different.

But Gran's kindness was short-lived.

"Don't be thinkin' you're fixin' to tag along with me every time, now," she said sharply. "Ya ain't cut out fer town folk. Ya hear me?"

Esther nodded, her excitement fading into the familiar pull of resignation.

"Yes'm," she said, her eyes dropping to the weathered wood beneath her.

The mule trudged forward, heaving the wagon onto the narrow dirt path that twisted through the hills. The woods receded, giving way to open fields where wildflowers danced in the breeze.

As they traveled, the scent of peach blossoms wove through the air, their delicate petals spilling over a wooden fence that lined the road—a fragrant barrier against the encroaching greenery.

The rhythmic click of the mule's hooves echoed, the sole sound methodical as they drove past the procession of fruit trees.

Esther couldn't help but feel a shift deep inside her. Here, the air appeared lighter, as if it, too, had cast off the darkness of the woods.

Beyond the fruit trees, the Old Reed Estate came into view, blending into the landscape as though it had always belonged there.

Clarissa Johnson's house bore the gentle wear of time, yet stood untouched by ruin.

It was a two-story structure, set back from the road with a long gravel drive. There was a simple, inviting charm to it, much as an old friend might wait at the door, ready to welcome you home after a long journey.

The estate had always remained a mystery to Esther, something just out of reach. She was certain it held more than what could be seen—filled with untold stories hidden beneath the worn floorboards and behind the weathered walls.

She sometimes let herself wonder what it would feel like to wake up there in the morning, to press her face against those tall windows.

Clarissa, a full-figured Black woman in her mid-sixties, moved across the front porch. Her skin, velvet-worn, still carried a whisper of the beauty it once held. Near her, square white columns framed a row of hanging pots, the lush ferns tumbling over as if they'd grown wild.

As she swept, a long silver braid down her back swayed with each stroke.

When the wagon came into view, she paused, resting her weight against the broom handle.

Her calm, knowing eyes followed Gran and Esther as they passed, her gaze unhurried, as though someone who had seen a lifetime of such moments.

Not a word was shared, not even a nod, only the silence between them, thick and familiar, as if it had somehow been silently agreed upon.

Esther had always felt a pull at her when it came to that woman, a thread of connection she couldn't explain, though not a single exchange had passed between them. She could see that the figure on the porch carried herself with dignity, a strength as steady as the land she claimed.

But there was a wall between them, like the old fence that ran along the road. They stayed on opposite sides, connected by land but never crossing.

The buckboard rolled on, passing the caretaker's home. Small, with a stone façade, it stood close to the road as if it didn't dare ask for more space. Roses, not yet blooming, sat in neatly trimmed bushes that softened the rough edges of the building.

In the yard, the morning air filled with the sound of laughter as two lively children ran about. Ten-year-old Benjamin Huggler, with his dark, serious features, and his spirited six-year-old sister Rebecca, a whirlwind of black hair, played their games of pretend.

They galloped across the green grass like wild horses, the ground soft beneath them as they whinnied and chased the wind.

As Esther and Gran rode past, the children's laughter faded, their small feet scurrying to the fence. Wide-eyed, they watched, curious and bright as the day itself.

Benjamin, his chin resting on the rail, let a shy grin creep across his face. Rebecca, always eager, waved with both hands as if she were greeting the entire world.

Esther's lips curled, lifting her cheeks.

Their cheerful spirits stirred something she kept dead inside most days, a part of herself she seldom let escape. Unable to resist, she lifted her hand to wave back.

But Gran's elbow jabbed hard into her ribs, knocking the gesture clean from her—a rough reminder of the line that still divided them.

"Pay no mind to them…" Gran muttered, slipping in a word Esther had never heard before, though its meaning was clear. Gran's tone was as cold as the shadow she cast.

"Yes'm, Gran," Esther whispered, though the ugliness of those words painted the air gray with discomfort.

They felt mean, unwarranted, and not fit for such beautiful children. The words sat in her chest as if they were stones, and no matter how she swallowed, they wouldn't go down.

"Devil don' put his seed in 'em. Cursed 'em with that dark skin," Gran mumbled with disdain.

Even with Gran's harshness lingering, Esther couldn't help but glance back at the children, who had quickly returned to their play.

A small smile slipped across her lips once again—as the wagon carried her farther away. That moment of connection had felt good. Their joy. Their innocence. The way they laughed suggested that the world still held a goodness she'd hoped for.

As they traveled on, the road unfurled before them, snaking through the foothills and drawing them farther from the Blue Hollows.

Esther tugged at the loose denim of her ill-fitting overalls, her fingers brushing against the dried dirt caked on her pant leg. She tried to rub it away, but the grime was stubborn, determined to stay. Gran sat rigid beside her, eyes fixed ahead, unmoved by the bumps and sways of the trail.

The strain of what lay ahead in Larkin twisted tight inside Esther, a knot she couldn't undo. The wagon rocked beneath them, and she shifted, hoping to shake off the discomfort, but it clung to her, stubborn as the mud on her worn knees.

She had wanted to come, desperate to see life outside of the hills, but she knew it didn't come without a price.

It was springtime, and she was sure it had been at least a year since she had last been allowed to go to Larkin. Each visit seemed farther apart than the one before. But what lay ahead had to be crossed, managed as best it could—if that's what you could call it—before she might let herself enjoy the trip.

The wagon gave a loud creak as it rolled over a protruding rock, jarring her from her thoughts for a moment. But she drifted back easily, remembering the small drawing she had made that morning—a sparrow's nest.

Like that nest—fragile and tender—she, too, perched on the edge of survival, vulnerable to the wind and rain.

But within that tiny home, there was something fierce—a will to protect, to hold on to life, even when the world was hell-bent on destruction.

Esther wondered if she would ever find her own courage to build a life that was hers.

The thought seemed distant, almost impossible, as she glanced over at Gran's stern profile.

Chapter 2: Dark Dealings

The old church loomed over the plowed fields, a forgotten relic, its once-bright white paint curling into brittle strips that fluttered in the breeze like little ghosts. The steeple, rusted and jagged, pointed crookedly into the sky, a broken mast stranded in a sea of tilled earth.

It stood stark against the well-tended house beside it, as a faded shadow of what it once was.

Clive Jones' residence remained pristine. A white picket fence, too clean for the dust-filled air, wrapped around the building. Springtime flowers bloomed, the garden almost defiant in its order, making the house feel detached from the fields around it.

The wagon jostled past the church, its wheels thudding over the uneven ground until it slowed to a stop. The mule lowered its head—an opportunity to nibble on a patch of green.

Gran's face tightened, eyes narrowed, and with a grunt, she climbed down from the buckboard, her boots hitting the earth with a dull thump.

She moved quick and rough. Without a word, she walked to the sideboard and smacked it firmly with her hand, the sharp sound cutting through the air with clarity.

A warning, plain as day.

"Ya stay put," Gran said.

Esther nodded, huddled small on the wagon seat, watching her grandmother disappear around the corner.

The air was warm and smelled of the promise of a storm, despite the sun blazing on Esther's back. An icy knot built in her chest, making her tremble in the sweltering humidity.

Time dragged on, each second stretching until she felt sure it would snap.

Finally, Gran reappeared—but she wasn't alone.

Clive Jones followed her, and his very presence sent a shiver down Esther's toes.

In his mid-forties, with the years etched into his round features, he had clearly overindulged in excess of everything. Thin hair clung to his slick face, and the fabric of his tight-fitting suit was shiny, pulling at the seams.

In his hand, he held a lantern, though it was midday.

His mouth curled into a greasy smirk as he eyed Esther, pleased to see her.

Agitated, Gran yanked the wagon's backboard loose, slamming it down with a sharp crack. The wood groaned, but she didn't care. She was angry, and when Gran was upset, it settled in the air like a storm cloud.

"Ya get yer lazy ass out 'n start haulin' them jugs to the cellar," Gran snapped with authority.

Esther slid off the seat, her hands already reaching to grab the cold stoneware.

Their rough texture steadied her as she worked to block out Clive's focused gaze. Unwanted, it lingered on her like something dirty.

Set on avoiding even a casual exchange, she kept her eyes down, focusing on the task in front of her.

Gran snatched the lantern from the man's hand, sparking it into life with a swift flick of her wrist. The flame flickered as she turned her gaze back on him, her expression set hard as stone.

"The least ya could do, Clive, is help," Gran growled, "seein' as how you've been stealin' my money."

He chuckled, leaning lazily against the wagon. His smirk widened, turning more devilish.

"Now, Auntie Pearl, I ain't stealing nothin'. Law's crackin' down on runners, and white likker don't fetch what it used to."

Gran's eyes narrowed.

"Ya ain't paid me fer two loads. Pawdad ain't got no coffee to drink, and Esther done clean wore out her winter shoes."

Her tone dropped to a dangerous whisper that sent chills racing up Esther's spine.

"Can't even afford to make mash."

Clive's gaze shifted to the girl's bare feet, his expression twisting into a sneer.

"Now, are ya sure she'd even wear them?" he asked, pulling the lantern from Gran.

Pretending she didn't hear him, Esther tightened her grip on the load, making her way toward the church cellar.

Her movements were slow and deliberate as she focused on keeping the liquid steady.

Clive's heavy footsteps trailed close behind, echoing as he followed her down the stairwell.

The entrance waited ahead, its wooden planks worn smooth from years of use.

Clive stepped past her with an exaggerated flourish, flinging the door open as if mocking a gentleman, before stepping aside.

Esther paused at the threshold as the cellar yawned before her, the darkness swallowing the weak light.

Inside, the air was damp, carrying the scent of earth and old wood. A low ceiling and narrow walls closed in around her, tightening the space and making it feel even smaller than it was.

Gran brushed past her, hurrying to the far end where rows of jugs stood scattered in disarray. She gestured at them with a grunt.

"Ya need to stack 'em tighter," she demanded.

Esther nodded and set down her load. She reached for the jug Gran had pointed out, but as she lifted it, something felt off—it was far too light. She froze in confusion.

"Gran—these ain't got nothin' in 'em," she said.

Gran's head snapped up, her mouth drawn down.

"What?" She grabbed the jug from Esther's hands and shook it, the emptiness quiet in the small space.

Her face twisted in rage as she whirled around just as Clive descended the steps, the last of their load balanced in his arms.

"All you got is empties!" Gran's temper rose. "Where's all the likker I brought ya last time?"

"Calm yerself. I ain't keepin' it all here. What if there was a raid or something?" he said, oozing sweetness.

Gran's glare lingered on him.

But she relented, grumbling as she stomped back up the stairs, leaving her granddaughter alone with him in the suffocating dark.

Esther swallowed hard, the taste of the stale air holding to her tongue.

The flickering lantern cast long shadows across the walls, ghostly jagged shapes.

But it wasn't the shadows she was afraid of—it was her cousin Clive.

His eyes haunted her, not looking away as he watched her every move. His very presence wrapped around her—a dark cloud.

"How come ya ain't brushed your hair all pretty for me today?" Clive's voice slithered out with a mock affection.

Esther stayed silent, focus locked straight ahead as she hurried toward the stairs.

But before she could reach them, Clive blocked her path, his broad body creating a wall that filled the space, preventing her from getting past.

"Ah, my sweet Esther," he said, his breath hot against her ear. "Come here and show me a lil' bit of affection."

Revulsion shuddered through her, but she met his eyes, her own filled with fire despite the terror coiling inside her.

"Why'd I do a silly thing like that," she said, her voice trembling but strong, "when I hates ya?"

Clive's smile faltered for just a moment, his hand creeping toward her, but Esther was quick.

She jerked back, slipping out of his reach, her body hitting the earth wall of the cellar.

"Ah, no, you don't," he said, unfazed by her remark.

Before he could say or do anything more, Gran's voice cut through, sharp as steel from the top of the stairs.

"You let her be."

He paused. The smirk slithered back onto his face as he turned to the door, to Gran. There was a malice that burned bright in his eyes.

"I'm just talking. All I'm doing is talkin'." He looked back at Esther. "Did I hurt you, my precious? Now ya know, I'd never do a thing like that."

Esther didn't answer, her body stiff as she pushed past him, hurrying up the creaky stairs.

Gran watched, her expression unreadable, before turning her attention back to Clive, who followed behind.

Gran stretched out her hand, waiting.

"Ya forget, I know your nature, and it's a wicked one. Preachin' mornin' till night don't change a thing," she said.

The silence between them swelled, hinting at more than the words spoken, as Clive glared back at her.

"Now hand me what's mine. I ain't got a cent to my name," the woman finally said. "Need some things fer this girl as well."

Clive's smug look faltered as he begrudgingly pulled a few crumpled dollars from his pocket, shoving them toward her with an irritated look.

She took the money, not saying a word. Her eyes were tight as she counted the bills, then stuffed them into her apron, her movements quick and hard.

Esther stood by the back of the wagon, her heart pounding wildly as she watched the exchange. The tension between her grandmother and cousin was something she didn't want to be a part of.

She knew this wouldn't be the last of it—Clive would never forget the defiance either of them had shown him.

As they climbed up into the wagon, Gran's face stayed locked in those hard lines that had carried her through years of struggle.

But when Esther glanced over at her, she noticed the creases etched into her brow—so subtle most wouldn't see, but unmistakable to her. She wondered what churned behind that tough exterior, what thoughts Gran kept hidden beneath that steely gaze.

Even with their dependence on Clive for running the moonshine, Gran stood tall, unbending in the face of his intimidation, calling him what he was. But it didn't stop Esther from worrying or from feeling the tension that came with empty pockets, or the thin thread of survival the Primms clung to.

Esther had heard whispers of prohibition, stories of men who'd risked everything only to lose it all—lives cut short by fleeting profit.

That history sat heavy on her shoulders, reminding her that every day they walked a fine line, knowing full well it could snap without warning.

Chapter 3: The Gift

The small town of Larkin had seen better days. Tucked deep in the rural stretch of Tennessee, it held on to its stubborn charm, a patchwork of old and new. Some folks clung to their ways, their creaky wagons rolling along dirt roads, just as they had for generations. Others had let go, traded in horses for the hum of engines, the slow creep of modern life inching its way in.

But even here, far from the battlefields of WWII across the ocean, the war had found them. It cast its shadow over Larkin, pressing on every face and tightening every belt. Finances hung by a threadbare edge, the uncertainty of the times drifting through the dust-filled air.

Esther and Gran made their way down the town's main strip, their old wagon standing out—a relic in contrast to the sleek automobiles parked here and there.

As they neared Paulson's Mercantile, Esther felt a small flutter in her chest. These visits didn't come often.

The shop was modest, its storefront marked by a hand-lettered sign hanging over the entrance, worn but still legible. As the bell above the door jingled, the women stepped in, baskets clutched in their arms. Inside, the air smelled rich—ground coffee and dried tobacco, a variety of scents that enticed shoppers.

Margie Mae Paulson, a round, middle-aged woman with a ready smile, looked up from a small ladder as they entered. Her hair, neat and styled, and her double-breasted dress hinted at the latest city fashions—a minor rebellion against the conservative world of the countryside.

"Well, hello, Pearl," she greeted Gran, disbelief threading through her tone. Her eyes shifted to Esther, the smile widening in recognition.

"Esther, isn't it? Ain't seen you in ages. Thought ya might've up and moved."

Gran waved off the small talk, cutting through.

"Don't suppose any of 'em baskets sold?"

Margie Mae's grin flickered, dimming with her words. "No," she said, regret in her eyes. "Sure wish somethin' had… Might be worth takin' 'em to Jasper—tourists always passin' through there. They'd likely snatch 'em up real quick. Y'all do such fine work."

Gran's laugh came bitter and sharp.

"She ain't got no weaver's hands. Too damn dumb."

Each word landed with a cold, hard blow, aimed perfectly to wound. Esther kept her eyes down, refusing to show how much they stung.

The shopkeeper glanced at Esther, her disapproval sparked by Gran's cruelty, not the girl herself.

"Well now," Margie Mae said, searching Esther's face. "I reckon you've got a gift for somethin'. Lots of things to do in this here world."

Esther shook her head, giving a weak smile, her shoulders drawing inward, as if trying to vanish entirely.

Her grandmother's harshness was nothing new, but she secretly wished she wouldn't do it in front of other people. She wanted the people of Larkin to like her, to accept her, despite her backward ways.

Gran, tired of the small talk, changed the conversation.

"Need a couple pounds of dark roast and some sugar," she said impatiently.

Margie Mae nodded, turning to fetch the items. But as she moved, her gaze lingered on Esther, soft and kind.

"She's a bright woman," she added over her shoulder, her words filled with sincerity. "I can see it in her eyes."

Gran paid her no mind, her attention already elsewhere in the store.

But Margie Mae's words hung in the air, a gentle offering that Esther didn't quite know how to receive. She gave another smile to the shopkeeper, briefly locking eyes with her. Margie Mae, noticing her response, gave her a playful wink, making her smile grow.

This was the part of the trip into town that Esther looked forward to. Over the years, the kindness of the storekeeper had meant more to her than she could ever have known. She remembered, as a young child, Margie Mae leaning over the counter and giving her a handful of jelly beans, her face beaming— a rare treat for a poor child from the hills.

Drawn to a display of fancy soaps, Esther made her way over to the front counter. She eyed the pretty packages, each bar wrapped in colorful printed paper and tied with a fancy ribbon. Her fingers traced the smooth surface, drawn in by the beauty of its floral wrapping. She lifted one to her nose, letting the sweet scent wash over her. For just a moment, she allowed herself to linger in that small pleasure—the delicate soap between her hands, the world outside forgotten.

Margie Mae, however, noticed the way Esther's eyes lingered, her expression one of yearning.

As the two women left the store and headed back to the wagon, the shopkeeper followed, her footsteps a whisper on the front stoop.

Gran, already fussing with the hitch and the mule's harness, moved with the steady assurance of someone well-versed in the craft.

Esther stepped toward the buckboard, ready to climb up to her seat, when Margie Mae caught her arm. Startled, she looked down to find Margie Mae's warm, knowing eyes meeting hers.

With a quick glance to ensure Gran's attention was elsewhere, Margie Mae slipped a small, prettily wrapped bar of soap into Esther's hand.

"Shh—this is for ya, hun," she said. "Every girl deserves to feel pretty now and then."

Esther stared at the gift, her heart swelling with a mix of gratitude and surprise that she hadn't known she could feel.

Though small, it held a depth of kindness.

With care, she tucked the soap into the pocket of her worn overalls, her fingers wrapping around it as if it were a treasure, something to hold close in a world that often gave so little.

"Thank ya," Esther said, her voice no louder than the footsteps of a mouse on the floor.

Their eyes met briefly, and in that exchange, Margie Mae saw the vulnerability the girl from the hills tried so hard to hide—the part of her still yearning for the gentleness she rarely found. With a last nod, the woman stepped back, letting her climb into the wagon.

Gran, none the wiser, finished her inspection with a grunt and took her place beside Esther, snapping the reins.

As they made their way towards the mountains, the sky thickened with the promise of an approaching storm. Heavy clouds gathered on the horizon, their edges tinged with the ominous hues of impending rain. A tension settled over the landscape, the kind that made even the trees hold their breath, waiting for the inevitable downpour.

The first drops splattered against the wagon's weathered wood, cold and stinging, as they traveled the familiar dirt road that wound through the countryside like a ribbon of brown earth.

Gran's mood, already sour, curdled further as the rain fell harder. She snapped the reins with a harshness that made the mule jerk forward, her drawl rising to cut through the storm's growing noise.

"Get up! Move, ya lazy beast," Gran shouted, her anger biting against the drum of rain.

"Should've left Larkin sooner, shouldn't have dawdled like we done," she added.

Esther didn't notice her grandmother's words—her thoughts were on the small, precious thing hidden in her pocket.

She slipped her hand inside and touched the soap, feeling the ribbon tied to it, a delicate reminder of a kindness she hadn't expected. For a heartbeat, she dared to peek at the bar, her eyes lingering on it before she quickly stuffed it back into hiding.

But Gran's keen vision caught the movement. Suspicion flared, a spark to dry kindling.

Her hand shot out, rough and demanding, clamping down on her wrist like iron.

"What ya got there, girl?" Gran's voice was sharp, her eyes pinning Esther as she searched for guilt in the way she clung to the pocket.

She tugged hard, attempting to pry the soap from her granddaughter's grip.

"Nothin'… I ain't got nothin'," Esther said, fear lacing her words. Her fingers pressed the bar deeper into the thin fabric, trying to hide something precious from a hawk's claws.

Her grandmother wasn't buying it.

She growled low, yanking the reins so hard the mule jerked to a stop, its hooves sinking into the rain-soaked earth.

Mud splattered as Gran swung her full attention back to Esther, her face twisted with an anger that had long learned how to turn itself into punishment.

"Ya steal somethin'?" her voice cracked with the snap of a whip.

"I ain't steal nothin'. It's mine," Esther said, though her heart beat like the wings of a trapped bird, desperate, frantic.

She tugged away, trying to maintain the distance she could feel slipping away between them.

Gran's eyes burned.

"I saw it. You took somethin' that ain't yers."

"Liars and thieves rot in hell—you want the devil at ya door?"

"Hand it over!"

Esther's defiance broke free with a cry, and in one swift motion, she scrambled out of the wagon, her feet hitting the ground with a squelch as the mud gave way under her.

She stood firm, though her whole body trembled, refusing to shrink back any further.

"I said—I ain't no thief. I ain't lied neither," her voice shaking, but there was steel beneath her fear, a resolve that hadn't shown itself before.

Gran's fury erupted, spilling over like a pot left too long on the fire.

She jumped down, grabbing the nearest stick with a snarl.

In seconds, she was on Esther, her arm raised high as she brought the weapon down with brutal force.

Her words came out in harsh, jagged bursts, laced with judgment between each strike.

"Do I look like a fool?"

"Ya think I'm stupid?"

"Evil done already grabbed hold of ya, girl. And it's gonna whoop ya down—whoop ya down till there's nothin' left but ashes!"

Each blow drove Gran's words deeper, her rage as fierce as the downpour that fell in sheets over them, drowning out every sound.

Every sound but her voice and the crack of the stick hitting skin.

Esther curled in on herself, wrapping her arms tight around her head as if she could fold into nothing, shrinking from the blows.

She didn't fight back, didn't cry out—just took it, the way she'd learned to, letting the pain wash through her body—rain over stone.

Her silence was her shield, her only defense.

Then, slicing through the storm, a deep and powerful voice rang out.

"STOP!"

"What are you doing to her?"

Gran froze, the stick still poised in mid-air. Her breath caught in her throat as she turned toward the dominating sound.

Standing just beyond the fence of his own yard was Ian Huggler, a tall, broad-shouldered German man in his mid-thirties.

His presence was commanding. His eyes, dark with anger, bore into her, making it clear he'd seen every bit of it.

The man's children, Benjamin and Rebecca, peeked out from behind his legs, their expressions filled with fear and confusion.

"Ya… keep out of our business!" Gran said, though her tone trembled as she met Ian's unwavering gaze.

Ian, with deliberate calm, removed his hat, his stance firm.

"You wouldn't treat an animal this way," he said.

He gestured toward Esther, still curled tight on the ground, her body trembling, small and cornered, as though she were a helpless creature.

"She's defenseless and in pain," the stranger said.

Gran hesitated, the fire in her flickering, just for a moment.

She looked at her granddaughter's thin form, pressed hard into the earth.

A shiver ran through the old lady, quick and sudden. For a split second, she felt something—guilt, maybe—but she shoved it down deep where it couldn't touch her.

"She ain't yer concern," she said, trying to reclaim her power, the edge in her words creeping back toward anger.

But Ian didn't flinch.

He took another step forward, his eyes hard and unyielding.

"I CAN NOT let you beat her. Put the stick down!"

His words were akin to a commandment, spoken from some place higher than either of them.

The air between them buzzed with tension, the storm overhead paling in comparison to the tempest brewing between Gran and the German man.

Neither of them was willing to back down. The moment stood still, and even time didn't dare interfere.

As the clash dragged on and the rain poured down, a deep, burning shame rose inside Esther. Like all this was her doing, her mess.

Who was she to think she could ever have more?

Slowly, she uncurled herself from the mud, her body aching with the blows, yet she willed herself to stand.

In her hand, the small bar felt heavier than before—a blessing and a curse.

She stepped forward, shaky but determined, holding the soap out toward the old woman.

Her delivery was weak, but grew stronger as she spoke.

"It's mine, Gran… She gave it to me. I wasn't about to go to hell over nothin'."

Gran's eyes flicked from Esther to the bar.

Without a word, she snatched it from Esther's hand, her grip rough and unforgiving. In a show of power, she flung it into the bushes as if it didn't mean a thing. The act was final, as though slamming a door shut.

"Get in the wagon!" Gran said, her tone brooking no argument, her control reasserted with that one firm command.

Esther obeyed, her body moving without thought as she climbed up to the buckboard, her legs weak and reluctant.

She stole a quick, uncertain glance back at Ian, standing by the fence, his eyes following them as though he could close the distance with just a single step if he willed it so.

Never wavering, he stood there, rooted to the ground, watching them fade beneath the low-hanging clouds, his face giving away nothing.

As the wagon clattered farther down the road, Benjamin tugged at his father's pocket, his brow furrowed with questions too heavy for a boy his age.

"Papa, that ol' woman's eyes looked burnin' mad."

He paused, his confusion deepening as he went on.

"I don't get why her girl just lay there, lettin' her whoop on her like that."

Before Ian could find the words, Rebecca hugged him tight around his waist, as if she needed to squeeze the bad things away.

Ian cast one last look at the wagon disappearing beneath the storm clouds, the burden of his thoughts deepening the lines across his sun-worn brow.

"Son, it's over now," he said, his tone dragging low with the weariness of the encounter.

The man guided his children toward the cottage, its soft light spilling out as though a shield, keeping the dark at bay.

Benjamin couldn't shake what he'd seen.

"You suppose she gets whooped every day?" he asked.

Ian let out a long breath, resting a hand on his boy's shoulder.

"We should talk about something else. Something… pleasant. Something nice."

"Well, I can't think of nothin' pleasant. Nothin' that feels nice either," Benjamin said, not wanting to give up.

A cheerful Rebecca started jumping up, her eyes shining as bright as the sun after a long storm.

"I know somethin' nice, real nice!"

Ian looked down at his daughter.

"What's that, sweet girl?"

"I sang Auntie a song today," she said, her expression bubbling with pride. "It's all about how Auntie always tries to chase the chickens and ends up trippin' over her own feet. She said she's gonna remember it forever."

Ian chuckled, scooping Rebecca into his arms and pressing a soft kiss to her head.

"Thank you," he said.

With a mischievous grin, Rebecca cupped his face in her small hands, pushing his cheeks up into a wide smile.

"See, Papa? You're happy now."

He let out a playful grunt, and she squealed with laughter. Her joy lit up the moment, even coaxing a small smile from her brother.

Chapter 4: The River's Warning

Rain came down, quick and mean. Each drop hit the earth with force, as if sent from above to wash away the world's sin—to cleanse all that had gone wrong.

Gran and Esther trudged on, their bodies bent against the cold, wet air.

Ahead, the river—once a whisper winding through the trees—had swelled into a beast, all fury and teeth, crashing hard against the rocks, a force too strong to be tamed. It surged forward, burdened by the storm's anger, carrying what it had no choice but to bear.

Gran, stubborn as always, didn't blink. Her gaze fixed straight ahead, and without a shiver of doubt, she steered the wagon toward the riverbank.

The mule's eyes rolled back, wide with fear, nostrils flaring at the scent of danger. Esther felt it too —the same fear that rooted them in place—two creatures cornered with nowhere to run.

With an iron will, Gran pushed the beast forward.

"I don't think we should go in," Esther said, trembling as she eyed the wild, angry waters ahead.

"Don't be ridiculous," her grandmother said. "Pawdad be waitin' fer his supper."

But Esther's panic only deepened as she stared into the dark, swirling current—no longer a quiet river but something alive and feral, ready to pull at anyone who dared to cross.

The animal, sensing Esther's trepidation, dug its hooves deeper into the mud.

Gran, however, wasn't one to allow hesitation from man or mule. With a hard snap of the reins, she forced the beast forward.

The animal lurched, muscles straining against the icy torrent. Gran held fast.

But each time the mule faltered, Esther gripped the buckboard's side tighter, her knuckles turning white.

Water crept up to the height of the wagon's axles. The force of the current pressed against them, determined to tip them clean over.

The wheels struggled to hold on, slipping and sliding on the slick riverbed as the wagon swayed, a ship lost at sea. The old wooden frame groaned, but not as loud as the river's roar.

"I'm scared, Gran. We should wait," Esther said, her voice strained, pleading for her grandmother to listen.

"Just a damn river," Gran said, hands firm on the reins. "Ain't nothin' I'm afraid of."

Gran's words, strong as they were, did nothing to calm Esther as the sound of the rushing current filled her head, drowning out everything else—until, at last, they reached the far bank.

Still reeling from the narrow escape, Esther finally released her grip. Gran, however, gave no sign she'd even noticed. Eyes ahead, the mule moved quicker now, eager to leave the river behind.

Overhead, the storm brooded darker with each passing moment—the sky hanging low and heavy, as if night had fallen too soon.

By the time they reached the Primms' cabin, the rain was coming down in drops as big as acorns—the mountains closing in where few dared to venture.

Their home was a small, ramshackle thing, battered and bent from years of harsh living. The wind seemed to push at it from all sides—the downpour only making its frailty more certain.

Swollen and warped from neglect, the wood sagged inward, as though the very bones of the place had grown tired of standing. Even the weary porch moaned under the weight.

An old man, Pawdad, sat beneath the hanging eaves in his favorite cane rocker—a lanky frame slumped to the side as though he had dozed off.

His gray beard, wiry and wild, hung low, damp with rain, while beside him his faithful hound, Bones, lay curled tight, oblivious to the downpour. Ezekiel Primm looked carved straight out of the mountains themselves, hard as granite.

Gran hoisted an armful of supplies from the wagon, grunting with effort as she hurried up the steps to the porch. The boards beneath her creaked as though ready to give way.

As she passed Pawdad, she gave his rocker a hard kick.

"Get up, ol' man. I'm fixin' to get ya something to eat," she said, her tone lacking softness, just the plain necessity of the thing.

But Pawdad didn't stir. The chair rocked back and forth with the force of her boot, yet her husband remained still, his head resting against the headrest, as though he hadn't a care in the world.

Gran stepped into the shack, thinking nothing of it, guessing he was asleep or indulging in his favorite brew.

Inside, the cabin was as rundown as the outside had warned, walls bare but for a few yellowed photographs, their edges curled with time, and a faded quilt hanging crooked on one wall.

The front room held the clutter of years, bits and remnants of a hard life spent scraping by. The air was thick with the smell of damp wood and past smoke, the evidence of countless fires lingering in every corner.

Gran busied herself at the stove, hands moving with the ease of someone who had lit that old potbelly a thousand times over. The fire took quickly, crackling to life as it cast a dim, flickering light.

Esther, cold and worn thin by the day, slipped toward her corner, where her unmade bed waited.

With Gran's back turned, she pulled out her hymn book, thumbing to a page she hadn't yet claimed. Her callused fingers traced along it as she began outlining the bar of soap, remembering its fancy wrapping and delicate ribbon. Each detail was sketched in soft pencil.

The gift had felt like a dream she wanted to remember.

Meanwhile, Gran worked with the same steady rhythm, her hand diving into a can of lard, tossing a thick handful into the flour. The repetition was in her bones—timeworn.

Soon, a pot on the stove gave off a savory scent, filling the room, stirring memories of harder times, when a meager, warm meal was all they had to soothe a soul.

But the peace was fragile, breaking as Gran's sharp eyes caught Esther's distraction. Without missing a beat, her words sliced through the calm—swift and cutting.

"What ya doin'? Stop wastin' yer time and go get yer Pawdad, girl. I swear, yer useless as a stump. He gonna freeze himself out there if you don't."

Esther shoved the book under her blankets and hurried out the rickety door, the sound of rain swallowing her whole the moment she stepped out.

She wasn't gone long before she rushed back in, her face pale, eyes wide and frantic.

"He ain't wakin' up, Gran. I shook him and he ain't movin'… not a bit," Esther added.

The old woman, tired from the day, glanced up from her work. She waved a dismissive hand.

"Girl, he done drank himself to slumber. Pick him up and bring him on in here," Gran said, her voice sharp as a whip.

Esther tried to suppress the growing dread that twisted a deep knot in her stomach.

She'd seen Pawdad drunk before, passed out with a jar of moonshine still gripped tight in his hand.

But this time—this time felt different.

There was a stillness in the air that made her heart race.

With an urgency she couldn't ignore, Esther turned and dashed back outside, rain soaking her skin as she hurried across the porch.

She knelt beside Pawdad, shaking him again with more force. But his body, usually quick to stir with a grumble, stayed limp in her hands.

Panic clawed at her chest, her breath catching as the truth settled—heavy and unshakable.

She stumbled back inside, her voice trembling as she spoke.

"He ain't got no jar by him, Gran… and I felt his pipe. It's cold as ice. I don't think he's smoked all day."

Gran froze mid-motion, fingers tight around a canning lid she was using to cut biscuits. Her face hardened, and in that split second, the impatience in her eyes gave way to something darker.

"God damn it! Bring him in here, now!"

Esther's feet didn't wait for her mind to catch up.

She was out the door again, moving fast, the urgency in Gran's tone pushing her as if a gust of wind were at her back.

When she reached Pawdad, her heart sank again.

His face was slack, his eyelids only partly shut, leaving his eyes exposed in an eerie stillness. His skin—so pale it looked almost blue—sent a fresh wave of dread surging through her.

She fell to her knees beside him, her hands unsteady as they brushed against his foot. It was icy, the warmth she'd always known, even in winter, gone as if it had never existed.

Esther rubbed his ankle, desperate, pleading with fate to feel something—anything—but it was no use.

"He's all cold," she whispered.

Gran stood in the doorway, her face set hard with determination, but her body told another truth. Her shoulders, once proud, slumped just enough to betray the dread—a burden she'd never let her voice carry. Even the iron in her eyes couldn't smother the fear.

She crouched beside Pawdad, her hands trembling as they reached for his.

She shook him, calling his name, her tone cracking under the strain of years together.

But there was no response.

No movement.

No life left in his body.

Gran pressed her ear against his mouth, desperate for the faintest sign of breath, but he was silent.

Pawdad was gone.

Her hands hung limp as she rose, her gaze fixed on the man who had shared her life. She looked down at him, the weight of years of unspoken words heavy in the silence between them.

The rain fell in a steady rhythm, a drumbeat against the porch, its sound weaving through the heavy fog.

Esther, still kneeling beside him, looked up at Gran, tears welling in her eyes, searching her grandmother's face for guidance.

But her grandmother said nothing.

She just stood there.

As the hours stretched on, Esther lay restless in bed, the storm still clinging to the house.

Her stomach growled with hunger, the smell of the uneaten biscuits a cruel reminder of the day's bitter end. Fear kept her from asking, kept her still. She didn't dare disturb the quiet that had settled between them.

She stole a brief look at Gran, wary of lingering too long.

Pearl Primm seemed adrift, her gaze fixed on the flickering lantern in the corner. Pawdad's death had hollowed out something within her, as though the very part that knew how to fight had been stripped clean.

But still, she refused to let a single tear fall.

Later, when Gran retired to her room, Esther lay restless, tossing and turning on a thin cot. She flopped onto her back, hands behind her head as she stared upward, seeing nothing. Pawdad's face lingered in her mind—unclear, elusive. It clung to the edges of memory, drifting like smoke from a chimney into the dark night sky.

He hadn't been one for talkin' much. His words had been measured and spare, as if he were rationing them for when they mattered most—moving through her days a shadow she could never quite catch. Now, he left nothing behind but the quiet spaces where he once lingered.

Sometimes, when Gran's tongue lashed too sharp, he'd straighten and give her a look that could bend iron, and the room would still. Most times, though, he'd turn his head to the side, as if he couldn't see the hurt she put down, that it wasn't his to fix. Esther hadn't decided whether he didn't care or if it pained him too much to try.

There was a bitterness in him, a feeling that life had cheated him out of something. It was something she had never understood. His stories—old tales spun from some distant place—belonged to a world far from the one they knew.

And as the years wore on, his memory slipped.

He'd call her Annie sometimes, using her mother's name as if it belonged to her. A name rarely spoken.

Gran had always kept her mouth sealed when it came to her daughter. And when she did speak of her, it was cold, saying only that it would have been better if she had died.

Unable to lie in her bed any longer, Esther pushed herself upright and moved to a small window in the front. Outside in the dark, her Pawdad's empty rocker sat still. She thought of him—the way he'd sit there, lighting his pipe with a skinny stick, or how he'd stare out at the mountains, his eyes searching for something long gone.

There had been times her grandfather had shown her kindness, slight gestures that held more warmth than her grandmother ever had—brief moments that made her feel she mattered.

Esther reflected how she'd never seen affection between him and Gran. They'd lived side by side, yet the space between them was a river they had never crossed.

The closest they came to tenderness was when Gran took the old scissors to his hair, her hands moving slow but sure, like she'd done it a thousand times. When she was done, she'd step back, give him a once-over, and tell him he looked handsome. That word alone, slipping from her lips, would pull a soft smile from him.

Sometimes Pawdad would read from an old, worn Bible, his deep resonance rumbling through the room, filling it with tales of battles and kings, stories that felt too mighty for the worn-out walls around them. He favored the verses that crackled with fire, the ones that stirred deep fierceness within him.

But Gran, with a slight smile, would shake her head and say the Good Book might've turned out better if a woman had written it.

It was one of the few things she'd said that made Esther laugh—a glimpse of something softer in her grandmother, a side rarely seen.

Beyond the small cabin, the rain beat hard, its cadence falling in step with an ache that had taken root.

Pawdad was gone, and the world felt different.

A quiet fear—an uncertainty—gnawed at her.

How would they survive without him?

That thought sent a chill straight through her.

Chapter 5: Into the Current

Nothing had changed in the night. The rain kept on, indifferent as time itself. It swept over the hillside with no mercy, scrubbing the earth clean, bit by bit, until it wore down to rock.

Esther hunched forward, her narrow frame straining as she fought to back the mule and wagon toward the Primms' battered shack.

Every inch the animal gave, it took two back, its hooves slipping in the waterlogged ground. She couldn't tell if it was resisting out of sheer stubbornness or exhaustion from the previous day.

But Esther's will was stronger.

The downpour pelted her skin, but she pressed on, knowing Gran had expected her to get it done and soon.

On the porch, Pawdad's body lay still, covered by a sheet so thin it might as well have been rain itself. The fabric clung to him, soaked through, offering no protection.

Even the heavens above showed no mercy—not for the living, and certainly not for the dead.

Next to the body, Bones sat unmoving, his old eyes fixed on the man as if the passing of life meant nothing in the loyalty of dogs. His fur was slick and heavy with rain, but he didn't flinch— just stayed there in silent vigil, keeping Pawdad company.

As if summoned by the moment, the shack door groaned open. Gran stepped out in her Sunday best, a black dress that clung to her frame. The fabric pressed neatly, given the day.

Around her neck hung a string of pearls—pearls Esther hadn't thought about since that day she'd glimpsed them in an old photograph, a memory of better days long gone.

Gran's face held nothing but stern resolve, no trace of grief showing through that mask she had worn for years.

"Well, go on then—put 'im in," she said.

Esther held. Her eyes locked onto the still form.

Never in her life had she imagined this moment—never thought she'd be standing here in the downpour, tasked with lifting her grandfather's body as if it were some ordinary thing to be done.

She swallowed hard, dreading what came next.

But Gran's voice gave no room for anything else, only action.

Esther stepped forward, the rain blurring everything in her sight, wet hair falling across her eyes. It was hard to see the man who had once been such a tall pillar. Her arms shook as she bent to grasp the edges of the drenched sheet, pulling against the heavy fabric.

Pawdad's body was lanky, stiff with the stillness of death. She struggled against it, as though dragging a fallen log. Her fingers slipped as she tried to wedge him onto the wagon's wooden bed.

The linen caught on the splintered wood, tore as she tugged. Exhausted and breathing heavily, she refused to give up, finally managing to heave him all the way to the back of the buckboard.

His legs still hung over the back—too long for the small wagon.

Teeth rattling from the cold, Esther retreated to the porch, her eyes searching desperately for her grandmother's face. She wanted something—anything—that might guide her through what came next.

But Gran only stood there, her umbrella offering little against the downpour.

Without a word, the old woman made her way to the wagon, climbing up with a stiff body.

"Ya gonna drive me there. I ain't drivin' myself, ya dummy," she mumbled over her shoulder, adjusting herself on the seat.

Surprised, Esther quickly followed, settling beside her grandmother, her grip firm on the slick reins.

The moment unfolded like a timeworn ritual, steeped in history and significance.

Gran carried herself with a knowing, a deep-rooted understanding passed down through generations of kin.

Though Esther felt very much an outsider, adrift and uncertain in this silent tradition, she had no fine Sunday dress to offer her respects, no outward reflection to mark her presence in this solemn affair.

Bones, refusing to be left behind, scrambled up into the wagon and lay at Esther's feet. The animal seemed to feel it all—the somberness, the quiet. He made no sound, just closed his eyes and put his head down.

Esther, afraid to speak, held a question close, tucked away. She had seen the small, somber family graveyard perched on the hill. There, her grandparents had mournfully laid to rest their two young sons—tiny young'uns taken too soon.

The thought of placing Pawdad there seemed almost natural. But then she remembered his last wish—it echoed back to her with perfect clarity.

He had said that when the Lord saw fit to take him, he was to be laid next to his mother, who had died when he was just a teen. As though the earth could weave together the scattered threads of their family in the next life.

The women pressed on toward the river, the road turning treacherous beneath them. What had once been a familiar trail now rose against them, churned to ruin by mud and slick stones.

Refusing to ease, the rain pelted harder, turning the dirt into a swirling mess that threatened to flip the wagon.

Water gushed through ruts carved deep by years of use, forming small rivers of their own.

The mule staggered forward, hooves slipping in the sodden earth, driven on by Gran's cracking commands.

She didn't falter, forcing the animal on, while Esther gripped the reins, rigid with strain, guiding them over what had once been a road.

As they drew near the water, Esther's chest tightened.

The sound started low, building into a roar, a rushing torrent—so ominous it set her teeth on edge.

The river had swelled since the night before, the rain feeding it until it was no longer something they could reckon with.

It churned and thrashed beneath the morning fog, a dark, restless force, its power lurking beneath the mist.

Just waiting.

Esther tugged at the reins, bringing the wagon to a sudden stop at the edge. The mule's mane bristled with unease, his flanks heaving.

Her heart thudded as she swallowed hard.

"Gran—we can't cross," she said, her voice straining to rise above the roar.

"We's buryin' 'im today," Gran said, not looking at her, voice like ice.

Esther's eyes locked on the dark, swirling water, which almost seemed to laugh at them as it crashed against the riverbank.

It wasn't just a river anymore—it was a threat, cursing out a warning that they had no business being there.

The mule could hear it too. He tried to back away, but the thick mud stuck to him, climbing up to his knees and flanks, coating him as he fought to break free.

Gran, stubborn as always, refused to listen.

She grabbed the small whip beside her and struck hard at the mule's haunches without a shred of mercy.

The animal let out a bray in protest, fear etched in its eyes.

"Gran, stop! It's too high," Esther said, her words faltering. "We'd best wait till tomorrow, or the day after."

But her grandmother was resolute, eyes fixed ahead. In one quick motion, she yanked the reins from Esther's hands.

"We ain't waitin' fer Pawdad's body to stink all up," Gran growled, cracking the whip again.

Esther watched in horror as the mule stumbled forward, its legs shaking, its head pulling back, struggling against the harness as it inched dangerously toward the edge.

Desperate, she tried to pry the reins free from the old woman, to stop this madness, to stop the animal.

But before she could, the poor beast spooked.

With a wild cry, it bolted, yanking the wagon straight into the rushing river.

The current swallowed them in an instant, gripping the buckboard and dragging it downstream with a power neither woman could control.

Water surged into the footboard, rising violently around her legs and pulling at her clothes.

The raging torrent left them helpless.

Esther screamed, the sound swallowed by the roaring waves.

Gran, unmoved by the chaos, sat still, gripping the reins as if sheer will could steer her fate.

"Get out. Swim to the shore. Take yer dog too," she mumbled.

Esther's mind stumbled over the words, her wide eyes fixed on her grandmother.

"Gran." Her voice cracked, a plea more than a question as she hesitated.

"I said swim—girl!" Gran snapped with sudden fierceness. "If ya mean to live, swim!"

For a moment, a flicker of tenderness passed through the old woman's eyes, a whispered confession of love arriving too late.

But the light vanished, giving way to the steely resolve Esther had always known.

Before she could react, Gran seized Bones by the scruff, flinging the dog into the churning water.

Esther had no time to think, only to act.

She followed, hurling herself from the wagon.

The river hit her like a hammer, driving the air from her lungs, and for a moment, she was nothing but a rag doll tossed in the icy water, limp and helpless.

Bones' fur brushed her leg, a lifeline in the middle of the madness.

She grabbed at him with all the strength she had, pulling him close as they battled together.

The current was a living monster, sucking them under, but Esther thrashed back, her body aching with the effort.

She could feel the river trying to claim her, clawing at her clothes, dragging her under.

But she fought back, inch by inch, forcing herself toward the shore.

The girl from the hills fought for a life, a life that belonged to her, a gift she had never opened.

Her limbs burned with effort, her chest tight as she gasped for air, but she wasn't fighting just the river—she was fighting for the very breath she had yet to claim.

Esther wanted to live, to hold on to the small pieces of herself that had always slipped away downstream.

This life was hers, and she wouldn't let the water or anything else take it from her.

When her feet found the slick, muddy bottom, she clawed her way up the bank, dragging her dog with her.

She dropped down, chest still, not moving—but then…

She sucked in a deep, aching breath that filled her lungs, like the first cry of a newborn—fresh and sharp.

It was a breath that carried the fire of being alive.

But there was no time to recover as she rolled over, eyes darting toward the river.

Esther saw her—a stubborn silhouette in the back of the wagon, clinging to Pawdad's shirt collar.

The old woman's face was as calm as stone, her body half-submerged in the rising water. It sent a chill through Esther deeper than the river's cold.

It whispered of resignation, of a choice made and a path picked.

"Gran!" Esther's scream tore through the air. "Get out, Gran! Get out! Why ya ain't gettin' out? Swim, Gran! Swim!"

Gran didn't stir.

She sat in the old wagon as if she belonged to the river, as though she'd made peace with its decision.

Her face was relaxed as the current pulled her closer to the falls.

No fight. No panic.

Just surrender as the backboard jolted hard, slamming against a big rock.

The impact was sharp enough to crack wood, snapping the hitch clean. The poor mule, wide-eyed and frantic, broke free and paddled to the shore, leaving the battered wagon to its own fate.

It drifted, helpless, toward the edge, where the river dropped off into the unknown.

Desperate, Esther ran along the bank, her feet slipping on the wet ground, roots catching at her ankles. But she didn't stop.

Every step, a battle against the earth itself.

A low branch caught her, pitching her down into the mud. Her knees stung, but she scrambled up, forcing herself forward.

"Gran!" she yelled, her voice more of a rasp now. "Please!"

But Gran's ears weren't listening anymore—she was somewhere else entirely.

Somewhere beyond the river's roar, beyond Esther's cries, her lips moving, the sound of *"Amazing Grace"* rising faintly over the water.

The hymn wove itself into the rush of the current, as if the river and the song had always belonged together.

Esther's breath caught in her chest, forcing herself to acknowledge what she already knew. Gran had already let go.

There'd be no pulling her back from the beast's grasp. No saving her from the falls. She would stay with Pawdad to follow him where the living couldn't go.

As if caught between waking and sleep, Esther watched the wagon approach the hiss of Cedar Falls.

The river grew hungrier, pulling harder—now ready to claim its prize.

Gran's delivery didn't falter, though.

The hymn drifted across the water, as if guided by a higher purpose to reach her granddaughter's ears, a way of making peace, perhaps asking forgiveness.

Esther's heart clenched as the buckboard slipped to the edge. She stood helpless, her feet stuck in place.

And then, in one swift motion, the wagon tipped—its fragile frame no match for the power of the falls.

The water gulped them whole, dragging them both into the unknown.

"Nooo!" Esther cried, her voice breaking in half.

It was too late. The river had them.

No mercy. No pause. It just kept rushing on, as though they had never been there at all.

Esther's eyes moved to the place where they'd disappeared.

Bones pressed his wet nose into her leg, letting her know he was still there, with her. His warm breath against her skin pulled her back from the edge of numbness.

With a hitched breath, she glanced down at him. The dog's eyes filled with something akin to worry, the kind only a creature like him could express.

She knelt, her hands wrapping into his fur, burying her face in his neck.

Chapter 6: The Harbor

The storm eased, slipping off like a weary traveler at its journey's end. Stubborn clouds tugged apart, revealing a pale sliver of sky against the gray. What lingered was an uneasy stillness—the land hushed, its mouth bound.

Esther stood there, knowing she couldn't stay—she had to move, had to find someone, tell them what the river had taken.

But as she turned, eyes scanning the wilderness that stretched out around her, the truth seeped in. She was alone, with no clear path in sight, no sense of where to go.

Then she saw it.

Off in the distance, just visible through the trees, the Old Reed Estate rose. Its tall, weathered roof stood as a beacon, cutting through the gloom—a lighthouse for the lost.

It was a house she had only ever seen from afar—a place that never seemed meant for her kind. Too grand, too far removed from the life she knew.

But now, when all appeared lost, the Old Reed Estate stood tall and sure—a promise she hadn't known to believe in.

With Bones at her side, Esther ran.

Her legs were exhausted. Her body raw. Still, she pushed forward.

The underbrush caught at her ankles, tearing her skin, but she wouldn't stop. The estate wasn't far, yet the journey stretched on as if it would never end.

She staggered up the hill, the grand old place looming above her, the back door within sight.

Every breath burned as she climbed, each step driven by the need to reach the door before her body gave out.

Nearby, two men labored against the storm, their hands smeared with mud as they fought to clear a ditch swollen with rainwater, threatening to engulf the orchard.

Abram, a Black man in his early thirties, wielded his shovel with determined strokes. Each scoop of wet earth filled the sack that Ian held steady. They moved in sync, sweat glistening on their skin, the work grueling.

A faint cry drifted through the air, barely audible, but enough to stop Abram, his grip stalling mid-motion.

He twisted at the sound, his brow furrowing.

"Ain't that one of them Primms?" he asked.

Ian followed his line of sight and spotted her—Esther—her form darting toward the house.

Wet dirt streaked her clothes, plastered to her slender frame as if the river had taken possession of her.

Her face was pale—hauntingly so, and marked by desperation.

His eyes narrowed, recognizing her, the image of their last meeting still fresh in his mind.

Her dog followed close behind, his drenched coat plastered to his sides as he pressed on after her.

Reaching the back door, Esther pounded with all her strength, her fists slamming against the wood in a wild rhythm.

"Please! Somebody, help! Please!"

The door swung open, and Clarissa stood there, surprised.

"What's happened, child?" she asked, eyes scanning the girl's soaked form.

Esther gasped for breath, chest heaving as she tried to form the words that felt caught in her throat.

"Help me!" she sobbed, her voice breaking. "She went over the falls… they—they went over the falls."

And then, as if her strings had been cut, her body crumpled onto the wooden porch, too weak to carry on any longer.

Clarissa's eyes widened, her mouth parting in shock just as Ian appeared.

Without hesitation, he dropped to his knees beside Esther, his hands firm on her shoulders, his gaze locking with hers, urgent and steady.

"Who went over the falls?" he asked, his tone carrying a force that sliced through the panic.

Esther's mouth opened, but no sound came. Her head moved side to side as if the truth might slip free again, but all she found was silence.

"Somebody swept away?" Ian's voice pushed through, sharper this time. "Over Cedar Falls?"

Esther's head dipped once, and with it came the tears she couldn't hold back, her heart splintering.

Ian's face darkened as his gaze locked with Abram's, a silent understanding passing between them.

Without a word, both men knew what had to be done.

They took off in long strides toward the river, the sound of their boots cutting through the still air like a promise—one they might not be able to keep.

Esther tried to stand, her legs quivering under her. Clarissa reached out a gentle hand, steadying her.

"They'll take care of it, honey," she said, her tone a soothing balm.

Esther let herself collapse against the woman, her body shaking.

"The river," she mumbled. "It's taken all the family I got. I ain't got no one now… no one."

Clarissa embraced her with a fierce tenderness. Her own heart ached in rhythm with the girl's.

She brushed her fingers through Esther's damp hair, her silence a sanctuary.

In that moment, Clarissa became a steadfast light amidst the turmoil—a haven against the dark void.

She glanced over just as Mitzy, Abram's young wife, approached. With a child balanced on her hip and a basket of wet laundry tucked under her arm, she moved with a hesitant grace.

A solemn look passed between them.

"Mitzy, will ya go and fetch Benjamin and Rebecca? Bring 'em inside, quick-like. Matter of fact, we all best head in," Clarissa said.

"I gotta go get my Gran," Esther whispered.

The old woman's arms tightened. Her voice, though gentle, carried a firmness that brooked no argument.

"Honey, I think we should just sit and wait. The menfolk will do their best. If bad is gonna happen today, it already has."

She held Esther close, her eyes reflecting a deep well of compassion.

"God has most likely done His will as well," Clarissa added.

Then she sighed, aware of her hands cradling the girl from the hills. It felt as if they'd found where they belonged, as though they'd discovered what they'd been searching for all along.

The thin girl seemed helpless and fragile—a hatchling that had tumbled from its nest.

With a quiet resolve, Clarissa ushered Esther into the Old Reed Estate.

Esther had nothing left, like an empty shelf stripped bare. The fear that once held her back from crossing that forbidden threshold was gone, leaving only a hollow resignation.

She let the woman from the porch guide her into the house.

The one who always wore her hair in a long braid.

The one she'd only ever glimpsed from a distance.

Chapter 7: Loss

Evening sank over the hills, wrapping itself around the landscape, unhurried. The rain had dwindled to a light drizzle, a steady murmur against the earth. Somewhere out there, in the trees that stood tall, an owl let out a mournful hoot. It echoed through the countryside—a sad, lonely reminder of the day's loss.

Ian's battered blue truck, a Ford Model BB that had seen its share of hard miles, sat on the main drive of the Old Reed Estate, its frame creaking as it settled under the weight. In the back, two bodies lay motionless, wrapped in white sheets that clung to their forms—the last embrace of life.

Sheriff Marty Ronell leaned against the vehicle, his frame softened with age, a protruding belly pressing against the buttons of his brown uniform. His thick, dark mustache twitched as he removed his hat and shook off the rain with a quick, practiced motion before shoving it back on his head, indifferent to the sagging brim.

Beside him stood Deputy Frank Burgess, a wiry man with sharp, beady eyes that missed nothing. He shifted his weight from one foot to the other, glancing sideways at the sheriff. Every few moments, his gaze darted toward the road, eager to get moving.

Sheriff Ronell noticed, but didn't budge.

"We'll go when Clarissa gets here," he said, as if that was the only explanation needed.

"What's takin' her so damn long? We could've been halfway to town by now," Frank added, his voice tight with frustration.

The sheriff shook his head, a smile tugging at the corner of his lips.

"Frank, you oughta know better by now—you can't rush a woman. It only makes 'em slower."

Frank rolled his eyes, muttering something under his breath, but let the matter drop.

Not far away, Esther sat on the porch swing of the Old Reed House, a thick blanket wrapped around her slumped frame, a warm mug cradled in her hands. Her weary eyes were distant, lost in the gray light that drifted on the horizon, where the day had faded into dusk. Beside her, the hound sat watch, his nose twitching as unfamiliar scents drifted on the air.

Across the yard, Ian lingered by the lawmen, his arms folded firmly across his chest. Wet strands of dark blond hair clung to his forehead, still damp from the cold river where he and Abram had pulled the bodies.

He looked down, eyes narrowing at the thick mud caked on his boots—a reminder of the day's grim work that left him drained. With a scuff of his heel against the gravel, he worked to dislodge the clinging muck—with little success.

What could easily be called an awkward silence hung around the men, settling in as it always did when there was nothing left to say.

The quiet stretched on.

Then, breaking the monotony, the loud clop of hooves on gravel came into earshot, drawing their attention.

Abram appeared, coming up the drive, leading the Primms' weary mule by a rope, the animal's head hanging low, its steps heavy with exhaustion.

Ian's eyes flickered with surprise at the sight of the scruffy beast as his friend drew closer.

A grin spread across Abram's face, his steps carrying an air of satisfaction.

"I found him munchin' in a pasture," he said, his tone carrying the triumph of a man who had brought back something worth keeping.

The two lawmen exchanged a glance of amusement, despite the task at hand. Even Ian's stoic expression softened into a brief smile.

"Good job, I guess," Ian said, though his face soon returned to its serious demeanor, the grin vanishing as quickly as it had appeared.

"Figured we could put 'em in the barn," Abram added.

Reluctantly, Ian nodded, letting his gaze drift back to the road. The mule, along with everything else today, was just another responsibility—one more task on a day already burdened with too many.

Sheriff Ronell turned to Ian.

"I appreciate ya takin' them down the hill," he said, his gruff tone carrying a hint of gratitude.

Ian nodded again, peering at the bodies in the back of the truck, the reality of it all sinking in deeper.

"I don't mind," he replied, his German accent slipping through, a reminder that, despite his time here, he remained an outsider, a man apart.

Deputy Frank scoffed as he jabbed at his teeth with a toothpick, his eyes narrowing.

"Don't know why those crazy fools tried to cross during the spring runoff. They shoulda known better."

The sheriff grunted in agreement, his gaze sweeping over the Old Reed House, its shutters creaking in the wind, as if they, too, were nodding to the absurdity of it all.

"Speakin' of them, where's the Primms' granddaughter?" the sheriff asked.

Ian glanced at the porch, surprised to see the swing empty, the blanket draped in a lumpy heap over the seat.

His gaze shifted, scanning the area until he spotted her fading figure in the distance, walking up the road with her dog trailing behind, their forms almost indistinguishable in the dimming light.

"There," Ian said, nodding towards the road. "She must have hopped the fence."

"Are ya kiddin' me? Where the hell does she think she's goin'?" Sheriff Ronell grumbled as he straightened up, hands resting on his hips.

Deputy Frank chuckled, a sound that fell flat.

"I think she's headin' home," he said, a trace of amusement coloring his words, as if he found some small humor in the girl's quiet defiance.

The sheriff sighed, rubbing the bridge of his nose, trying to ward off the inevitable headache. His shoulders slumped, a man tired of chasing after the ghosts of the day.

"Ah, guess I needa take her down to Larkin. Maybe Preacher Clive can find her a place 'til the river drops."

As the men stood by the truck, their voices low with the weight of responsibility, the front door of the house creaked open.

Clarissa stepped out onto the porch, pausing for a moment as the cool air touched her face. Ian's children followed behind her, their figures moving like shadows. Dressed in a housecoat and apron, Clarissa's calm expression faltered. Her chest tightened as she caught sight of the abandoned blanket.

"Benjamin, Rebecca," she called out, her voice a mix of concern and determination. "Run after her and tell her to come back here."

The children needed no further urging. With a quick nod, they leaped off the veranda, their small feet carrying them down the road after Esther. The sound of their footsteps, nimble and light, echoed in the evening's stillness.

The old woman watched them for a moment, her hands tightening around the porch railing. She couldn't bear the thought of letting that poor girl walk into the mountains alone, not after everything that had happened.

Steeling herself, Clarissa turned, purpose driving her steps as she made her way toward the truck where the lawmen lingered. Her pace quickened, her resolve growing with every stride, until she stood before them, her presence commanding, demanding to be heard.

"She's stayin' here," she said.

The sheriff glanced up, surprise flickering in his eyes at the force behind her words. He was used to folks deferring to his authority, and Clarissa's assertiveness caught him off guard.

"Now, Miss Clarissa, ya ain't responsible for that girl," he said, his tone a mix of firmness and caution, as if trying to reason with a storm that had already made up its mind.

"Oh yes, I am," she said, unyielding.

Her face hardened as she went on.

"She's kin, and I'm gonna take care of her."

The sheriff shook his head, a sigh escaping as his tone softened, perhaps out of respect for the resolve he saw in her eyes.

"Look here, her cousin Clive lives down in town. He'll make sure someone looks after her," he insisted, his words meant to persuade, but they fell flat.

Clarissa didn't budge, her eyes narrowing as she stood her ground.

"I said I would take care of her. She's my kin as well," she reiterated, her inflection carrying a quiet strength that left no room for doubt.

Deputy Frank snorted, eyes darting between Clarissa and the sheriff.

"That right? Well, I heard somethin' like that once 'fore but didn't believe it. Now ya tellin' us it's true?" he asked.

"Yes, sir," she replied, a shadow of sadness escaping her eyes, a glimpse of a past she rarely let surface.

"For heaven's sake," the deputy muttered, shaking his head, skeptical.

Clarissa ignored him, her focus shifting to the truck.

She walked around to the tailgate, her steps firm, though a slight tremble betrayed her hands as she reached for the sheet.

Pulling it back, she revealed Pawdad's face. Her expression softened, bittersweet as she looked down at him.

"This here is my brother," she said. "My half-brother. Though we barely spoke a handful of words our entire lives."

Sheriff Ronell, unshaken and growing impatient, grunted as he rubbed his chin, his eyes drifting toward the setting sun.

"Well, I'll tell ya what, I've got supper waitin' for me and really don't give a damn what went on in yer family tree. Keep her here as long as ya want. You tire of her, send her on down to Preacher Clive's."

The lawman turned to Ian, giving him a nod, tapping his hat.

"We'll be expectin' ya to bring down the bodies shortly," he added, his voice spent, as he pivoted on his heel and headed for the driver's side of his patrol car.

With that, the sheriff and his deputy climbed into the cruiser. The engine sputtered to life, and they drove off, the sound of the road beneath the tires fading into the distance.

Ian and Clarissa stood by the old blue truck, the somber air hanging thick between them. He traced his hand along the bed rail, fingers brushing the chipped paint, before turning to her, his voice low.

"Clarissa, do you think she'd want to say her goodbyes? I can wait," he offered, a decency in his tone that belied the strength of the man behind it.

Clarissa sighed, her eyes drifting up the road where Benjamin and Rebecca had chased after Esther.

"She's lost… terrified, Ian. I'm certain she's not ready to face 'em like that," she said, her voice carrying the sorrow of understanding—the burden of knowing what fear can do to a person.

Ian nodded back, all too familiar with it himself.

In the distance, Benjamin sprinted up the road, his legs pumping with the urgency of a boy who knew the importance of his task.

His face was resolute as he reached Esther, gently tapping her arm, trying to pull her back from where her thoughts had wandered.

"Auntie says ya need to come back here," he said, breathless.

Esther didn't respond right away. Her gaze remained fixed on the road ahead, her eyes distant and unfocused, overwhelmed by the day's chaos.

"Oh, no… I need to git goin'. Gotta find a way to get home 'fore dark," she mumbled, as if speaking more to herself than to the boy beside her.

Benjamin looked up at her with big brown eyes, worry visible on his face as he searched for a clue about what to do next.

"How? Ya ain't gonna be crossin' today, least not again," he said, his words small but insistent.

Before Esther could answer, Rebecca darted forward. Her small hands clutched the hem of her dress, as if holding it tightly could somehow make her move faster.

"Benji," the little girl called out. "Ya tell Esther to come back to the house?" Her words nearly tripped over themselves in her haste.

"I did," Benjamin said. He tensed, trying to hold onto a situation that felt too big for him.

"Why ya even comin' up here?" he added, glaring at his sister with a moan.

Ignoring him, Rebecca looked up doe-eyed, her big brown eyes as sweet as dark honey, aware of the power they held.

"Ya are comin' back, right?" she asked Esther with a sincere plea.

Benjamin, gathering his courage, added, "Don't ya want to look at yer Gran and Grandad before they put them in the dirt?"

Esther remained torn between the new safety of the Old Reed House and the dark, lonely road ahead.

The thought of her grandparents' lifeless bodies flickered in her mind, sparking a deep, paralyzing fear that wrapped around her—a twisted, overgrown vine.

Rebecca reached up and took Esther's hand, hoping to break her out of the trance. Her small fingers warmed the chill that Esther hadn't even noticed.

"Yer gonna come stay with us fer now," Rebecca said, deciding for her.

The words carried a tenderness that seemed to echo in the soft chorus of the evening—a mix of peepers calling from a nearby ditch, with the last notes of birdsong still lingering.

Esther looked down at the little girl, and for a moment, the world focused on just the two of them—Rebecca's innocence piercing through the darkness of despair. The care in her young eyes awakened something deep inside her.

It reached a place she had kept sealed tight—a door shut against the wind. But now, dust was creeping in, carried by a breeze she couldn't keep out.

No longer able to resist, she sighed and allowed herself to be led back toward the house.

Each step felt heavy, as if mud from earlier still clung to her bare feet, pulling her down with every move.

Esther avoided looking at the truck as she walked past, deliberately steering clear of it, her feet almost stumbling while her fingers dug into her palms.

Unable to bear the sight of what was inside, she felt a wave of nervous dread wash over her, her breath growing shallower and shallower. It was already hard enough seeing Pawdad's sunken face, his features haunted and distant. But the thought of looking at Gran—well, it petrified her.

The image of Gran in the distance—singing, waiting for the end—remained vivid, replaying over and over, a cruel trick of memory.

No, Esther told herself, squeezing her eyes shut. She had seen enough.

Watching her, Benjamin, insightful for his young age, sensed her unease and straightened his shoulders. He marched over to his father with the seriousness of a man.

"I think she's made her peace with her kin already," he said, his voice steady.

Clarissa, taking in the wisdom of her young great-nephew's words, gave a slight nod and encouraged Rebecca to lead their new guest toward the house.

Esther drew a deep breath as they neared the front steps, the squeal of unfamiliar boards beneath her feet heightening her apprehension.

Just as Esther was about to step into the house, Rebecca tugged on her pant leg, making her pause. The girl looked up, her small hands stretched out. In them, she held a bar of soap—the same one Gran had tossed in anger the day before.

"I saved it for ya," Rebecca said, her eyes wide and hopeful, as if she were handing over a piece of herself along with the little package.

Esther's heart clenched as she saw the carefully tied bow, almost too much to bear.

"Ah… ya found it," she said.

Rebecca nodded, her angelic smile widening.

"Yes, ma'am. I tied the bow all pretty again," she said with childlike pride.

Tears welled up in Esther's tired eyes, but she tried to hold them back as she took the gift.

"Thank ya kindly," she said softly.

Rebecca, pleased, slipped her small hand into Esther's once more, her eyes gazing up with a solemn expression.

"Now that I found somethin' of yers and gave it back to ya, that means we gonna be friends… Alright?"

"That's somethin' friends do," she added, her words filled with a simple truth, spoken with the innocent belief in the power of friendship.

Esther stood there, the words hanging in the air like her tattered blue coveralls—just a worn shell that concealed the girl beneath.

She had never known the comfort of a friend, never felt the kindness this little child now offered so freely. The mix of distrust and desperate yearning in her heart left her teetering as if on a tightrope stretched over a yawning chasm.

For twenty-three years, Esther's grandparents had kept her entirely cut off as if marooned on an island in the Blue Hollow Hills.

They had seeded her mind with fearful thoughts—that the people of Larkin, or anywhere, would never accept her. Never like her. That she was unworthy of even the most basic needs or desires.

"Don't have no friends," Esther whispered. The words slipped out before she could pull them back. Embarrassed, she hated how lonely it made her sound.

Rebecca tilted her head, her tiny fingers tightening around Esther's hand.

"Then that means I am yer best friend, since I am the first," she said with a simple certainty.

Esther gave a shy nod, uncertain of the protocol and uncomfortable with repeating the phrase.

Rebecca was undeterred, beaming up at her. Then, with a gentle tug, the young girl drew Esther into the house.

The air inside was warm, with meat roasting and fresh bread filling the space. But as Esther stepped inside, the adrenaline that had kept her going suddenly faded, and her knees buckled as she caught herself on a wall.

Everything blurred—the comfort of the house threatening to break her.

Rebecca's hand closed around hers again, and Esther felt as if she were leaning on the small girl—a child binding her to this new and foreign life.

There was a strength in Rebecca's small body, a warmth that radiated from her. In that moment, Esther drew from it, courage sparking like a hidden flame, steadying her for what lay ahead.

Chapter 8: A Bath and a Story

Upstairs, Clarissa's bathroom was a sanctuary, a place where the weariness of hard living could be washed away.. Steeped in old-world charm, the room reflected the practicality and warmth of the 1940s.

Walls, a creamy white, absorbed the light of countless days, despite the evening's dimness. Muted hues, softened by lace, filtered through a small frosted glass window.

At the center of the room stood a large, claw-footed bathtub, its white porcelain surface gleaming—a relic from a time when luxury spoke of elegance, not excess. It invited comfort—something Esther had never known in a bath before.

A wooden stand beside the tub held a folded towel, a small glass jar of bath salts, and the paper wrapping from a bar of soap—now discarded.

The soap itself, wet and fragrant, rested in Esther's hands as she soaked in the warm water, her body submerged up to her chin. The warmth seeped into her bones, loosening the knots of tension that had been her constant companions.

A strange, unfamiliar feeling settled over her. She had always taken her scrub-downs in a tin tub set in front of the stove or in the icy waters of the creek. Those baths were practical, quick, and often accompanied by the shivering chill of mountain air. This, however, was wonderfully different.

The water enveloped her, and the soap had a sweet scent, a sharp contrast to the harsh lye bars her grandmother made.

She drew the bar closer to her face and breathed in deep, savoring the scent.

Careful not to disturb the tranquility of the moment, Clarissa quietly opened the door and stepped inside.

"How ya likin' the bath?" she asked, laying a blue dress over the arm of a chair and placing a pair of beaded moccasins on the ground.

With a smile, Esther opened her eyes and looked up.

"I never lay down in a bathtub 'fore. I'm likin' it mighty fine," she said.

Clarissa returned the smile with quiet satisfaction, her kind eyes hinting at unspoken longing. She wanted Esther to like this, to like her, but wouldn't say it aloud.

"I'm glad to hear that. A good soak can do wonders after a day like today," she said. "I couldn't find any shoes that'd fit ya, so I brought some old leather slippers, 'til we can get ya some in town."

She reached down, picked up the moccasins, and held them out for Esther to see.

"They're mighty worn, but they still got some use in them," she went on. "They belonged to my grandmother."

Esther's eyes went wide as she took them in, a stark contrast to her bare feet or the rugged, ill-fitting boots she usually wore.

"Yer granny was an Indian?" she asked.

Clarissa nodded as she pulled a small wooden chair close to the tub, settling in with a quiet sigh. The seat creaked under her weight as she folded her hands in her lap, as if she were about to share a story.

"She was Cherokee," Clarissa said, her voice full of admiration and love, each word a thread in the fabric of their shared history.

Esther stilled to listen, sensing it was more than an old fable. It was a piece of the old woman's soul, a fragment of the past carried down.

"My grandfather was a slave, born in Georgia under the harshest of conditions," Clarissa continued, her voice steady. "He experienced nothing but the chains and the whip for most of his young life."

She paused for a moment, letting the gravity of those words sink in.

"But one day, he found the courage to run. Dangerous business, runnin' from a master, and he knew the risks."

Clarissa's eyes drifted away, lost in reflection, as she continued.

"He couldn't stand the thought of spendin' his whole life in bondage, so he ran. Didn't have a clue where he'd end up, but that didn't matter—just knew he had to get away."

Esther soaked in the story, her fingers tracing the rim of the bathtub.

"My poor Grandpappy moved through the woods at night, livin' off the land. Eatin' whatever critters he could catch. Never knew when they might find him. After weeks of runnin', he stumbled upon my grandmother's people—the Cherokee. They were strong and proud, and understood the dangers in hidin' a runaway."

Clarissa paused, resting a hand on Esther's arm. "They thought of tellin' him to be on his way… but it wasn't easy once they saw the fear in his eyes."

"Then, my great-grandfather, a respected medicine man, saw him in a powerful dream—a dark-skinned young man lookin' for freedom."

"That same mornin', my grandmother told her father about her own dream, her heart certain as the rising sun. Ama knew that strange man, the one called Isaiah, was gonna be her husband."

"The Cherokee saw it as a good omen, a sign from the Great Spirit," Clarissa said, rocking her head in agreement. "So, they hid him, riskin' their lives for the person they believed would become one of their own."

Scenes from the past unfurled in Clarissa's mind, each detail painted itself on a vast canvas. Esther could almost see it too—every stroke filling the quiet spaces between her words.

"But those were dangerous times," Clarissa continued, her voice laced with sorrow. "The government started roundin' up the Cherokee, takin' 'em off the land that had been theirs for generations."

"Isaiah, after tastin' freedom, couldn't bear the thought of bein' shackled again. He'd fought too hard, bled too much to let any man take that from him."

"When the soldiers came roundin' up my grandmother's people, Isaiah took Ama by the hand, and they hid in the river, the tall reeds coverin' their scared faces."

Esther had never heard a story like this before, and as Clarissa spoke, she felt herself being pulled toward memories she had tried to drown long ago.

She vividly recalled hiding as a child, crouched in the dirt beneath the shadows of the wooden porch. Terrified of her Gran's fury—always holding a stick. Although the circumstances were different, the fear was the same, connecting her to the story in a way she hadn't expected.

"They were lucky to find this place," Clarissa went on. "The landowner, Augustus Reed, wasn't like most folks 'round here. He was a man of quiet principles, a hidden abolitionist who didn't believe in slavery."

"But bein' in the South, he had to keep those beliefs locked up under his roof. Holdin' such convictions in these parts was dangerous. So, he kept to himself, kept his family close, and lived a life of quiet defiance."

Clarissa sighed, searching for his eyes in the recesses of her memory. She knew if she could find his eyes—long lost to time—it might bring forth his full face. The memory of the man who changed the fate of two desperate souls.

"When my grandparents first set foot on his land, they didn't know what to expect," she continued. "But Augustus saw somethin' in them—maybe it was their strength, or maybe he just couldn't stand by any longer. He offered them a place to hide, a chance to build a life away from the cruelty they'd known."

"Augustus had only one son, Jeppson Reed, but that boy was cut from a different cloth," Clarissa said, a wistful edge to her voice.

"Jeppson was a rebellious seed, wild as the wind. Didn't wanna settle down and sure didn't have his father's quiet sense of duty. Restless, he was always lookin' fer somethin', but it sure wasn't responsibility."

Esther tilted her head, the glimmer of a memory surfacing, like spotting a penny on the floor that had gone unnoticed.

"I've heard that name before," she said.

Clarissa nodded, offering a sad smile that spoke of an open wound that had never quite healed.

"Jeppson Reed was yer Pawdad's father, though he never claimed 'im outright. Truth be, we ain't sure how many children he fathered in this county. He never wanted just one woman—guess he wasn't one for wedlock."

Like opening an old, dusty box of memories, the old woman leaned back in her chair and sorted through them. There was a longing in her voice—a need to unburden herself, to put the pieces together in front of Esther.

"My mama loved Jeppson somethin' fierce," Clarissa said. "They grew up together. She never married, either, just kept workin' in his house her whole life. She was loyal, even though he didn't deserve it. I'm certain he knew I was his child, but he never offered me his name, just the same…"

Clarissa rose from the chair, rolling her shoulders as if to shake off the pain that had clung to her for years. Taking it as her cue, Esther stood from the tub. Clarissa stepped forward, lifting a worn towel to wrap around her.

But as she did, Clarissa stopped cold, her eyes locking onto Esther and the ravaged skin of her back.

It hit her like an icy wind blowing in from the window, rattling the door and cutting straight through her.

With a trembling hand, she instinctively reached out to touch the undeniable evidence of sad cruelty. Her face tightened, torn between disbelief and sorrow.

The poor girl from the hills had weathered a savagery no human should endure. From nape to tailbone, her back was a landscape of scars—some deep, others raised, some silvered with time, and others still angry and red—each one a silent testament to abuse she'd borne for years.

"Oh—honey…" Clarissa gasped, her words trembling. "I never knew."

Her eyes welled with grief and anger, some of it reflected inwardly.

"I would've done somethin'. I would've come and got ya, no matter what yer Gran and Pawdad might've wanted," she added.

Esther quickly pulled the towel around her shoulders, as if trying to conceal what Clarissa had already seen. The thought of anyone pitying her made her uneasy, a nakedness that shone brighter than bare skin.

"Always wondered why my kin didn't like ya so," Esther said in an apologetic tone, hoping to distract Clarissa from what she'd just laid eyes on.

Easily reading her unease, Clarissa continued, though her voice faltered.

"'Bout forty years ago, yer Pawdad went to see Jeppson. Told 'im he was due somethin', figurin' he was his son and all. Jeppson, always a man of few words and fewer attachments, didn't argue much. But instead of embracin' the bond they might've shared, he offered yer Pawdad that piece of property up on the hill and nothin' more."

"Washin' away the debt with the Blue Hollows. Thinkin' that handin' over a small parcel of earth could make up for all the years of neglect and silence. And that land, rocky and hard to farm, wasn't much. But yer Pawdad took it, more out of pride than anything else," Clarissa said, resting her hands on her hips.

"No different than hangin' sheets on a windy, dusty day—you know it ain't worth the trouble, but you do it anyway, outta sheer stubbornness, thinkin' you can make somethin' outta nothin'."

Esther knew full well what she meant. Though Clarissa hadn't known him in the flesh, she understood Ezekiel Primm with the precision of an arrow.

The stories Esther had heard all her life, the resentment that seeped out of Pawdad, the longing in his eyes—it all made sense now.

The pages of his life had finally found their book.

Esther stood still as Clarissa carefully lifted the dress over her. The woman's hands moved with the tenderness of a mother caring for her child. The fabric whispered as it settled over the girl's thin shoulders, and Clarissa stepped back, a small, approving smile softening her face.

"There," Clarissa said. "That'll do."

A question that had been gnawing at Esther slipped out.

"How'd you come by this place?"

"Well… my mama… she took real good care of Jeppson. Fed him, cleaned him, nursed him when he was laid up all them years," Clarissa said. "Never once did she falter. Never once did she leave his side. Guess he tried to make amends the only way he knew how—by leavin' her this place. Too late, maybe, but it was all he had left."

There was a break in Clarissa's voice, an opening that bared the depth of an old hurt.

Esther searched for words, but none came.

Instead, she just looked at Clarissa. Her eyes spoke for her, filled with sympathy and an understanding of what Clarissa truly meant.

And Esther wanted to believe in the goodness Clarissa was offering her, to embrace it. But trust was a brittle thing—its broken pieces hard to gather.

When Esther finished dressing, hair brushed, Clarissa stood back, a swell of mixed emotions rising in her. The girl reminded her of a young sapling—fragile yet resilient, weathered by more storms than most. The wind had bent her, stripped her leaves, and worn at her roots, yet the core remained unbroken, clinging stubbornly to life.

And like a mother's calling, Clarissa felt the deep urge to protect her, to shield her from the winds that had battered her spirit, to help her grow strong.

As they reached the door, Clarissa paused, resting a gentle hand on Esther's shoulder.

"Honey, ya look so beautiful," she said, her voice rich with affection.

Those words—rare and foreign—had never belonged in Esther's life.

Without thinking, Esther raised her hands to her face, her fingers brushing over her cheekbones, feeling the warmth of her own skin as if trying to connect to the compliment. She felt the rays of Clarissa's words warm her, letting them settle into the cracks of her heart—seeds finding fertile ground.

Then, with a playful nudge to her hip, Clarissa added, "Let's go downstairs," her grin widening as she winked at Esther.

Chapter 9: A Feast

At the center of the home sat the dining room, a beating heart within four walls. It pulsed with tradition, warmth mingling with a quiet grandeur that felt like Clarissa herself.

Though generations had passed through, this space had become her own. Their presence lingered, but it was Clarissa's spirit, still in body form, that imbued the space and was etched into every nook.

A long, dark table stood at the center of the room, set for dinner. Its surface gleamed under the soft glow of the electric light. Draped in a crisp, white linen tablecloth, the place settings showed meticulous care. Each porcelain plate and piece of silverware was perfectly positioned.

As Esther lingered in the doorway, she thought about how she'd always wondered what the inside of the Old Reed House looked like. Folks in their proper clothes, with manners all polished, coming together in this way.

But the sight before her exceeded anything she could have imagined. It was as if she had stepped from the pitch of night into the noonday sun.

Looking down at her dress, it felt stiff beneath her hands as she tried to settle it against her skin. Damp strands of dark hair clung to her back, still heavy from the bath. Bruises, some fresh, some fading, covered her arms and legs—marks from the evening before, and from days long past.

She took a deep breath, her heart hammering in her chest as she crossed the threshold, feeling as though every eye was on her— watching, judging, measuring her worth.

But there was no turning back now. She must do this. She must face them.

As Esther entered the dining room, nerves prickled beneath her skin. The closeness of the others stirred a misplaced sense of caution within her. She tried to steady her unsteady legs, reminding herself that they were just people—people as hungry as she.

On the far side of the house, Ian coaxed the front door open, taming the creak so it wouldn't disturb the tranquility.

He stepped inside, his shirt crisp and clean, freshly ironed for the evening. His boots barely made a sound on the wooden floor as he moved toward the table, each step unhurried.

His gaze swept the room, a playful smile forming as he raised his eyebrows at his children, who grinned back.

Then his eyes landed on Esther. His smile grew wider, the rough edges of his face softening. He had a rugged charm, one that he wore well.

Was this really the same rain-soaked girl he'd seen before? It was a testament to Clarissa's powerful magic—she had a way of restoring people that Ian had witnessed firsthand.

Under his gaze, Esther shifted, the pink rising in her cheeks. Her fingers tugged at the neckline of her floral dress, as if to hide the heat that crept up.

Esther felt exposed, eyeing the exit, but too afraid to leave.

Luckily, Rebecca came to her rescue.

"Esther, come sit by me!" Her bright, eager voice broke the tension.

"Esther can sit where she sees fit, Rebecca," Ian said.

But she was insistent.

"No, Papa, we're best friends, and best friends sit by each other."

The girl from the hills froze, unsure of what to do, her gaze darting between Ian and his daughter. She didn't want to stir up trouble, but the little girl's large, wishful eyes were hard to resist.

With a small nod, more to keep the peace than anything else, she said, "I'll sit here by…"

"By your best friend," Rebecca finished for her, beaming in triumph.

Wearing a hesitant smile, Esther took the seat beside the girl.

Every movement, every breath felt exaggerated—an actor uncertain of her role onstage.

Ian gave his daughter a pointed but gentle look.

"Don't pester her," he said.

Shaking her head, Esther said, "No, it's fine. Rebecca… my best friend Rebecca." The words sat strange on her tongue, a language she didn't understand.

Rebecca glowed—her cheeks so high they appeared bright enough to light the entire room.

"See, Papa. She wants to sit by me."

Benjamin, who had been watching closely, chimed in, his voice earnest.

"We're friends too," he said. "I smile at you when ya ride by. Remember?"

Esther nodded, a hint of joy slipping through and revealing itself in her expression.

"I remember," she said. Benjamin's shy, fleeting smile had been important and not gone without notice—a tiny treasure she put in her heart.

Edging closer to Esther, Rebecca leaned in, her whisper full of mischief.

"Ya can say you're his friend, but just be pretendin', okay?"

Before Esther could respond, Benjamin's foot shot out under the table, connecting with his sister's leg. Rebecca grunted, her eyes narrowing at her brother, who sat there with a satisfied smirk on his face.

A laugh slipped from Esther's lips as the tightness in her chest eased. The siblings' playful bickering brought a strange, unexpected comfort.

Soon, the savory warmth in the room distracted her, pulling her gaze to the feast before her. Clarissa moved quickly, placing hot dishes on the table—golden roasted chicken, creamy mashed potatoes, corn pudding, and fresh vegetables.

It was a sight beyond anything Esther had ever seen—except maybe the wake for her grandmother's sister when she was just a child. But even that was nowhere near as fine. No fancy linens, and the food wasn't as pretty as Clarissa's.

Clarissa offered grace, thanking God for the bounty and mentioning Esther, saying, "Thank you for safely delivering this here girl to this house. We're mighty happy to have her here."

It felt strange to be mentioned at the table like that—almost exposing, making her want to crawl beneath the surface and hide.

Not having fully shut her eyes during the prayer, Esther looked up, catching Mitzy smiling at her with a knowing warmth in her eyes. The toddler in Mitzy's lap twisted around, but she didn't look away.

As the plates and bowls circled the table, Esther was too shy to take a thing. It felt wrong, as if this feast didn't belong to her.

Rebecca noticed her hesitation and gave her a light nudge.

"Go on, take some," she said.

Clarissa's voice carried across the table, warm but firm.

"There's plenty to go around, Esther. Help yourself."

Gathering sparse courage, Esther reached for the serving fork. Her hands trembled as she placed a small piece of chicken on her plate. The simple act felt strange, as though she was taking something that didn't belong to her.

But when she took a bite, the flavors were rich—unlike anything she'd ever tasted before. Encouraged, she took another. The warmth of the meal seemed to seep into her very bones, soothing the ache of loneliness—a hunger that had never carried a name.

Clarissa sat at the head of the table, steering the conversation as she'd done a hundred times before. Her voice was smooth and loving, drawing folks in, her questions gentle but sure, nudging Esther to speak.

The small talk flowed as easily as the blackberry wine, sweet and smooth. Esther took a sip, feeling the warmth slide down her throat, rich and thick, like honey. It left a lingering sweetness that clung to her tongue, making her want another sip.

"Have you always lived in the Blue Hollow Hills, Esther?" Mitzy's voice asked.

"I… I think so," Esther said, her eyes fixed on the plate in front of her.

Abram, who'd been quiet most of the meal, spoke up then. His deep tone held a kind of knowing.

"Hard life up there, I reckon," he said.

Esther only nodded, keeping the words trapped inside. She didn't want to talk about her life up there, didn't want to drag it into this warm, bright room.

Rebecca, a happy chatterbox, leaned in close.

"Ya know, Auntie makes the best banana puddin' in the entire world," she said, her eyes wide. "Ain't nobody makes it like her."

"It's real fine," Esther said, despite it being the first time she'd ever tasted it.

The Primms didn't have sweets much, since Gran had to save most of the sugar for making corn mash.

Food for them had no joy. It was stark, born out of what they could get, not out of love or care. Their meals mainly were venison, plain potatoes, grits, beans, and whatever wild critter Pawdad could bring home. Portions were small, and Esther had grown comfortable with the gnawing pain of hunger in her belly.

Gran had always given the best cuts to Pawdad, saying a man needed his strength to hunt.

Esther learned early how to catch wild game, despite being a girl. She could fire a gun if it came to it, and once she'd shot a black bear that had broken into their cabin in the dead of night, busting down the door like it owned the place.

Not a scrap of that bear went to waste.

Sitting at the table now, tasting the richness of the food before her, Esther couldn't help but wonder if anyone here had ever eaten bear.

Rebecca smiled at the praise, her chest puffing up with pride.

Clarissa, with a playful smirk, pointed her finger at Rebecca.

"Now, don't you go spillin' that secret, young lady. I know you've been spyin' on me."

Rebecca burst into laughter, her joy so full it spilled over, catching everyone around her.

Esther couldn't help but think how strange it was—this place down the hill from her own house, yet the folks here were completely different. They spoke to each other softly, kindly. She hadn't heard one mean word out of anybody's mouth.

She watched as Abram teased Ian about the heap of mashed potatoes on his plate, calling him someone by the name of Paul Bunyan. That got everyone really going.

Ian, grinning, played along. He grabbed another enormous piece of chicken, saying he didn't mind, but since he didn't have an ox, Esther's old mule would have to do.

Unable to contain herself, Esther giggled louder than she intended. Her hand flew to her mouth to stifle the sound, but it only bubbled up more.

Ian's laughter followed—bold, hearty, and rich. The way his eyes lingered on her, sparkling with amusement, told her all she needed to know—he clearly enjoyed charming people with his quick tongue.

Esther couldn't help but think of Gran. She'd filled her head with all kinds of warnings about folks with dark skin. Tired stories passed down like gospel, spoken as if they were carved in stone.

Gran would talk about a curse, one so deep that no amount of prayer could ever wash it clean. But Esther never took it in. Something about it always felt wrong, off in a way she couldn't explain. If she were honest, she wanted nothing to do with Gran's God. He didn't sound anywhere close to a good man—not the way Gran spoke of him.

And now, sitting here, surrounded by the beating hearts of good folk, she could see it clearly.

Those tall tales seemed the most ridiculous lies ever told. All it took was stopping and listening to the rhythm of their hearts.

And Miss Clarissa wasn't just kind—she was family. Pawdad's little sister. That truth cut through every story Gran had ever told.

If this was the Devil's house, Esther thought, then maybe hell wasn't half as terrible as Gran had always warned her.

Clarissa, with her gentle ways and willingness to share, carried a kind of godliness that Gran, with all her harshness and judgment, could never hold. There was a light in her that Gran's words never touched. How could someone such as Clarissa be anything but good?

And what of Ian's children? Esther didn't rightly know what Gran had called them, but from what she could tell, Benjamin and Rebecca were mixed. They were happy, loved, and full of life— everything Gran had claimed they couldn't be.

And Ian? That strange way of speaking that slipped out from time to time—his accent—wasn't strong enough to confuse her. Esther didn't know where Germany was, but in this house, none of that seemed to matter.

As dinner came to a close, she rose from the table, her hands already reaching for the plates and cutlery. But before she could gather anything, Clarissa's hand, warm and gentle, found her shoulder.

"No, darlin'," Clarissa said.

"You've had yourself a hard day. There's plenty of work waiting around here, but tonight, you rest."

Esther looked at her, hesitation flickering in her eyes. She wasn't used to being told to rest. There were always tasks, always something needing doin'. The idea of stopping, of being allowed to sit still, felt strange—unsettling, almost wrong.

But the warmth in Clarissa's eyes told her this wasn't rejection or being cast aside. It was care—pure and simple.

So, Esther nodded, too tired and worn down to argue, and let herself lean into it, just this once.

Clarissa turned to Rebecca and Benjamin, who had already begun clearing the table.

"You young'uns take Esther upstairs to the small room. Make sure she's settled in nice-n-comfortable."

Rebecca's face lit up, and she grabbed Esther's hand, tugging her toward the stairs. Benjamin followed.

The climb up the stairs was quicker than Esther remembered. Before she knew it, she stood in the doorway of a small, neat bedroom. It was simple, but everything in it seemed touched with care. A bright, cheerful handmade quilt lay on the bed, a lamp with a fringed shade sat on the bedside table, and a vase of cut springtime blooms added a soft touch.

Rebecca stood by the window and whispered in a sweet tone, "Esther, look, that's our house. You can see it from here." She gestured toward the dark outline of the small stone home.

"That way, you can find us tomorrow, okay?"

Benjamin, quiet and unsure, noticed a tiny spider crawling across the floor. He didn't say a word, just stepped forward, his movements deliberate, and squashed it underfoot.

Then, without a fuss, he pulled a worn handkerchief from his pocket, wiped the remains away, and gave a small, proud grin.

"Don't worry about that spider curling up to you tonight," he said. "I took care of it."

Rebecca gave her hand one last squeeze before letting go.

"See ya tomorrow," she said, hopeful and happy.

Saying goodnight to the children, Esther shut the door. She had never had a room to herself. Not in this way, with privacy.

The space held its warmth, whispering promises of comfort, but the dream felt unreal—a kindness she didn't know how to hold on to.

Quiet settled over her, as the mist that clung to the Hollows, familiar but unwelcome.

Dinner had been nice, different—no one had looked through her, no one had made her feel as though she wasn't worth the food they fed her.

Clarissa had laid out the table as if she were serving kings from the Good Book, every dish an offering without a price.

But just as that thought took root, Gran's voice surged up from the corners of her mind, sharp as a nail. It warned how the devil could dress himself up fine, how he could sweet-talk his way into your soul.

Esther clutched the thick quilt as if its weight could silence the echoes in her mind. She tried to cling to the good feeling from earlier, willing it to stay, to lull her into sleep, but it was slippery and refused to let her catch it.

As she lay there, she fought not just Gran's voice, but the ones she made in her own mind—whispers that urged her to go back to the water, to join Gran and Pawdad where the current was strong and sure.

It told her that Clarissa's house wasn't real, that she'd never truly left the river's grasp. Maybe she hadn't. Perhaps she was still trapped in the water's pull, passing over herself—a spirit who didn't know she was gone.

Her imagination ran wild as the old oak outside cast moving shadows, clawing at the walls—reaching for her.

And the sound of the torrent's roar echoed in her ears, a haunting refrain. Over and over, she replayed how she could have done things differently. Why didn't she grab Gran and pull her out with her?

Flashes of Pawdad's face tormented her too, pale and still, as if the earth had already claimed him and set the maggots to work. The life had drained from his eyes, leaving nothing but the emptiness that comes when the soul has taken its leave.

She prayed that if she were alive, they wouldn't come back for her, not in dreams or shadows. Esther's imagination was worn thin, her thoughts tangled in a web she couldn't escape.

She pressed a pillow over her face, trying to muffle the scream that clawed at her throat. But it stayed buried deep inside, refusing to be freed.

In those silent, sleepless moments, the boundary between past and present, reality and nightmare, blurred.

She didn't know how to stop becoming her own ghost, haunting herself. Or maybe she had been for a long time, not living in the earthly realm, just drifting—part in and part out of it all.

She wanted to cry, to let the sadness pour out, but the tears refused to come. The truth settled over her, cold and inescapable.

"I am the ghost," Esther whispered to herself.

Chapter 10: The Orchard

The morning sun was already high when Esther stirred, the quilt clinging to her, damp from the sweat of a restless night. Unease lingered—a phantom presence, an echo she couldn't shake, no matter how hard she tried.

The room, quiet and serene, seemed different in the daylight—less strange, but still not hers.

She sat up, her eyes tracing the straight lines of the window frame as nervousness crept in. Had she overslept? This wasn't the way to start off in a new place—not like this.

Idleness had never been in her nature—the call of work was always there, lingering in the back of her mind, urging her to rise and get moving.

Gran would have smacked her with a broomstick by now, her voice tearing through the morning chill, screaming at her to bring firewood in, or make sure the smokehouse was tended to.

The brisk mountain air would have met her face before she could even focus, and she'd be moving, hands working without thought, because there was always more to be done.

But no one had awakened her, leaving her to her slumber.

Maybe they were cross at her, fixin' to give her a talkin' to. Gran's constant name-calling still rang in her ears, despite now dwelling with Jesus.

"Useless girl, a waste of skin and bone, that's all ya are," she would say, her voice sharp enough to cut through the veil even now.

As she moved to rise, Esther's eyes were drawn to a dress, neatly laid over the chair in the room. Clarissa had clearly been there.

The evening before, during dinner, Mitzy had mentioned that if Esther didn't mind some hand-me-downs, she had a few things that might fit. She'd laughed, commenting about how her hips had spread since having a baby and how she wasn't sure she'd ever be that size again. Her husband, Abram, only smiled and said he didn't mind, which earned him a playful smack on the arm from Mitzy.

Esther slipped into the pretty dress, worried that such a nice article of clothing would easily become damaged and dirty with physical labor. Her overalls, worn beyond their use, were nowhere to be seen, suspecting Clarissa had done away with them.

The urgency to hurry and finish dressing played in her head again, her fingers moving not fast enough as she fumbled with the last of the buttons.

She eyed a hairbrush, clearly another thing Clarissa had left out for her. Esther paused, gripping the brush hard, and pulled it through the tangles in her hair, as if she could smooth out the knots inside her stomach.

As she moved from the bedroom down the staircase, Esther listened. The house was still, except for the faint sound of dishes clinking in the kitchen. Clarissa was already busy, just as Esther had worried.

Determined to avoid the older woman, Esther slipped out the front door like a thief, shutting it quietly behind her. She even held the doorknob, just as she had seen Ian do, careful not to draw Clarissa's attention.

Outside, the day was brighter than expected, chastising her for her tardy rise.

Bones greeted her on the porch, wagging his tail, happy to see her. She gave him a morning scratch on the ears, grateful for a familiar face.

"Stay," she told him, and he did obediently.

The air carried a coolness, laced with the sweet scent of blossoms, gently drawing her toward the grove. The orchard stretched out before her, a stunning sight that made Esther catch her breath.

Row upon row of trees, dressed in their springtime coats, with bright pink blossoms cascading almost to the earth.

Yet the storm from the day before had punished the fragile trees, and broken branches littered the ground. Here and there, blossoms had been torn from them, their pink petals now scattered across the earth—delicate wasted promises.

Esther headed toward the upper orchard, her steps slowing as Ian and Abram came into view up ahead. The two men were deep in the rhythm of their work, sleeves rolled up, sweat glistening on their brows.

Ian, with a firm grip on the pruning saw, worked methodically, choosing the exact spot to trim away the damaged wood. There was a focused intensity in his eyes, as if he didn't take pleasure in wounding the trees, but knew what was best for them.

Abram moved in silence, bending low to gather fallen limbs, tossing them aside effortlessly, as if it were second nature.

The girl paused, watching them. Their movements were steady, grounded in the earth itself, as if they had become part of the land. Esther hesitated. The idea of interrupting was unsettling.

Joining in just didn't feel right, like she'd be barging in on something old and unspoken between them and the soil under their feet.

She'd never had to ask for work—tasks had always come naturally, woven into her days. But here, everything felt uncertain. She didn't know where she belonged or what hands like hers were meant to do in a place like this.

Esther inhaled deeply. Her fingers brushed against her chest, feeling the steady rise and fall. Her pulse thudded beneath her palm, its rhythm unsettling. She squared her shoulders and lifted her chin, masking the fear spreading through her with the intensity of wildfire.

When she approached the two men, she stood silently.

Time dragged on, each second painfully slow as she waited for them to notice her.

Finally, Ian looked up, his gaze catching on the willowy girl standing only a short distance away—her presence a surprise in the stillness.

He finished his task, then paused, setting down his saw and straightening up. Abram followed suit, resting his hands on his hips, eyeing her curiously.

Giving a small smile, Ian said, "Well, hello. Is there something you need?" His voice was pleasant but held a hint of distraction, clearly drawn from his work.

"What ya want me to do?" Esther blurted out, instantly regretting the tone she had used.

The men exchanged a glance, something unspoken and almost humorous passing between them.

Then Abram turned to Esther, speaking before Ian had a chance to answer.

"Ain't no need for ya out here," he said. "Ya grievin', so go on back inside and grieve."

Ian quickly interjected, his tone softening.

"What he means is that we're just finishing up here. Appreciate the offer, though."

Shooting Abram a look of disapproval, Ian knew it was too late. His friend's words had been too curt.

The expression on Esther's face bore the mark—her lips twitched inward, the barest hint of a downturn, as if the sting of rejection had stolen the warmth from her.

It was a sadness easily read by the tall German man.

She let her hurt harden quickly into defiance. She wasn't used to being turned away, and the fear of being seen as a burden terrified her.

"Never rested a day in my life," she said. "Laziness is the devil's business and… I'm stronger than I look."

"I can chop down a tree quicker than most men, I reckon."

Abram raised an eyebrow, his tone a blend of sarcasm and skepticism.

"Well, we ain't choppin' any trees down today. Go see if Clarissa's got somethin' fer ya to do."

Bristling at the suggestion, Esther quickly responded, her voice sharper.

"Oh, I don't do womanly work so well."

Abram folded his arms and said, "Is that right?"

Taking a swig from his canteen, Ian nearly choked on the water. He could see Abram digging his own grave—and fast.

"Women's work is only for smart folk," Esther shot back.

It was something Gran had drilled into her many times. But the moment she said it out loud, it twisted inside her, reminiscent of the time she'd eaten pokeberries as a child. It sounded wrong, and she knew it.

Frustration simmered—this wasn't how she had imagined it would go. She thought they'd just hand her a chore and let her be.

Instead, she was at a loss, overwhelmed by a feeling that made her want to fly toward the hills, to run fast and far.

All she could hear was the echo of doubt—these people didn't really want her. They saw no value, not even in the labor she offered.

Maybe it was because she was so thin, so worn down, weary like the old mule in the barn.

As Abram was about to say something else, Ian interrupted, taking control of the conversation that was clearly heading in the wrong direction.

"Tell you what," he said warmly. "My children have taken a liking to you—and whether or not you want that much attention, I apologize."

He paused for a moment before adding, "Maybe you could check in on them from time to time. If you don't mind."

The suggestion instantly surprised Esther. She hadn't expected Ian to offer her such a job, let alone trust her with something so personal—his young'uns.

Sensing her hesitation, though not knowing the exact cause, he reassured her the best he could.

"They won't break. They're past the breaking age," he said, confidence laced with humor.

Before she had even agreed, Ian gestured toward his home beyond the orchard, the roof barely visible through the trees, his hand lingering as if to draw her attention there.

"See that house over there? They oughta be in there. If they aren't, just holler their names, and they'll come running."

Taking a moment, Ian added, "Or… they might be over at Clarissa's, trying to sweet-talk her into a treat."

Esther followed his gaze. The simple stone facade, with its weathered texture and aged wooden shutters, had a warm glow in the sun, not at all unwelcoming.

The thought of being useful to someone, especially to the man who seemed to run things for Clarissa, felt like a good thing. If this was his request, she'd oblige. The idea of spending time with his children was oddly appealing—they weren't intimidating, and they made her laugh.

"Well… alright then," she said slowly, though her voice held a note of uncertainty. "Ya sure you don't need my help here?"

Ian shook his head, his smile widening.

"We'll get by."

She nodded, as though they had just struck a bargain, and spun away. Relief washed over her as she walked swiftly from them, her steps almost an escape. Keep walking, she told herself. Do as he asked.

Once she was out of earshot, Abram's brow furrowed as he watched her walk off.

"You sure she's up to watchin' after 'em?" he asked.

"Oh, it's not them I'm worried about," Ian said, a grin tugging at his mouth.

He turned back to the peach tree in front of him, examining the bark.

"I fear she doesn't know what she's in for, though," he added with a light tone.

"That little girl of yours could talk the ears off a deaf man, that's for sure," Abram said, letting out a deep, rumbling chuckle that echoed through the air.

Ian shook his head, grinning as he pulled a rag from his pocket and wiped the sweat from his neck.

"Like I said, I'm not worried about them."

As Esther walked toward the cottage, the sound of Abram's laughter faded behind her, leaving her alone with her thoughts.

Relieved the whole confrontation was over, she couldn't help but wonder why she'd gone out there in the first place. They clearly didn't like women meddling while they were workin'. And women's work—how in the hell was she supposed to do that right? She had never really learned to cook or bake—Gran had made sure of that. But she'd done just about everything else.

Something else gnawed at her, too—that blond man had smiled a lot, and she wasn't used to that. His smile bothered her— the way he held it, gaze locked on hers, never looking away.

As she continued toward his house, she kept trying to figure it out.

Maybe what really vexed her was that she liked Ian's face, she confessed to herself. Couldn't find a darn thing wrong with him. Was it the way his eyes smiled even when he talked? She'd noticed it at dinner the night before—how he listened when she spoke, not dismissing her.

Esther knew little of male attention, but back when she was younger, Gran had taken her to Larkin more often—sometimes to revivals, other times to visit her great-aunt Jones. She had noticed the way men stared even then, but as her body grew into that of a woman, those trips became few and far between.

On the rare occasions they went, a couple of strangers—young men—had tried to talk to her, flashing quick smiles. She'd felt awkward, unsure of what to say, and when she dared smile back, Gran had publicly shamed her for it.

Maybe it was because she didn't quite fit in with the townsfolk, but her grandparents never gave her the chance.

Then there was her cousin Clive—she knew all too well what his stares meant, and that was perhaps the main reason Gran had stopped taking her to town.

Gran had made her feel responsible for his attention, even though Esther had never asked for it. When she was younger, Clive had been overly familiar, telling her she was a "*pretty lil' girl.*" At the time, she'd enjoyed hearing it—no one else ever told her that.

But now… now she detested him!

"Don't tempt the devil with your ways," Pearl Primm would always say, reminding her it was her job to be meek and quiet in spirit.

Esther once asked her grandmother how she met Pawdad, and how she was supposed to find herself a man someday.

Gran let out a rough laugh and said, "You're a fool, girl, if you think any man would want you fer a wife. A man'll only want one thing from the likes of you."

Esther hadn't understood it then, but now, as she walked away from Ian's smile and Abram's scrutiny, those words echoed with a bitter clarity. Maybe Gran had been right all along. What was there in her for anyone to want?

Chapter 11: Laughter

A large oak door loomed before Esther, its hand-crafted brown surface imposing and weighty. It stood with a solid presence, as if declaring it wasn't in the mood for visitors today.

Esther hesitated, staring at it as if it were a formidable foe. These were children—ones who had warmed to her the day before. They weren't intimidating—she reminded herself—but still, her nerves held her back.

That thought should've given her courage. But courage was a fleeting thing, slipping through her fingers like blackbirds scattering from a field.

Her eyes drifted down the dirt road that stretched before the house. She remembered how, just two days ago, those same children had witnessed Gran laying into her. Shame curled in her gut at the memory. She instructed it to go away, but it didn't listen very well.

It would be easy to turn back, whistle for Bones, and take off down that road again.

But up on that hill, there wasn't a soul waiting for her. She kept tellin' herself to stay, but it wore her out, plain and simple.

With a breath that hardly filled her lungs, Esther knocked, knowing real courage would never come. She waited, ears straining for any sound, but there was nothing.

After a moment's hesitation, she pushed the door open. Ian had told her to check on them, after all, and she wasn't one to shy away from her duties.

The hinges made a creaking noise as she stepped inside. The house welcomed her with a cozy, well-lived-in warmth, the kind that spoke of a family that called it home.

There was a light, lingering scent of past fires mixed with a musty yet pleasant aroma, a smell that drifted in but didn't stay too long. Shelves lined the walls, filled with books of all shapes and sizes. Esther had never seen so many. A castle wall, an impenetrable fortress of words she would never breach.

In the center of the room, Rebecca and Benjamin sat at a sturdy wooden table, each with a book open in front of them.

They looked up, surprised, when she entered.

"Yer pa said to look after ya," Esther announced, stepping into the space.

Benjamin, ever the serious one, eyed her thoughtfully.

"We don't need someone watchin' us." He shrugged. "We stay out of trouble most times."

Rebecca, however, broke into a wide, welcoming smile, clapping her hands in joy.

"Esther, you came!"

She jumped up and ran over to Esther, wrapping her arms around her waist as if she had known her forever.

Looking up into Esther's eyes, she said, "Are ya gonna teach me to read better?"

It was easy for Esther to hug the sweet little girl back. It felt natural. But the question pinched at her heart—a wound prodded that had never quite healed.

"Oh, no, I never learned how to do that," she admitted, her voice tinged with regret.

Benjamin's eyes widened in disbelief.

"Are you foolin' me?" he asked, incredulous. "Didn't yer pa and ma teach ya?"

Esther shook her head, a pang of sadness tugging at her.

"I never knew my ma and pa," she said.

Rebecca's smile faltered, her gaze softening. Her voice was small and tender as she asked, "Ever?"

Esther took a deep breath, steadying herself before speaking again.

"My ma ran off when I was just a baby," she said, the words falling from her tongue. It felt strange, almost wrong, to share such things, so personal, with these children.

Rebecca's face fell, and she gently touched Esther's arm.

"Oh, that's so sad," she said. "That happened to me, too."

Benjamin, who had been listening, tensed.

"Mama didn't run off," he interjected sharply, his young voice laced with somberness. "She died. It's not the same thing."

With that, he slammed his book shut and pushed back from the table, clearly upset as his brows drew together in frustration.

He journeyed towards the front door, picking up his homemade slingshot.

Rebecca glanced at Esther, her expression apologetic.

"He doesn't like to think on sad things," she said.

Esther nodded, understanding the boy's reaction all too well. She hadn't been there more than a few minutes, and already, she felt as if she'd let Ian's children down, making them feel bad.

Uncertainty gnawed at her—what was she even doing here? This was a disaster. Maybe women's work was meant for the smart ones after all.

Benjamin paused in the doorway, his back to the room. Regret flickered across his face as he half-turned. For a moment, his shoulders sagged before he asked, "Ya feelin' bad about yer Gran and Grandad?" His voice softened, an apology lingering there.

Esther swallowed hard, trying to find the right words.

"I think so," she admitted. "Never woke up nowhere 'cept my home. Feels sorta… different."

Benjamin nodded, seeming to understand more than he let on. He shuffled his feet a little, eyes fixed on the floor.

After a pause, he glanced up before asking, "How come yer Gran never taught ya to read?"

Esther sighed, the memory of her Gran's frustration rushing back.

"Oh, she tried," she said. "But I just never got the hang of it. It only made her cross."

For the first time, Esther truly realized how much her lack of interest in readin' had stemmed from Gran's frustration. All those years, she'd felt stupid, but now she gave herself some grace. Maybe if someone kind, like Clarissa, had been patient with her, she might've picked it up.

Pawdad had tried a couple of times, but Gran would always say, "He didn't have time to be foolin' with a child. He had better things to do, such as hunting."

Rebecca, eager to lift the mood, offered a bright smile.

"Well, it takes a long time to learn it. I'm just startin', but Benji can do it by himself now," she said, as if her brother's skill was her own achievement, too.

Benjamin's brow furrowed, as if he were working out a solution.

"Maybe my pa could teach ya some words," he suggested, a bit of his father's practicality showing through.

"He's real good at that kinda thing, used to be a teacher, y'know. He can read and write in both German and English."

Esther blinked in surprise, the offer catching her off guard.

"He must be really smart," she said, her voice laced with a mix of admiration and uncertainty.

Benjamin nodded enthusiastically.

"I will ask him," he said, already turning toward the door.

Panic shot through Esther at the thought. The last thing she wanted was to draw more attention to her shortcomings.

"Oh, no, don't," she said, her tone rising in alarm, pleading. "Please don't."

Rebecca, sensing Esther's distress, hastened to reassure her.

"Don't be frightened," she said, reaching out to stroke Esther's hand, her touch gentle. "My pa is real nice."

But Esther couldn't shake the fear and embarrassment that gripped her.

"No, I just don't want to," she said, her words trembling. "Please don't. Just don't say nothin' 'bout that to him. Please."

Rebecca's sweet eyes filled with concern as she noticed the uneasiness in Esther's voice. She nodded, almost resembling a little mama, just as she'd seen Aunt Clarissa do, and reached out to grip Esther's hand.

"We ain't gonna say a word, honey," she said, her words firm with reassurance. "We're best friends, and best friends can trust each other. Right, Benji?"

Benjamin, confused by Esther's reaction, nodded reluctantly.

"Well, I think it's just silly," he said, his voice tinged with frustration as he tried to understand why anyone wouldn't want to learn. "Words aren't scary."

With that, he turned and walked out the front door, letting it bang shut behind him.

Watching him go, Rebecca placed her tiny hands on her hips and faced Esther with a reassuring smile.

"Don't worry," she said. "Benji won't say a thing. I'll make sure of it. If he does, I'll tell Papa it was him that hit the truck window with a rock."

"Oh no, don't do that," Esther interjected, trying to dissuade the little girl from her plan, unsure if Rebecca was serious or just playing.

"That's nice of ya and all, but don't get your brother in trouble. Wouldn't ya be sad if he got a whoopin'?" she added.

"Oh, my papa wouldn't whoop him. He just gets real serious," Rebecca said, a sudden light sparking in her eyes.

Pulling a chair from the table, she climbed up, her hands gripping the edge for balance as if she were preparing for a grand performance.

She straightened her shoulders, her face growing serious as she imitated her father's stern expression. Raising her arm straight, she shook her small finger back and forth, her voice dropping into a deep, authoritative tone.

"Son… I'm real disappointed in you," she said, pausing for effect. "Why'd ya go and do something so silly?"

Esther couldn't help but chuckle as Rebecca continued her performance. This little girl was a spark, that was fer sure.

"Now you're gonna have to pick two rows of weeds in the garden," Rebecca continued with a big laugh. Her brown curls bounced as she shook with giggles, the sound filling the room.

Benjamin returned just as quickly as he had left, catching the tail end of Rebecca's impression. He smiled, amused by her portrayal.

He walked over to help his little sister down from the chair, but not before Rebecca scolded him one more time.

"Did you tear the knees out of your nice britches? That's three more rows for you!"

"Get down," Benjamin said, pulling her off the chair. "You're the one who's so silly," he teased, tousling her hair.

When Esther was younger, she used to pretend she had a sister with a spirit much like Rebecca's—someone to run through the woods with, someone to share secrets with.

She would often talk to her, as if she were as real as the day, and sometimes, her sister would even appear in her dreams, as vivid as her imagination.

But the reality of it—the way Benjamin and Rebecca played and bickered—was something she had never known.

There was something special in the way Benjamin, even when frustrated, still looked after his little sister. The way he gently pulled her off the chair, making sure she wouldn't fall. It filled Esther with warmth, their brightness bleeding into the darkness she had carried for so long—vivid warm colors, hues of every kind, stroking over gray.

Distracted, Rebecca glanced at a shelf, then back at Esther.

"Do ya wanna play a game?" she said, her voice brimming with enthusiasm.

Esther paused, uncertain. Games weren't something she'd ever played—at least not the kind Rebecca was thinking of. But the eagerness in the little girl's eyes made her reconsider.

Nodding, Esther agreed and followed Rebecca's instructions, pulling down the box from the shelf.

While Rebecca and Benjamin cleaned up their books, making room on the table, Esther's gaze wandered to a row of framed photos carefully arranged on a nearby shelf.

One picture drew her in—a small snapshot of Ian and his wife. She picked it up, studying the youthful faces. Ian looked much younger, and his wife, wearing a pretty hat, had a joyful smile—the same smile that Rebecca's face now wore.

Full of excitement, Rebecca's voice brought her back to the moment, urging her to join them at the table.

"I don't know how to play. Yer gonna have to teach me," Esther replied, her uncertainty clear, as she set the photo down.

"I'll show ya how," Rebecca said, as her enthusiasm only grew.

"Okay," Esther agreed, feeling a bit more at ease. "Show me how it's done."

Rebecca set up the checkered board, explaining the rules as she went along. Esther listened, trying to take it all in.

The game seemed simple enough, but it required a strategy that Esther wasn't sure she had. Still, she was determined to try it, if only to see Rebecca happy.

As they played, Esther relaxed more with each move. The simple act of sliding the round checker pieces around and planning her next step had a surprisingly calming effect.

The game gave Esther something to focus on other than the turmoil that had been swirling inside her since she arrived.

Rebecca was patient and encouraging, offering tips and advice without making Esther feel foolish. It was a tenderness Esther wasn't used to, but one she appreciated.

Benjamin soon joined them, watching and contributing with occasional sound advice. His presence had a charming influence, and Esther found herself enjoying the game more than she had expected. There was something about the way the three of them interacted that felt natural, as if they had known each other far longer than just a day.

Eventually, the activity ended with Rebecca declaring herself the winner, her face lighting up with a triumphant grin. Esther laughed loudly, an authentic sound, not held back or stifled, and as light as the children's.

As the afternoon unfolded, the three of them found a comfortable rhythm in their chatter. They spoke of the animals they'd seen around the farm, and the games they enjoyed playing.

Esther even told the story of the black bear she had shot. Rebecca's eyes went wide with delight, her energy contagious. She showered Esther with questions, then leapt up to mimic the bear crashing through the front door, her glee spilling into the room.

Benjamin, quieter by nature, listened closely. But when he spoke, a note of doubt crept into his voice.

"Did ya really kill it by yourself?" he asked, clearly skeptical.

Esther noticed the uncertainty in his tone. With a playful smile, she teased that she could bring down the bear pelt from the cabin if he needed proof. That seemed to put Benjamin at ease. He nodded, then asked if she thought she could hit anything with his slingshot. Esther grinned and promised to try it the next day.

When the afternoon light softened and shadows stretched across the land, Clarissa, ever mindful, sent Mitzy to fetch the children and Esther, concerned they might have missed more than one meal.

On the back porch of the Old Reed House sat a simple platter—chicken salad sandwiches on thick slices of homemade bread, deviled eggs beside them, and jarred peaches glistening in the fading light. Each bite carried the taste of the day's work and care.

The children, not wanting the fun to end, convinced Esther to picnic with them. Using a big blanket, they spread it wide over the grass, making enough room for everyone. Clarissa, Mitzy, and her little baby, asleep in her arms, joined as well.

As they were finishing up, Ian and Abram walked over, done for the day. Ian stretched, letting out a playful growl, his eyes landing on the remaining food. He rubbed his stomach, clearly hungry, his posture and dirty shirt a testament to the hard work he had put in. Despite it all, he wore an easy grin, happy to see people enjoying themselves.

Clarissa, already up, instructed the men to wait while she brought out some more sandwiches.

Ian plopped down on the blanket as he let out a satisfied sigh. Without hesitation, he reached for the jar of peaches, his large hand dunking inside and pulling out a sticky slice, juice running down his fingers. Mitzy gave him a mock-disapproving look, her eyes narrowing with playful concern.

"Clarissa's gonna catch you, Ian," she said, a teasing smile tugging at her lips.

"Naw, she won't," Ian replied, a mischievous glint in his eyes as he reached for another slice.

"Especially if I eat all of them." His grin grew wider, defiant, as he sucked the juice from his fingers, ignoring the huff from Mitzy.

Turning his attention to Esther, who sat with her legs tucked beneath her, only inches from his feet, he lounged back on one elbow, his gaze warm.

Looks like they didn't tie you up or anything," Ian said, pretending to be serious.

Esther's smile widened, though she felt a little confused. Did he mean anything by that, or was he just tryin' to ruffle her feathers? Either way, she didn't mind. It made her feel like she belonged.

He continued, "What prohibited activity did they try to convince you to do today? You know, what kind of trouble were they up to?" He asked. "And don't let them fool you about the river, either. They know better, especially right now."

"Oh, nothin' too wild. Savin' that fer tomorrow," Esther said, trying to keep a straight face. When she saw the real look of concern in Ian's eyes, she finally let a smile slip.

Clearly, despite her isolation, Esther was a girl who could give as good as she got when she felt comfortable, and Ian appreciated that kind of wit.

Hearing his father, Benjamin came up, a play gun fashioned from a twig in his hand, his small feet rustling the grass as he approached.

"We know better, Pa. And we wouldn't tie up Esther… Well, unless she wanted us to, like she was a pirate or somethin'," he said, glancing up with a grin, his voice full of earnestness.

Ian's eyes crinkled with a smile.

"Let me see what you got there?" he asked, his voice light.

As Benjamin approached, Ian's arm shot out, the suddenness of it catching his son off guard. He pulled Benjamin into a playful headlock, the boy's laughter bursting out in peals.

Worried, Mitzy scrambled to move the food tray out of the way just as Ian rolled, with Benjamin squirming and giggling as he tried to break free. When Ian shifted back, Esther quickly grabbed her glass of iced tea and set it aside, just in time, as the blanket pulled beneath their quick movements.

"Sorry," Ian mumbled, looking up at Esther for a split second, his grin sheepish as he continued to tickle his son. Benjamin's laughter echoed, his high-pitched giggles infectious as he wriggled under his father's grasp.

"Pa, you smell," Benjamin complained, scrunching his nose and attempting to push away.

"What? That's just the natural scent of pure handsomeness, son," Ian laughed, leaning closer, his armpit hovering near Benjamin's face. "You should try smellin' Abram."

Abram, lying completely sprawled out on the cool grass, groaned without opening his eyes.

"This shirt could crawl home by itself," he muttered, his voice carrying a playful resignation.

"He ain't lyin' neither," Mitzy chimed in, her eyes sparkling as she smirked at her husband.

Abram turned onto his side, calling his wife over with a lazy crook of his finger, his lips curving into a smile.

"Come over here and give me a kiss, woman," he said.

Mitzy shook her head, glancing down at the baby asleep on its blanket beside her.

"He's asleep," Abram urged, his eyes half-closed and a pleading note in his voice. "Please don't make me get up."

Sighing dramatically, Mitzy crawled over to him on her knees, the grass tickling her fingers. She gave him a quick peck on the lips, but Abram pulled her in for a longer, deeper kiss, his arm wrapping around her waist.

Esther quickly looked away, her cheeks warming at the public display. She turned her head just in time to meet Ian's gaze—his eyes twinkling with amusement.

"You're gonna have to get used to that," he whispered, leaning in slightly. "They forget we're here all the time."

Esther shook her head in disbelief, smiling back at him. She let her eyes wander to the baby, curled up and content.

"So, ya sayin' this little sprout is just the first of many?" she teased, her accent thickening.

"Exactly," Ian responded, his brows raising as a wide grin spread across his face.

"I'm thinkin' a good even dozen before they're done."

"Good Lord," Esther laughed. She couldn't believe she said something so shocking, but he seemed to think she was funny, which only encouraged her more.

Ian chuckled as he reached for the peach jar, his fingers brushing hers for a moment. He pulled out another slice, pausing briefly.

"You didn't want any more, right?" he asked.

"No thank ya. Never ate so much in my life," Esther replied, sincerity in her eyes.

With a grin, Ian leaned in a little closer.

"Let me tell you a secret—Clarissa will feed you if you so much as blink with a hint of hunger. Swears she can see it in your eyes," he mused.

"Even if you're not hungry, you might as well just eat—she won't rest 'til she's seen you take a bite," he added.

Esther laughed, shaking her head knowingly.

"Ha! I'm not surprised in the least bit. Should have wagered with Abram," Ian laughed, leaning his head back in disbelief. "So, what did she say?"

"Pretty much what ya said, maybe somethin' 'bout seein' a hole in my belly," she whispered, looking to make sure Clarissa couldn't hear her.

"Yep," he replied with a confident nod, reaching for the last peach in the jar, then triumphantly shaking it in the air for Mitzy to see.

"Well, ain't ya a good boy, Ian," Mitzy said with a playful, sarcastic smile.

As Ian was about to set the jar down, Esther, feeling unusually bold, pointed at it and said, "There's still some juice."

Without missing a beat, Ian picked it up and chugged the last of the liquid, then looked over at Mitzy with a grin.

"Did you put poor Esther up to that?"

Mitzy laughed as Abram groaned, rolling onto his back.

"Oh Lord, two of them? Just what this place needs," he muttered, raising his hands together in playful prayer.

A smile danced on Esther's lips. These people were funny—outright entertaining.

It reminded her of how she had traded jokes with her Pawdad from time to time—though only when they were off hunting on the hillside alone. He hadn't minded, maybe even enjoyed it, sometimes lookin' for an excuse to take her along. She remembered a time she'd made him laugh so hard he cried, tellin' her, "Best not let Gran hear that, or she'll think ya wicked fer sure."

But being part of a group like this, not hidin' out, that was something new.

It felt nice.

Just then, Rebecca came skipping over, her feet barely touching the ground, her curls bouncing as she twirled once and plopped down on Esther's lap.

"Rebecca, don't just sit on her," Ian scolded, his tone affectionate.

"I don't mind," Esther said, giving Rebecca's shoulder a gentle squeeze. The little girl lit up, her eyes bright.

"I made something for ya, Esther," Rebecca announced, pulling a small, wilted bracelet from her pocket.

"I was gonna make you a crown, but I couldn't find more of them flowers," she explained, carefully slipping the bracelet over Esther's wrist.

"Ya like it?" she asked, her voice hopeful.

Esther looked down at the fragile flowers, their petals slightly crumpled, and her heart swelled.

"I love it," she said softly, her voice thick with emotion. "Thank ya."

And she meant it—she loved everything about this place, this moment.

Esther couldn't help but reach up and touch the smile on her own face, an expression that grew into a wide crescent, lifting her cheeks. It felt comfortable there, like it belonged on her lips.

This might have been the best day of her entire life—freedom to feel joy, to carry it openly.

Freedom.

She let the idea rest in her heart, breathing it in deeply.

Despite the loss of her grandparents, she refused to let them take this away from her. They had taken enough.

If Gran had truly sacrificed herself, severing the bind that held Esther to her, then she would accept that gift. She wouldn't waste another day.

For the first time in her life, the girl from the hills didn't wish to be anywhere else but here, in this moment at the Old Reed Estate.

The earlier encounter in the orchard was already forgotten—she just needed to figure out how things worked here. Her role was different now, and she didn't mind.

Esther even found herself looking forward to seeing Ian's kids the next day. They had made plans for an adventure—the children were eager to really show her around.

If this was heaven, she thought, she'd stay forever if given the choice.

Chapter 12: Threads of the Past

The afternoon sun dipped low in the sky, filling the rural estate with a honeyed amber glow. It washed over the land—an oil painting bathed in rich, soft colors, ethereal. Weeks had passed since Esther had been born of the river into this new life. Though the dark parts of her past still whispered from the corners, she had found a kind of solace. It grew as a seed in a plowed field, nurtured by the emerging routines and bonds she was tending.

That day, the scent of freshly laundered linens filled the warm spring air, giving the land a serene, almost otherworldly calm.

Standing by the clothesline, Clarissa's plump figure moved steadily, her strong arms unpinning sheets that fluttered in the breeze.

Bringing in clean, crisp linens had always been one of Clarissa's favorite tasks—a soothing simplicity, such as taking down the billowing sails of a seaborne ship. The light carried through the fabric, giving it a soft glow. Joy was clear in the corners of her eyes.

In the background, the sounds of children's laughter filled the space as Esther played with Benjamin and Rebecca. Bones, despite the gray in his muzzle, barked and dashed around with the children, his tail wagging furiously.

Esther joined in, chasing the kids by a large oak tree. She reached for them, letting them get away, as Rebecca's squeals echoed down to the orchard.

Collapsing into the damp grass, she laced her fingers behind her head as Ian's children giggled and tumbled over her legs. They wriggled as if fueled by the sun.

It didn't help that the shaggy dog, still buzzing with excitement, circled them a few times before finally settling down with a satisfied huff when Esther called him.

Esther watched the leaves of the oak tree sway above her, their movement hypnotic. Out of habit, she listened… hoping to hear God say something.

It didn't seem to matter as much as it used to—making her feel a little guilty—like she cared only when there was a longing deep in her soul.

With a sigh, Esther pulled herself to her feet and walked over to where Clarissa was still bringing in the last of the laundry. Glancing up as Esther approached, Clarissa put her hands on her hips.

"Y'all tired out?" Clarissa asked.

Esther shrugged, brushing a few stray strands of hair from her face. "No… well, maybe a bit."

"They'll run ya ragged if ya let 'em," Clarissa chuckled.

There was a warmth in her gaze, a kind of affection that had grown clearer as the days passed. She had taken to Esther like one of her own, and it showed in the way she spoke to her, tending to her with care.

Watching the children under the shady tree, Esther felt the question she'd been holding back rise to her lips.

"What happened to their ma?" she asked hesitantly.

"Their mother was my niece," Clarissa said, a shadow of sadness passing over her. "Our beautiful Adeline… she was the daughter of my late husband's sister. When Obadiah and I took her in, she was just a little girl, barely old enough to understand what had happened. Little, just like Rebecca."

There was something almost sacred in the way Clarissa spoke of Adeline, as though the memories were delicate flowers that needed to be handled with care, not speaking her name too loudly.

"We never had children of our own," Clarissa went on. "So, Adeline was our blessing. She was such a bright spark of a girl—always had a book in her hand and big ideas in her heart. She wanted to be a teacher, ya know, like Ian. Was goin' to school up north, full of hope and plans for the future."

Esther thought of the woman she would never know, someone who was part of the history of every person here but her.

"She met Ian up there?" she asked, recalling how the children had mentioned a city by the name of New York.

Clarissa nodded, a faint smile playing at the corners of her mouth.

"Yes, she did. They fell in love—hard and fast, like young folks often do. Got married and settled down, thinkin' they'd build a life together. But times were tough, and when work dried up, they had no choice but to come down here. We had work for Ian in the orchard, and they made the best of it."

Esther couldn't even imagine a city. Even though the children had shown her pictures, her eyes had never seen beyond the Blue Hollow Hills and Larkin.

"And their ma… is this where she died?" she asked, trying hard to give the question the care it deserved.

Clarissa's smile faded, replaced by sorrow.

"Yes, darlin'," she said softly. "She's buried in our graveyard with the rest of our people. It was such a very hard time for all of us. Losing her… it was like losin' a piece of myself."

"How… how'd she die?" Esther pressed, though she hesitated, worried the question might bring Clarissa more distress.

"We never rightly knew what took her," Clarissa admitted. The old woman paused, remembering. "She slipped on a wet road and hit her head—one day she was fine, the next she couldn't even stand, legs wobbly like a new colt."

"Ian… Well, Ian did everything he could to save her, rushed her to the town doctor, but…" Clarissa sighed and looked away, the truth almost too heavy to speak.

"That damn doctor refused to see her," Clarissa went on, her voice edged with bitterness. "Said it was on account of her bein' married to a white fella."

"Ian rushed to another town—a man he knew would see Black folk. He thought she'd fallen asleep in the car, didn't want to wake her, cause her head had been achin' somethin' awful. But when he got there…" Clarissa trailed off, her voice breaking. "It was too late."

"The doctor told Ian it wouldn't have mattered—that there would have been nothin' he could've done anyway—tryin' to help the poor man from feelin' responsible." Clarissa's face wore the story in her falling tears, her eyes brimming as she spoke.

Esther couldn't imagine the agony Ian must have experienced, watching the woman he loved slip into the unknown, knowing there wasn't a thing he could do to save her.

"That's not right, not right at all," Esther said.

Clarissa nodded. "It was a terrible thing, honey. And it broke Ian down hard. Fer a long time, I wondered if he'd ever let his grip on her go, let her rest in peace. But slow-like, his happiness returned.

"But it was mighty difficult, 'cause Rebecca was just a little babe. She wanted her momma somethin' fierce. And Ian would stand and rock her for hours, tryin' to comfort her the best way a man knows how.

"He told me once that her tears felt like they were tearin' him up inside. He was both heartbroken and angry at Adeline for leavin' 'em."

Clarissa's words cut to the center of Esther's gut, slicing deep and making it bleed—bleed for him, for all that had been taken.

It was a strange thing, because everything about Ian spoke of strength—not just in body, but in mind.

The thought of him tore at her, making him feel more real, as if he weren't just the man with broad shoulders and powerful hands.

Esther had noticed him always watching, making sure he attended to everyone. She could tell how much Clarissa meant to him—he valued her words, careful not to take advantage of her generosity. And he was such a good father. Perhaps a bit sterner than his smile would let on, though.

He'd told Esther just yesterday, "Don't let them run you, you run them." Whatever that meant.

But most of the ideas were hers, like playing in the muddy ditch catchin' frogs in mason jars, which Ian wasn't particularly fond of when he found them lined up on his porch.

Esther looked over at the children, so full of life, energy, and mischief. But there was a sadness there too, a lingering grief Esther now recognized more deeply.

"I never knew my pa," Esther said, almost as if speaking to herself.

Clarissa's gaze softened even further as she reached out to touch Esther's arm. "Maybe it's best ya didn't, child," she blurted, her words brief—closing the door on any questions.

Esther glanced up at her, a frown creasing her brow. "What do ya mean?"

Clarissa sighed, nodding toward the setting sky.

"Oh, look at those storm clouds," she said quickly, eager to change the subject. "I'd best get these down."

She hurried to the clothesline, pulling off a clothespin and letting the sheet dip to the ground.

Esther wasn't sure what Clarissa had meant, but it was clear she wasn't willing to say more. And Clarissa didn't like her work disrupted—she did everything at a quick pace, as if she was racing against the sun.

"Girl, I've got a nice roast in the oven, and I reckon Ian and Abram might not make it back in time for supper. Will you walk down to the lower orchard, find them, and tell 'em dinner's nearly ready?" Clarissa asked, placing the last sheet into the basket and heading toward the back door.

There were only a few unspoken rules at the Old Reed Estate. One of them was that when Aunt Clarissa cooked supper, everyone had best be there on time and cleaned up. She wanted to see their shining, cheerful faces looking at her as she sat to eat.

Nodding, Esther set off to deliver her urgent message.

Chapter 13: Copperheads

A wandering wind picked up as Esther passed the grove, the peach trees dancing quietly in the fading light.

Her steps slowed, keeping pace with her thoughts as she walked, replaying her earlier conversation with Clarissa. Esther kept thinking about how sadness didn't always show in people's eyes, and how Ian never revealed his brokenness.

She wondered where Ian had laid his wife to rest and whether someone had marked the spot, so she could find it and pay her respects. Esther wanted to introduce herself—to tell Adeline how much she adored her children. Maybe she could even bring her some daisies.

It felt strange to want to visit someone she had never known, especially since she didn't find the idea of seeing Gran and Pawdad's graves pleasant. She hadn't bothered to ask where they rested, nor had she shared Pawdad's last request with anyone.

A chill crept up her spine at the thought. If Gran could read her thoughts from the other side, it wouldn't be out of the question for her to come back and haunt her, calling her ungrateful.

When Esther finally arrived at the bottom of the lower orchard, it was empty, save for a dilapidated storage shed and a few trees standing sentinel in the soft afternoon light.

She spun around, searching for any sign of life, but the old truck was nowhere in sight. Esther wrinkled her nose in frustration.

As she was about to return to the house, a flicker of movement on the horizon caught her eye.

On the other side of the back road, where the land flattened and opened to fields, she saw men working near a wire fence. Their figures stood silhouetted against the sky, bending low over the earth.

Just beyond them, she spotted the familiar blue truck. Curiosity, or perhaps duty, urged her forward as the dirt lane widened, leading her closer to the workers.

Shovels clinked rhythmically against the ground, and voices murmured, carried on the breeze. The scent of perspiration from hours of toil mingled with the rich, loamy aroma of soil recently unearthed.

A large ditch, freshly dug with mounds of earth piled high, stretched parallel to the newly turned field. A few unfamiliar vehicles sat parked nearby, their presence jarring against the natural landscape.

Esther wondered who these men were and why they were working on land that likely belonged to Clarissa.

As she walked down the road, nearing the fence, one man glanced up, his eyes locking onto hers. He straightened, his posture shifting from work to something else, something that made Esther's skin prickle.

"Well, look at that," the man called out, his voice rough. "We got ourselves a visitor."

A few of the other men looked up, curiosity piqued, their expressions hard to read but unsettling all the same.

One of them, younger than the rest, with a smile that didn't seem sincere, stepped closer to the fence, his hands gripping the wire as if testing its strength.

"Hey there, miss," he said, the words slithering out with an edge that made Esther's heart skip a beat.

"You're real pretty. What's your name? Where ya from?"

Esther's breath lodged in her chest, her feet seemingly glued to the earth. She hesitated, unsure whether to answer or just keep walking towards Ian's truck, but something warned her to stay silent.

Her pulse quickened, and the unease from moments ago bloomed into something more—fear.

"C'mon now, don't be shy," another man added, his voice coaxing, but his eyes sharp. "We're just tryin' to be friendly."

The straggly younger man leaned in, his gaze sliding over her like an unwanted touch.

"Yeah, we just wanna talk. Ain't nothin' wrong with that, is there?"

She took a step back, but the distance between her and the fence felt too small, too fragile. The men's laughter cut through the air, thick with something sinister.

One man spat into the dirt, his gaze trailing over her with a lazy, unsettling confidence.

Another hooked his thumbs into his pockets, shifting his stance as his eyes narrowed, tracing her every move.

The third ran his tongue across his yellow teeth, a deliberate gesture that made her feel ill.

She wanted to defend herself, to say anything, but the words wouldn't come. Esther's mind froze—a deer caught in the sights of a hunter.

Then, like a crack of lightning, a voice cut through.

"Keep your eyes down!" the foreman barked, his words sharp and commanding, snapping the men back like dogs yanked on a leash.

He strode over, his expression a mix of anger and control, and Esther felt a rush of relief as he put himself between her and the men.

"Y'all got work to do," the foreman said, his stare narrowing at the group. "Ain't got time for this nonsense. Get back to it."

The men grumbled, their shoulders sagging as they turned back to their tasks, but not without casting one last glance at her, something unspoken lingering in their eyes.

The foreman turned to her, his expression softening just a little.

"You best be careful around here, miss," he said, not unkindly. "These men ain't the type you want to be chattin' with."

Esther nodded, her voice still lost to the tightness in her chest.

She took another step back, retreating further from the barbed wire.

Then she saw him—Ian.

His tall figure cut across the landscape—like a guardian sent to protect.

He had been speaking with another man, someone with authority, a man in a suit jacket. But the moment Ian had seen the exchange by the fence, his demeanor shifted, his eyes narrowing.

Without a word, he broke from the conversation, his strides long and purposeful, as he closed the distance between them.

The sight of him, all broad shoulders and stern resolve, made Esther's heart flutter with a mix of relief and something else she couldn't quite name.

When Ian reached her, he didn't speak right away.

Instead, he took hold of her arm—not harshly, but with a firmness that conveyed his worry.

He led her down the road in silence, then leaned in close, his voice a low, protective growl in her ear.

"Stay away from them, Esther," he said, his breath warm against her skin. "They're bad men, dangerous. You hear me?"

She nodded, her eyes wide, feeling the energy from him—a strong wind, shaking her as she listened.

"I didn't know," she said, her voice small. "Clarissa wanted me to call you for supper."

Ian's expression softened, but only a little.

"It's all right," he said, though his tone still carried an edge of concern. "But you listen to me now—you don't come down here again, not while those men are working. Understand?"

Esther swallowed, the seriousness of the situation becoming clearer.

"Yes, I understand," she replied, her voice steadying.

"Good," Ian said, his grip on her arm loosening but not letting go. "Now, go sit in the truck and wait for us. You're not walking back alone."

Esther hesitated, glancing back at the men still working in the distance, but the look in Ian's eyes told her there was no room for argument.

She nodded again and headed toward the vehicle, her pace quickening as she put more distance between herself and the unsettling encounter.

As she climbed into the old Ford, the worn seat felt cool beneath her. It helped ease the lingering tension in her muscles. But the fear remained, a small ember glowing in the pit of her stomach.

She watched as Ian and Abram finished their conversation with the man in the suit. Ian was clearly expressing something that made him heated, and Esther suspected it had to do with the interaction by the fence. He pointed in that direction, shaking his head, a clear sign it wouldn't be tolerated.

Esther's mind replayed the scene. The way the men had looked at her, spoken to her.

It was a look Clive had given her many times before—one she had never encountered from anyone else, and certainly not from a group of men. It was a mix of want and disregard, making her feel like nothing more than a passing curiosity, something to be toyed with.

When Ian and Abram joined her in the truck, there was a charged silence between them. Despite the quiet, the men seemed in sync, their facial expressions mirroring each other's.

As the truck rumbled to life and started down the dirt road toward the house, Esther sat wedged in the middle, her hands folded in her lap. The warmth of Ian's presence was on one side, the quiet strength of Abram on the other.

The mood inside the cab was thick, palpable with the scent of soil and sweat, weighted with the tension of what had just happened.

Ian gripped the steering wheel in the center with one hand, as if he wanted to rip it off. The old leather creaked under the pressure of his grip.

Esther noticed the muscle in his jaw tighten, pulling his brow into a deep furrow. His eyes were locked on the road ahead, burning with simmering intensity.

Finally, he broke the silence, his voice low but brimming with frustration. The sound echoed through the truck's cab, sharp and cutting.

"Clarissa leased out the wrong damn land! Good land, too close to the orchard," Ian said, speaking more to Abram than to Esther, though she listened.

"It's a done deal. They're already working," he fumed. "I told her to let me read the final contract."

Ian jerked the vehicle onto the side road leading up by the orchard, taking the corner too fast.

The tires spun on the loose gravel, causing the Ford to lurch to the side. Esther braced herself against the dashboard as Ian spat out, "Shit," his voice low and tense.

This was the first time she had seen Ian lose his composure. He had always shown such restraint.

"They're goddamn prisoners," Ian continued, his frustration spilling over. "Part of some work program to plant corn. The government's paying them to work the land, and now they're apparently paying us for letting them use our dirt."

As if trying to reason with himself, Ian let out a sigh.

"Lord knows we need the money."

Abram nodded, his brow furrowed.

"I know, Ian, but those men… they're too close. It ain't safe for the womenfolk and the children."

Ian sighed, the sound heavy with the burden of responsibility.

"I know, Abram. What am I supposed to do? I don't like it any more than you do. But Clarissa has already signed it, and I don't think we can break the contract. We can't afford to break it."

"We need that money, Abram. Last year's harvest was too damn thin from frost."

Esther's heart tightened as she listened. She hadn't realized how precarious things were for the Old Reed Estate.

It wasn't until she heard the men speak that she understood the magnitude of the situation. The farm wasn't just land. It was their means of survival, and that livelihood was struggling, despite Clarissa never letting on.

Esther had never been privy to the goings-on of the estate and now felt as if they had finally let her in, even if unintentionally.

Ian's hand left the steering wheel for a moment, and he reached out, resting it on her knee—a gesture of both reassurance and concern.

He looked at her, his eyes filled with a mix of protectiveness and worry.

"Esther, listen to me carefully. Those men—they're dangerous. Never go down there, ever. You understand? It's not safe."

The warmth of his hand, the earnestness in his voice, made something inside Esther shift. It wasn't simply a command. It was protection, genuine.

For a moment, she thought of Pawdad and how he'd never been this protective, this watchful, leaving her to fend for herself more often than not. The comparison was stark.

Esther nodded, her voice a whisper. "I will, Ian. I didn't know. I just...."

"You've got to be careful, Esther," he reiterated, noticing the way she seemed to shrink under the weight of his words.

But as he tried to reassure her, he realized his hand had lingered too long on her bare knee.

Suddenly aware of the inappropriateness, he pulled it away, his fingers brushing awkwardly against his pants as if unsure where to place them.

As the truck bounced over the uneven road, Esther gazed out at the fading light, the shadows lengthening over the grove. The wind whispered through the cracks in the windows, carrying with it the faint scent of the peach orchard. The land was beautiful, but it was also full of dangers she hadn't expected.

Abram shifted beside her, breaking the tense silence.

"All we need is some of those no-good bastards creepin' around. How the hell are they gonna keep those men in line? Men like that—they ain't worth the damn food that's wasted on 'em. I love Clarissa, but sometimes, I swear, that woman is too damn trusting."

He paused, realizing Esther was sitting right there, listening to every word. His eyes narrowed as he turned to her, his tone blunt and firm.

"Keep this to yerself, ya hear? Let Ian handle Clarissa. Don't go stirrin' things up."

Esther nodded, understanding the gravity of his words.

She wasn't about to stir the pot, not when everything already felt so fragile.

Ian nodded, his gaze fixed ahead, the truck's engine growling low as they neared the estate.

"And Esther, you need to make sure Rebecca and Benjamin stay clear of the lower orchard. It's too close to where those men are working, and I don't want them—or anyone—anywhere near that fence."

Esther had already reached that conclusion on her own. His previous concern was now turning to irritation. It irked her when Ian sometimes spoke to her as if she were a child, especially when giving instructions for Rebecca and Benjamin, as if she were incapable of making her own judgments.

The men had caught her off guard, as she had never encountered such a group before. Nevertheless, she was adept at steering clear of threats. She knew how to avoid places where copperheads might hide.

When it came to Ian's children, she would never put them in harm's way.

Noticing Ian's impatience for a response, she said, "Yes, sir," her tone edged with frustration.

As the vehicle rumbled down the drive, the house came into view, standing tall against the dusky sky. The windows glowed with the soft, welcoming light of evening, a glaring contrast to the unease that lingered in the cab.

Rolling to a stop by the old barn, the vehicle crunched over the gravel as Ian cut the engine. The sudden quiet enveloped them.

Abram was the first to move, his hand reaching for the door handle.

Then, with a decisive slam, he shut the truck door, oblivious to the fact that he had forgotten to leave it open for Esther, leaving her in the cab with Ian. The suddenness of his action felt off-putting, though she wasn't sure if it was deliberate.

Ian remained seated, his arms resting on the steering wheel, his gaze fixed on nothing, lost in thought. He seemed unaware of her awkwardness as she debated whether to try getting out on her own.

As she sat, Esther took the opportunity to study his profile. His face was ruggedly handsome, accentuated by a neatly trimmed beard that framed his strong jawline. She watched as he breathed through his nose, periodically squinting as though some thought unsettled him. For a moment, she wondered what he was thinking about, but eventually decided she should make her presence known, shifting on the seat just enough to remind him she was there.

Finally noticing her, Ian moved to exit the vehicle, opening his door and holding it for her as she climbed out. He mumbled an apology that seemed to address both his and Abram's oversight, and perhaps more.

Stepping out into the cool evening air, Esther caught the faint scent of woodsmoke from Clarissa's house, drawing her in. At a loss for words, she made her way toward the back porch, eager to escape the discomfort of the moment without needing to respond.

Ian watched her go, his eyes lingering as he leaned against the truck for a moment.

He had noticed it before but never let himself fully acknowledge it, trying not to think about it.

But Esther was a *beautiful girl*. In fact, she was far more than the average pretty, and that realization worried him even more.

It struck him then how the unsavory men at the fence had looked at her, gawking with ugly desire, like a pack of wolves drawing in their prey. It made his gut twist. She wasn't just some kid—they'd seen her as a young woman, fresh meat. That thought unsettled him more than he'd care to confess.

Abram walked up to Ian, sensing a shift in his mood. He placed his worn hat on his head with a slow, deliberate motion and exhaled. Taking his position beside Ian, he followed his gaze, his expression tightening at the scene before them.

"She's a good girl, Ian. But don't know how much sense she got. If one of those fellas caught her alone…" Abram shook his head.

Ian sighed, running a hand through his hair.

"Yeah, I know. If anything bad happened to her, Clarissa would never forgive me," Ian said.

The two men stood there for a moment before Abram gave Ian a pat on the arm, heading off.

The evening echoed with crickets lifting their nightly chorus, and somewhere in the distance, Esther's dog barked, shattering the quiet.

Ian was thankful for the old hound, knowing that Bones' vigilance would ensure no one could approach the house or its grounds unnoticed. He pushed off the truck, his boots sinking into the dirt as he went to get cleaned up for dinner.

As he walked, he couldn't shake the thought of how Esther had addressed him as "sir" in the cab.

It felt formal, as though he were an old man. He wondered what age she perceived him to be. At thirty-five, he questioned if his sun-darkened tan made him appear older than he was.

Regret washed over him for letting his temper flare in front of her. He'd seen the way her eyes widened when he barked, the flicker of fear unsettling him.

It wasn't right for her to be afraid of him.

Often, she'd bite her lip when he gave her simple instructions, like telling her that the children shouldn't run through Clarissa's house.

She was clearly attempting to adapt to life on the estate, striving to fit in and relate to everyone. But there was a feral-ness to Esther, a wild, untamed quality that set her apart.

Part of him wished she would stand up to him more, similar to how Adeline had. Adeline had asserted herself when he overstepped, never letting him get away without hearing an earful and telling him what she thought.

Ian paused at his front door, his hand resting on the frame as he took a long moment to scan the porch.

The light was fading, casting shadows across the stones, and he was half-expecting to spot a few more critters his children might have brought home from their latest adventure with Esther. He sighed, a faint smile tugging at his lips, recalling the mud-covered jars lined up just the day before.

He didn't mind them having a good time, but six jars of frogs? That seemed more than a little excessive.

Especially considering the state of the porch afterward—mud smeared everywhere, and peepers hopping about—lids not secured. His patience had worn thin by then, and he was quickly becoming "not a fun papa," as his daughter Rebecca had pointed out, her words sticking with him longer than he'd have liked.

As he leaned down to take his boots off, another thought perplexed him—something peculiar and out of place, lingering just at the edge of his mind.

Why was he comparing Esther to Adeline?

After all, Esther was just a girl—wasn't she?

Chapter 14: An Unexpected Encounter

July rain poured down with fierce passion, carried by strong currents of wind, its musky scent weaving through the Old Reed Estate. Thunder rumbled ominously, melding with the smoldering summer heat of Tennessee.

Esther stood by the kitchen window, watching lightning flash across the sky, heralding the storm's arrival. Inside, the air pressed warm and damp, as though the tempest outside had already seeped into every corner.

A short, sleeveless white nightgown clung to her skin, still damp from the evening bath, as if it, too, was trapped in the thick humidity.

Her dark hair was pulled back, wet and clinging in spots as she sought relief from the heat. It revealed the delicate oval shape of her face, usually hidden beneath unruly waves.

Lightning split the dark sky, a flash illuminating trees bowing in the wind. Esther's eyes stayed fixed as she nibbled on a cookie, savoring the flavor.

Suddenly, a loud bang shook the house.

The old wood groaned in protest as the overhead light flickered, threatening to go out and casting eerie shadows across the kitchen walls.

Then a fierce gust of wind howled against the windows, rattling the panes as if the storm was trying to force its way inside.

The noise startled her, making her skin prickle.

Storms such as these often bothered Esther, their ferocity awakening memories deep within. Most likely, it was the stories her grandmother had whispered to her as a child—tales of spirits that roamed the hills during tempestuous weather, waiting for the thunder to mask their approach as they sought a way inside.

As a small girl, she believed those fables, each one crafted to scare her into submission, to keep her from wandering too far. But as an adult, the remnants of those fears surfaced in times like this.

As if on cue with the next flash, the back door flew open with a violent gust, slamming against the counter with a bang that echoed through the room.

The sound made her heart race as she hurried to shut it, the wind whipping around the space—a wild creature, scattering papers and rattling the pots hanging from the rack.

But before Esther could reach the door, Ian's tall figure materialized in the doorway, drenched from the storm, his clothes clinging to his muscular frame, water streaming down his face.

She bumped into him, startled, her body tensing as she collided with the solid wall of his chest.

A small scream slipped from her lips, quickly muffled by the booming thunder that followed.

Ian's hands were on her shoulders in an instant, his grip holding her, preventing her from stumbling backward.

"God, I'm sorry," he said.

"Thought ya were a ghost or somethin'," she said.

"Boo…" he teased with a playful grin, his eyes sparkling with mischief as he leaned in slightly, trying to lighten the moment.

Taking a deep breath, Esther braced herself against the stove, the cool metal grounding her. Then a rich laugh bubbled up, her head tilting to one side. She squinted at him as if truly sizing him up as a ghost.

"Yep, reckon ya are," she said playfully.

Smiling back, Ian felt the urge to explain his late arrival in the kitchen.

"I saw a light on and needed my ledger for tracking the rain. I measure it and write it down, so we don't over-water the trees and split the fruit," he said, self-conscious of having shared too much.

He gestured toward the small table piled with notebooks and pens, the remnants of his earlier calculations, as if to prove his intention. Unable to stop, he went on.

"It's important to record it, especially with storms like this. Can't let all of our hard work go to waste."

Esther nodded. She didn't mind listening to his lengthy explanation. Something was compelling in his passion for the trees, the way he spoke with conviction. It drew her in, making the storm outside fade into the background.

"We're getting close to harvest, and we've got a nice bumper crop going. Don't want to mess that up," he continued. "Maybe you're good luck—or it's Clarissa's old-time magic." His eyes held hers with a seriousness that made her wonder how much he truly believed in those words.

"I saw her sprinklin' cornmeal in the orchard, sayin' words I'd never heard before," Esther said.

Ian nodded, a knowing look that implied he understood precisely what she was talking about.

"Yes. I've learned over the years not to question her ways. I wouldn't put a curse past her," he mused.

Esther smiled. She enjoyed watching him talk—it was easier to understand him now. And most times, his accent wasn't noticeable, just a soft echo in the cadence of his words.

Still dripping from the rain, Ian glanced around for a towel. He spotted one of Clarissa's dishtowels hanging on the stove and reached for it, wiping his forehead and chin.

With a look of concern, Esther drew her brows together, confident Aunt Clarissa wouldn't have wanted him to put his scent all over her flowered dish towel.

Ian, realizing his mistake, carefully hung it back up, smoothing the fabric with his rough hands.

Then he pressed a finger to his lips in a comical "shh," as if pleading, "Don't get me in trouble." Esther's smile widened as she shook her head.

Ian was so funny when he wanted to be. Not when he was barking orders. But when he let his personality shine, everyone couldn't help but be drawn to him, the way folks gather close to a fire on a cold night.

"I ain't gonna be responsible if she chases ya out with a broom," she teased.

He chuckled, leaning into the easy banter. He hadn't planned on running into anyone in the kitchen, especially not this late, but the encounter turned out to be a welcome reprieve from his evening chores.

And Esther had an easiness about her, a warmth that made conversation effortless. Over the past couple of months, they had become what he considered something like friends.

But as his eyes wandered over her pretty face and soft expression, a sudden awareness struck him.

Her nightgown, damp from the lingering humidity and bath, clung to her in a way that was too revealing.

The fabric, sheer in the dim light, traced the delicate curves of her figure, the outlines of her complete feminine form unmistakable beneath the thin material.

Ian's breath caught, and he tried to shift his gaze, his thoughts scrambling.

The last thing he wanted was to embarrass her, and he was certain she was utterly unaware. The realization made him feel both awkward and protective, his pulse thrumming a little faster as he struggled to maintain his usual composure.

He cleared his throat and studied the floor, working to find something, anything, to say.

"I… I wanted to thank you. For what you do for my children. At night, they can't stop talking about you."

He shifted, chuckling softly. "You've even convinced Benjamin you're a better shot than his old father. Said if there's ever a bear, I should hand you the gun—just to be safe."

She laughed, though she noticed Ian's eyes seemed to drift oddly past her. Puzzled, she turned to see what he was looking at, forcing him to shift his gaze back to her.

"All I done was hit a squirrel with his slingshot," she said, wrinkling her nose. "I really like yer young'uns. Bitty makes me laugh so hard, I nearabout peed myself today."

"She's got you calling her that?" Ian asked, amusement softening his tone, smoothing out the tension lingering between them.

Esther bit her lip, worried that she'd overstepped.

"Oh, I'm sorry," she began, "Hope ya don't mind…"

Ian waved off her concern with a shake of his head.

"Not sure why we even bothered giving her a name when she was born," he said. "Since the day she uttered her first word, she's been changing it weekly. Once she had all the pickers calling her Tulip. But Bitty… Bitty is her spare name, in case she can't think of any flower names."

"Well… Benjamin says Ian ain't your real name, so I guess ya got a spare, too," Esther said with a sly grin.

Ian just shook his head, pretending to be betrayed.

"Benjamin's got a big mouth."

"I can't remember what he said it was," Esther pressed, curiosity sparking.

Looking up sheepishly, as if confessing a great secret, he mumbled, "Immanuel."

"Ya don't like it? Sounds like a fine name."

"Oh, it's fine—if you're leading a choir or founding a university," Ian quipped. "Too much name for everyday Americans. You try introducing yourself as Immanuel Huggler without getting a few raised eyebrows."

"Reckon it'd make sellin' peaches kinda hard," she said with a smile.

"Exactly, Addie suggested Ian, said it would make me sound less…" He paused dramatically, letting the word dangle.

"Ornery?" Esther offered with a teasing smile.

"No!" he said with a defiant grin. "I was gonna say stern. Apparently, I've got the face of a schoolmaster—and not a pleasant one."

She just smiled, her expression urging him on.

"At least I'm not stuck with Ignatz, like my younger brother. He goes by Freddie now—can't say I blame him! Ignatz sounds like he should be running a sausage shop in Berlin," Ian said, chuckling at his own joke.

"Is he the fella in New York?" she asked, sounding as if she knew the entire story.

"Yes," he said, narrowing his eyes with mock seriousness. "Either my children talk far too much, or…" He glanced at the cookie jar. "You've discovered their weakness—Clarissa's molasses cookies."

Esther laughed, her voice a soft, carefree melody, and he felt himself lost in it for a moment.

But as her laughter faded, Ian's eyes betrayed him, drifting down to her nightgown once more.

He caught himself in an instant, but it was too late.

Esther had seen where his gaze had fallen.

Her eyes darted down, shock rippling through her—the nightgown little better than wet tissue, the thin fabric leaving no mystery.

Their eyes collided in a single, suspended heartbeat as they both acknowledged the truth—the truth of her peach-colored skin.

With a sudden whip of his head, Ian snapped his gaze to the wall.

Mortified, Esther turned sharply toward the table, arms crossing over her chest. Her heart pounded as her cheeks flushed, her palms growing slick with sweat.

"I needa be goin' to bed now," she whispered.

Ian searched for the right words, wanting to apologize, to soften what had just passed. But they both knew the truth. So, he held himself rigid, a faint, uneasy smile crossing his face.

"Okay then. Have a good night," he said quietly.

"Night," she answered in a clipped tone, refusing to turn and face him.

Working not to look in her direction, he walked over, grabbed his book from the side table, and moved toward the back door.

But before he left, his stomach let out a loud growl, making him pause. With a guilty glance toward the table, he reached for the cookie jar. He tried to hurry, but the lid slipped, clattering against the counter.

"Sorry," he muttered, a boyish smile breaking through as he fumbled the lid back on. With one more quiet goodnight, he stepped out the back door, biting into a cookie as he went. The door clanked shut behind him.

Esther waited, holding her breath, until she heard the final thud of the screen door before she allowed herself to exhale. Slowly, she turned and peeked through the window, careful not to be seen, her eyes tracing Ian as he disappeared into the rain-soaked night.

The storm raged on, but her thoughts were far from the weather, her mind swirling with the strange interaction that had just unfolded.

As she climbed the stairs to her bedroom, that unfamiliar feeling lingered, settling in her chest. Something had shifted between her and Ian. It was subtle, almost imperceptible, but undeniable—a thing that hadn't been there before.

She tried to dismiss the thought, telling herself it was nothing, only a fleeting awkwardness.

But as she slipped under the covers, the pattering of rain against the window served as a reminder. Her memory played it over and over. Ian's eyes. The way he'd looked at her. It haunted her peace.

She couldn't help but ask—did he see anything in her? And she wasn't talking about the eyeful he most likely got tonight.

She wondered if it was possible for someone like him to smile at her the way he smiled at Adeline in those old photos.

Would any man ever look at her that way?

Was she worthy of that kind of smile?

What about the broken parts she kept hidden?

The scars she bore—how could any man find her body beautiful?

And the old secrets she carried.

Outside, Ian trudged through the downpour, the storm mirroring the turmoil inside him.

He worried that the trees would take in too much rainfall, swelling and bursting, leaving the fruit vulnerable to rot. Their thirst was insatiable at times, even when it wasn't good for them.

Much like himself.

He had always seen Esther as someone in need of guidance and protection, a young woman trying to find her way into a new world.

But tonight, he had seen her in a different light—both literally and figuratively—and it left him feeling unsteady.

As he reached his cottage, he paused, his eyes lingering on the faint outline of Esther's window where she was likely already in bed. The rain pressed through his shirt, but he paid it no mind, standing motionless beneath the downpour, staring up.

He knew he'd have to work hard on himself. This playful flirtation, this fascination—it had no future, and he wanted to avoid hurting the girl from the hills.

His heart would always belong to Adeline.

"Damn you, Addie," he said under his breath, the words carved with lingering grief. "Damn you for dying," he said as he shut the door behind him.

Chapter 15: Summer's End

The late summer sun had climbed to its zenith, flooding the Appalachian hills with light and warmth—one last seasonal embrace.

Peach trees, once heavy with fruit, now stood bare, their branches still holding the ghost of the harvest that had passed. The last of the trucks and pickers had rumbled away, leaving behind only the whisper of toil in the dust that settled on the dry earth.

The heat lingered, thick and potent, but with the pick done came a yearning for escape—a brief respite from the relentless grind.

Ian's old blue truck growled along a forgotten road, its tires kicking up clouds of grit as Esther and the children sat in the back. Their laughter fluttered like birds taking flight, defying the truck's steady hum.

Her makeshift shorts, cut from old pants, flapped in the wind as she leaned back, letting the breeze tangle her hair.

The truck bed, though rough and weathered, became a cradle of simple delight, their anticipation pulsing with each jolt of the uneven road.

Driving with a relaxed expression, Ian kept his eyes steady on the road, except for the occasional glance in the rearview mirror.

Clarissa sat beside him, one arm draped over the windowsill, letting the wind play with the loose strands of her hair as it brushed across her face.

The rhythmic grumble of the engine filled the space between them, a steady, comforting sound that matched the gentle sway of the truck as it navigated the winding road.

"You know, it was real nice havin' an extra pair of hands this year," she said. "Esther worked hard, didn't she? Didn't shy away from any of it."

Steadying the steering wheel, Ian rolled down his window, letting in some air. He smiled and nodded at Clarissa.

"She sure did," he said. "Didn't wilt in the heat, that's for certain."

The breeze tousled his hair as he settled back against the seat.

Clarissa could see the relief in his demeanor—the long days in the orchard, the endless hours under the sun had finally ended, and it showed in the way he carried himself. And the trip today wasn't a chore but a delight, a chance to unwind and let the exhaustion of the past weeks drift away.

"She's a good fit 'round here," Clarissa added. "Don't seem like the kind who'll tire of this life too soon."

Glancing at her, Ian gave her a thoughtful look.

"No, she doesn't." His voice was even, but his mind was already working through what she might be aiming at.

Clarissa had a way of dropping subtle hints—brief comments that left him pondering long after she'd spoken. He could recall times when she'd said things like, "Esther would make a wonderful mother," with that knowing look in her eye.

Ian never quite knew how to respond to statements like that. What was he supposed to say? It wasn't like Esther was a broodmare, after all.

And he knew the idea wasn't absurd, maybe even natural given her proximity, but something inside him resisted.

During the pick, he'd watched Esther pick harder than any of the other workers—her determination relentless. She had more drive in her than he'd expected, and sometimes he had to stop her, remind her to rest for fear she'd push herself into heat exhaustion.

Usually, his concern was met with a playful challenge, Esther tossing a smirk his way and teasing him about not being able to keep up.

"What's the matter, Ian? Can't outwork a girl?" she'd said, her eyes dancing with that familiar spark.

And he'd grin back, shaking his head, wondering how someone so seemingly delicate could possess such a tenacious spirit.

It was in those moments, amidst the banter and laughter, that he realized just how much he enjoyed looking at her face.

But even then, the thought of her in a different light—of what she might mean to him beyond today—well, he didn't want to think about it. It felt like a chore, something heavy and complicated that he wasn't ready to deal with.

As these thoughts swirled in his mind, Ian glanced down at his wedding ring, the band still resting on his finger. It was a simple piece of gold, worn and weathered, much like the memories it represented—his everlasting commitment to the love of his life, Adeline.

The pull of that ring, both physical and emotional, reminded him of a promise he'd made, a bond that hadn't faded with time.

But here was Clarissa—always trying to mend people, push people, always looking for ways to stitch the world back together in the way she thought it ought to be.

Ian respected that about her. He admired it even, but it also left him feeling off balance, as if he was always one step behind in a conversation he wasn't sure he wanted to have.

Noticing his unease, Clarissa offered him a soft smile, letting the conversation fade into silence. But he knew her well enough to realize she was still watching him, waiting, confident she'd stirred up his thoughts.

As they rounded a gentle curve, the road opened up, revealing a hidden lake, its surface shimmering—a sapphire under the midday sun. The water sparkled, cool and inviting, a dramatic contrast to the dense green of the trees that framed it.

It was a slice of paradise, untouched and pure, and as the truck rolled to a stop, the lake called to them, promising the simple, unspoken joys of summer's last embrace.

Abram, Mitzy, and their little boy had already claimed their spot beneath the broad arms of a sprawling oak, its shade casting a cool spot from the sun's gaze.

The savory scent of roasted chicken filled the air, mingling with the fresh tang of the lake and the earthy perfume of pine. It was a potent mixture, a reminder of simpler pleasures tucked away in this quiet corner of the world.

Ian, despite the uneven ground, found a suitable spot and parked the truck with careful precision. He moved quickly, circling the vehicle to help Clarissa out, always the gentleman as he guided her to solid footing.

Rebecca, aware of her own charm, stretched out her arms from the back of the truck, her face expectant and eager as her father gently lifted her down in response.

Benjamin, full of boyish independence, launched himself from the bed, landing with a soft thud on the grass.

Esther watched him with a hint of pride, her own readiness to leap just behind him.

But before she could act, Ian was there, his presence filling the space beside her. Without a word, his hands found their place at her waist, lifting her down with the same effortless strength he'd shown his daughter.

As her feet touched the ground, his hands lingered, the warmth of his touch sending a tremor through her, stealing her breath. She wondered if he had felt her reaction.

He was always spooking her like that, catching her off guard.

The sensation clung to her as he let her go, reaching for a picnic basket. A feeling that refused to fade as she worked to behave unbothered. But Esther now lived for those fleeting times when she could be near him.

When his accidental yet electric touch would send a ripple through her.

A brush of his arm as he walked by—

A casual bump when he was hurried and distracted—

Or the way his foot would knock into hers at the dinner table, always followed by a soft apology.

She had noticed that during the peach harvest, Ian had checked on her more often than the others, constantly reminding her to pace herself.

Once, he'd made her sit under a tree, his concern plain as he pressed his canteen into her hands and demanded that she rest, insisting she drink.

She remembered the cool metal against her lips, knowing it was the same canteen he'd just drunk from, the taste of the water mingling with something more—maybe the taste of his mouth.

There had been a day when curiosity got the better of her, and she had followed him. Careful to stay hidden, she watched him make his way toward the small hill just beyond the road in front of the estate. He had walked slowly, reaching down to pluck wildflowers as he climbed toward a small fenced graveyard. The worn path bore witness to years of solitary visits.

Concealed by the trees, she saw him settle beside his dead wife's grave. His shoulders dipped as his head bowed, lips moving in a private conversation not intended for earthly ears.

After he'd left, Esther hesitated before making her way to that same spot. The graveyard was quiet, shaded by old oaks, a peaceful spot removed from the world.

Kneeling by Adeline's grave, she traced the delicate flower carved into the headstone.

"They're real good young'uns—Benjamin and Rebecca. I don't know ya, but that lil' girl of yers must be a lot like ya."

Esther paused, her fingers lingering on the cold stone.

"Now Benji, he's got his daddy's ways, through and through," she said, her voice just a breath against the stillness, a subtle smile playing at her lips.

The wind stirred the leaves, and for a moment, Esther listened, confident that Adeline had answered back in agreement. She felt a strange pull as she lay down on the ground beside the grave. It was odd, this sensation in her chest, this feeling of connection. In her heart, Esther was certain they would have been friends.

Pulled from her thoughts, Esther heard the children squeal with delight, already darting toward the lake's edge. Their laughter rang out across the water, snapping her back to the present.

"Be careful now, ya wait for yer pa," she called out.

Mitzy, ever the adventurous one, dipped her toes into the lake, testing the temperature with a grin.

"Ya gonna swim?" she called back to Esther in challenge.

Esther eyed the cool, inviting expanse of the lake, the water shimmering under the midafternoon sun.

"I don't know," she said, uncertain.

The thought of swimming in front of everyone, especially with Ian, made her feel self-conscious.

But Ian, catching her hesitation, stepped up beside her, close enough that she could feel the warmth of him.

"Oh, come on, Esther. It's so damn hot today," he teased, a smile curling at the corners of his mouth, tempting her with the ease of his charm.

"Maybe I'll stick my feet in," she conceded, trying to push away the nervousness that followed her everywhere.

"Well, I'm goin' up to my knees," Mitzy said, already wading into the shallows as she laughed.

Before anyone could react, Abram came soaring through the air, swinging off a rope tied to an old, sturdy branch.

He let out a triumphant holler, released himself at the perfect moment, and crashed into the water with a resounding splash, sending cool droplets raining down over the entire group.

The children shrieked with delight, and a startled laugh escaped from Esther.

Ian, caught up in the carefree spirit of the afternoon, stripped off his shirt and tossed it aside as he made his way toward the water.

But just as he was about to dive in, he turned back to Esther, his eyes lit with a wicked twinkle that made her heart skip.

"Look, Esther, you're already wet. What's a few more drops?" he quipped.

Before she could muster a strong reply, he reached out, his hand closing around hers with firm but gentle insistence, pulling her closer to the shoreline.

"No, no, no…" Esther protested, trying to dig her heels into the ground, but he was too strong, his laughter mingling with hers as he finally decided to scoop her up in his arms.

Her protests turned into breathless giggles as he trudged into the water, the coolness closing in around them.

Far enough out, Ian released her, dropping her into the water. She sank quickly beneath the surface, the icy shock enveloping her.

Concerned, he grabbed her arm and whipped her up, afraid he might have accidentally drowned her.

As she broke through, she sputtered with laughter, the initial surprise giving way to exhilaration and a rush that made her feel alive—more alive than she'd felt in a long time.

What followed was a playful water battle that quickly spiraled into a full-blown tussle, the cool lake water churning around them as laughter echoed across the shore.

Esther, her initial hesitation long forgotten, dove headfirst into the fun, her competitive spirit flaring to life as she tried—unsuccessfully—to dunk Ian.

The thrill of the challenge ignited something fierce in her, pushing her to lunge at him with all the determination she could muster.

But Ian, with his simple strength and quick reflexes, sidestepped her every attempt, his grin widening with each failed ambush.

He expected her moves before she even made them, his eyes dancing with amusement as he let her believe she might have the upper hand.

Benjamin, not wanting to miss out on the action, barreled into the fray with all the enthusiasm of a boy set on toppling a giant. He splashed through the water, his small but determined arms aiming for his father's legs in a valiant effort to bring him down.

Esther knew they didn't stand a chance against Ian's sheer strength, but that wasn't the point. The thrill was in the attempt—the shared joy of the moment, the laughter that bubbled up with each new wave of water.

They attacked from different angles, their strategy as unpredictable as the ripples that spread across the lake's surface.

Esther lunged for Ian's shoulders, her hands reaching out to unbalance him, while Benjamin wrapped his arms around Ian's waist, determined to be the one who brought him down.

Ian, reveling in the game, countered their every move with ease, his laughter mingling with theirs.

In one swift motion, he lifted Esther off her feet once again, holding her just above the water, his strength effortless yet gentle.

With a broad grin, he leaned in close, his breath warm against her ear, and whispered, "Amen," a promise of what was coming next.

With that, he dropped her back into the lake. This time, Esther was more prepared, pinching her nose before she went under.

Undeterred, Benjamin redoubled his efforts, splashing water at his father with renewed vigor, shouting encouragement to Esther between breaths.

Ian let out a deep chuckle, low and rolling.

"You want a good dunk too, Benji?" he teased as he pretended to lunge toward his son. Benjamin squealed, scrambling away in mock terror.

Rebecca, delighted by the fight, splashed water from the shallows, her voice ringing with enthusiasm.

"Get 'im, Benji, get 'im!" she cheered, her small hands sending waves of water in their direction.

Drenched, Esther conceded, "Yer too damn strong! Don't think I can whoop ya." But the glint in her eyes suggested she wasn't done trying.

Amid the playful chaos, the game shifted.

What began as a quick catch to keep her upright became a hold Ian didn't release.

His fingers splayed at her waist as though testing how it felt to keep her there.

For an instant, the whole world narrowed—the water, the shouts, the children—everything gone but her wet blouse under his palms and the way her breath broke against him.

With a rash impulse, he leaned in and pressed a brief kiss against the top of her head, her damp hair carrying the faint scent of lake water.

It was so fast, so natural, that for a split second, it felt like the most ordinary thing in the world.

But almost as soon as it happened, he froze, realizing what he'd done.

His heart stuttered. *What the hell had possessed him to cross that line, even for a second?* His body had acted before his mind could stop it, and now he could only pray she hadn't noticed.

But she had, her heart thudding in her chest. She tried to tell herself it was just a friendly gesture. And yet, the soft pressure of his lips lingered, sending a tingle down to the roots of her damp hair, making it harder to dismiss.

Esther blinked, fighting to steady herself as Benjamin's hands gripped his father's waist again, tugging with all his might. His eager excitement sliced through the air.

"Bite 'im! Bite his arm, Esther!" Benjamin urged.

She blinked again, the trance breaking as her eyes found Benjamin's eager face.

"Bite him?" she asked, still caught off guard.

"Yeah! Do it!" Benjamin insisted, his determination unshaken.

With a half-smile, Esther leaned in and gave Ian's arm a playful nip, expecting him to release her.

But Ian didn't budge. His eyes flicked down to her, and his lips twitched into a smirk.

"Did you just… bite me?"

Esther opened her mouth to respond, but nothing came out. The teasing words she had ready vanished under his steady stare, leaving her uncertain. The moment stretched between them, his smirk deepening as he waited, clearly enjoying her silence.

Finally, speaking with a slow voice, Ian said, "You're a wild one, aren't you?" The words were thick with meaning, settling over her like a challenge, leaving her unsure if she should laugh or retreat.

Before she had the chance to react, his arms released her, his touch slipping away.

"Well, it's time to baptize you, boy," Ian said, his grin returning full force.

He scooped up Benjamin in one smooth motion as the boy let out a loud holler. With a swift toss, he hurled him into the deeper part of the lake.

The splash that followed broke the tense spell, joy rippling back through the air.

Cold, Esther made her way to the bank, her breath still coming in uneven bursts.

She couldn't help herself as she watched Ian—watched how water droplets shimmered in the sunlight, glinting like tiny diamonds as they cascaded down his broad torso, his muscles rippling with every effortless movement.

Careful not to stare at him too long, she slowly made her way out of the water.

A cool breeze found her, sweeping over her damp skin, sending a shiver straight through her.

Quickly wrapping a towel around herself, she rubbed at her arms and squeezed the water from her hair. Settling at the edge of the picnic blanket, she allowed her gaze to drift back to the lake where the group was still at play.

With the sun on her face, she tilted her head back, eyes closed, savoring the warmth as if everything had aligned perfectly—a scene plucked from a dream.

But she felt it then—a feeling she couldn't describe. It crept over her, dark, crawling up her spine and prickling at the nape of her neck.

The wind, gentle only moments before, now rustled sharply through the trees. It carried an eerie note, as if whispering something unsettling in her ears.

Esther's eyes popped open. Her gaze swept the lake's edge and the tree line beyond, sharpening as unease settled deep in her chest. She tried to will it away, but her body refused, every muscle tightening against her will.

Then, a low rumble echoed beyond the trees.

At first, it was so faint—blending seamlessly with the distant calls of crows—that it barely registered. But as the noise grew, a small glare flickered in the distance.

Her eyes narrowed.

An unfamiliar car crept along the rutted dirt road that wound its way around the lake. The shiny vehicle looked out of place in such a secluded spot, where the only traffic was the occasional wagon or an old truck.

As it drew nearer, Esther swallowed hard, an icy knot forming in her stomach. The car crawled forward, deliberately slow— slowing even more as it reached her.

Two men inside.

Then she saw their faces.

Recognition struck like a gunshot.

Her cousin Clive.

And beside him, an odd companion—Deputy Frank Burgess.

Of all places. Why here?

Esther's gaze darted back to the group by the lake, her instincts screaming for her to retreat, to return to their safety. But she felt pinned to the ground, her legs refusing to move.

Clive, the more brazen of the two, leaned out the passenger window as the car idled. His eyes locked onto hers.

The intensity of his silent, unblinking stare made her skin crawl. She had tried to forget he even existed—had scrubbed him from her memory. But here he was, looking at her the way he always did, as if she belonged to him.

Forcing herself not to flinch, not to give him that power, she turned her back to him, wrapping the towel tightly around herself. Maybe if she dismissed him, he'd just leave. Let her be.

For a moment, there was nothing.

Then came the slow crunch of tires on gravel as Clive and Frank drove off without a word.

Esther glanced over her shoulder, watching until the car vanished. Her heart kept its frantic pace, the encounter lingering, dark and heavy. She considered telling the others, certain they had all seen the vehicle yet hadn't been overly concerned.

But what would she say? That the trees had whispered a warning? That her cousin's stare terrified her? The thought itself felt absurd, even in her own mind.

As the afternoon went on, it passed without incident—quietly, almost gently.

Yet Esther felt herself drawing inward. She could cast off the encounter with her cousin, forget it like she always did.

But Ian stayed in her thoughts, refusing to be pushed aside.

She had dreamed of him, turned him over in her mind until she was nearly undone by it. And today, when they had been so close, touching, it only made the ache worse. What she had wasn't enough. She longed for more.

Overwhelmed, she slipped away from the others for a while, choosing a tree at the far edge of the meadow. There, she sat with her hymn book open, her pencil moving across the page as she released her frustration.

As the sun dipped lower, casting the lake in a warm glow, everyone began packing up.

The day's excitement slowly gave way to an evening surrender.

Mitzy's toddler, worn out from all the activity, fussed, his tiny face scrunched in sleepy discomfort. Attentive, Esther picked him up and cradled him in her arms. The baby relaxed almost instantly, his small fingers curling into her hair as he drifted off to sleep while she rocked him, humming a tune she made up on the spot.

Ian, busy gathering the last of the blankets, glanced over. He paused, smiling, taking in the scene before him.

The tenderness with which she held the child made him think back to Clarissa's words. He wondered why that old lady had to plant such ideas in his mind—a damn fool notion.

"Well, look at ya, Esther," Mitzy said as she came to retrieve her child. "Holdin' 'im like he's yer own. Might have to watch out, or he'll be callin' you mama 'stead of me."

"Sure is a sweet lil' thing," Esther said wistfully as she gently handed the sleeping child back to his mother.

Mitzy winked at her. "Well, if ya ever need a practice run, ya know where to find us."

Ian, still watching, caught Esther's gaze for a moment, sensing a storm gathering beneath the surface, though its nature eluded him.

There were times when something in her seemed to switch off—when her smile faltered and the light in her eyes dimmed. He'd noticed it before, those quiet withdrawals when she thought no one was watching, as though she believed her absence could pass unnoticed.

Sometimes he wondered if she was truly happy here, among them. Perhaps she needed to spread her wings, to soar beyond the foothills of Blue Hollow, where the sky stretched wider and the world promised more than they could ever give her.

He feared that if Esther ever longed to leave, Clarissa might clutch her too tightly, unwilling to let her go.

And he wondered, too, if Esther's tireless need to please was only a veil, hiding her true desires—those buried longings she scarcely admitted to herself.

She had been swept into a life carved by fate, a path not of her own choosing.

And he wasn't sure if she realized she had any say in it at all.

Chapter 16: A Night of Confusion

Waxing high above the hills, the Grain Moon bathed the Old Reed Estate in soft, silvery-blue hues. Under the old oak tree, its light draped the ground like delicate lace, perfectly still in the quiet air.

Esther sat on the wooden steps of the back porch, her fingers idly toying with the edges of her fan as she tried to cool herself. Bones lay at her feet, eyes closed, occasionally flicking his tail in response to the distant sounds of the night.

The evening should have been peaceful, yet a deep restlessness stirred within her.

After weeks of back-breaking labor, pushing her body to the limit to prove she could keep up with bringing in the fruit, she felt a different kind of exhaustion.

She had kept her deep desires for Ian locked away, buried in the cellar of her mind, where they would knock on the door, trying to get out, and she would tell them she would return later.

But after their day at the lake—his coy behavior, the kiss on her hair—it felt as if everything had reached a breaking point. Frustration welled within her, borne of yearning. She longed for his full attention, the way it had briefly surfaced in the water.

Why did he always act in ways that confused her? It made her wonder what he truly meant, only for him to turn into serious Ian again after carefree moments.

From a distance, she watched his silhouette move toward the barn, blankets in hand from the old truck.

His gaze lingered longer than it should have, a fleeting connection that left her even more unsettled.

Taking a long, steady breath, Esther leaned back on the step, her hands covering her face. With her eyes closed, she let the memory of a dream wash over her—part nightmare, part something good. She breathed slowly through her fingers, blocking out the moonlight as she tried to recapture the images from her slumber.

She had woken that morning with every detail etched in her mind, vivid and unshakable. In the dream, her imagination had painted Ian just as he appeared today at the lake, his presence so real it almost felt like a premonition.

He had called her by name, his voice cutting through the thick mist where she was lost and afraid.

She had wandered, searching for something she couldn't find, until his hand finally reached hers, pulling her from the shadows.

She remembered cradling his face in her hands, the warmth of his skin grounding her in that strange, foggy world.

His smile—tender, familiar—was the one she had been longing for.

But then, in the dream, a dark beast with no eyes grasped her by the ankles, its hold cold and unyielding. It dragged her into a deep, shadowy lair, pulling her farther from the light above. The darkness closed in, thick and suffocating.

The memory of that night terror lingered, its grip tight on her mind. Yet she kept returning to the moment Ian called for her—his voice a rope she clung to.

Sitting up, Esther swept her hair aside as a restlessness seized her legs. It was a feeling that had haunted her for as long as she could remember, woven into her very being—the urge to run, to climb the cliffs of the Blue Hollows, and vanish. She wondered if acting on it might loosen the grip, finally shaking it free.

The clink of the porch door pulled her from her thoughts as Clarissa stepped out.

"You sure are quiet tonight, darlin'," Clarissa said as she handed Esther a glass of iced tea. "Got somethin' on your mind?"

"I reckon I do," Esther said.

Clarissa followed the girl's gaze toward the soft glow of the barn lights and smiled knowingly.

With a gentle hand, she passed Esther another glass.

"Honey, take this out to him, would ya?" she said. "Tell him he's done enough for the day."

Esther hesitated briefly, then nodded. She instructed her dog to stay, rising to her feet, the drink steady in her hands. But before taking a step, Clarissa spoke.

"Ya know, I seen ya watchin' him."

Esther froze, a jolt running through her as if her aunt had laid her secret bare.

"Girl, I reckon you're just what he needs," Clarissa added.

Esther turned to face her, brows knitting.

"Ain't rightly sure what ya mean."

Clarissa let out a sigh. "I thought Ian would spend a lifetime just draggin' his feet, holdin' on to what was gone. Figured he'd never allow himself to see what's standin' right before 'im. But today… Hmm, today told me different. Somethin' brewin' 'tween the two of ya."

Clarissa's words instantly unsettled her.

Unsure how to respond or even if she should believe them, Esther nodded and turned toward the barn, her mind buzzing.

As she walked, she thought back to her aunt's words, but they only amplified her restless energy.

At the barn's entrance, where the large doors stood open, she paused, letting her eyes adjust to the dim light. The air inside was cool and earthy, the familiar scent of hay and old wood.

Ian was there, as always, lost in his chores. Slipping into the shadows, Esther couldn't help but be drawn to the way his body moved, each task unfolding with an ease, a natural rhythm as though the evening itself bent around him.

Her gaze followed him across the barn as he gathered a pile of hay and carried it to her old mule. His hands, calloused yet tender, gave the animal an affectionate pat—a gesture that made her chest tighten.

Unaware she was there, he kept working. She lingered, caught now by the way his chest shifted beneath his button-up white shirt, or the way he bent down—the fabric of his pant legs taut across his thighs, as if it might tear under the strain. It held her there longer than she intended.

"How long have you been standing there?" Ian's voice rose, breaking through her thoughts, startling her.

"I… I…" Esther's breath tangled in her throat, nerves rattling her until she finally eked out the words. "Clarissa wanted ya to have this. She said to tell ya not to be doin' no more work tonight."

Esther stepped forward, extending the glass of tea straight out to him.

He took it with a grateful nod, sipping before setting it on a nearby shelf.

"Well, I'm almost done, but tell her thanks."

Esther shifted on her feet, her knees unsteady. She wasn't sure what had come over her, only that she wasn't ready to leave the barn, her words slipping free before she could rein them in.

"Ian… can I ask ya somethin'?"

He hesitated—something in her tone cautioned him.

"Yes?"

"Do ya think I'm pretty?"

His face tightened, his hands moving to his hips as if to steady himself. He looked at her—really looked at her—and for a moment, he seemed at a loss.

"Sure," he finally replied in a careful voice.

She took a reckless step closer.

The wanting inside her was at a precipice, breaking out, coming unhinged.

She told herself to run, to bite back what she was about to say, but her mouth betrayed her, spilling the request.

"Ya wanna lay down with me?"

Ian nearly choked on her words, his breath catching in his throat as the boldness and gravity of her question crashed between them.

He let out a strained laugh, uneasy, as if grappling with the shock.

"What… what're you saying?" He swallowed hard. "Do you even know what you're asking?"

She regretted it the second her words hit the air. Esther's face fell, as though sinking into a deep well, the embarrassment drowning her.

Instantly, she whipped around, desperate to escape the encounter.

Despite his shock, the crushed look on her face told him she had been serious, and his awkward laugh had been the wrong response.

"Esther, wait!" he called after her, his voice a mix of urgency and his own unease.

Outside, the night air clung warm to her flushed cheeks as she hurried across the yard, fleeing the barn and the tangled mess she'd just made.

She fought back tears, her teeth pressing hard into her lip, hating the way they pricked at her eyes—just another sign of weakness she couldn't afford to show.

The salty sting burned, not from hurt but from the storm of frustration rising inside her—at herself, her own ignorance, and the sticky web of feelings tearing her in every direction.

"Just leave me be," Esther demanded when she heard Ian's heavy footsteps behind her.

For a desperate moment, she eyed the hills in the distance, but she forced herself to keep walking toward Clarissa's house, knowing he wouldn't let her disappear into the night.

"Wait," Ian pleaded, catching up to her and grabbing her arm. "I didn't mean to make you upset."

He struggled to find the appropriate words, his mind racing, attempting to understand what had just been asked of him. And he could hardly believe they were having this conversation—right now, right here.

It felt so intimate.

How had it come to this?

But deep down, he knew. At the lake, he'd played into it—flirting with her, wanting to touch her, more familiar than he should've been. There had been moments where he'd crossed that line, letting himself get caught up in it—it had felt good. Now, he could see what it had led to.

Esther refused to look at him, and it unsettled him. He wanted her to know he was sincere, to see it in his face, in his eyes, but she wouldn't give him the chance—her gaze firmly on the ground, refusing to give him that satisfaction.

"Forget what I said." Her tone was cool, masking the turmoil inside.

He sighed, his grip on her arm loosening as he leaned in, choosing his words with the utmost care.

"I appreciate the offer, if that's what it was, but… it doesn't work like that."

He paused before adding, "Well, it shouldn't."

Esther didn't need him to explain what she already knew. She felt foolish, and the gentle tone he used—like he was talking to one of his children—only irritated her more.

"I don't know what to say to you," Ian admitted, his voice heavy with regret. "I don't want to hurt you."

But those words had the opposite effect—making her heart bleed like an open wound, sincerity only slicing at her pain. She fought with all her might to close it off—and fast—but it wasn't easy.

"Ya could never do worse than what's been done to me," she whispered.

"God—Esther! That's not what I want," he said, frustrated. "I just… I see you sort of like a child, in a way."

There. He had spoken his truth. Ian had finally put into words the reasoning that had kept him from fully entertaining the idea of her, beyond his love for Adeline. It wasn't just loyalty—it was the way he saw her connection to the world, a fragility he wasn't sure she even recognized in herself.

How could she truly know what she wanted?

At that moment, she looked up at him, tears shimmering in her eyes. Her expression spoke of a rawness, a vulnerability she had never shared with him. It was deep, not just the shallow fancy of a young girl.

It radiated from her, sending out in waves, unexpected and powerful.

And when she spoke, it was slow with a defiance mired in pain.

"My whole life, people have been lookin' down on me. My words are always wrong and… I can't read 'em. Gran near worked me to the bone since I took my first step. But no, Ian, I ain't no child… I never got the chance to be one."

Ian remained in place, held to a spot on the gravel road.

He regretted his words—how clumsy they'd sounded—and how he hadn't truly acknowledged what she was offering him. She wasn't just offering her body to him—she was offering something more, something with meaning.

Guilt pooled in his chest, and he felt an urgent need to make it right, to ease the hurt he'd caused.

"I'm not saying you're a child, but…" he began again, his tone gentler, but she cut him off before he could finish.

"If I ain't a child, then what the hell am I?" she said. "I feel everythin', even you."

She could no longer hold back the tears in her eyes; one escaped, moving down her lightly freckled cheek as she quickly wiped it away.

He wanted to hug her, to comfort her, but he hesitated, thinking it might make things worse. He wanted to fix this. Fix their friendship. Go back to before today.

Ian felt utterly overwhelmed.

For once, words had failed him—something Esther had never managed before. It felt as if she had sewn his mouth shut.

"Well…" Esther's voice cut through the silence sharply, almost as if she were answering for him. "I guess ya don't know what I can or can't do," she said.

She pulled her arm free, leaving him standing there as she slowly walked toward the house.

His hands found his hips again as he watched her go.

He'd tried to apologize.

What else could he possibly do?

Would he tell her that he could teach her to read? That he had somehow been oblivious to something so important? He hadn't even noticed the signs that she struggled, perhaps because he had seen her with a book in her hands—and not just today.

That realization pained him deeply. For all the care he gave to everyone, especially Esther, how could he have missed what she needed—something he of all people could have so easily given her?

As the back door clanked shut behind her, Ian's thoughts churned. What else had slipped past him? What other parts of her life had he not noticed?

Inside her room, Esther collapsed onto her bed, her body trembling as she sobbed out loud. The ache in her chest was consuming—tearing at her—a clawing wild beast.

Ian hadn't wanted her. Why would he?

Gran had been wrong—no man even wanted her for the one thing she had always said they would.

Meanwhile, Ian finished up in the barn, but the stillness only unsettled him more. He kept going over their conversation, her bold question rattling around in his head. He couldn't get rid of it. What she'd asked him… how he'd reacted.

And he couldn't deny it—being wanted, desired by a woman again—it stirred something in him, something that had been buried since Adeline had passed.

There had been a few moments over the years when he could've let himself be with a woman, but he'd chosen not to. He wasn't about to use someone to fill that void. That wasn't the type of man he was. He prided himself on doing right.

And those women, he'd told himself, weren't interested in him, not really. They wanted something reckless, maybe even dangerous, and he wasn't about to be caught up in that. He knew better. Didn't need trouble coming to his doorstep.

But Esther—God, she was different. There was a beautiful goodness about her, something real and alive. That's what made it so damn hard.

Why'd she have to come into the barn tonight? He was tired. Worn out. He just needed sleep, not all this turning around in his head.

Now he had to figure out what to say to her come morning. But how could he go from her asking to "roll in the hay" to sitting down at Clarissa's table, passing the bread as if everything were normal?

And his children… they adored her—clung to her. Sometimes, it felt as if they liked her more than him, that they'd choose her without a second thought if they had to.

Ian, a man who always had to have a solid plan of attack in front of him, had none. He was at a complete loss.

Maybe by morning, with daylight on it all, he'd have some clarity. Perhaps Esther would pretend it never happened, meeting him with a sweet smile as if nothing was amiss, but he highly doubted it.

As he shut the barn door, making his way home, Ian kept his eyes straight ahead, not allowing himself to look up at her window. No, not tonight. He'd already gotten himself in enough trouble, and he'd show some restraint, for what it was worth.

Chapter 17: Confronting the Past

Soft morning light filtered through the thin curtains in honeyed rays, warming the kitchen with a gentle glow. The scent of fresh coffee wove together with the earthy aroma of eggs and biscuits filling the air.

But inside, Esther felt anything but.

She sat quietly at the kitchen table, her bare feet idly rubbing her dog's back as he lay at ease near her. Her mind was still reeling from the previous night's conversation.

And it didn't help that she'd snuck down for a bottle of Clarissa's blackberry wine—its lingering effects still buzzing in her head, adding to the fog of it all.

Ian's words played over and over, like a needle stuck in the groove of an old record, replaying the confusion and hurt she just couldn't shake.

Every time she tried to let it go, it twisted itself deeper, making her feel foolish. How had she let herself get so hopeful, so obsessed with him?

Across from her, Clarissa sipped her coffee, eyes soft but searching, not prying. The silence between them wasn't uncomfortable, but there was an unease in Esther, and it worried her.

She'd sent the girl out to Ian the night before with that iced tea, never imagining it would stir things up. But now, looking at Esther's sleepless eyes, she knew something had shifted, something that wasn't good.

The faint scent of blackberry spirits lingered in the air, but Clarissa didn't say a word. If Esther had leaned on it for a bit of comfort, Clarissa wasn't one to judge. That girl didn't need anyone telling her she'd done wrong. The look on her face already said enough. She was beating herself up more than anyone else ever could.

Their quiet was soon broken by the swing of the back door, its clank echoing through the kitchen as Benjamin and Rebecca burst in, their faces lit with that early morning excitement only children seemed to have.

Right behind them, Ian stepped in, his footsteps slow as he assessed the room, his gaze lingering on Esther's back as he tried to read her temperament.

Purposefully refusing to even look at him, Esther turned her gaze toward the window. She had promised herself to just get over it last night, to move past the sting of his words. But with him standing just a few feet away, the hurt still clung to her, raw and unshakable.

Rebecca, happy to see her best friend, wrapped her small arms around Esther, pressing her cheek firmly against her face. It had become their morning routine over the last several months. Esther smiled softly, her hand stroking the girl's back. The warmth of the hug was a fleeting balm, soothing the ache in her chest, if only for a moment.

Rebecca pulled back, her smile turning quizzical. With an innocent tilt of her head, she remarked, "Esther, you smell like berries."

Clarissa, ever warm and steady, rose from her seat, her voice trying to lift the mood—sunlight through a cloud.

"Well, sit yerselves down, you two," she called out, her smile wide as she moved toward the stove. "What ya fancy for breakfast this mornin'?"

Benjamin and Rebecca quickly took a spot at the small table.

"They ate already," Ian interjected, his voice gentle but firm. "Don't let them fool you."

Rebecca's grin stretched wide, her eyes twinkling with that playful defiance only children can get away with.

"We like your food better," she confessed, not the least bit ashamed.

Ian gave her a look—half amused, half stern.

"Rebecca."

Clarissa chuckled, brushing off Ian's concerns with a casual wave.

"Ian, ya know I love cookin'. Why ya gonna deny me that? Ain't nothin' better than watchin' a young'un gobble down a good meal."

He sighed, rubbing the back of his neck as he always did when he felt caught between being polite and being firm.

"I just don't want you feelin' like you have to…"

Clarissa wasn't having any of it. She walked right up to him, her expression soft but resolute, cupping his face between her hands in a way only she could.

"I love ya, honey. You's the best man I know, but let me do what I love."

Despite the sunshine spilling from Clarissa and the children, a mood lingered in the kitchen.

It clung to Esther like a storm cloud, darkening by the moment, pressing in on her until even the warmth of the morning couldn't reach her.

While Clarissa busied herself with the children, fussing over the stove, Esther sat there, feeling the walls close in on her.

The familiar smell of coffee and breakfast, usually so comforting, now seemed to choke her. Even Rebecca and Benjamin's sweet, uninhibited laughter—their carefree chatter—felt far away, as if it belonged to another world, distant from where she sat.

Esther's gaze found its way to Ian, briefly lingering for a moment before she forced herself to look away.

The memory of their conversation from the night before stung, sharp as a bee sting right in the center of her chest, the ache unresolved.

She had misjudged everything with Ian, and now she wasn't sure they had ever truly been friends at all.

Maybe he'd only ever been kind to her out of pity—for the poor girl he'd stopped getting beaten by the side of the road, trying to save her from a life she'd never asked for.

Dark thoughts chewed at her insides, hollowing her out, and for a moment, she felt like a stranger in the very place that had started to feel like home.

Her mind, always quick to turn on her when she was at her weakest, whispered cruel things, pulling her deeper into the shadows.

For Esther, it became unbearable—the weight of it all, the pretending, the isolation. She needed to escape the kitchen, needed to escape herself.

Clarissa, sensing the mounting tension in the awkward silence between Ian and Esther—usually filled with their cheerful morning banter—quietly guided the children toward the stove.

But it was too late.

Without a word, Esther pushed her chair back abruptly. The harsh scrape of wood against the floor clashed with the cheerful hum of the room, throwing the mood off balance.

She stood, her movements stiff and awkward, as if her body had forgotten how to move naturally.

Bones, her old faithful dog, picked up on her restlessness, his tail thumping lazily against the floor as he followed her toward the back door.

Esther barely registered the act of stepping outside as she crossed the threshold.

She needed space. She needed quiet. A breath to untangle the knitted mess of feelings crowding her chest—emotions piled like an overstuffed basket of yarn, spilling out with every step she took.

The porch creaked beneath her bare feet as she made her way down the steps, Bones padding softly behind.

Ian, who had been leaning against the kitchen wall, arms folded, trying to wear his usual calm as if it were a second skin, waiting, watching, hoping the tension from the night before had settled.

But he knew, in a heartbeat, that the storm inside Esther hadn't quieted with the dawn. If anything, it had grown, untamed, as a wildfire crawling through dry grass, reaching out to consume whatever lay in its path.

Outside, Esther spotted a stick. Mindlessly, she bent down, fingers brushing the dirt. She picked it up and tossed it across the yard.

She hoped, perhaps, that the motion would shift something in her, offering a brief release.

But Bones, usually quick to chase anything she threw, just lay there, his head following the stick's arc before settling back in the grass. His tail gave a slow, half-hearted wag as if to say, *Not today*.

"Well, go get it," she said, frustration slipping into her voice. "What ya waitin' fer?"

Bones didn't stir, his eyes already closing, choosing to rest over her restless demands.

Esther sighed as her gaze wandered over the yard, landing on the old barn in the distance. It stood there, solid and worn, staring back at her—a blatant reminder of everything she was trying to escape.

She hadn't noticed Ian approach from behind, his usual strides tempered into quieter steps. When he spoke, his voice broke the silence, carrying a tone that sounded almost rehearsed.

"I think we should talk."

Esther stiffened, her back straightening as if bracing for what was to come.

She didn't want to turn and face him, though it would have been the courteous thing to do. She didn't trust herself to meet his eyes.

"I don't wanna talk right now," she replied, her voice flat, detached.

He stepped closer, not easily swayed.

"Are you still mad? Esther, I came out here to say I'm sorry… if I hurt your feelings. But…" He paused, long enough for it to feel deliberate, as if he was about to school her.

She felt the weight of his words, the apology lingering, not quite sincere. That single word—but—carried a subtle unease, something that made her stomach tighten.

"Said I don't wanna talk," she said.

But Ian wasn't one to back down, especially not when things felt unfinished and he wanted to speak his peace.

"I think I've done some things that might've confused you," he admitted, his voice steady but tinged with regret.

Frustrated that Esther hadn't turned to face him, he moved in front of her, taking charge as he would when yielding the land beneath his hands—firm and reproving.

"But Esther… what you said, well… it wasn't proper for a young woman to say. Something you shouldn't ask a man."

When she finally raised her eyes, it was clear she hadn't taken his chastisement well.

Her brows furrowed, annoyance flashing across her face.

"I know that… Ian. It's not like I said it to one of the men workin' down on the fence."

Her tone was something Ian had never heard before.

Where was the submissive Esther he knew? She was sharp. Fiery.

"Esther," he said, more out of shock than anything else. It wasn't a question, nor a statement—just disbelief hanging in the air.

"I hope you'd know better than that."

He paused for a moment, catching the faint smell of wine on her breath, which further caught him off guard.

"Have you… been drinking?" he asked, his tone chiding her further.

By now, Esther had let her mouth run, so she opened the gate and gave it the whole field.

"Why do you always have to be so bossy? Pushin' everyone around? You can tell me what to do when I'm workin' in the orchard, but ya can't tell me what I should say."

Ian just stood there. She'd done it again—sewn his mouth shut.

Bossy? What did she mean by that? He was in charge of the estate. It was his responsibility, his duty.

What had started with a tender approach now grated on him, scraping against his pride. She was stepping out of line.

"Esther, you need to control yourself," he said, his tone hardening.

But his words were like pouring fuel on the fire.

"Aw, shut up, Ian," she snapped. "Ya ain't my father. Matter of fact, ya ain't nothin'."

With that, Esther turned and walked away toward the front of the house.

Esther couldn't believe what she had just said. It echoed Gran's tone, slipping off her tongue with an ease that startled her.

But she was tired of being nice, tired of swallowing the thorn that pressed against her chest.

The air between them felt too thick, too charged.

She needed space, distance, before more words came crashing out.

But Ian's footsteps followed, heavier now, crunching in the gravel, his voice demanding as it cut through the tension.

"Esther, come back. We're not finished."

She had nearly made it to the front drive when she noticed the approaching vehicle.

The sun glinted off the polished chrome of the police cruiser, its black-and-white paint job stark against the gravel road.

She stopped as it pulled up the driveway toward her, coming to a halt about ten feet away.

Her heart skipped a beat, an icy dread seeping into her veins as she recognized it.

The engine of Sheriff Ronell's patrol vehicle turned off, and the sudden silence amplified the tension in the air.

Without hesitation, the sheriff and his deputy, Frank, stepped out, their expressions serious, eyes zeroed in on the girl.

Sheriff Ronell wasted no time, striding purposefully toward Esther, his gaze unwavering. His badge, a sign of his authority, gleamed in the light.

"Girl, I got some questions for ya," he said.

Ian had followed her out front, ready to continue whatever argument had been brewing between them, though he hadn't wanted it. Still, he was prepared to finish it.

That was until the sheriff arrived.

In an instant, the fight drained out of him. The look in the men's eyes told him they weren't here for a friendly visit.

No, they were here for Esther. She was in trouble.

"You know brewing moonshine is illegal?" Sheriff Ronell's words were sharp, cutting through the air as he approached Esther, who stood there, timid and unsure.

"We know you and yer Gran were up there doin' it on that hill," he continued. "Now, I know yer Gran is dead and all, but you're still here to answer for it—fer yer law breakin'."

Not knowing what to do—whether to run or just stand there—Esther's eyes darted to Ian, and fear was plain on her expression.

She needed guidance, unsure of the truth she was now faced with.

Gran had always warned her, "Keep your damn mouth shut. Don't say a word 'bout it, if they ever ask ya."

But right now, Esther wasn't sure if the look on her face might say something she didn't want them to know.

Ian's demeanor shifted, defensive. The sheriff had rolled up on private land, questioning someone under his care—Clarissa's niece, no less. But he wasn't sure if pushing back was the right move.

As Esther's eyes searched his, silently pleading for help, His mind scrambled, trying to find the best approach.

Frank interjected as he joined the conversation, eyeing Ian's posture for a sign of whether he should be on guard.

"Local hunter said he found a spot… where ya been hidin' your setup," Frank said.

"You say a hunter found this spot?" Ian cut in. "What's he doing hunting up here? That's Primm land," he challenged.

Frank's eyes narrowed, clearly irritated by Ian's interference.

"Vic Porter was huntin' hogs and came about it, not that it's any of your business," Frank retorted sharply.

Sheriff Ronell, placing his hands on his belt, took control of the conversation.

He fixed his stern gaze on Esther, his eyes steady and unyielding.

"Now, Miss Primm, we all know ya might have a little…trouble understandin' certain things, but ya still know the difference between right and wrong, don'tcha?" His voice softened, just a touch.

"It's time to fess up."

Esther's throat felt as if it was closing up, fear and shame swirling in her chest, making it hard to breathe. She wanted to speak, to defend herself, but the words wouldn't come.

"Right?" Sheriff Ronell pressed, his patience wearing thin.

Ian stepped closer to the willowy girl standing helpless in the drive. Leaning in, he asked, "Esther, do you know what they're talking about?" His voice was low, almost pleading, hoping she'd deny it, but the worry lingered in his chest—afraid she wouldn't.

"Yes, sir…" Esther whispered, her voice barely above a breath.

The truth of her past—the old copper distillery and all the consequences that came with it—bore down on her.

Sheriff Ronell nodded, satisfied, as if he'd gotten all the confession he needed just by looking into her eyes.

"Well then, girl, I see it two ways—you take us up there on that hill and show us the exact spot… or we climb up and down that damn hill 'til we find it ourselves. And I promise you, we'll be mighty mad about wastin' a good day."

Like a bug under a glass jar, Esther had no choice. She was caught.

With a shameful expression, she nodded.

"I'll show ya," she said, her voice heavy with defeat.

Dammit, Esther, Ian thought to himself.

He'd hoped she wouldn't say anything—neither deny nor confirm. But it was too late. He couldn't believe the reasoning that had run through his mind. The hills were vast—he'd hoped they wouldn't find the spot. She could've shown him later, and they could've destroyed all the evidence.

The thought hit him hard—he was actually considering breaking the law to protect her. But it wasn't justice, he reasoned.

Esther wasn't some calculating hillbilly moonshiner. She was a girl forced into this life by the very people who should have kept her safe.

Not willing to leave the trouble solely on her shoulders, he stepped forward, his voice steady. "I'll come with you."

But Sheriff Ronell was quick to shut him down.

"You're stayin' put—this is out of yer hands."

And with those final words, the sheriff led Esther to the car.

That vacant, distant look filled her eyes again—the same one she'd worn that night on the road in front of his house. It painted her face in a way that made Ian's heart sink. The brightness that had glowed in her for months now flickered, quickly diminishing.

Frank, always the opportunist to prove his prowess as a lawman, tipped his hat to Ian, a mocking grin plastered on his face.

"Have a good day now," he said, his tone dripping with sarcasm.

As Esther climbed into the back of the sheriff's car, her heart raced.

The life she had tried so hard to leave behind had caught up with her, and there was no running from it now.

Esther had only gone back to the hills once since that day in the river. She had returned for her hymn book, the only thing she cared about.

Nothing else—not a single thing—did she want from that old place.

She had told no one where she was going, just walked up there alone, disappearing for hours.

When she came back at dusk, Ian was waiting in the upper orchard. He'd told her plain that it wasn't all right to take off like that, said it had given Clarissa a fright.

Told her they'd even gone down to the fields where the men were working to see if she'd gotten herself into some trouble. It left her feeling as if she had wasted his day—and that's precisely what he meant.

But now, she had to go back—back to the place where she had been little more than a shell of a person. Her life there had been a quiet torture, one she hadn't fully understood until living at the Old Reed Estate. The thought of it made her skin crawl. Despite the beauty of the mountains, the old shack had been only a prison, and the moonshining her chain.

At the forefront of her mind, she didn't care if they destroyed everything. Gran had always said they would. Go ahead, she thought, burn it all down.

The car's engine roared to life, and as they pulled away from the estate, she felt a deep bitterness well up inside her, aimed squarely at Gran and Pawdad. It felt as though they were coming back from the dead to make her pay—to pay the tax on their misdeeds.

As the sheriff's car disappeared down the road, Ian watched it fade, his chest tightening with dread. How was he going to tell Clarissa? And the kids? What was he even going to say? The children didn't need to know the details, but Clarissa—this would tear her apart.

He wasn't sure how first-time offenders were punished, but the thought of Esther in jail unsettled him, made his chest tight. Clarissa was sure to be terrified.

And then there were the fines. Esther didn't have the money for that. She had refused to take a wage for the pick, saying that Clarissa had given her all she needed.

The harvest this year had been successful, but that money was already spoken for—directed toward the debts they'd piled up from the year before.

Feeling the burden settle deep inside him, he walked toward the house, getting ready once again, just like he did the night before, bracing for the storm.

Chapter 18: Burning Bridges

The August sun beat down over the hills of Eastern Tennessee, casting jagged patches of light between the dense pines of the Blue Hollows.

Sheriff Ronell and Frank made their way through the thick underbrush, moving swift with purpose.

The hidden moonshine still had been a well-kept secret, tucked away deep within the hillside where few would venture. But today, its days were numbered.

Esther walked ahead of the men as she guided them to the spot where Gran had taught her the art of brewing illegal liquor.

Each step, a walk to the gallows.

Dread pulled at her bare feet as she climbed the once familiar path, now overgrown. She thought it fitting how quickly the hills were reclaiming what had always belonged to them.

Like they had known what the Primms were doing was wrong and were now determined to erase any sign of them.

The surrounding forest felt oppressive, the tall trees looming as silent judges.

When they reached the moonshine still, hidden under a thick layer of leaves and brush, Sheriff Ronell let out a low whistle, impressed by how well it had been concealed.

Frank wasted no time, grabbing a sledgehammer from his pack and swinging it with all his might.

The sharp clang of metal against metal echoed through the woods, reverberating off the trees and sending birds fluttering into the sky.

Esther watched in silence as an era came to an end. The copper pot had been part of her life for as far back as she could recall. With each arc of the hammer, a piece of her past was shattered, the connection to her Gran severed with brutal finality.

For a brief moment, a sadness settled over her as they punched a hole through the heart of the kettle. It wasn't the loss of the thing itself, but something deeper, something she couldn't name. It felt as though they were violating something sacred, tearing apart the last piece of Gran—her body, her limbs—bit by bit.

Though she knew it had to be done, watching it didn't come any easier. She hated it—hated that the old still stirred pity in her.

Why should she feel that way? It had rubbed her knuckles raw from scrubbing it clean, its fire tended with care, and still, all it ever did was mock her.

It was always hungry, never fed enough mash, never full. And it never would've been, if the river hadn't saved her.

She'd still be here now, doing what she'd done for years. It was ugly, a thing that devoured her bit by bit. She hated it with every ounce of her being.

As a matter of fact, she hated it all.

She hated the place she had once called home.

It was never a home—just a shelter from the rain.

She hated the girl who had lain in the front room, all skin and bone.

She thought about how she wanted to kill her off forever—that version of herself that whispered, promising that if she could just survive one more beating, she'd find solace somewhere.

The girl no man would ever truly want—especially the one who could only see her with pity.

Esther grew tired of the voices in her head. Tired of feeling small.

She was angry. Mad.

Watching the lawmen, making sure they were engrossed in their task, Esther decided it was time.

This might be her only chance, and she had to act quickly.

Without a sound, she slipped into the brush, her movements careful and deliberate. She knew where she was going and what she was doing.

Her heart pounded in her ears as she ran, her feet ghosting over the forest floor, barely a sound to betray her.

The trees blurred, their branches reaching out, skeletal and grasping. But every boulder was etched in her bones, a map carved deep in her body.

She didn't slow, not until the old shack came into view.

It stood there, fragile and cold, a shadow of something long gone—a stark contrast to the vibrant green of the forest that had almost forgotten it.

Esther burst through the door, breath coming in quick, shallow gasps, heading straight for the dusty table.

A lantern sat there—its paint long worn away. The metal was bare and cold, but it was still filled with fuel—like it had been waiting for her.

Trying to welcome her back.

She grabbed the box of matches from a rickety shelf.

Her eyes swept over the old photos—portraits of Gran and Pawdad in their younger days.

A truth, sharp and cold. Not one of her. Not one of her mother, as if neither she nor Annie had ever existed.

And then, the voice inside her head started laughing.

You don't have the courage.

Taking one last glance, Esther knew what she had to do.

With the lantern in hand, she smashed it against the floor. The glass cried out, a sharp crack echoing through the room.

Its precious fuel, its lifeblood, spilled out, flooding the grooves of the wooden planks, soaking in fast. The scent of kerosene rose, sharp and pungent, filling the air.

Her hands trembled as she struck a match against the stove. The small flame flickered in the dim light. There was no hesitation as she let it fall, dropping the match onto the fuel-soaked floor.

The fire caught in an instant, claiming the old shack in its last embrace. The flames spread fast, as though the cabin had always been destined for this moment.

Esther stumbled outside, the porch creaking beneath her feet, as if asking, "Why? Why had she done this?"

The same porch she'd hidden under as a child, not for joy, but for survival.

Standing a few feet from the inferno, she watched as the flames devoured everything she had ever known. The roaring fire tore through what had stood for years, dry timber catching like kindling in an instant.

Smoke billowed up. Dark clouds twisting and dancing, mocking what once was.

She surprised herself—there wasn't a flicker of regret.

Nothing pulled at her.

There was nothing left she wanted from that place.

Not even a memory.

The darting flames mesmerized Esther, her eyes following as they slipped into the hidden corners of the roof.

Her gaze stayed fixed on the fiery dance. Before she realized it, her feet were already carrying her forward.

Each step was slow, deliberate, as if the fire itself were drawing her in. It pulled her closer to its dangerous beauty. The heat warmed her skin, while the crackle of burning wood filled her ears.

She didn't hear the frantic footsteps of Sheriff Ronell and Frank rushing up behind her.

"What in the God-living hell?" Sheriff Ronell shouted, grabbing Esther by the arm and yanking her away from the speeding blaze, his face twisted in disbelief.

The flames reflected in his wide eyes, the heat making him squint as he took in the sight of the burning building.

Frank arrived a moment later, letting out a sharp bark of laughter.

"Well, hell—she done gone and set the whole place on fire," he said, amusement clear in his voice as he watched the destruction.

Sheriff Ronell shot Frank a look of disbelief before turning it on Esther.

"Why'd ya do that?" he demanded, his eyes flicking back to the roaring fire. "Goddamn it, girl! I wasn't gonna burn down yer home. Why the hell did ya have to go and do somethin' like that?"

His voice was sharp, cutting through the crackle of the flames, but Esther didn't flinch.

She stared at the blaze, her face empty, the fire's glow dancing in her eyes.

Sheriff Ronell let out a long breath, exasperation and frustration carving lines into his face.

"I don't know whether to arrest ya or send ya to an insane asylum," he muttered, shaking his head.

Frank stepped in closer, speaking low in the sheriff's ear, the snap of wood burning nearly drowning him out.

"Marty, this girl ain't right. This place has twisted her up. She needs help, real help. A good place where she can get some education, some structure. Learn how to live as a real person, not some wild thing."

A flicker of softness crossed the sheriff's face, a rare crack in his seasoned exterior.

He nodded, the reality of the moment settling in.

Frank gave a firm pat on the sheriff's shoulder, leaning in again.

"Her cousin Clive said he'd take her in. Give her a good place, make sure she stays on the straight and narrow."

The sheriff nodded once more, his gaze darting back to the flames.

Turning to Esther, he said, "I swear, next to yer Gran ridin' the falls…"

He shook his head again, a look of bewilderment on his face.

"This is the craziest damn thing I ever seen," he added, half to himself, half to the fire.

With the fire nearly spent, devouring the last remnants of Esther's past, soot clung to her—a second skin.

As the flames died down, the lawman and Esther turned and made their way toward the vehicle.

The pop of the embers grew faint, replaced by the soft crunch of dirt beneath their boots.

Nearing the car, the sheriff glanced down at Esther's bare feet, caked in dirt.

"Girl, where's your damn shoes?"

"At Clarissa's house," she said, not meeting his eyes.

Agitated, the weary sheriff growled under his breath, "Of course."

The drive down the dirt road was rocky, the silence thick between them. When they crossed the creek, it was all but dry, just a trickle running through the rocks.

Esther stared out the window, her thoughts far off, drifting as the familiar landscape rolled by, untouched by what had burned behind her.

As they approached the Old Reed Estate, her heart sank. The house loomed closer, yet it seemed unreal, as if it had only ever existed in a dream—never truly hers to hold.

From the backseat, she called out in a small, almost childlike voice to the sheriff,

"Am I… gonna go to jail?"

Fear clung to her words, uncertain of her fate.

He answered with a muffled gruffness, his voice more worn out from the day than filled with anger.

"No, but you're done livin' with those people."

"Why? They ain't done wrong to me," she said.

"They don't have what ya need. Ya need yerself a real life. To be around regular folks. You've spent enough time in these damn hills," he said, his words weighted with judgment.

She wanted to argue, wanted to push back, but the sheriff's stern eyes in the rearview mirror silenced her.

The sun was still high as the police cruiser crept up the drive, stirring the summer air.

Ian sat on the front porch step of the big house, his arms folded across his knees, his gaze locked straight ahead, unmoving.

His jaw was clenched tightly, the muscles in his face stiff, as if he barely contained the tension hidden beneath his rough exterior. Sweat glistened on his forehead, but he didn't wipe it away. He simply sat still.

Clarissa rocked beside him in her favorite chair, her foot tapping against the floorboards, the only sound breaking the silence.

The atmosphere grew suffocating as they waited for news.

Rolling to a stop in front of the house, the sheriff cut the engine. He stepped out, set his hat on his head, and rounded the back of the vehicle to open the door.

Esther climbed out, moving sluggishly, her steps void of their usual vigor, the life drained from her.

A soft haze formed around her as the sun caught the light, her black-streaked dress standing as a witness to her deed.

She refused to look up, instead keeping her eyes pinned to the ground, afraid to face the disappointment. She had brought shame to their good name, to the Old Reed Estate—a place too good for the likes of her.

Clarissa gripped the edge of her rocker, her heart heavy. It was a mercy she had sent the children off with Mitzy, knowing the sight of Esther like this would have upset them so.

After sitting unmoved for hours, Ian finally stood—something he hadn't done since Abram had held him back, stopping him from rushing into the hills when they first saw the smoke.

"Ain't nothin' you can do," Abram had told him, firm but calm. "They're just burnin' the old moonshine stills."

But Ian had known better, had seen the thick column of smoke rising too high, too big for something small.

As Ian moved toward Sheriff Ronell, the tension radiated from him, rippling through the air like heat rising from the ground.

The tall German's agitation was plain, his anger directed squarely at the lawman.

Ian's strides were long, deliberate—predatory in their intent. He was a man barely holding onto control, and Frank, the deputy, could see it.

Frank climbed out of the vehicle despite orders to stay put.

"Before you start in on me," the sheriff said to Ian, his hands raised, voice steady. "Just know, it wasn't me that set that goddamn house on fire." He paused, bracing.

Ian's eyes narrowed.

"I think you'll need to explain." His voice was low, his body taut, ready for whatever confrontation might come.

The fire on the hill had left him with a rage, burning hotter inside than anything the flames could touch.

He had heard the stories of lawmen burning down homes— especially when people crossed the wrong lines. And it reminded him of darker memories from his youth in Germany: soldiers setting fires to villages during the war.

It pulled him back to every stare, every warning he and Adeline had faced when they first arrived in the South.

It was a reminder, sharp and unwelcome, of the divides carved long before their feet touched this land.

"She set it all ablaze," the sheriff said, his words slow, deliberate. "'Fore we even had time to stop her."

He let out a long sigh, his eyes rolling as if he couldn't fully believe it himself.

"Thought she was gonna walk right into it."

Esther stood a few steps away, hearing all she needed. She hadn't meant to set herself ablaze—she had just wandered too close.

Frustrated, she started walking toward the door, her steps quick. She didn't want to linger, didn't want to hear the disappointment or shock that might spill out. Better to keep moving, to outrun the consequences of her poor judgment. And it didn't help that a bitter humiliation simmered inside her, still reliving the memory of the previous night's encounter.

"I'm gonna get my things," she said, her tone flat.

She didn't want a scene, didn't want to have to explain herself. The only thing she wanted was to get in and out of the house as quickly as possible. To just disappear.

The thought of facing the children, of seeing their wide, sad eyes, made her stomach twist. It would break her down, she knew that much.

Clarissa stood in silence—her heart being torn from her chest. The moment the sheriff said Esther had lit the fire, she thought, damn straight. *And why shouldn't she, after all they had put her through?* But she kept those words locked inside, holding them close, where they couldn't stir up more trouble.

"You best be quick. Don't go gettin' any harebrained ideas about runnin', or I'll lock ya up fer good. Ya hear me, girl?" Sheriff Ronell barked.

A man who'd long since lost his patience.

Esther nodded, her face set, her eyes avoiding the surrounding stares. She pushed past them all, slipping into the house.

Ian, still bristling, felt his temper flare again but forced himself to draw a steady breath. This wasn't the time for fighting. He needed to reason with the man, not lash out.

"What kind of trouble is she facing?" he asked, voice thick with concern. "You know her situation. She didn't know better."

Sheriff Ronell's face hardened.

"She ain't goin' to jail, if that's what yer askin'," he said, his tone blunt.

"But she ain't stayin' here neither. She needs more than what y'all can offer her."

Both Ian and Clarissa felt the weight lift, the news that Esther wouldn't be taken to jail, a fleeting breath of relief in the stifling heat.

But the relief was momentary, quickly swallowed by the sadness that filled Clarissa's eyes.

Her heart sank as she absorbed the sheriff's words. Her niece—her sweet, troubled Esther—was being taken away from her. Shaking, Clarissa moved toward Ian and took hold of his arm, her fingers gripping tightly, looking for support.

"Where's she gonna be?" Her voice cracked, her throat dry.

"Cousin Clive," the sheriff said, his voice rough with finality. "Y'all best leave her there. I'm tired of this Primm nonsense. It's clear ya can't control her. Lucky she didn't set the whole hill ablaze."

Clarissa winced at the harshness, her hand on Ian tightening.

Inside, Esther darted through the narrow hallway, her footsteps heavy on the wooden floor.

She burst into her room, eyes scanning the small space for the few possessions that truly mattered. Her hands moved quickly, gathering clothes, her hymn book, and a small picture frame of Rebecca and Benjamin, a gift they had given her.

She fought the tears threatening to break through, biting her lip to keep them in check. There would be no crying—not now.

Moments later, she pushed open the front door, her steps urgent, as if the faster she moved, the quicker she could escape the shame and pain clinging to her.

She didn't stop, didn't meet their eyes.

She made a straight line for the sheriff's cruiser.

There'd be no goodbyes, no last words.

Ian followed the sheriff, his eyes locked on Esther. His body was still tense, but aware—knowing this wasn't something he could solve, could fix.

Not now. Not for her.

When she reached the car, she looked up, catching his gaze briefly. There was a sadness in it she didn't want to acknowledge. She turned away quickly, scanning the yard until her eyes landed on her dog.

A sharp whistle cut through the air.

Bones bounded toward her, ears perked, his paws kicking up dust with each stride. Without hesitation, he leaped into the backseat.

Before Esther finished climbing in, she paused. She couldn't help herself—she had to see Ian's face one last time.

The face she had dreamed of, though no smile.

He stood tall, his light blue eyes held on her.

All Esther could think was how she'd brought it all down on herself—her ignorance, her weaknesses. She wasn't sure if he was still cross with her from earlier, certain she had pushed his good nature too far. But she tried to smile, to let him know she'd be okay. Her lips silently formed the words—I'm sorry.

That was it. That was all she'd let show.

And she couldn't—wouldn't—look at Clarissa.

If she did, she knew it would break her, shatter her completely. Aunt Clarissa had given her love and a home she'd never known before.

With one arm resting on the roof and the other gripping the doorframe, Sheriff Ronell stood by his vehicle, his weathered face unflinching. His posture radiated authority, every inch of him direct. When he spoke, he aimed his words at Ian, making sure Clarissa could hear.

"Ya best leave that girl alone. Let her get herself settled, get civilized, 'fore any of ya think about messin' with her."

He turned, eyes cutting sharply into Clarissa. "Because I won't tolerate her actin' out again. Ya understand me?" His gaze left no doubt—his word was law, and it wasn't a threat, it was a promise.

With a sharp nod to Frank, they were off, the car kicking up dust as it rumbled away.

Ian and Clarissa were left standing, watching the haze as the car vanished down the winding road.

As quickly as Esther had come into their lives at the Old Reed Estate, she had left.

Ian glanced over at the older woman, tears slipping down her worn face as her shoulders trembled. He walked slowly to her, his head hung low. Aware of the strange and surprising ache in his own chest.

When he pulled her close, her usually sturdy body felt frail, shaking in his arms.

"Ian, they took my girl," she whispered through her sobs.

He had known it would break her. With no words to mend it, he just held her, letting the silence wrap around them.

In his heart, he knew this pain wasn't Clarissa's alone to bear. Esther had planted her roots here, had become part of the land, part of the life they'd all built. She had woven herself into the tapestry of the estate.

Already bracing himself, Ian knew telling the children wouldn't be easy. They had faced more loss than most. He thought of little Rebecca—losing her best friend, how it would cut so deep.

He even allowed himself to mourn the thought of Esther—the timid smile she wore as she'd bring him his lunchtime pail each day.

He had never told her she was pretty, though he'd thought it a hundred times.

Last night, when she asked, he had only said "sure," when all she had needed was a "yes." A real one.

But she was gone.

And that conversation no longer mattered. Nothing left to sort through, no thoughts left to untangle. It had all been settled—sadly.

Now, Ian could just go on loving Adeline and her memory.

Chapter 19: Prison

Esther sat in the back of Sheriff Ronell's car as they traveled down the winding road toward Larkin. Warm air rushed in through an open window, only adding to the swelter. Indifferent, she let her hair whip around wild, as though caught up in a tornado.

Bones, sitting beside her, didn't seem to mind.

Once Pawdad's hound, he had become her faithful companion—the only one to bear silent witness to the hardships she'd endured. She knew Bones wouldn't judge her for burning down that old shack. He'd seen the way Gran laid into her plenty of times. Once, he'd even tried to lick the marks left on her raw, red legs.

As the vehicle passed an old graveyard, Esther wondered if her grandparents lay there. Right then and there, she vowed never to visit them, never to clear their headstones.

Go ahead and haunt me, you mean ol' bastards, she thought. You've ruined what little joy I ever had—her mind echoed bitterly.

She wasn't sure where they were heading, but her suspicions lingered. It hadn't been by accident that Frank had shown up with the sheriff the next day. Her cousin was the only one who knew about the moonshine they'd been making, tucked away where no one else should have found it.

Now, all she could think about was how she'd navigate life with the one person she hated more than anyone else in the world.

She felt cursed just thinking of her cousin Clive.

Running away had crossed her mind more than once. The idea of bolting from the car and disappearing into the dense woods, never to be found, was tempting. But she knew better.

They would come looking for her, and Clarissa's home would be the first place they searched. She had already brought too much trouble to their doorstep.

And where would she go? She had no money, no plan, and had known nothing but the hills of Blue Hollow.

The harsh reality was that she was trapped, with no means of escape. She hadn't listened to the wind's warning as it whispered through the trees by the lake. She hadn't wanted to. It had tried to tell her—the ache in her legs begging her to run.

But now she was caught.

This game of cat and mouse felt like the checker game she'd played with Ian's children.

Each move was calculated. Each piece, slowly sacrificed. Until finally, there was nothing left but the corner from which she couldn't escape.

As they neared Clive's home, her fears were confirmed. The lawmen—they were cut from the same cloth as her cousin, she thought bitterly.

The small white house next to the old church looked innocent enough, with its neat picket fence and carefully trimmed yard. Yet to Esther, it felt like a prison, just as confining as the one she had just burned down.

When the sheriff's car came to a stop, Frank was the first to get out. His usual smug expression was plastered on his face.

He opened the door for Esther—not with the courtesy of a gentleman, but with the cold detachment of a warden overseeing the men by the fence.

Gesturing toward the front door, he said, "Git goin', girl."

Her dog leapt out, trailing behind as she made her way.

Esther's heart hammered as she whispered to herself to be brave. But facing that door now, she wasn't so sure. She had never stepped inside Clive's house.

Gran had warned her as a child, "Even if he offers ya somethin', don't ya go in there. Ya hide in the cornfields if ya got to."

Esther glanced back at the fields, the corn growing high, stretching up toward the sky. The green stalks rustled in the wind, whispering as if they knew what was coming.

Deputy Frank followed closely, sensing her hesitation. With an open hand, he nudged her forward, urging her up the sidewalk, herding her toward the porch like one would drive a wild animal into a corral. She slowly climbed the small set of stairs, but before she could steel herself, the door swung open.

There stood Clive in a freshly pressed shirt, hair slicked back, as though he'd been waiting for this moment. His eyes lit with a twisted satisfaction that sent a shiver clear to her toes.

"Well, here she be," Frank announced with a grin, clearly enjoying the situation more than he should have.

Clive didn't say a word, just nodded, and motioned for Esther to come in.

The door closed behind her with a finality that felt like the clanging of an iron pen. She was alone with him now, her dog left on the porch with Frank, her last bit of comfort taken away.

Clive's home was small, cramped, and filled with a sense of foreboding that seemed to seep into the very walls. The stench of musty furniture lingered, mixed with something else she couldn't quite place—but it made her skin crawl.

"Welcome home, Esther," he said, his voice dripping with mock sincerity.

"This ain't my home," she replied.

His smile faltered, just for a second, before he masked it with a look of disappointment.

"Ah, why ya always gotta be so mean to me?"

Then he gave Esther a full once-over, eyeing her soot-covered dress and the wild tangle of her hair before chuckling softly.

"I'd offer ya a seat, but looks like you'd stain it."

She said nothing. She didn't want small talk—she wanted a way out.

"Where's my space?" she asked, her eyes scanning the front room.

Clive made his way to the sofa, leaning casually on the back, as though it were something he owned—and now, so was she.

"Well, this here couch is for sittin'."

His eyes narrowed, a dangerous glint flashing in them.

"This house only has one bedroom."

"Fine enough," she shot back, her voice tight with defiance. "I don't mind sleepin' on the floor."

Clive's lips curled into a smile, but it wasn't friendly.

"Tell ya what, precious, why don't ya take a bath, and we can sit here together. I'll read from the Good Book fer ya. How'd you like that? We could even have some peach pie and get to know each other better."

Her stomach lurched at the thought.

"I ain't sittin' next to ya," she said, stepping back, her body tense, ready to bolt.

"Now, Esther, I'm only doin' what the Good Lord would ask of me—tendin' to His lost lamb."

His voice was slick with false sweetness, coating his words— molasses gone sour.

Esther could feel the lie in his tone, knowing his kindness was just a skin he slipped into for the game.

He stepped closer, inch by inch, testing her resolve, his eyes gleaming. As the space between them shrank, she knew she was right, had always been—Clive enjoyed her discomfort. His hands were stretched out, fingers spread wide—a dark version of the Lord's comforting call.

"Esther, are you God's lost lamb?"

His words coiled around her.

"Kinda looks like you are," he continued. "Standin' there all quiet, unsure of where to go, what to do. But don't fret—yer good cousin Clive's here to take care of ya. Will see to ya needs, won't let ya outta my sight."

Her knuckles whitened, nails biting into her palms as her mind raced, wanting to break free, but he was right—there was nowhere to go. She'd only ever met a handful of folks in Larkin, and they were strangers all the same.

As he stood there, head tilted to one side, gawking at her, she thought of Ian's warning. His words echoed in her mind. "They're bad men, Esther. Stay away from them."

But how could she stay away when the worst one stood right in front of her?

She was nothing more than an offering—handed over by men whose word was law. They didn't need a reason, didn't care for the truth. If they wanted to, they could lock her up, throw her in the slammer. And the sheriff had made his demand known—she was to live with her cousin, Preacher Clive Jones. A man respected in the community. Untouchable.

"I'll be fine," she said as her voice wavered. "I don't need yer help."

Clive, amused, shrugged, as if her resistance was nothing more than sport to him.

"Suit yourself, but remember, Esther, this is your home now. Ya think of tiptoein' out in the middle of the night, and I'll be so overcome with worry—might have to send a few fellas to look fer ya."

He paused, his voice dropping dangerously low. "I once promised yer Gran I'd watch after ya… and by God, I intend to do just that."

His words were a death sentence, each one sealing her fate.

Irrevocably trapped—Esther was stuck in Clive's clapboard prison, a cage disguised with a picket fence and rose bushes.

Chapter 20: Never Sweet

September withered away as the last of the cornfields rustled with dry stalks. The old white church stood watch, a weary guardian over the fading fields. Inside, the scent of polished wood filled the air as purple and pink dahlias adorned the altar.

For years, the small rural chapel had been the spiritual heart of the community. Generations of local folk had filled its pews each Sunday, the oak benches worn smooth by years of faithful attendance.

Today, the congregation filled every seat. The elders sat up front, while Esther tucked herself in the back row near the wall, wanting to hide and keep her distance.

Clive stood at the lectern, his hefty figure dominating the small space behind it. He clutched the Bible tightly, as if it were a weapon to wield against the very sins he preached about. His voice boomed through the sanctuary. Every corner brimming with self-righteous fervor.

"I'm a rich man standin' here today," Clive said, his false humility making Esther's stomach churn.

"Blessed with his Savior's holy resurrection. But filth and evil are so temptin'! For earthly man must resist! He must! He must overcome his carnal temptations so that he may someday reside in the holy light of our dear Lord," he intoned.

Esther kept her head down, her hands clenching the worn edges of the hymnal she had taken up more as a shield than a guide to worship.

Every word that spilled from Clive's mouth felt as though it was poison, a toxic mix of fire and brimstone meant to instill fear rather than faith. She had heard these sermons before, each one more condemning than the last, as if Clive needed to constantly remind his flock of their unworthiness while elevating himself as the only path to salvation.

"Do ya hear me, brothers and sisters?" His voice rose, his fervor intensifying as he gestured dramatically to the congregation as he continued.

"Do the Lord's words ring true to your plugged ears? Pray each of ya tonight that ya may find peace with God's word and accept His fate, His design to heal your sinner soul. I bless ya in His name, Amen."

The final "Amen" reverberated through the small church, and the congregation stirred, murmuring their responses as they stood and prepared to leave.

Esther lingered in her seat for a few more moments, feeling lost amid the sea of people. Clive's sermons always made her feel as if she were sinking underwater, drowning a little more with every word he spoke.

When she finally stood, she felt light-headed, as if even the air in the church had been sucked out by her cousin's overbearing presence, leaving the room gasping for breath.

She followed the others outside, squinting at the bright midday sun.

Long tables were arranged on the lawn near the building, with women already laying out platters of pulled pork, potato salad, and a variety of pies. The smell of home-cooked food filled the air, blending with children's laughter as they played, their shoes kicking up dust in the dry grass.

Esther wandered around the side of the church, looking for a quiet spot away from the crowd. She needed to clear her mind and be alone. A place on the back steps seemed private enough, so she sat. Pulling her knees to her chest, she wrapped her arms around them.

The cheerful noise outside twisted a knife deep inside her, cutting at her loneliness like a blade.

Benjamin and Rebecca felt like ghosts now, their faces flickering in her memory.

Her mind drifted. She missed those days—running through the orchard, creating mischief under the sun. They felt so distant now.

She remembered once when Ian, with a twinkle in his eye, quickly joined in the play—splashing them with water from his canteen as they darted past the trees.

With a hearty laugh, he denied the deed, claiming it must have been a lone rain cloud overhead. She'd looked up to a clear blue sky, and when she shook her head, he winked back, grinning.

But it was the plan she and Benjamin had devised that still brought a smile to her lips. It had been carefully timed, each move in place, waiting for the perfect moment. Benjamin had hidden in the loft of the old barn, a bucket filled with cold well water, his boyish grin spreading across his face.

Ian, unsuspecting, wandered in for his evening chores. The moment he stepped underneath, Benjamin let it all out. The shock on Ian's face was worth it as he muttered a string of curse words, followed by a chuckle.

She had watched from the barn doors, trying to stifle her own laughter. When Ian spotted her, he asked if this was her doing. She only shrugged with a playful smirk and said, "Who do you think lifted the bucket?"

God, how she missed those days. They had been heaven. The Old Reed Estate and all of those faces.

Footsteps interrupted her thoughts as she turned to find a group of men just rounding the corner. Their laughter was loud and boisterous. Passing around a mason jar, each man took a long swig of what was clearly likker. Quickly, she averted her eyes, hoping they'd pass by without noticing her.

But, as she'd feared, Clive lagged behind the group. He stopped abruptly a foot away, his shadow casting over her like a dark cloud. She didn't need to look up to know it was him—she felt his menace.

"Why ya hangin' out here?" he asked. "Womenfolk keep out front—that's where they're meant to be."

Esther kept her gaze downward, refusing to look at him.

"I didn't know ya'd be back here," she replied flatly.

"Didn't ya?" he teased, nudging himself closer, his shoes touching hers. "Ya sure you weren't lookin' for me?"

Esther's chest tightened, but she forced herself to stay calm— this had become a daily thing.

"I promise ya, I ain't lookin' fer ya nowhere—ever," she mumbled, looking up enough to shoot him a side eye.

Clive chuckled, a humorless sound—his pride clearly pricked.

"Good Lord, yer such a spiteful thing. Ain't ya got a bit of gratitude in ya? Who d'you think was givin' yer Gran money so ya wouldn't starve to death up on that hill? Always paid Aunt Pearl more than the goin' rate—outta the goodness of my heart—and this is what I get."

With that, he pushed at her foot again, but this time Esther moved it out of reach.

She had resigned herself to this life—dodging him and avoiding him as she must.

And Clive was a snake, a copperhead, and she knew she had to be careful, to play along until she found a way out of this nightmare.

Undeterred, his tone shifted, becoming sickeningly sweet.

"Tell ya what, why don't ya go down in the cellar and bring up one of them big bottles fer me. Ya know where I keep 'em. Do that, my precious, and I'll leave ya alone for the rest of the day, as that seems to be what ya want."

He paused as she weighed her options.

"Well, is it a deal or what?" he pressed.

Esther felt conflicted, not wanting to go out of her way for him, nor provoke him. With a slight, conceding nod, she stood and headed toward the cellar.

The old wooden door creaked when it opened. The damp smell of earth wafted out as she looked into the darkness.

With little light reaching the back, she knew she'd have to find the jugs by memory, recalling the wooden table that blocked the crawl space where he kept them.

Inside, Esther gritted her teeth and dragged the heavy piece of furniture aside. Just as she made enough room to squeeze through, something brushed against her back.

Startled, she whipped around, her heart leaping into her throat.

Clive stood behind her, a leering smile half-shadowed by darkness.

She heard his breath before he spoke.

"Whatcha doin' down here?" he whispered.

"Ya sent me down here," she shot back, refusing to be toyed with despite the fear rushing through her.

She squinted, her eyes straining to adjust as he stepped closer, pressing the roundness of his belly against her.

"Did I now? Must've forgotten," he said with mock surprise. "Ain't it funny how ya always end up where I want ya?"

She felt his foul breath hot on her neck as he leaned in, his hand reaching out to stroke her hair. Esther flinched at his touch.

"Ya… ya promised ya'd leave me be," she pleaded in a shaky voice.

Clive ignored her protests, his hand sliding down to brush against her cheek.

"Esther… do ya remember the first time?"

His words made her blood run cold, dragging up memories she had tried to bury, now resurfacing with a vengeance.

She had been just a girl—too young to understand, too scared to fight back, even through her tears. But she wasn't that girl anymore, she told herself, though the thought felt thin, her fear still clawing at her.

"You were so sweet to me," Clive continued, his voice soft, almost coaxing. "How come ya can't be sweet like that no more? It's been such a long, lonely time. I miss you."

Esther's stomach churned with disgust—sure she'd lose its contents any moment. Everything he said was a lie.

"I ain't never been sweet to ya," Her voice trembled. "Not then… not now."

"Now—don't go actin' all high and mighty," Clive breathed, each word crawling toward her. "I've seen the way you look at me, darlin'. You can play innocent, but we both know the truth, and I've been about as patient as I'm gonna be."

His hand reached out to grab her again, but Esther refused to let him corner her.

Fueled by adrenaline, she shoved past him and hurried for the stairs.

She didn't stop until she was outside.

The daylight struck her like a temporary deliverance, a reminder she could still fight back. Her heart raced as she hurried toward the safety of a group, gasping for air, her mind reeling.

But the fear quickly gave way to a burning anger—at Clive, at how he'd poisoned her life for years, stalking her whenever she left the hills.

She wanted to scream, to tell someone—one of the women passing by with their carefree smiles, maybe even someone like Clarissa. But the words lodged in her throat. She had never told a soul. People didn't speak of such things. It wasn't a story she could share. It was her shame to carry.

Her cousin Clive had pursued her, hunted her, for as long as she could remember. Now she was trapped in his lion's den, pretending she'd come out unscathed. But deep down, she wasn't so sure.

The urge to cry kept pushing up inside her, but she forced it down, the way she always had.

For a fleeting moment, her thoughts flicked to Ian—how he'd shielded her once, not out of love, but out of common decency. He was a man who'd never stoop to the vile things Clive was capable of. He had honor.

She rested against the rough bark of a tall tree, eyes turned skyward, searching for a sign, hoping something would cut through the noise of her thoughts. But the only sound that reached her was Gran's words, echoing in her mind like the old woman had cast a curse on her, telling her she was only good for one thing.

But Esther had tried to give that one thing to Ian, and he hadn't wanted it.

Perhaps Clive was the only one who really ever would. The dark thought lingered, unwelcome.

In that moment, she found herself wishing she had walked into the flames—just as Sheriff Ronell claimed.

Maybe it would've been easier to let the fire take her. Easier than living with the constant worry. Every single day.

Chapter 21: Bones

The evening at Clive's house began like so many others. A mood thick with suffocating dread, as Esther tried to bide her time.

Distracted, she clumsily placed her empty glass near the edge of a table. It teetered and then toppled, hitting the floor with a sharp crack as shards scattered at her feet. She quickly bent down to gather the pieces.

"Ya stay back, Bones," Esther mumbled.

But her dog lingered nearby regardless. His eyes stayed on her as if she couldn't shake him so easily.

Since coming to Clive's, he had become a constant in her life now—always watching, waiting, silently witnessing what she was enduring.

Other than those Sunday mornings when she was forced into a pew, Bones shadowed her everywhere—his paws never far behind.

Sometimes in the yard, he would bark at her, insistent that she play with him, breaking through her sadness when she couldn't.

She was sure he'd taken on her peace as his duty. And when she faltered, he'd rest his head on her knees, forcing her to look into his dark, solemn eyes as though they had the ability to heal.

And tonight was no different. Grateful to be alone in the house for the moment—the only evidence of her cousin was the dull thud of the front door as he left.

Esther prayed he wouldn't return until morning, as he did now and then. Only then could she breathe easier, sleep better, knowing he wasn't under the same roof.

But hours later, when the door rattled open again, her heart leapt into her throat.

Clive stumbled in, reeking of alcohol, his steps uneven as he passed by the kitchen without so much as a glance in her direction.

He headed straight to his bedroom, shutting the door behind him.

A small wave of relief washed over her. Maybe he was too drunk to notice her tonight. Maybe she could curl up on her pile of blankets on the kitchen floor and slip into sleep. But it wasn't easy. She had grown always watchful, her body tense, her nerves on edge.

She tried to push it aside, telling herself she was safe—that Clive had mostly kept his distance, settling for leering eyes and oily words, perhaps believing his so-called charm could wear her down. Yet the unease refused to leave her. It grew, crawling deeper under her skin as the night dragged on.

She tried to distract herself, pretending she was back in her bed at Clarissa's, enjoying the comfort she'd quickly taken for granted. She smiled, recalling how her aunt was always particular, insisting on fresh sheets once a week. "Sleepin' should be a luxury," she'd say, without fail.

And Esther didn't mind the chore of fetching bedding from Ian's house. Sometimes, if the kids weren't with her, she'd linger longer than necessary.

He'd often forget to have his linens ready, giving her a chance to sneak into his bedroom. She liked the way his body smelled, how his scent clung to his pillow. Once, she pulled it close to her face, breathing him in, lost in a moment that wasn't hers to take, and he'd nearly caught her. She'd sworn to herself she would be more careful, but truth be told, she didn't regret it a bit.

She prayed those memories would stay with her tonight, wrapping around her... like one of Clarissa's crisp white sheets, keeping the darkness at bay.

When Esther lay down on the spot she'd claimed in the corner of the small kitchen, she pulled a thin blanket over her shoulders. It was old, holding a smell she could never wash away, no matter how many times she laundered it. Bones settled at her side, his warm body the only thing that made her feel even remotely safe in this place.

Closing her eyes, she willed sleep to come, praying to God to watch over her and grant her peace.

But the peace she sought was fleeting.

In the dead of night, a low growl jolted Esther awake.

Her eyes snapped open, and she saw Bones standing protectively beside her, his fur bristling, his eyes fixed on something in the doorway.

She squinted into the darkness.

Her shoulders tensed as she tried to piece together what she was seeing.

A dark figure loomed in the doorway, swaying slightly.

The outline of a man all too familiar.

Clive stood there. Naked—his eyes glassy with intoxication.

For a moment, Esther couldn't breathe.

The sight of him, the realization of what he intended, sent a sharp panic through her entire body.

But before she could react, Bones let out a deep, menacing growl.

He edged forward, positioning himself right between Esther and the threat.

The dog's ferocity briefly gave her hope.

Clive stalled, his eyes shifting to the animal.

Then, without a word, he turned and stumbled back to his room, the door slamming shut behind him.

Still breathing in shallow bursts, Esther reached out with trembling hands to touch Bones, grateful for his protection.

But something told her this wasn't over, that Clive wouldn't let it slide. He was becoming increasingly brazen and demanding. And the image of his dark form, without a stitch of clothes on, lodged hard in her gut.

The rest of the night passed in a haze of sleeplessness—too scared to close her eyes for more than a few minutes at a time.

She lay there, straining to catch every creak of the house, every rustle of the wind. Bones pressed close, refusing to lie down. He stood guard, body rigid, as if he too sensed the danger waiting beyond the door down the hall.

Morning seeped in through the blue café curtains, its pale light spilling across the kitchen. Esther pushed herself up, every muscle aching, her eyes raw with exhaustion. But there was no time to rest. Clive would be waking soon, hungry for his breakfast, and she had to brace for whatever the day might bring.

Standing, she stretched her arms, then walked to the window. She gazed over the morning landscape. The fields lay bathed in soft, golden light—almost idyllic, if not for the ugliness shadowing her.

And then she saw him.

Clive.

He was walking toward the house, his boots caked in mud, a shovel slung over his shoulder.

For a moment, her mind didn't grasp the significance of the shovel.

She was too focused on the empty space at her feet where Bones should have been.

Panic gripped her as she searched the room, the house, calling out for him in a desperate voice.

"Come here, boy. Come here."

But Bones was nowhere to be found.

Esther's throat tightened as she leaned out the back door, whistling for him, knowing he sometimes followed Clive out. Her voice rose in desperation just as her cousin stepped onto the porch—his expression dripping with satisfaction.

"Ya seen my dog?" she asked, trying to keep the fear out of her voice.

He glanced at her from the corner of his eye and set the shovel down with a clank. Then, slow and deliberate, he pulled off his muddy boots, one after the other, each thud echoing across the porch like a warning.

"I think he ran off this mornin'," he said, his tone flat, casual— almost bored. "Saw him headin' through the pasture."

Esther's breath caught in her throat, and she forced down a hard swallow.

"What ya mean? Ya run him off?" she demanded, though she already knew the answer.

Clive shrugged, a smirk tugging at the corners of his mouth.

"Now, why would I do that?"

He stepped past her into the kitchen, his expression dark and frightening, void of any light, making Esther's knees go weak with terror.

"Since ya just standin' around, why don't ya fix me some eggs?" he added.

She didn't answer, turning her back to him. Her hands clung to the counter, her body threatening to give way, but she stayed upright, refusing him the satisfaction.

But the truth. The truth of what Clive had done crashed over her like a landslide, stripping away the last of her strength, the very last of her will.

Bones hadn't run off.

Clive had removed him, and with him went the last bit of safety Esther could ever claim.

Tears welled up in her eyes, but she held them back. It wasn't easy, like trying to cup water in her hands. And Clive was watching, a sick pleasure dancing off him.

Working to steady her hands, Esther placed the skillet on the stove, her movements stiff, almost mechanical as she lit the burner.

His gaze still pinning her back, Clive scooted his chair closer with a low, guttural grunt, settling in like a man expecting to be served.

She wanted to scream, to run. Wanted to fight back against the injustice of it all, but she knew it wouldn't change a thing. He held all the power now, and there was nothing she could do to stop him.

As the eggs sizzled in the lard, Esther felt a hollowness settle in her chest. She had been defeated, wholly and utterly, and the sense of doom that followed was overwhelming.

Bones had been her last line of defense, the only thing that had stood between her and Clive's advances.

Now, with him gone, she knew it would only be a matter of time.

Finished with the food, she placed the plate in front of him without a word. His sinister grin said it all. He stared, hungry for a reaction, daring her to respond, but she didn't lift her eyes.

Then, without a backward glance, she walked out of the kitchen.

Her steps were slow, legs weak as she made her way outside, down the porch stairs, seeking safety in the open air.

Hiding herself on the side of the house, she slumped back against the white siding.

The dam inside her finally broke as she gasped out an agonizing cry. Tears, the ones she'd held, unleashed, bursting free, soaking her face.

She sank down inch by inch, until she was crouched low in a ball, hugging her knees tightly to her chest.

Clive's cruelty was more than she could hold.

Bones, her good dog, her gentle dog, her only friend.

How was she supposed to survive?

Why did she ever have to go to Clarissa's?

Why did she have to know a life so different?

Before, she had learned how to turn it all off—the pain, the emptiness. She'd mastered it, like pouring ice water over her heart, freezing it just enough to keep it from bleeding.

But now, that voice, the one she thought had burned up in the cabin's flames, was back.

Louder than ever.

Clarissa never really loved you. If she had, she would've come for you. She would've taken you away like she promised.

The voice grew sharper, crueler.

She didn't want you there. You were just a burden.

Clarissa had only helped because she was a good Christian woman. She must be relieved now, with her gone—no more trouble, no more mess to clean up.

And Ian—damn him, too!

Why did he have to pretend as if he cared?

Just like Clarissa. Pity for the girl from the hills.

The one too dumb to read, too backward to fit in with town folk—always saying the wrong things.

Who was she to think someone like him—smart, educated— would ever want her? A girl who couldn't even grasp common sense.

He was right. She was a child. A proper woman wouldn't have been so foolish as to throw herself at a man. Ask a man to lie with her.

What kind of girl does that?

Not one who was pure. Not clean. Not used up.

Esther knew it now—Gran's God was punishing her, punishing her for wanting the sins of the flesh.

Why had her body asked for it? Her body, so scrawny and freckled, ugly to the core.

It was God's wrath, and she deserved it.

Maybe when she'd crossed the river, she had died. Perhaps she was already in hell.

And the devil? He was just playin' with her now, having his fun.

The dark words continued, swirling in her mind, pulling her down, just as she had dreamt.

The abyss was deep, dark, swallowing her whole.

She could feel it now, tightening around her chest, claiming her.

This time, there would be no escape.

Chapter 22: A Deal with the Devil

Wind tore through the streets of Larkin, lifting autumn leaves into swirling gusts. The air was thick with the sharp scent of smoke and decay and carried the bite of approaching winter, as if the last traces of summer warmth were being chased away.

Esther tugged her coat tight as she stepped out of Clive's shiny new car onto the road in front of Paulson's Mercantile.

Clive, already moving ahead, kicked up small piles of fall debris without glancing back.

For a moment, Esther allowed herself to hope she might see someone—anyone—from the Old Reed Estate. A face she knew, a familiar smile. But they were nowhere to be found, as if they'd vanished altogether.

Inside the mercantile, the wind howled through the door, the bell ringing in protest. Wooden shelves stood like watchtowers, stacked high with goods, while a chalkboard with hand-scrawled prices added a rustic charm. The muffled laughter of customers offered a comforting contrast to the approaching storm.

Margie Mae, the store's chatty owner, was laughing with a pretty red-haired girl at the counter. The girl flipped through a magazine, her fingers gliding over the glossy pages, drinking in the city's latest styles. She carried herself with effortless confidence, each move calculated. Her red lips were daring, accentuating her sharp, pretty features.

Esther couldn't look away. The way the girl moved seemed carefully crafted, as if she were aware of every gaze drawn to her. Even Clive had fallen under her spell, his eyes trailing after her as if nothing else existed.

So much so that Esther hadn't noticed who stood just ten feet away.

Her breath caught as she shifted her gaze.

It was him.

Ian.

He stood there, unaware, a blue shirt showing beneath his dark jacket.

She wasn't used to seeing him dressed up. The jacket stretched across his broad shoulders, lending him a formality that quickened her pulse.

In an instant, the world around her disappeared—Clive, the store, all the noise.

All she could see was the tall German man. He had never looked more handsome, and in that instant, every feeling she had chained deep inside came tearing free.

Her heart was alive, unwilling to be tamed.

She wanted to call out to him, to feel the warmth of his presence, the safety of his smile. But her feet stayed planted. Her voice remained silent, her teeth clamped down on her tongue.

Clive, oblivious, wandered toward the back, disappearing into one of the side rooms.

It gave Esther room to breathe. Still, she was too afraid—too afraid to say his name out loud.

So, she just stared at him, his tall form now dominating the space, while she hovered by the store entrance. Her hands twisted at the frayed hem of her coat as her eyes clung to him.

The scene in front of her—another world where she was only a spectator.

For the past couple of months, everything had unraveled in ways she couldn't control, leaving her like a ghost in her own life.

Esther watched as the red-haired girl turned her head to catch Ian's eye, claiming his attention. And Ian, standing there, wasn't blind to it. He seemed to take it in—the way her smile met his, each one returned like an unspoken exchange.

"I know, he's just my favorite movie star," Margie Mae chimed in, her eyes twinkling with amusement as she glanced at the magazine. "Look at that charmin' grin."

The girl leaned over the counter, her posture leaving nothing to the imagination, her words spilling into the air as she chatted with the store owner.

"Yes'm, he is a good-lookin' man," the red-haired girl agreed, casting a sidelong glance at Ian. "Maybe not as handsome as Ian here, though."

"You're trying to get me into trouble," he said, deflecting the compliment with ease.

A pang of jealousy twisted inside Esther, but she tried to push it away.

Margie Mae chuckled again, clearly enjoying herself as she eyed Ian.

"Well, goodness me. Look at that sheepish grin on his face."

He just shook his head.

"You ladies sure love to keep a man on his toes," he teased. "But I've got to run over to the feed store before it closes. I'll be back later to pick this up." He set a small bundle of things on the counter.

The women laughed as he gave them one of his big, broad grins.

But as he turned to go, his eyes landed directly on Esther.

His expression softened, his brows lifting in recognition.

He was happy to see her.

Drawn to her at once, he cut straight across the floor, moving so quickly he nearly collided with her before stopping short.

"Esther…" His voice was gentle, warm.

But as he gazed down at her, his expression shifted, giving way to concern as he took her in.

"Hello, Ian," she said quietly, the words carrying more than they revealed.

His brow furrowed as he studied her face, searching her eyes for answers she wasn't ready to give.

"It's so good to see you. How've you been? You look well."

The question hung awkwardly between them.

She nodded, the knot in her throat too tight.

She wasn't alright—far from it—but she couldn't bring herself to admit that. Not here. Not now.

He leaned in closer, his voice dropping.

"You sure he's treating you okay? Do you need anything?"

Before she could answer, Clive reappeared. His shadow cut through the room, each step deliberate, carrying a grim authority. He was coming straight at her, as though he knew—always knew—exactly where she'd be and what she was up to.

Something deep inside Esther shifted—an old reflex, carved by years of knowing when to shrink, when to disappear.

She took a step back, creating a safe distance between herself and Ian.

"I'm fine," she mumbled, her voice empty of conviction.

Clive's eyes flicked between them, a sly smile slowly creeping up his face as he watched her retreat toward him.

Ian didn't look convinced, but he didn't push the matter. He nodded, his expression still troubled.

"Well, it was good to see you," he said, his voice softer now, tinged with regret. "I'll tell Clarissa you said hello."

Then he eyed Clive, giving him a solid stare.

But Clive was undeterred as he put on his salesman voice.

"Never seen ya at services. You oughta join us. The Lord's always willing to embrace another prodigal son."

Ian just laughed him off, not wanting to get caught up in his trap as his eyes returned to Esther.

"I'll tell Benjamin and Rebecca you asked after them as well," he added.

Esther nodded, but her eyes fell to the floor so he wouldn't see how his words pained her. Just the sound of their names was enough to wash a sadness through her.

And it didn't help that she could feel Clive watching her, could sense the satisfaction leeching out of him, seeping into every corner of the room. She hated it—hated how he could manipulate her so easily, how he could make her feel small and powerless with just a look.

Just then, when it seemed things couldn't get any worse, the red-haired girl appeared, her arms stacked with packages.

"Help me out? Bought me too much to hold," she said, her bright smile aimed directly at Ian. Before he could reply, she pressed the brown paper–wrapped parcels into his hands.

He glanced toward the window, where the wind whipped around wildly. Always the gentleman, he nodded.

The girl gave a flippant laugh, as if she'd just trapped herself a man, and pushed the shop door open with her free hand.

Following behind her, a strong gust of wind hit him immediately. With clumsy movements, he struggled to juggle the packages.

Just as he slapped at a parcel sliding down his thigh, Esther looked up. Unable to hold her amusement, she let a small smile slip free.

And he caught it, returning it quickly with a broad grin.

Their eyes locked for a moment—like steam rising from a kettle, warm, fleeting, vanishing into the air.

Then he was gone.

The door shut, and Ian left with the pretty girl, their footsteps fading along the sidewalk.

Lingering on them, Esther secretly wished she could trade places with the girl—to leave with him, to slip into that easy world of laughter and wind.

But the reality of that dream came crashing back down when Clive pulled at her arm, ushering her away from the glass. His grip reminded her that the warden was always calling and wouldn't be ignored.

Esther played in her head the words she wished she'd had the courage to say—what she was desperate for Ian to hear, but hadn't dared to speak.

"Ian, please," she would've said, her voice trembling but determined. "Ya don't know what he's been doin'… what he's capable of. I need ya to stop him. I can't live like this anymore."

She would've told him everything, every filthy detail, laid it all out for him to see. She would've begged him, broken, raw. "I don't care what it takes—just get me out of here, before it's too late."

Instead, she had said nothing.

This had been her chance. He was the only one she could've reached out to, but he'd been distracted by the red-haired woman.

Her chest tightened as another wave of jealousy stabbed at her.

Seeing him with that pretty girl—it was just a cruel reminder of everything Esther would never have.

She pulled away from Clive's grip and went to the counter, trying to distract herself.

But thoughts of Ian fought their way in, each one striking a dull ache.

And that damn hussie—struttin' around like she owned the place, full of herself as a spring chicken. Who'd she think she was? So riled by the red-haired girl, Esther didn't even hear Margie Mae call her name at first.

"Esther dear, it's so good to see ya!" Margie Mae chirped.

Esther turned to find the shopkeeper beaming at her.

"How have ya been? I saw ya at church last Sunday and wanted to have a chat, but ya ran off," Margie Mae added.

Before Esther could respond, Clive cut in with a cutting tone.

"That's Esther, always runnin' off, avoids socializin' like the plague."

Margie Mae playfully frowned, clearly disapproving of his chastisement.

"Well, we can't have that now, can we?" she said.

Esther offered a weak smile, but something on the counter quickly caught her attention.

It was a vibrant magazine, with a glamorous, beautiful woman on the cover, her dress elegant and perfectly tailored.

Esther's fingers itched to pick it up, to flip through the pages and escape into anything beyond her own life.

"Isn't she just beautiful?" Margie Mae asked, noticing her interest. "And look at the cut of that dress. Makes her look so slim."

"I've never worn anything like that in my whole life," Esther said in a soft, wistful voice.

"Well then, ya gotta see what I have over here by the window," Margie Mae said, her enthusiasm infectious as she grabbed Esther and led her to a dress hanging on the wall.

"Now," Margie Mae went on, "it ain't as fine an article as that one in the magazine, but it's pretty darn close. And look at the print."

The dress was a lovely shade of red, with tiny dark blue flowers sprinkled across the fabric. It was simple yet sophisticated, and Esther couldn't help but admire it. But as quickly as her admiration appeared, she pushed it aside, knowing it was out of her reach. She turned back to the magazine, her fingers grazing the pages as she flipped through them once again.

Clive had been watching her. He moved in close, his voice low, calculating.

"You want that?"

Esther looked up at him as he eyed the magazine. Clive had been working her for some time, always searching for something she wanted, something he could twist into leverage to make her more submissive. She knew every promise he made, every slight gesture of kindness, came with a price.

"The magazine," he clarified, his tone laced with something that made her uneasy. "I'll buy it for ya, if ya want it real bad."

She knew precisely what his intentions were. He was trying to strike a bargain with her, plain and simple. You comply, stop fighting every time I come at ya, and you can have this. It was always the same—his way of breaking her down bit by bit.

"I don't know…" she said, tired of never winning this game. Every inch of her wanted to resist, to fight back, but there was a type of exhaustion setting in.

"Well, ya want me to buy it for ya or not? Make up yer mind. A lot of nice pictures in there," Clive said in an impatient voice.

Margie Mae chimed in, unaware of the tension.

"My goodness, Clive, now isn't that sweet of ya! Should let him get that for ya, honey. You'll learn more about fashion and fellas in there than anyone can tell ya in this here place."

Clive chuckled darkly. "If she could read."

With a scoff, Margie Mae said, "That's okay, darlin'. The pictures are the best part. I never really read the articles myself."

Clive's eyes remained locked on Esther, silent, waiting for her to break.

"What ya say? Think ya like to have that?" he finally added.

Esther considered her options—what bleak, hollow choices she faced.

She had seen how the pretty girl in the shop wielded power with her beauty and feminine charm, how effortlessly she commanded attention.

And Esther's approach over the past months had been the opposite—making herself less appealing, hoping it would dismay Clive, hoping he'd lose interest. But it hadn't worked. If anything, he relished her weakness.

She kept thinking about how even Ian couldn't resist the saucy charm of an alluring woman.

It was in that moment that she formulated her own plan. She would no longer let herself be pushed into the corner of the checkerboard. No more hiding.

She would fight the only way she knew how—with the one thing she had left.

Her body.

That was it.

Esther would do exactly as that red-haired woman had done. Play her part while being clever enough to survive. She would bite her tongue, close her eyes, and endure the poisonous touch of Clive.

She'd win this game, no matter the cost. And when she did, they could all go straight to hell.

"Alright," she said.

Margie Mae clapped her hands in delight.

"Oh, honey, yer just gonna enjoy it so much. Don't know what ya started, do ya, Clive? A new edition comes out every month."

Esther forced a smile, but it never reached her eyes. She could feel Clive's gaze boring into her, and she knew—knew—that in accepting his gift, she had bound herself to something far darker.

But what choice did she have? She was alone, and if she could twist some control from this tornado, she could preserve herself— what scraps were left.

Clive had always wanted one thing from her.

Well, she would let him have it.

He'd been taking it, anyway, and fighting him had left her feeling broken, each encounter inflicting more pain than the last.

If that's what it took to survive, she'd give him what he wanted, but this time, she'd be the one in control.

If she was already in hell, how much worse could it be to sell her soul to the devil? The line between survival and surrender had blurred so long ago that it no longer mattered.

She would figure out how to control the devil, learn his weaknesses, and get what she needed from him. If Clive wanted to own her, she'd make sure she owned a piece of him, too.

As they left the store, the magazine clutched tightly in her hands, Esther fought to hold it against the wind that tried to snatch it away.

The weight of her grim decision fought to settle inside her, calling her back to reasoning. But she refused to give it a home now, casting it to the wind, no longer caring where it drifted.

For the first time since arriving at Clive's, she felt a flicker of strength—of power.

If no one would love her, and Clive was the only one who wanted her, then she would have to make the best of it.

Just as she was about to get into Clive's car, a cold gust of wind hit her hard, sending a shiver down her entire body—a warning. She didn't question whether it was God trying to talk to her. She was angry at Him. Bitter.

Where had He been when she lay beaten and broken?

Did He ever stop Gran from whipping her, Clive from hurting her, or the sheriff from taking her from the only people who had ever truly been kind to her?

No. He had left her to fend for herself, left her to this life of cruelty. If God had abandoned her, then she'd have to survive on her own terms now, no matter what it took.

Back at Clive's house, the sky darkened into evening, and the wind picked up again, wild and biting. It lashed the trees against the walls, branches breaking free as though nature itself was screaming at her.

The windows whistled—distant cries, and the house shook beneath the storm's fury.

The lights flickered as the electricity battled to stay on.

Esther sat perched on the edge of the frayed sofa, her eyes fixed on the glossy pages of the magazine in her lap.

Every turn revealed something new—a life that existed far beyond the confines of the Blue Hollows and Larkin. It was a dream, shimmering and unreachable.

The women on the pages were strong, powerful—the men, handsome and confident. She whispered to herself, "This is the world I want to be part of."

Their happy smiles looked effortless, as if they didn't have a care in the world. Her fingers traced the outline of a pair of elegant shoes, admiring their sleek design. For a moment, she let herself imagine what it might feel like to wear something so fine, to step into that other world where her pain and past could not follow.

But the fantasy was short-lived, shattered by the sound of Clive's heavy footsteps as he entered the room.

Esther's whole body tensed as she heard him circle behind the sofa. She didn't move, didn't look up, but she could feel him hovering above her, the smell of his sweat growing stronger as he drew nearer.

He placed a heavy hand on her shoulders, his touch not rough but possessive. She held her breath, not daring to move.

"You sure do like that magazine, don't ya?" he said.

She didn't respond.

His voice dropped lower.

"Ya like pretty things? Well, I'd like to buy ya nice things if ya let me."

She could hear him breathing—certain he was smiling.

"Who would have guessed, Aunt Pearl keepin' ya hid up there in rags. What ya really were wantin' was to be a fancy gal."

Esther's hands gripped the pages as she kept repeating in her mind, "Ya knew this was comin'. You can play this game. Sacrifice this piece of yerself so ya can win." The words echoed—a mantra, a bitter reminder of the path she had chosen.

She had to endure this so she could make it out. There was no room for girlish weakness now.

He released her shoulders and walked toward the hallway, his footsteps slow, drawn out.

She finally looked up, her movements slow, hesitant.

He stood there, hand outstretched.

Her eyes dropped back down to the magazine still open in her lap, its pages a cruel contrast to the truth closing in on her. She felt her resolve crumble.

The life she dreamed of was quickly being replaced by the crushing weight of what was about to happen.

She swallowed hard as she rose. Already she felt herself retreating, her mind pulling back—a betrayal of her flesh, abandoned to endure what it must.

With cold trembling fingers, she reached out and took his hand, sealing her fate with that single touch.

Clive led her into the shadows of his room.

She let her mind drift to Ian again—thinking she'd close her eyes and let the thought of him buffer her from the act.

He had been so close, yet impossibly far away.

Chapter 23: Walking Next to the Devil

Many months had drifted by, and spring had crept back into the Tennessee hills in 1942, breathing a fragile life into the land still scarred by winter's grasp.

But within Clive's home, the change in seasons was a distant echo, barely noticed, barely felt. Time had folded into itself, a haze of days and nights that bled together for Esther, who now awoke each morning to the oppressive confines of Clive's bedroom.

The room, once stark and empty, now felt cluttered, overrun with things she hardly recognized as her own. Magazines, flaunting their false promises of beauty, lay scattered across the floor. Shoes stood in neat rows, like soldiers awaiting orders. Dresses hung carelessly, their bright colors only mocking the darkness that had found a home inside her.

Among them, the red dress from the store—a vivid reminder of the moment she'd surrendered, piece by piece, to a fate she never asked for.

Esther stirred, her eyes slowly opening to the early light filtering through the thin curtains. The gentle glow that bathed the room revealed the warmth of spring, but it offered no comfort.

She rose from the bed, sheets slipping away as she sat up and gazed at the disarray. With even, practiced motions, she dressed, brushed her hair, and pinned it back—the routine nearly automatic.

As she sat at the vanity mirror, she almost didn't recognize the woman staring at her. Her hair was styled, her face polished, but none of it felt real.

Leaning closer, she traced the lines of her face with trembling fingers.

Something had changed in her eyes—something hard and lifeless had taken root. The innocence, the fire, the hope that had once glimmered there was gone, replaced by a dull, stone-like quality. She had learned to survive by doing what Clive expected, by becoming what he wanted.

In doing so, she had buried the girl she used to be.

In a low whisper, she said to herself, "I'm a ghost."

The words lingered in the air, barely audible—unseen, unheard, drifting through her own life.

The devil knew how to play the game better than she ever could. For every piece she gave, he took two.

And now she was sitting here in the corner of the room.

She rubbed her forehead, the ache from last night's alcohol—a supposed remedy for her angst—still lingering. Clive had been all too eager to get her plastered, insisting she was easier to manage when liquored up. It had become nearly daily, and she wondered if she had let two beasts own her now.

Her dark thoughts had also become her constant companion. Esther would think about ways to escape. But they all involved a permanent residency in hell.

One night, she drank beyond even reckless, hoping to blur the world around her permanently—putting out the light forever—but it hadn't worked. She told herself that if it was an accident, then God wouldn't be able to hold it against her.

Clive's loud voice rang out from the other room, drawing her from her thoughts and shattering the silence that had settled over the house.

"I'm headin' over to the church," Clive said, his voice commanding. "Don't be too long."

Esther didn't respond as she slowly rose, searching for a matching pair of slingback shoes.

They had a small open heel with a strap around the back, something Esther's feet had finally grown accustomed to.

At first, she had found them uncomfortable and restrictive, the straps digging into her skin and leaving her heels sore and raw. But her desire to match the part, to be seen as a proper lady, had pushed her past the discomfort. The blisters had healed, and the shoes had become just another part of the role she had learned to play.

As she finished getting dressed, she heard the door close behind Clive. The sound echoed through the quiet house, and for a moment, she felt the weight of solitude pressing down on her. However, it felt empty, not comforting.

She realized that even the balm she had once found in being alone had vanished, leaving only a shallow solace that twisted thoughts into something painful.

Later that morning, the small rural church was filled with the familiar hum of murmured prayers and rustling hymnals as the Sunday service came to a close.

Esther sat in the front row, her posture rigid, her hands folded neatly in her lap. Her dress, one of the finest Clive had bought her, draped elegantly over her figure, and her hair was styled in soft waves that framed her face. To anyone looking on, she appeared the picture of a refined, contented woman.

But inside, Esther was numb. She had become a master at hiding her emotions, at masking the turmoil that churned within her. Her days were filled with the routine of survival, each one blending into the next, marked only by passing seasons rather than any genuine change in her life.

As the congregation began to rise and file out of the church, Esther moved to join them. Before she could make her way out the door, a hand gently caught her arm.

She turned to see Margie Mae, her face lit up with excitement.

"Esther dear, I've got a wonderful idea!" Margie Mae said. "How about ya come with Ralph and me to a show in Jasper? It's not a long drive, and I've just been dyin' to see His Girl Friday."

Esther blinked, her mind slow to process the invitation. It was rare for anyone to ask her to do something that didn't revolve around Clive. He had, however, allowed her to visit Margie at the mercantile under the guise of learning how to fix her hair just right. Esther had enjoyed the time, but Clive cut it short, saying she'd learned enough to get by.

The thought of going to a real film stirred something deep inside her—something she hadn't felt in ages.

"I've never seen a real film before," Esther said.

Margie Mae's eyes widened in surprise.

"Are you kiddin'? Now ya surely gotta go!"

Before Esther could respond, Clive appeared behind them, his presence casting a shadow. His eyes narrowed as he looked at the two women, his expression one of thinly veiled displeasure.

"Gotta go where?" Clive's voice was calm, but there was a challenge behind it that Esther recognized all too well.

Margie Mae, undeterred, beamed up at him.

"I was just tellin' Esther she oughta come along with Ralph and me this weekend over to Jasper. We're gonna see a show. Isn't that a swell idea?"

For a moment, Esther felt a flicker of bravery. The thought of escaping, even if just for a few hours, filled her with excitement.

"I'd love to go," she said, her voice confident.

But the bravery was short-lived. Clive's hand clamped down on her arm, his grip firm. Her heart sank as she looked up at him, the unspoken understanding between them—an icy blade.

Margie Mae, sensing the tension, shifted uncomfortably.

"Well… it sounds like we'll both be goin'. Hate to miss out," Clive hissed, his voice sharp with irritation.

Margie Mae forced a smile, trying to keep the mood light.

"Wonderful, that's just wonderful," she said.

As they left the church, Esther fell into step behind him, trying not to let her shoulders slump as she played her part.

But her thoughts slipped away from Clive and back to Larkin, to the brief time she had seen Ian last fall, an ache she'd never fully healed from. Always wondering what might have been.

In those early months after she was forced to live with her cousin, Esther kept her hopes alive by searching for Ian in every shadowed corner of town.

Each trip to the mercantile was tinged with desperate anticipation, her mind rehearsing the words she'd use if she ever saw him again. Every face in the crowd pulled at her, her heart leaping at the faintest resemblance—only to drop, each time, in the same old disappointment.

There was a time she would have given anything to see him, to catch even a glimpse of him, Clarissa, or anyone else from the Old Reed Estate.

That home had been a place where, for a brief moment, she had felt safe. But in the end, they had left her to the shadows, as though wiping her from their hands was the easiest thing to do.

Margie Mae, usually the hub of town gossip, had told Esther that Ian had left for the city—New York, of all places—to work with his brother.

When Esther asked if he was coming back, Margie hadn't been sure. In a way, it eased a part of her. She wasn't sure she wanted him to see the person she had become.

Shame clung to her like a second skin, one she couldn't peel away. She was different now—used-up. The girl Ian had known was no longer there. Replaced by someone scarred so deeply it was as if a hole had been burned clean through, daylight spilling out of the wound.

Would he pity her now, or, worse, turn away in disgust?

She was a shell of herself, scattered into unrecognizable pieces, a mason jar smashed on stone.

She let Clive use her now, hardly resisting.

After he had taken her dog to pasture, Clive had come at her for the first time. Esther had even pulled a kitchen knife on him.

But he had only laughed, snatched it from her hands, and turned it toward her, pressing the blade to her throat, his grin widening.

"God ain't gonna punish me for killin' ya, a forsaken woman," he had said.

And Clive's threats carried a danger she couldn't deny. He wasn't to be messed with.

Esther was sure he was behind local people who had plumb disappeared—or been found dead—after crossing him.

He wasn't just a bootlegger—he was the devil walking beside her.

Chapter 24: A Night to Remember

A week back from New York, and Ian was finally settling into the rhythm of being home. Gladly trading the smell of smoke and steel for the loamy scent of soil.

While there, Freddie, his younger brother, had hustled up a job for him, translating German into English. The pay had been just enough to cover the wartime taxes and even slip a little extra into his pocket. Managing a high-end nightclub, Freddie was the kind of fella who thrived on charisma and connections, always in the thick of things.

But Ian had longed to return to what he knew best—working under the sun, hands thick with dirt, the rhythm of the land beneath his feet. While he'd been gone, Abram had covered for him, tending the estate, but now he meant to ease that burden.

The thought of facing yet another brick wall had left Ian feeling trapped, longing for the vast expanse of greenery. The hills of the Blue Hollows had beckoned him, their distant vistas whispering for his return.

Odd, since he had once loved New York—but that had been with Adeline.

Exciting at first, the Big Apple had been a whirlwind of noise and bodies. Life moved fast there, even under the cloud of war. People still clung to the glamour of city life, gathering in bars and theaters, laughing too loudly, ignoring the cracks forming under their feet.

Freddie reveled in it. His bachelor pad was always alive with the soft chatter of pretty women and the steady flow of friends, coming and going like the tide.

Ian had been drawn in briefly—his more serious nature softened by the luxury of time away from responsibility. He had even let himself kiss a girl, taken her out for dinners, and, for a moment, tried on Freddie's easy life for size.

But the city wasn't home.

On quiet afternoons, he'd steal away to Central Park, to stand under trees that couldn't know the hills of Tennessee, but tried.

And the ache for his children, entrusted to Clarissa, had gnawed at him daily—a guilt he couldn't shake, knowing he wasn't there for them. Missing out on their stories and faces.

Something else—someone else—tugged at a corner of his heart too.

Squeezing it until he could no longer ignore it.

The girl who hooked herself into the core of him. Piecing the broken pieces back together, sewn with thick thread. Then, gripping it tight, despite his denial that it had ever happened. A hold he had never expected, nor could he ever break.

Beautiful and unforgettable—Esther.

She had haunted him since the moment he had left.

Her soft features lingered in his thoughts, pouring into the silence of his days.

A girl in New York had been sweet, even pretty, and he had liked her well enough. But every smile she gave only made him miss Esther more, wishing it were her instead.

He dreamed of Esther running through the orchard, her tangled hair whipping in the wind as she laughed. The way her doe eyes lifted to him when he spoke—or when she said his name

He missed her.

And it lingered with him—a long, persistent pain. One he no longer wished to be free of.

He also couldn't shake the memory of the last time he'd seen her, how it clung to him like wet clay, molding itself into something he couldn't fully explain, something that nagged at him.

Despite hearing through the grapevine that she was doing well—thriving, even—he needed to see it for himself. To see her.

Ian had made up his mind. He'd drive to Clive's, walk right up to the door, and say hello. He'd do it the next time he was in Larkin. Damn the sheriff and his small-town posturing. He wasn't God, and he wasn't a judge to decide where a grown woman could go or who she could see.

As he stood in Jasper, loading the last of his supplies, the decision was final. He would see her. Nothing would stop him.

By the time he'd finished securing the last of the dry crates in the back of his old truck, evening had settled in. The main street of Jasper came alive with the buzz of weekend guests. Ian paused, letting the hum of the town soak in as the soft glow of streetlights flickered on, casting long shadows across the pavement.

The air carried distant voices and the occasional honk of a car horn. Wind wove through the street, stirring a strange restlessness within him.

He ran a hand through his hair, the cool night brushing against his skin as he straightened and looked around. It was nothing like New York, yet it held its own kind of charm.

Leaning back against his truck, he weighed whether he should grab a bite before heading home, the long drive ahead. Clarissa would likely have something put away for him, but the hunger gnawing at him wasn't sure it could wait. His eyes wandered to a small diner across the street, the warm light spilling onto the sidewalk, tempting him.

He mulled it over, weighing whether it was worth the money. Then he shook his head—he could wait. With a heavy grunt, he rallied his tired body, shoved off the truck, and headed for the driver's side.

But the sound of an approaching car caught his attention. He turned, eyes narrowing as a sleek white Buick pulled into a spot about thirty feet away.

The headlights sliced through the twilight, momentarily blinding him before the engine quieted and the lights dimmed. It was familiar—he thought to himself.

Curious, he watched the doors open. Ralph stepped out from the back seat, holding it open for Margie Mae, who emerged with her usual lively energy. Clive followed, his movements deliberate as he scanned the area, always surveying like a man used to control.

But it was the last figure that made Ian pause.

At first, he didn't recognize her—just a beautiful woman stepping out of a car, her movements elegant and poised.

Then, as the light shifted and caught her face, the realization hit him hard, tightening his chest.

It felt unreal, something he had conjured by sheer desire.

There she was.

It was her—Esther.

She stood there, adjusting the hem of her dress, then applying a touch of lipstick, her movements slow and meticulous.

But this wasn't the Esther he had known.

The woman before him was striking, dressed in a way that commanded attention. Her hair framed her face in sleek, deliberate waves, as her dress hugged her figure—both elegant and provocative.

Ian found himself captivated, unable to look away.

There was a magnetic pull in the way she moved, a grace and poise that appeared almost out of place against the backdrop of the small, busy street.

She looked like one of the women from the city, the kind who strolled down Fifth Avenue with shopping bags draped over their arms like conquests. And she moved with a confidence that made heads turn—slow, sure, and all without a word.

He noticed the group of young men, mid-laughter, fall quiet when they saw her, their gazes lingering—captivated by her beauty.

These were the kind of men who knew their worth, the type who would court a woman like her. One of them, tall and confident, tried to catch her eye, flashing a smile that could have easily charmed anyone else. But she didn't even glance his way, brushing off the attention without a second thought.

Who was this girl? What had happened to the Esther he'd known?

A mix of emotions stirred in him. He found himself transfixed by her transformation—how she carried herself as if a woman who belonged in the spotlight.

It left him silently overwhelmed, torn between the woman she'd become and the memory of the girl he had known.

It was then that Esther looked in his direction.

Saw him.

Their eyes locked, and in that instant, the world paused, holding for them.

Everything stood still.

As though they were two people frozen for a photograph. A snapshot printed on glossy paper. The moment etched permanently into time.

The noise of the street, the people passing by, even the faint breeze—all of it faded away. Only the connection between them remained, alive, raw, and in an inexplicable form.

Eyes looking into eyes.

The confident veneer Esther had so carefully constructed seemed to waver. In its place, a flicker of vulnerability appeared—an echo of the girl he had once known, soft and uncertain, just for a moment.

And they simply stared at each other.

He felt an overwhelming urge to go to her, to close that distance and bridge the gap that had silently grown between them over the months.

But before he could move, the moment was taken from him. Clive emerged, grabbing Esther's arm and pulling her away, leading her toward a group moving up the sidewalk.

When her gaze shifted away, Ian couldn't let it go. Something deep inside him urged him to follow.

Keeping a safe distance, he trailed behind them, watching as she occasionally glanced back over her shoulder, a small, tentative smile playing on her lips.

Margie Mae and Ralph, who had hurried up the sidewalk, were waiting by the theater's box office, chatting animatedly—a vivid contrast to the charge building inside Ian.

He watched as they spoke with Esther and Clive, exchanging pleasantries before entering the theater.

Ian stood back, torn between the practical urge to turn away and the undeniable pull to follow.

The scent of freshly popped popcorn filled the air, his hunger returning at its call. He stood there, the rustle of ticket stubs and murmurs of anticipation moving around him.

Esther had disappeared inside, and all he wanted was just to keep looking at her.

After months of lingering thoughts, she felt like a mirage.

For a man who had always considered himself confident and bold, he had felt a hesitant, unfamiliar intimidation in her presence. It wasn't uncomfortable, though. In fact—he had to admit—he liked it.

After a moment of internal struggle—which wasn't much of a battle at all—he gave in and bought a ticket. With a big bag of popcorn in hand, Ian slipped into the dark theater, his heart beating hard as he crossed the threshold.

Inside, the atmosphere was hushed. Flickering light from the screen cast dramatic shadows across the rows of seats, while the reel clicked steadily in the background.

As his eyes adjusted to the dim light, he searched the room until at last he found her. Relief mingled with longing as he took a seat across the aisle, one row ahead—near enough to feel her presence, yet far enough to mask his eagerness.

After the newsreel, the film began. Ian tried to get comfortable in his narrow seat, stretching his long legs into the aisle, though he didn't mind. His focus was solely on the girl seated diagonally from him.

And Esther knew he was there. Even in the dark theater, he was impossible to mistake. She knew his form—had studied it from afar. The way he moved, the way he carried himself—etched into her memory.

She couldn't believe it was him—he was back. She had thought her eyes were playing tricks when she saw him by that old blue truck. Yet now he was here, close enough to breathe the same air.

Her heart ached at the sight of his face. And what was he doing? Had he really come to see a movie in Larkin, too? Ian was acting strangely, in a way she hadn't seen before.

Esther had quickly grown accustomed to the wanting looks from men since altering her appearance. She couldn't lie—it was exciting. But she was forced to temper it, knowing it unnerved Clive—as if her newfound attention were his to control.

But tonight, Ian's gaze had held hers, long and unbroken. Different. He had never looked at her that way before. And now he sat only a few feet away.

She was grateful Clive hadn't noticed, distracted more than usual tonight. So much so that after they'd all been seated, he excused himself, claiming he'd return before the movie ended. His sudden departure left Margie Mae and Ralph puzzled as to why he had even come at all.

Her cousin's absence, though, only made the experience more enjoyable.

Just as the film's leading man came on, Margie Mae broke through Esther's distraction. She leaned close, her voice bubbling, "That's Cary Grant! Oh, why don't they make more men as handsome as 'im? I could just kiss that face silly."

It took Esther a moment to answer. Her eyes had slipped to Ian, taking in the chiseled edge of his profile and the small curl at the back of his neck, his hair longer than he usually wore it. A flutter rose in her chest, as though tiny wings were beating inside her.

"Oh yes, he is mighty handsome," she said, not knowing if she was talking about Cary Grant or the tall German.

As the movie unfolded, Esther enjoyed the playful banter between the main characters. She admired Rosalind Russell's chatty personality, and it reminded her of times at the Old Reed Estate, when she'd tried to tease Ian in a similar way—though maybe not quite as clever. She found herself wanting to take notes from the actress.

But just as she was getting truly drawn into the film, Esther felt something hit her lap, looking down, she found a piece of popcorn.

Unsure of how it had made its way there, she wondered if Ian had playfully tossed it at her, as he was clearly munching from a bag.

Her eyes went back to the screen, yet his gaze clung to her, making the film blur into nothing. Back and forth they went, stealing glances, as if both feared being caught in the act.

And then there was the other man—the one from the group that had passed her on the sidewalk. Maybe she'd gotten it wrong, and he was the one who had tossed the popcorn, eager to catch her eye too.

The brunette man had positioned himself in her line of sight as well. It was strange—two men vying for her attention at once. And she couldn't deny he was attractive, his gaze lingering just enough to be noticed while his friends goaded him on.

Almost as if to punish Ian—for the red-haired girl from Larkin, for leaving, for everything—Esther let herself smile at the stranger.

She made sure Ian saw it—a playful taunt, held just long enough.

She knew she was tempting fate, but his reaction when she glanced back at him made it worth it.

There was a flash in his eyes, like he knew exactly what she was doing—and it only made her want to toy with him more.

The film passed in a blur for Ian. He couldn't focus on the story—it wasn't the film's fault, he just couldn't lose himself in it.

Beyond distracted, his thoughts kept returning to Esther—her laugh, the way she had always playfully challenged him, and her dark blue eyes.

He thought of the time she had offered herself to him in the barn. He had let himself imagine it—his body resting on hers, their lips pressed together. But he forced the thoughts aside, willing his mind not to indulge in it.

It wasn't until New York that they returned with a fury, flooding his mind during lonely nights and consuming him with a hunger that was hard to bear.

The truth rose up inside him, forcing him to acknowledge something he could no longer deny.

For a fleeting moment, he had thought of accepting her offer— and feared that if she hadn't come at him so abruptly, he might not have been able to turn her down.

And now, it was really starting to bother him, watching some bloke eye Esther, the girl from the hills—the girl he suddenly realized he wanted more than ever.

What unnerved him even more was how she encouraged the man's attention. That smile she flashed at the stranger—it chipped away at Ian, eating away at his calm.

He couldn't believe how much he wanted to be the only one she smiled at… like that. The jealousy was fierce and unexpected, and he hated that it had crept up on him so easily.

While he wouldn't fully acknowledge it, there had only been one other girl who had ever stirred rivalry in him—and he'd given her his last name.

When the film ended, Ian lingered in his seat, waiting until the theater had almost emptied before making his move.

His eyes followed Esther and Margie Mae as they left together, arms linked, their voices lively as they chatted. Ralph walked a few paces ahead of them, eager to get home.

Ian quickened his step, catching up to the women just as they reached the sidewalk.

"Oh—hello, Ian," Margie Mae greeted him. "How ya doin' this evenin'?" Her smile was bright, the kind that invited conversation.

Ian's gaze went straight to Esther.

"I'm well," he said. "I thought I saw a familiar face. I wanted to say hello to Esther."

Esther looked up at him—a smile playing on her lips, though surprise flickered underneath at his boldness.

"Hello," she said softly, as if they were strangers meeting for the first time.

"I noticed you in the theater," Ian added, his words halting, searching for more.

"Yes," Esther replied.

For a moment, he thought he saw a flicker of the old Esther beneath the polished exterior—the playful one who always knew more than she let on, maybe even enjoyed watching him stew.

Margie Mae, always eager to keep the conversation going, chimed in.

"Oh, ya came to see a show too?"

He nodded.

"Decided to at the last minute," he said.

"Wasn't it delicious? The actors were so witty," Margie Mae continued. "Have you seen any of Mr. Grant's other pictures?"

But Ian's attention belonged only to Esther, leaving Margie Mae's words hanging unanswered.

He leaned in, his voice softened.

"I wanted to ask you something…" He hesitated, searching for the right words. "Well, I thought I'd ask if you'd like to take a ride out to see Clarissa. She's been asking about you."

He paused, searching her face.

"I could come pick you up in town. We can make a day of it," he added.

"I think I would like that," Esther said, her smile growing.

Emboldened, he leaned in closer, his large frame towering over hers as he grinned, pleased she'd said yes.

"You wouldn't believe how much Benjamin and Rebecca have grown," he added.

Distracted, Esther was unaware that Clive had returned. From a short distance down the sidewalk, he watched in silence, a darkness etched across his face.

Clive's posture was tense and rigid—the mere sight of them together igniting something volatile within him.

His eyes locked onto Ian, dark and dangerous—a rabid wolf hovering over its prey. There was no mistaking the threat as he stepped forward, his presence impossible to ignore any longer.

Clive's hand shot out, grabbing Esther's arm with a grip so tight it made her wince. The fake smile he had worn earlier in the evening vanished, replaced by a scowl that twisted his features.

Pushing toward Ian, his voice dropped to a low, threatening growl.

"She ain't goin' anywhere with the likes of you," he spat.

Ian felt his temper flare at the public outburst. But he kept his voice steady, his words calm, edged with a quiet authority, like he'd been expecting this moment all along.

"Well, I didn't ask you," Ian said, his eyes narrowing as they locked onto Clive. "I'm asking Esther." His tone was firm, daring Clive to push him further.

In the air, an electric charge promised a confrontation.

Clive radiated a primal need for control.

But there was no hesitation, no intimidation in Ian's face—just an unshakable strength that signaled he wouldn't back down.

Clive's grip on Esther tightened. His words sliced toward Ian.

"You best listen to me. Listen good. I don't like repeatin' myself. She ain't havin' nothin' to do with you—or any of your people." He spat a huff through his teeth. "You're Goddamn trash, the lot of ya. And you ain't gonna taint her."

Esther's heart pounded as her eyes pleaded with her cousin.

"Please, Clive, I just wanna go see my aunt. I'll come back," she lied. Her voice trembled, torn between desperation and defiance.

It was more than a visit—it was a cry for freedom, a chance to slip his suffocating hold.

But Clive's response was swift. Venomous. His sneer deepened as he yanked her close, pulling her back into his shadow. His fingers dug in, sharp and painful.

"She ain't ya damn aunt. I've already told you that," he said with possessive fury. "I'm the only family ya got. And I've had about enough of yer mouth. Go git in the damn car!"

The command echoed like a chain, dragging her back to the reality she longed to escape.

Her mind raced, caught between fear of his wrath and the burning desire to reclaim her life. To see Clarissa. To feel the warmth of someone who truly cared. It was salvation, flickering just beyond her reach.

But every part of her knew that defying Clive would come with a price—one she wasn't sure she could afford.

Ian stepped forward, closing the distance between them, his presence commanding. His voice stayed level, but there was an intensity to it—tempered steel.

"I listened to you," Ian said. "Now you listen to me. She might be under your care, but that doesn't give you the right to dictate her life. And it sure as hell doesn't give you the right to throw her around on the sidewalk."

His gaze shifted to Esther, softening as he spoke directly to her. His words were deliberate, slow, so every one of them would reach her.

"I'll come and get you tomorrow," he said. A vow.

Clive's fury exploded—a guttural growl as he lunged at Ian, shoving him violently, grabbing at his collar.

"Stay the hell away from my house!" he snarled, as if he could break Ian's will by sheer force.

But Ian didn't budge. He didn't need to raise a fist—his presence alone made it clear who had the upper hand.

"Esther, wait for me down the road around noon tomorrow. I'll be there," Ian said.

His words were a promise—he would stand firm, no matter the cost.

Clive's eyes blazed with uncontrolled anger, twisting his face.

"Fucking dirty Nazi!" he hissed.

The words drew a gasp from the people who had circled to watch.

"She does as I say! Come anywhere near my place or her, and I'll shoot ya dead!" Clive added.

The venom in his words was palpable, a brutal warning that left no doubt about his intentions.

But Ian's determination was unwavering.

As the confrontation escalated, the air between them charged, ready to detonate—neither man was willing to back down.

The outburst on the town sidewalk took everyone by surprise, including Margie Mae and Ralph, who stood frozen in shock.

Ian, however, remained solid, a defiant smile returning to his lips, even as his hands curled into rock-hard fists.

"Aren't you a preacher? Thought murder was a sin in your book," he said.

Esther's voice sliced through the tension.

"Please—Clive, I wanna go. Just let me go… please. Only a few hours. Ya know I'll come back." Her voice faltered, softening to almost nothing at the end.

Ian watched as the defeat washed over her, her shoulders slumping as if the fight had drained out of her. She was going to submit, to shrink back under Clive's command, and it tore at him.

"Esther, you've got to know he doesn't own you," Ian said, trying to reach her. "No one does. You're free to do as you wish."

Clive's fury exploded.

As though Ian's words were blasphemy, never meant to be heard on this earthly plane.

Clive's teeth clenched as a vein throbbed on his forehead. His face flushed a deep red, and his eyes burned with a dangerous intensity.

It was like gasoline poured onto a roaring fire.

He shoved Ian again, harder this time, the force sending him stumbling back.

Ian straightened. Enough. His patience burned away, his eyes hard with resolve. His body coiled for the fight, legs braced in a solid stance.

Sensing the shift, Ralph stepped in, grabbing Clive's arm and pulling him back.

"That's enough," Ralph said, his voice firm, cutting through the tension before it went any further. "I'm sure ya don't want to spoil the evenin', Preacher Jones."

The intervention was like a bucket of cold water on the smoldering tension, momentarily dousing the flames before they could consume the night entirely.

Margie Mae quickly stepped in, taking Esther by the arm.

"Let's go, dear," she said as she guided Esther toward the car.

Flustered, Margie Mae went on about men and their lack of control in public, but Esther didn't listen.

All she could think about was Ian's words—words that had struck a chord deep within her. They stirred emotions she had tried so hard to kill off.

But as she got into the car, the weight of Clive's control settled back over her—a lead blanket.

Ian might have spoken the truth, but the reality of her life was far more complicated. She couldn't simply leave, couldn't escape the devil or his jailhouse.

When the last door of Clive's car shut, it closed with a finality that echoed in her chest.

As they drove away, a bottomless despair settled over Esther, as though the distance between her and Ian had grown too vast to bridge.

Tonight, she saw the way he reached for her across that great divide. His arms stretched as far as they could, but what he could never know was that the Devil had lashed her body tight with an invisible rope spun from fear.

Ian stood with his shoulders tense, hands on his hips as he watched the car disappear down the road, anger smoldering in him like a fire he couldn't put out.

He'd tried to reach her, tried to offer a way out. But Clive's grip on Esther was tighter than he feared.

The preacher seemed unnaturally possessive of his cousin, something she clearly wasn't returning. And there was a layer of genuine fear in her eyes as she looked at the man.

She had cowered to him.

Something was wrong. Deeply, unmistakably wrong.

"No!" he said to himself. There was no fucking way in hell this was resolved—he wouldn't let it be, he thought.

Unsettled, he knew the situation demanded action, and he would take it.

He'd be there tomorrow, as promised, hoping with everything in him that Esther would be too, though he knew she wouldn't.

Chapter 25: Boiling Point

The night was black as pitch, with only the headlights cutting through the dark as Clive's car barreled down the slick, winding road. Inside, an uncomfortable silence hung in the air, thick and suffocating.

The rhythmic patter of the heavy rain on the roof echoed the erratic beat of Esther's heart, each drop amplifying the unease growing inside her. She sat stiffly, her eyes fixed on the blurred scenery outside the window, trying to ignore the man beside her.

After dropping Margie Mae and Ralph off, she sat worried, knowing there'd be consequences for her defiance in Jasper. Her mind spun with the unknown. She couldn't shake the thought of what Clive might be plotting, what twisted plans were brewing in his mind.

He'd previously made threats about forcing her to marry him, boasting that she didn't even have to say "I do," not with the connections he had. That he could bind her to him without so much as a whisper of consent. And she feared he would make good on those threats—forever chaining her to his prison.

"It's God's will, Esther," he'd said with an unnerving smile. "The Lord made you for me. He brought us together—you should thank Him every day." His words, soaked in pious arrogance, still echoed in her thoughts, as though his warped sense of morality had excused every dark intention.

But Esther had vowed to herself that she'd swallow a bottle of poison before she would ever go by the name Esther Jones.

And tomorrow, there would be no chance to slip out unnoticed—Clive would make sure she never got near the door. His possessiveness had grown increasingly dangerous over the past few months, reaching a peak that evening at the theater.

Would he lock her up as a prisoner, cut off from the world now? When she'd acted up before, he'd threatened to keep her out at Pritchett Mill, working the moonshine stills until she was worn down to nothing, her spirit crushed by the grueling labor—isolated in a place where no one would ever find her.

Another time, he'd dragged her to a large, old house, far away in another county. Cars lined the dark and narrow road leading to it. Despite her fear, he had pulled her inside. People were drinking, and women in their underclothes moved among the patrons, soliciting them. They sat on laps, kissed the men, and acted lewdly.

It had been shocking, and Clive had wanted her to see it, even introducing her to a busty woman named Dixie Valentine. Dixie had eyed her as if she saw potential in her, and it sent a shiver through her entire body. Esther had begged Clive to leave, telling him he'd made his point once again—that she was at his mercy.

Or worse, he could do something truly final—end her life. Make sure no one else ever had her. And despite his threat of the brothel, she now knew he would never allow another man to touch her—he would see her dead first.

It wouldn't be out of character for Clive.

And Ian was coming to get her—she knew that much.

Then a chilling realization crept in—Clive could easily call in a favor, find one of those men who "took care of things." A man who owed him—just like so many others.

In Clive's world, everyone was ensnared, bound to him by something, and he might just get rid of Ian. Make him vanish, just like others had.

Take Buck Wheeler, a man from Larkin who'd supposedly been one of Clive's friends—though Clive didn't have friends, just people he eventually turned on. Buck had plumb disappeared one morning. Went out early and never came back. No trace. No car. Nothing but an eerie silence that settled over Larkin.

When Buck's cousin, Leroy, came knocking, asking if Clive knew anything, Clive had slammed the door in his face without a word. The smirk that followed told Esther all she needed to know—cold, indifferent, and grimly satisfied.

Being Clive's friend was dangerous, yet he charmed people, drawing them in like moths to a flame. But tonight, some of those people had seen the real creature.

She was sure it had unsettled Margie Mae—the way her smile wavered, barely masking her discomfort. It was as if she were silently asking herself, *Who the hell was this man?*

Esther regretted not taking her chance out on the street, letting Ian shield her from Clive's wrath. But her shame had gotten the better of her. She hadn't wanted to cause a scene in front of Margie Mae and Ralph, making them unwilling witnesses to her torment.

Now, it was too late. She had lost her chance again, and deep down, she knew Clive wouldn't give her another. There wouldn't be a third opportunity. He wouldn't allow it.

Suddenly, the silence was broken as Clive's hand slid onto her leg, his rough fingers rubbing against the fabric of her dress.

A shiver of disgust shot through Esther, and she shoved his hand away.

"I don't want ya touchin' me no more," she said, her voice firm.

He responded with a low, menacing laugh, as if her defiance amused him.

"I can tell ya somethin' right now, we ain't startin' all over with that shit," he drawled, his tone dripping with condescension. "How it is between us is how it's gonna be. We have us an agreement, you and I."

The car swerved slightly as he leaned back, adjusting his grip on the wheel.

"Had to handle a little business while y'all were enjoyin' the show," he said, voice casual but simmering with irritation.

"Took longer than it should've," he added. "If you'd drawn any more attention at the theater with yer actin' up, might've cost me more than time."

He shot her a sidelong glance as he went on.

"You like spendin' my money, don't ya? But you don't care what I gotta do to keep it comin'. You've got no idea what kind of trouble you almost stirred up tonight."

His grip tightened on the wheel, eyes narrowing in disdain.

"Some deals don't take kindly to attention. I guarantee that'll be the last time you go to Jasper."

Then he shot her a look of pure disgust, his lip curling as his gaze bore into her.

"Walkin' down that sidewalk… lookin' like some kinda whore. Kind of girl who'd spread her legs fer any man."

His words came slow, deliberate, each one hitting harder than the last.

Esther's jaw clenched, her hands balling into fists in her lap.

"I ain't agreed to nothin' with ya. And I ain't no whore," she said, her voice trembling.

Clive paused, then let out a mocking chuckle.

"Why, my precious Esther, are ya thinkin' of that man from town? That German fella? I saw ya gawkin' at him."

His voice turned icy.

"Ya think he would want ya if he knew… our dirty little secret?"

He squeezed her leg again, harder this time, as if to drive home the point.

"I ain't no fool, girl. Let's not lie. You'd be happy to lay down fer any man if he gave ya a ribbon to put in your hair. Be grateful I keep ya safe from yerself and the evil ya'd be doin' if ya were on the loose."

Esther recoiled, pressing herself against the door, trying to get as far from Clive as she could. Bile rose in her throat, and she forced it down.

He leaned closer, his voice lowering to a poisonous whisper.

"People might think ya dumb, but yer not." He let the words linger before continuing.

"You have Eve's wickedness in ya. It runs through those veins of that female body of yers."

He paused, letting the silence stretch, then went on.

"See—Satan uses those darling doe eyes to draw down the carnal man, forgetting himself like Adam." He let out a long sigh, followed by a crooked smile. "But when he prays, Jesus restores him again to the light… like the resurrection."

His hand moved from her leg up to her hair, stroking it with a false gentleness that made Esther's skin crawl. She remained motionless, trapped in her silence, not knowing how to fight back against his twisted logic.

Clive's hand slid down from her hair to her breast, his touch becoming more brazen, more entitled. He fondled her as if she were an object, something he owned.

"Unbutton yer front," he commanded, his voice thick with perverse anticipation. "Let me see some of Eve's fruit."

A tear slipped down Esther's cheek as she turned her head toward the window, the cold glass pressing against her forehead. An emptiness seeped into every corner of her mind, threatening to pull her under.

She listened to the growl of the car's engine, its rhythm a reminder of the road stretching endlessly ahead—offering no sign of escape, trapping her with him.

She thought of just opening the door and hurling her body out onto the highway, thinking it might be a better fate than what awaited.

But as Esther stared into the dark, rain-soaked night, something inside her began to shift.

She kept replaying Ian's words, how they burned through the darkness she'd known for so long.

He had told her there was freedom—one she hadn't even realized was hers to claim.

A choice.

And she trusted him. She knew he wouldn't lie.

His words—outstretched—reached toward her in the dark abyss, grasping at her fingers, pulling her from the depths that had swallowed her.

Beyond the shadows, sunlight waited to touch her skin and greet her.

Ian was trying to help her see what she had always refused to believe—that she could fight.

Fight for herself, even though it terrified her.

Fight for the life she thought she had surrendered to the dark.

The numbness that had enveloped her for so long started to crack, like a seed breaking through hardened soil.

It climbed with a silent, unstoppable force.

And with it came a slow-brewing anger, waiting to erupt.

It was a rage she hadn't allowed herself to feel in months, maybe ever—a fury buried under layers of fear and submission.

Now, as Clive's voice droned on beside her, that anger swelled, building, pushing hard against her insides.

It grew, a fast-spreading vine of indignation, twisting tighter and tighter with every word he spewed.

Esther's palms sweated as her hands clenched into fists. She fought to stay in control—part of her clinging to composure, while the other side pushed against it.

The words she had entombed deep clawed their way to the surface, demanding to be spoken.

She whipped her head to Clive, her eyes blazing with the question that had haunted her for so long. Her voice cracked as the words broke free.

"Did he die quick?" she asked. "I don't like to think of him sufferin'."

Clive blinked, momentarily confused.

"Huh?"

Her voice rose, jagged with sorrow.

"Ya done KILLED my dog, didn't ya?"

His confusion melted into cruel amusement as he laughed, a harsh, grating sound.

"I swear yer touched in the head. Sit back and be quiet."

Esther refused, her eyes flashing.

"Did ya kill my dog?!" she demanded.

Clive's laughter turned into a sneer.

"I didn't touch that ol' mutt."

But she knew the truth and claimed it, refusing to let him twist her mind anymore.

"I know ya done it! I knew it the day ya did!" she screamed.

His face didn't change, the malicious grin still riding his cheeks.

"What ya want me to say? That I knocked him real good with the back of my shovel? Didn't even let out a whimper. Just closed his eyes and laid down right quick."

Something inside Esther ruptured.

The dam exploded, and rage flooded her veins. Her vision narrowed, and with a scream that tore from the depths of her soul, she hurled herself at him.

Her fists came down with the force of a storm, each strike deliberate and heavy, carrying the weight of every moment she'd been silenced.

With every strike, years of swallowed pain poured out, her pent-up fury fueling each one.

He tried to block her blows, but she was relentless.

Her wrath burst free.

"I HATE YA!" she roared.

"I hate yer smell!"

"I hate yer face!"

"I hate yer very sound!"

The car swerved wildly on the slick road as Clive wrestled with the steering wheel, trying to regain control while fending off her onslaught.

The vehicle skidded, the tires struggling for traction on the rain-slicked pavement.

A sickening screech filled the air. Esther's blood roared in her ears as she felt the car lose control beneath them.

Then, in a split second that felt eternal, the car veered off the road, its front end dropping sharply.

Time slowed as they plummeted into a deep ditch, gravity thrusting them forward as if an unseen hand were pulling them into darkness.

The impact came, a bone-rattling force that threw them from their seats.

Metal shrieked, bending under the violent jolt, and the engine let out a high-pitched whine, as if it were a wounded animal.

Then came a sound—a heavy thump, resounding and final—followed by the groaning protest as it settled into the earth, its frame creaking under the strain.

With a sickening crack, Clive's head hit the steering wheel, his body slumping.

For a long moment, there was only silence, broken by the heavy patter of rain on the roof and the hissing of the engine as it cooled.

Esther sat motionless, her chest heaving as adrenaline coursed through her veins. She unclenched her fists—her knuckles white. Clive groaned beside her, but she didn't care. She had to get out—get away!

With shaky hands, she fumbled with the door, pushing it open. The cool, wet air hit her like a slap to the face as she stumbled out, her legs unsteady beneath her. She leaned on the car for support, making her way around to Clive's side.

Her mind swirled in a thousand directions, all of them instructing her to run, to vanish into the night.

Clive was slumped against the steering wheel, his face pale, his eyes glassy with confusion. He looked up at her as if he couldn't quite process what had just happened.

She just stood there, staring down at him with a mixture of hatred and pity. And for the briefest moment, she saw him not as the monster he was but as a pathetic, broken man.

But the flicker of pity quickly turned to loathing, consuming any trace of sympathy. Without another word, she turned and fled, seizing what was most likely her last opportunity.

As she ran, icy rain poured down in sheets, soaking through her dress and plastering her hair to her face. Her shoes struggled for traction on the slick road, holding her back. Without a second thought, she kicked them off, focused only on escape.

Desperate, she pushed forward, faster and faster. Her feet pounded against the pavement, the rhythm frantic and uneven, matching the wild beat of her heart. All that mattered was getting away—putting as much distance between herself and Clive.

The darkness closed in around her, an oppressive void eating at everything. Her breath was ragged, each gasp tearing through her.

She ran as if the devil himself were on her heels, her body fueled by a primal instinct to survive. Tears streamed down her face, mingling with the rain.

She cried out into the night, a raw, wordless scream, but the storm swallowed it whole, leaving her alone in the dark.

And still, she ran.

She ran until her legs gave out, until the car's blurry headlights vanished behind her. Until the empty hills and fields around her were reduced to the sound of her own sobs and unforgiving rain.

She thought to herself, *If I am to die, at least I tried. Tried to leave. Tried to break free.*

Miles away, the rain still fell in a steady downpour, the night now fully claimed by darkness.

Driving, Ian focused on the road, his headlights cutting through the gloom. The rhythmic sound of the wipers was the only noise in the cab, a monotonous backdrop to his thoughts. Jasper sat behind him, and the familiar, winding road to Larkin stretched ahead, the route as ingrained in him as the rows of trees in the orchard back home.

As he rounded a bend, a faint light flickered up ahead—just off to the side of the road. Almost hidden in the dark, barely visible through the rain.

He slowed his truck, brows furrowed. Easing to a stop, he shifted into reverse and carefully backed up until his headlights illuminated the scene.

Through the rain-streaked glass, he made out the shape of a car, its front end buried in a ditch, half-hidden by tall weeds swaying under the storm. The faint glow of its taillights cast eerie shadows across the ground, flickering as it struggled to cut through the tangled stalks.

Dread settled in his gut as he put the engine in neutral, pulling the handbrake. He stepped out, instantly soaked by the storm, his boots sinking into the mud. Darkness devoured the road, the rain distorting everything in it.

His eye caught sight of a figure—a man standing at the rear of the vehicle, leaning over the open trunk. His posture was peculiar, shoulders hunched forward, and Ian's steps faltered. Something wasn't as it should be.

"Are you okay, sir?" Ian called out, raising his voice to be heard over the hammering rain.

The man turned, his face hidden in the shadows as Ian tried to make out his features.

"I'm good. Thank you, but go on home," the man said, waving him off with a hand.

Ian didn't budge. The man's words were too casual for what the situation called for.

"Are you sure?" Ian pressed, taking another step closer, his eyes shifting toward the car's front end. "Looks like you've been in a bad accident. Let me help."

Clive stiffened, his body shifting from dismissive to defensive in an instant, positioning himself directly in Ian's line of sight to the trunk.

"Told ya I'm alright. Got someone comin' fer me," Clive snapped.

Then it hit Ian—hard and fast—a punch to the gut. The car, half-sunk in the ditch, was the same white Buick Clive had been driving earlier. His breath caught, eyes narrowing as the pieces rushed into place.

His gaze fixed on the figure before him—Esther's cousin, Clive.

Ian's pulse hammered in his ears, adrenaline flooding his veins. He couldn't believe it had taken him this long to recognize the man.

He noticed a trickle of blood sliding down from a split on Clive's forehead, his wild eyes darting everywhere but at him.

Ian whipped his head to the vehicle—it appeared empty.

"Where the hell is Esther?" he barked. "Esther? Esther!"

He called her name again and again, the sound lost to the storm.

"Where is she?" he pushed.

As if evil forces had aligned, the sky unleashed another barrage of pelting rain, drowning out everything but the rush of water filling the ditch. Even the rumble of Ian's truck engine was quieted by the deluge.

He cupped his hands around his mouth and shouted again.

No answer came.

His body darted around the scene, scanning the inside of the car again, checking the backseat. He moved to the shadows of the tall grass surrounding the vehicle, straining to see what lay beyond.

There was no sign of her.

And Clive didn't appear worried in the least. Where in the living hell was she?

Panic fused with anger, tightening with each breath as he worked his way back to confront the preacher.

Clive, seeing Ian's aggressive posture, held firm near the open back, raising a hand as if to block him from circling the car completely.

"Now, she ain't here. I already told ya that," Clive said, his voice strained.

The tone wasn't convincing, and it only fueled Ian's rising fear.

Soaked through, Clive's shirt clung to his round belly, wet hair slicked to his forehead, giving him a wild, disheveled look. He was a large man, stout, but Ian stood a good couple of inches taller at 6'4". Even so, Clive shifted his bulk, a feeble attempt to shield the trunk with his body. His stance was rigid and awkward, which only sharpened Ian's suspicion.

What was the man hiding?

Ian wasn't having it. No longer in polite society, he shoved right past Clive, who stumbled but pushed back, his wingtips slipping in the mud. He was no match for the tall German.

As he rounded the car, Ian's heart pounded in his throat. The trunk loomed ahead. The thought of possibly finding Esther stuffed inside made him ill.

But when he reached the open trunk, he froze.

Surprised by something else.

Filling the entire back of the vehicle, crammed full with crates, moonshine.

At least half a dozen, maybe more, stacked high, each one packed tight with quart-sized mason jars—most of them now in ruin. Their shattered pieces glistened, blanketing the trunk's floor. All of it submerged in a pool of clear white likker. The pungent scent drifted up, stinging Ian's nostrils as he stared down at the wreckage.

He stood there, mind reeling, struggling to grasp it all as he had prepared himself for the worst. But this… this mess of broken jars was something else entirely.

Clive watched his reaction, a smug grin curling at the edges of his mouth as he realized Ian had thought Esther might have been inside. The shift on Ian's face—from worry to confusion—delighted him, emboldening him as he leaned in, whispering low, "Surprise, you poor sap."

Ian's fury erupted. He was sick of playing games with this portly man who clearly hid a darker side. Turning slowly, Ian squared his shoulders, lifting them like a bull ready to charge. His expression hardened, his eyes locking onto Clive's with an intensity that left no room for misunderstanding. This so-called protector of Esther—her cousin—cared less about her than he did about his stash of moonshine.

"You're going to tell me now," Ian growled, his voice dangerous, as he took a step closer. "Where the fuck is she?"

Clive didn't budge, a smirk still playing on his face.

"God damn it, what did you do with her?!" Ian shouted. He was a man done with the preacher's smugness.

He surged forward, forcing Clive to stumble backward.

Clive's grin faltered, his bravado crumbling as he realized that whatever civility had restrained Ian in Jasper was long gone. Out here, nothing stood between them, and Clive wasn't so confident anymore.

"Left her at the Paulsons," the bootlegging preacher said, his back pressed to the car now. "She ain't here. Gonna pick her up tomorrow."

Ian didn't believe a word of it, not for a damn second. He shoved Clive hard against the car, his forearm pressing across the man's chest, pinning him to the metal.

"What did you do with her?" Ian's voice dipped to a lethal tone.

Clive squirmed, grunting as he twisted in a desperate attempt to free himself. But it was no use—Ian's grip was iron, built from years toiling under the sun. His forearm was a steel bar pressed against the man's chest.

For a moment, panic flickered in Clive's eyes, his veneer of confidence unraveling.

"I am a man of God," he whimpered, his voice cracking as he tried to appeal to Ian's sense of morality. His eyes were wide and pleading. "I swear on the Lord Savior, I did nothin' to her. I'll tell you the truth, she got scared, is all—ran off down the road."

"Why? What the hell would she be scared of?" Ian snarled, unconvinced.

He paused, studying Clive, but his excuses didn't sit right.

"What... what the fuck did you do to her to make her so afraid of you?" Ian pushed.

Clive's eyes darted, desperate and calculating, like a cornered animal searching for any escape, trying to read Ian's next move. He was trapped, but the instinct to manipulate still clung to him. His breath hitched, and for a moment, his voice trembled just enough to sound convincing.

"I—I swear, I didn't lay a hand on her," Clive stammered, his lip twitching with faux sincerity as he spun his lie. "Ya know how she is—gets all skittish, scared of her own shadow. Tried to calm her down, but she bolted, running off into the night. That's all it was, I swear. Plannin' on lookin' fer her soon as I pull my car outta the ditch."

Ian's grip didn't release as another wave of disgust surged through him. His jaw clenched, his nostrils flaring as he stared into Clive's deceitful eyes.

He could see through the pathetic act.

"You're lying," Ian hissed as his arm pressed harder into Clive's collar, rage fueling the force. He could feel Clive's pulse hammering beneath his fingers, but it wasn't fear—it was something darker.

Realizing Ian would never fall for his pitiful act, Clive's expression shifted. His whimpering facade dropped, and in its place, a sly, twisted grin tugged at his lips. His posture straightened as best he could, tension melting from his body. He was done pretending.

The real Clive stepped into the light, and it was uglier than Ian had imagined. He sneered, leaning slightly into Ian, as if daring him to dig deeper.

"I bet ya don't know a damn thing about that girl," Clive spat, a glint flashing in his eyes. His twisted smile grew, full of malice, as he continued.

"Wanna hear somethin'? A little secret?"

Ian's mind teetered on the edge, torn between the desperate urge to uncover the vile truth Clive held over Esther and the primal need to shield her from whatever filth was about to escape his lips.

His instinct to protect prevailed. He would not give Clive the satisfaction of seeing him falter.

Ian shook his head, refusing to bite.

"Just tell me which way she was headed," he said.

Clive's grin deepened, his eyes alight with sinister delight. He leaned in, his breath foul and hot against Ian's cheek.

"I think she's headed… to hell," he said, his voice dripping with vitriol, each word—a dagger meant to wound.

"And it's such a pleasant ride with her," he finished.

Something inside Ian snapped.

What restraint he'd been holding onto shattered in an instant, replaced by a primal rage surging through his veins. Without hesitation, he drove his powerful fist into Clive's stomach with brutal force.

The impact was immediate. Clive folded in half, his face contorted with pain. His body jerked, gasping for air.

But Ian wasn't done.

Before Clive could recover, Ian followed with a hard uppercut to his face. The blow landed square on his nose, snapping his head back. Blood sprayed in an arc, splattering onto the rain-soaked ground, mixing with the mud and moonshine at their feet.

Ian didn't pause.

With swift motion, he grabbed Clive by the shirt, his grip iron-tight. In a single decisive move, he slammed him against the side of the car, the sound of metal and bone colliding reverberating through the frame.

The sickening thud of Clive's skull hitting the car echoed into the storm. Blood smeared across the vehicle, a dark streak against the rain-soaked paint, as Clive crumpled to the ground in a limp heap.

Ian stood over him, chest heaving, the rain mingling with the sweat on his brow, fire still coursing through his veins. His rock-hard fists remained clenched, shaking with the aftershocks of rage.

He spared Clive one last glance, his lip curling in disgust at the man sprawled at his feet. For a fleeting moment, Ian considered finishing him off, but dismissed the thought just as quickly.

Esther was still out there—alone in the rain—and he had no time to waste.

The night was turning dangerously cold, the kind of chill that clung to the skin, pulling away what warmth remained. Drenched to the bone, someone like her could easily succumb to exposure, claimed by the elements before he could reach her. With only bare fields and hills for miles, there was nowhere for her to escape the cold.

Without another word, he pivoted hard, his boots grinding into the mud as he rushed back to his truck.

Every step was fueled by urgency, his mind fixed on one thing—finding her before it was too late.

Chapter 26: No More Fight Left

Darkness warped time and space, twisting everything into a blur. Esther stumbled along, lost, wandering blind in a world she didn't know.

She'd left the highway far behind and now found herself on an unfamiliar side road. Determined to make her way back to Ralph and Margie Mae's, but she wasn't sure which way to go—or where Larkin was, for that matter.

They lived about twenty minutes from town, recalling how Clive had complained about being so far off the main route. But now, out here, that distance felt insurmountable.

All she knew was that the rain refused to let up.

Her shoes were long gone, her legs caked in mud as she stumbled with each step, scanning the blackened horizon, frantic for a light, a house, anything. But there was nothing she could make out.

Still, she kept moving.

Esther was convinced that if Clive found her, he would do to her what he had done to her dog—kill her without a second thought.

The darkness inside him wasn't something she had to guess at—he'd shown it to her, a snake coiling around its prey.

And most times, his threats weren't screamed or hurled in anger—they were whispered in the quiet, delivered with precision, like a shadow suddenly revealed when the sun breaks through the clouds.

The warning he had hurled at Ian back in Jasper still echoed in her mind. She knew it wasn't just empty words—it was a promise. He couldn't control Ian, and he knew it. That thought alone would fester in Clive's mind.

Secrets had always been his source of power, his language. It was how he worked people, digging into the hidden corners of their indulgences and pulling strings behind their backs. He had mastered the art, sizing up every soul he encountered, calculating their worth and what he could gain from them.

He really was the devil, she thought.

And Gran—had she ever really tried to protect her from him?

It felt strange. Whenever her grandmother couldn't get what she needed from Clive, she'd bring Esther along for a delivery, using her as leverage—the one thing he couldn't have. Clive knew it too, always holding back just enough to push Gran to do that very thing.

Once, when she was seventeen, Clive had the gumption to ride up into the Blue Hollows, stand on Pawdad's porch, and ask if he could marry her.

While Gran had said, "No," it hadn't come out with much conviction, as if there had been a hint of negotiation. What hurt even more was Pawdad's silence. He left the porch when Gran gave him a look, as if telling him to back down.

Her cousin moved through the world with an air of untouchable confidence, convinced everyone loved him. People praised him for his fervor, his passion for the Good Book, though it was just another tool he used to bend others to his will. He loved to twist its words—and he could—to fit his needs, justifying even the darkest of his thoughts.

Esther didn't like Gran's God, but she knew Clive's God was something of his own making, created solely for his benefit.

The influence he had over his congregation was a force she had seen and naively tried to wield against him, as if she could actually fight him that way.

There had been a time she'd threatened him. Told him she'd stand before the entire church and tell them what he'd done, how he'd stolen her virtue and committed awful, lewd acts against her. But Clive had only laughed, his laughter echoing off the walls like a bell tolling doom.

That laugh—it wasn't just mockery. It carried an undertone, making her heed its warning. Then, with that wicked grin still on his face, he mumbled about how sweet she'd look fancied up in a pine box. He had said nothing more, letting the meaning settle where her fear lived.

His threat haunted her long after the ugly sound of his voice had faded.

Esther was convinced Clive's grip on her was something he couldn't release, like a hawk with its prey, talons sunk in deep.

He had been working on it for a long time, perhaps even before she was born. Patient and calculating, weaving his web over the years.

As a young girl, she remembered overhearing Gran talking to Pawdad, saying Clive couldn't have Annie, so he'd take her child instead. She knew then—he would never let go.

If Clive caught her tonight, it would be the end of everything.

He'd happily watch the life leave her body.

She had destroyed his new car, dared to defy him by running off, and exposed him for what he was.

Now, it felt as though he was hunting her, as if it were ingrained in his animal instinct. And when he caught her, he wouldn't just hurt her—he'd leave her broken and forgotten, her body abandoned for the scavengers that roamed these hills.

No one would ever find her.

Behind her tears, Esther's vision clouded as a pair of headlights pierced the darkness—but it was too late.

The lights cast a faint, eerie yellow glow, struggling to cut through the rain—more of a soft halo than a focused beam. Two eyes, searching.

She had been seen.

Feeling the light, she glanced back again, her heart racing—it was close.

What little strength she had left surged through her veins, a new wave of terror crashing over her.

With nowhere to hide, she veered off the road, her legs driving her up a small hill. At the top loomed a large oak, its branches spread wide, offering a fleeting sense of safety.

If she could reach it—just get to that tree—she could climb, knowing Clive couldn't follow as easily.

She clung to the thought, desperate for any hope.

But the ground beneath her was treacherous, the rain turning the earth into thick, mushy mud that held to her feet like grasping hands as though Satan himself were dragging her down.

She slipped with each step—each attempt to climb met with failure as the ground betrayed her. The harder she pushed, the deeper the muck seemed to pull her back.

Her legs trembled, both from exhaustion and the sharp edge of fear cutting through her. Her strength was fading fast.

Esther cursed herself for skipping supper, having eaten nothing all day. Food had become a chore, something that pleased Clive, so she had lost the will to bother with it.

The thought of him was persistent in her mind, eating at her.

He had once accused her of poisoning him when he'd come down with the stomach flu. She hadn't done it, though the notion had tempted her.

Gran had warned her about water hemlock—how it grew near the streams, how just a small amount could end a life—and she had wandered the nearby fields searching for it, but had never found any. And, truth be told, she lacked the nerve to act.

Clive had howled in suspicion, forcing her to prove her innocence by licking the dirty plate he'd left in the sink, his eyes cold and unwavering even after she obeyed.

But Esther couldn't think about him—he was here, behind her, gaining ground.

She worked to pull air into her lungs as her body screamed for rest, her legs heavy with exhaustion. Her mind spiraled as it played out how it would end.

Maybe he'd use his bare hands. Wrap them around her neck, snap it real quick.

The lights behind her grew, bouncing on the rocky road as they bore down.

She knew—knew for certain he'd seen her. And there was nowhere left to run.

Fate was knocking at her door—as her body gave out, giving up on her. The fight in her legs had dwindled to empty. Her mind called to them, but they were barely moving now, wobbly and unable to walk in a straight line.

Even if she made it up the hill, there wasn't enough left in her to climb the tree as she'd planned.

She stumbled again, struggling to pick herself up. The cold had settled deep in her bones.

Losing her footing one last time, Esther fell hard, her knees slamming to the ground. A rock jabbed into her, sending pain surging through her leg.

Not a dry article of clothing remained. Her sheer dress and undergarments were soaked through to her skin.

The roar of the engine sent a reminder of what was coming, calling her to her grave.

As the vehicle screeched to a halt, Esther felt the beat pounding through her—a paralyzing dread.

The door slammed shut with a final, resounding thud, pushing the doom deeper.

She looked back, her vision swimming as she saw a dark figure vaulting over the fence in pursuit. Desperate, she curled in on herself, a protective ball.

Preparing her mind. Making her peace.

"I can't fight ya… just can't fight ya. Can't fight no more," Esther sobbed, her voice faintly rising above the storm.

She buried her face in her hands, bracing for the worst, begging God to take her quick and sure.

Her thoughts darkened—if this was where she was going to die, at least it would be near a mighty tree. The oak would stand tall, marking her spot and memorializing her even if no one ever knew her grave.

But the man stopped a few feet away, his breath coming in sharp puffs, the rain blurring his figure into a shadow.

She squeezed her eyes shut, too terrified to look up.

And then… through the howling wind… his voice broke.

"Esther."

It wasn't the voice she had been expecting.

A familiar tone, gentle and warm, trying to call her back to the earthly plane.

Her mind, lost in confusion, tried to reason with itself—this wasn't the devil. It sounded like a guardian angel. Afraid to look up, certain heaven was upon her now.

"Esther… It's me. It's your Ian."

She held her breath, listening and replaying the words, trying to believe them.

Unsure if she could trust her own ears, she hesitated. Afraid to be wrong. Afraid to see Clive standing there.

Slowly, heart pounding, she told herself to be brave as she peeked out from behind her hands.

His face came into view.

The face she had last seen on the sidewalk in Jasper.

It was Ian.

His kind face, softened with concern—not cruel intent. His handsome face, his body real, flesh and bone.

With cold mud caked to her skin, she stared up, wide-eyed. The terror from moments earlier still played across her face, etched in a haunting gaze.

Cautiously, he stepped forward, his movements measured and smooth, as if approaching a frightened animal. He could see the fear, knowing she'd been expecting her cousin, unaware that he had been the one searching for her.

"I'm here," he said, his voice wrapping around her like a gentle embrace.

Crouching down, his hands found her shoulders, the warmth in his palms radiating into her frozen body.

He looked hard into her eyes, trying to reach her terror, speaking to it silently, telling it to be gone. Banishing it from her, as if his presence alone could drive it away.

"Please, don't be frightened," he said.

Without a word, she threw herself into his arms, clinging to him as if he were the only solid thing in a world that had drifted out to sea. Her anguish, the loneliness, it all came rushing out in a torrent of tears.

He held her tightly, his powerful body wrapping around her as he rocked her slowly, whispering words of comfort into her ear.

"Oh, Esther… my sweet Esther," he murmured, his lips brushing her forehead gently. "You're safe."

Ian took a deep breath, the relief from finding her unharmed washing over him.

"I've got you… I've got you," he intoned, the warmth of his embrace nourishing her tired and battered soul.

Through her sobs, Esther's voice was raspy, but he heard it.

"I left… I… chose, Ian." Her voice broke, the words fragile on her lips.

Hugging her tighter, he whispered, "I know."

Then, he pulled back slightly and looked into her eyes again, making sure she had heard him.

"I know," he repeated, wanting her to see that he truly recognized what it had taken for her to do such a brave thing.

When her cries subsided, replaced by a quiet exhaustion, Ian stood and reached down with both hands, carefully helping her to her feet.

Her body was shivering, her teeth chattering, as he pulled her into a full-body embrace. Holding still, he let her mold herself to his frame, offering what little warmth he could.

When Esther found her voice again, she spoke, the words more for herself than anyone else.

"I'm never goin' back to Clive's. I'll die 'fore I do."

He nodded, simply holding her—the girl from the hills.

Ian thought back to earlier—how Clive had brushed off her disappearance, claiming she was spooked. Ian had known better. And now, finding her here in this state, glued to the ground and bracing herself for something dark, he understood the truth.

Esther had been utterly terrified of her cousin.

It was as if Ian had reached the end of a book, with every sign now illuminated by the present truth.

One of those signs he had seen last fall at Paulson's Mercantile, but hadn't acknowledged it as he should have. Esther's posture had been slumped—eyes on the floor—like she couldn't stand Clive's very presence.

And still, he had left her there. The guilt ate at him.

Adjusting his arms around her back, he worked to pull the chill from her as his thoughts raced on.

It all now spoke of a truth—of what had likely been done to her. Of what she'd endured.

He swallowed hard, working to brush away the images, not wanting to tie them to the girl in his embrace.

No, the woman in his embrace.

As he drove home earlier that night, his mind kept circling back to how Clive would never let her leave. Ian had already resolved to find another way to reach her, never imagining it would mean searching for her in the middle of the night, through dark fields and hills.

He had almost given up, his gas running low, worried he would have to go on foot, when he saw an old, towering oak on a ridge. Somehow, he knew. Being a girl from the mountains, she'd be drawn to it, seeking safety. And when he saw her narrow silhouette, the relief was overwhelming. She was okay—shaken but not hurt.

"Esther, you're too cold," he said as he felt the deep chill that had settled into her. "I want to get you out of this rain and into the truck."

He steadied her as she swayed, her legs still weak, and guided her down the slope toward the old Ford. Taking slow steps until they reached a fence, he lifted her over. The golden headlights illuminated their path, casting blurred shadows on the road.

When they approached the truck, Esther glanced down, eyeing herself. Her pretty dress was now painted in dark splatters, clinging to her like a second skin.

"Oh—no," she said, despair creeping into her voice. "My dress... I look a fright, like I've been dragged down a ditch."

He paused, turning to her with a tender smile.

"No... Not at all," he said with sincerity.

He held open the passenger side door, waiting for her to climb in. But she stopped—looking up at him, as if giving him time to finish what he was saying. Her eyes held his, expectant.

He hesitated, a tightness pressing in his chest—nerves. Ian knew his words weren't enough to say what he needed her to understand, but he would try. Leaning close to her ear, he whispered, "You looked very beautiful tonight."

His warm breath lingered on her skin.

And the look in his eyes confirmed it was more than just a compliment—it was a kind of declaration. As if he were really saying, "You looked beautiful... to me."

It felt more real than anything he had ever said to her.

Hearing this, Esther's lips curved into a soft smile—the kind a woman wears when she hears just the right words, spoken just the right way.

She climbed in, her movements slow and deliberate, as if she were trying to hold on to the feeling for as long as possible.

Inside the cab, the smell of leather blended with the earthy musk of a man who had spent his day working hard. But there was something else—a faint trace of something unfamiliar. It was cologne, a distinctly masculine scent Ian had picked up in the city at his brother's suggestion. It suited him perfectly, complementing his dashing good looks, and Esther breathed it in.

Ian walked to the driver's side, silent as he prayed there'd be enough gas to get them home. He tapped the hood—encouraging his old friend, knowing there was nowhere to get any this late. The only extra fuel he had was stored in a shed by the orchard, and he'd forgotten to bring an extra can.

Sliding into the seat next to her, he glanced over. Despite being soaked like a kitten, he couldn't get over the fact that there she was, right next to him.

All those long nights in New York, longing for a girl so far away—now she was close enough to touch.

Esther, for a moment—perhaps replaying an old feeling— wondered if she had misread everything. Maybe she'd mistaken his care, his kindness, for something more once again.

Fatigue stripping away any filter she had left, the question tumbled from her mouth.

"So… ya think I'm pretty?" she asked, her tone laced with both suspicion and uncertainty.

It made Ian smile, catching a glimpse of the girl he adored, not bothered by the question. He could see how much she needed to hear it, and he didn't blame her. He had a lot to make up for.

And it didn't matter that it had made him nervous just a moment before. She wanted to hear it again, here and now. He liked the way she smiled when he'd said it, so honest and open.

He nodded. "Yes, very much." He said it slowly, with conviction, making sure she wouldn't doubt it.

If she needed to hear it again, he'd say it as many times as she wanted. It felt freeing to let the words go that he'd kept buried for so long.

Esther's brow softened, her smile edged with a hint of mischief, like he had just played right into her hands.

He couldn't help but think, *God, how I've missed her, that face.*

With that, the tension in her body eased as she leaned back into the seat, letting out a soft sigh.

Still worried about her, Ian reached under his seat and pulled out a thick, warm jacket. With gentle care, he draped it over her shoulders, tucking it in around her. She curled up into its warmth, batting her eyes before they closed, the exhaustion of the ordeal claiming her.

The truck's engine hummed, filling the quiet night with a comforting rhythm as they drove. After they'd made their way down a dark dirt road, Ian finally pulled out onto Miller Highway.

"It won't be too long now," he said, eyes drifting over to her. But she had fallen asleep, and he could hear the quiet cadence of her breath.

The rain continued to fall, but nestled inside the truck, there was a sense of peace—a fragile moment that felt as though it were timed in destiny.

He was bringing her home, where she belonged.

Chapter 27: A Storm Passed

Waking from a never-ending nightmare, Esther found herself within the embrace of Clarissa's home.

The early afternoon sunlight eased through the window, its warmth painting the familiar walls of the small bedroom in a soft, golden glow, bathing her in that delicate space between dreams and wakefulness.

Children's laughter drifted in from the yard—bubbly and bright. It was a treasured song, one she hadn't realized she had forgotten until it played for her again.

Rebecca and Benjamin.

Esther had lied to herself about how much she had missed them. She lay still, savoring the melody of their voices, the comfort of the bed beneath her, and the rare feeling of safety within the walls. If this were a dream, she didn't want to wake.

But the reality of the previous night settled into her—like a stone sinking into deep water.

Arguing with Clive. The crash. Fleeing into the storm.

And Ian.

Just as in her dream the year before, he had come to her, calling her by name, finding her in the dark.

The rest of the night was a blur, but she remembered waking up when he pulled into the driveway.

He told her she was home, and it felt good to hear—home. He mentioned something about running on fumes, saying he'd almost had to push the truck up the hill.

Clarissa had seen the headlights coming up the road. Rushing outside, wide awake, she had been worried about Ian. The moment she saw Esther, she wept, pulled her into her arms, and gripped her tightly. Everything had felt surreal.

Esther had been tired—deliriously so, not just from the frantic run, but from nights of never truly sleeping. Her body survived on only a couple of hours of stolen rest at a time.

Clive had forced her into his room, his bed, and since then, sleep had been impossible. His thunderous snores rattled the walls, pounding in her ears night after night. It was torture, seeping into the fragile edges of her sanity as she waited for dawn to break. And with it came his demands—breakfast served without question.

Sore, her body ached—muscles stiff, her stomach knotted with hunger. It had been days since she'd eaten more than a few bites, forced down not for nourishment but for mere survival.

Esther remembered how Clarissa had tried to feed her, setting down a warm bowl of soup in front of her. But her body resisted—too drained to cooperate. She couldn't summon the strength to lift the spoon. With a quiet sigh, Clarissa fetched a warm pan of water and gently began wiping the mud from Esther's feet. Her touch was soft, maternal, as if tending to a small child.

Ian watched from the doorway, his face set with concern in the dim light. After a moment, he stepped forward, his boots making no noise on the wooden floor. He knelt beside Esther, resting his hand on her leg.

"Come on, let's get you to bed," he said, sliding an arm around her to help her stand. She leaned into him, her legs unsteady but holding.

When they reached the foot of the stairs, he paused, glancing down at her. "Might be easier if I just carried you. What do you think?"

She shook her head.

"No… I can do it," she said, though exhaustion pulled at her.

Her legs trembled, but she gripped the banister with a firm hand. Ian kept his arm around her waist, not saying a word, and together, they slowly climbed.

Once they reached her room at the top of the stairs, he flipped on a lamp. Light washed across the walls.

He moved to the bed, ready to ease her in, but she collapsed onto it before he had the chance to pull back the covers. Too worn out to care, she lay still. With the folded quilt from the bottom, he gently tucked her in, making sure she was warm and settled.

Looking down at her with a smile, he felt the pull to curl up beside her, to hold her. But the gentleman in him held back. He hadn't even kissed her, and if Clarissa came in and found him there—well, that was enough to convince him otherwise.

With a quiet sigh, Ian dragged a chair over from the corner and sat down. He wasn't ready to say goodbye to the night, determined to stay a little longer.

His eyes remained fixed on her—her peaceful face framed by the soft lamplight. Gently, he rested a hand on hers, though she wasn't aware—her breathing deep, lost in sleep. He stayed like that, unmoving, watching her for what felt as though a good hour, before finally rising to make his way home.

In the morning, when Ian told the children that Esther was upstairs, their faces lit up with joy, thrilled to hear she was back. He instantly regretted it as they began begging him to wake her. Forced to be firm, he insisted she needed to rest. Eventually, he banished them outside to play, knowing that if he or Clarissa so much as turned their backs, they'd likely sneak upstairs and disturb her. Whatever the reason, she needed the sleep, and he knew it.

As the memories of the night drifted away, Esther stretched, letting her feet find the cool, polished floor. She remembered how it had felt the first time she arrived at the estate—familiar, comforting.

Rising to her feet, she went to the window, hoping to catch a glimpse of the children or anyone. Her eyes wandered over the horizon, the rolling hills, Ian's house, the barn, the spring garden, all bathed in bright light. It was so beautiful that for a moment, she didn't notice the group gathered in the driveway.

She leaned in closer, squinting to make out the figures.

Ian stood beside a dusty old car she didn't recognize. Abram was with him, along with Clarissa and two strange men, their backs turned. Something about their posture made her uneasy. It wasn't casual—not the way people slouch and talk when everything is fine.

One of the men turned, and she recognized him at once—Vic Porter, a fella who'd palled around with Clive from time to time.

Ian shook his head, his entire body tense.

As if he felt her gaze, his eyes flicked up to the window, holding hers for a brief, unsettling moment. Esther wondered if they were discussing her.

Perhaps Clive had sent them to collect her.

But she wouldn't be going anywhere. Not now. Not ever. She'd be more than happy to let them know they could tell that devil to go straight to hell.

A flash of resolve ran through her as she straightened. She would make her presence known and tell them exactly where she stood.

Ready to bolt out the door, she glanced down, startled to find she was only in a thin slip. The lace clung to her body, its revealing neckline far from appropriate for the company outside.

She didn't remember undressing the night before, but her dress now hung neatly on a nail at the back of the door. Clarissa must have seen to it.

Quickly, Esther readied herself, running a brush through her hair with less care than usual. She swept it up in a practiced twist. It wasn't perfect, but it would do. Slipping on a pair of shoes she had left behind, she steeled herself.

As she descended the stairs, the house was eerily quiet, save for the murmur of conversation outside. With a steadying breath, she pushed open the front door and stepped into the sun.

She would not be ignored.

When Esther approached the group, her eyes fell on Ian—on the way he looked stiffly back at her. It was almost as if he preferred she not be there. His face was serious, brows drawn, mirroring the other men near him. It unsettled her.

The moment Clarissa spotted her, she broke free from the crowd with a forced smile. It was warm, but something unspoken lay beneath it.

"Hello, honey," she said softly. "Been waitin' for ya to wake. Thought I'd never see that sweet face of yers."

She reached out a hand, gesturing toward the house.

"Got some warm biscuits waitin' for ya in the kitchen," she added.

Esther gave her an uneasy smile in return. Her eyes shifted beyond Clarissa's shoulder to where the men had fallen silent upon her approach.

"What's goin' on?" Esther asked.

Clarissa's smile faltered, just for a beat, before she reached out and gently took her arm, trying to steer her away from the group.

"Now's not the time, sweetheart. Let's get ya somethin' to eat. Ya must be starved," Clarissa said.

But Esther wasn't about to be brushed off so easily. She pulled her arm free, her gaze narrowing.

"I can see somethin's happenin'," she pressed, her eyes landing on Ian again, seeking answers. But he only gave her a slight shake of the head, his eyes silently pleading for her to let it go.

Abram, however, wasn't one for subtlety. His voice broke the tense silence, blunt and direct.

"Might as well tell her now, Miss Clarissa. Ain't no use in pretendin'."

The man beside him, Vic Porter, nodded in agreement, his slicked-back hair catching the light in a way that made him seem even more out of place.

"She'll find out soon enough," he said.

Esther's pulse quickened, an icy knot forming in her throat.

"Find out what? What are y'all talkin' 'bout?" she pressed.

Abram exchanged glances with the others before his eyes settled on her, and when he spoke, the words struck like a hammer.

"Yer cousin Clive is dead."

The words didn't register at first. It felt as though the air had been sucked out of the yard, leaving only the dull thud of her heart in her ears.

"Dead?" Esther whispered, her voice barely there.

A man she didn't recognize chimed in, his voice thick with a morbid tone.

"They found him layin' frozen out on Miller Highway."

Esther felt Ian's eyes on her, his concern palpable, a silent warning not to reveal too much. But her thoughts were a blur, spiraling with the impossibility of it all.

Vic, mistaking her shock for sorrow, tried to offer comfort, though his attempt only made Esther feel ill.

"We're real sorry 'bout this. Know y'all were close," he said.

Her mind kept replaying the words. Clive—dead? It didn't seem possible. She had left him alive, hadn't she? He looked up at her, maybe even spoke. Hadn't he?

She tried to shake herself free of the fog clouding her thoughts.

"Are ya sure?" she asked. "What… what'd they say happened to 'im?"

The other man just shook his head.

"Don't know rightly. Some kinda car crash, we think."

Esther swallowed, a lump rising in her throat as she looked helplessly back at Ian. But his face stayed hard, his gaze fixed on Clarissa—a silent message passing between them.

Without missing a beat, Clarissa stepped in, her voice soft and coaxing.

"Poor thing, you're in shock," she said, wrapping a protective arm around Esther's shoulders. "If y'all will excuse us, gentlemen, I need to be takin' her inside."

She gently steered Esther toward the house. As they walked, Clarissa leaned in close, her voice urgent and low.

"Don't say a thing," she whispered.

Esther let herself be led, though her mind was spinning. Clive was dead. It felt impossible.

Today, she'd been ready to tell him to go straight to hell, and now he was already there—dead on the highway.

She had wished for this a thousand times, prayed for justice, begged God for some miracle to end the torment he caused.

But now, standing in the wake of it, all she could feel was a sickening dread. It gnawed at her, whispering that she had played a part in his end.

As they stepped into the cool, shadowy interior of the house, Esther felt a wave of panic wash over her, dark and heavy. Her legs wobbled, grateful for Clarissa's steadying arm, as the shock settled in.

Clarissa guided her into the front room, a private space where the walls held their breath. She turned to Esther, finally reflecting the concern she felt.

"Ian told me what happened," she said, her voice low.

Esther searched Clarissa's face, as if she could find absolution there, or at least some understanding. But Clarissa pulled her into her bosom, holding Esther close as the tears came silently, shaking her thin frame.

"It's alright, child… be still. God is watchin' over us. He's delivered us thus far, ain't about to quit on us yet," Clarissa said.

As Clarissa spoke, Ian quietly entered the room. He nodded at Esther, his face set in hard lines, yet his voice was gentle.

"You did right not to say anything out there," he said. "Those fellas aren't just here to spread some town gossip. I should've sent Clarissa in to keep you from stepping out. That's my fault—I'm sorry."

Esther's pulse raced at his words. It was as if she were caught in quicksand, sinking her deeper into a trap she didn't know how to escape.

"I… I didn't do nothin' to Clive," she stammered, her voice shaky. "He was fine when I left 'im."

Before Ian could respond, the front door creaked open, and Abram made his way inside. His mouth was twisted into a grin, as if he were delighted by the news.

"Can ya believe that? Ol' Preacher Clive, dead as a doornail," Abram laughed, the sound harsh and grating.

The words hit Esther like a slap, and her body stiffened.

Clarissa stood up abruptly. Her eyes flashed with irritation, and she stepped toward Abram, her voice cutting as sharp as a blade.

"Hush up, Abram! Why ya gotta say such a thing?"

Abram raised his hands in mock surrender, the grin still plastered on his face.

"Aw, I don't mean nothin' by it. I just thought maybe Esther got tired of bein' his little pet. You know, like how he led her 'round like she was his prize—dressed up all nice for him," he said.

"Don't ya dare," Clarissa warned, her voice cutting through the rising tension. She could see the fire quickly building in Ian's eyes, knowing she had to act before the situation turned ugly.

"Ya say one more word like that, and you'll not set foot in this house again, ya hear me?" she added.

"Maybe we should settle this outside," Ian snapped, taking a step closer to Abram, his eyes narrowing.

But Clarissa's sharp gaze and outstretched hand halted him.

Ian looked anything but pleased with his friend, wanting to toss him out the door himself—or take him down a peg or two.

Abram hesitated, taken aback by their reactions, but he wasn't done saying his piece. His grin faded, replaced by something more serious.

"All I'm sayin' is, it sure is odd she shows up in the dead of night, and now that ol' preacher is cold on the road." He shrugged as though he were just stating the obvious, but the accusation lingered like smoke.

"Enough," Clarissa barked, her voice laced with ice. "Ya don't know a damn thing about what's goin' on, and ya best remember that before you keep runnin' yer mouth. Ain't your business. Now, I reckon you've got plenty of work to do today. So I suggest you get to it."

That tone from Clarissa was rare, and Abram felt it strike him square in the chest.

"Yes, ma'am. Never meant to make y'all cross," Abram said.

Still, a small sliver of defiance persisted as he headed for the door. He cast one last glance over his shoulder, his expression fraught with suspicion.

"I don't want no trouble for y'all," he said. "When Sheriff Ronell comes knockin'—and he will—y'all better have some good answers. I'd start by askin' Esther here what happened last night."

The door clicked shut behind him, and a heavy silence settled over the room.

Esther held her breath as Abram's words loomed over her.

Clarissa and Ian exchanged a worrying glance. They both knew that Abram wasn't wrong, nor would he be alone in his suspicion. If Sheriff Ronell started piecing things together, everything could spiral out of control.

Ian took a deep breath, looking at Esther.

"We need to be very careful," he said, the gravity of his words sinking in.

Chapter 28: Information

L arkin's small downtown had fallen into an eerie and unsettling silence. The usual buzz of activity was halted, now replaced by the murmurs of townsfolk sharing the grim news of Clive's death.

His parishioners were left in complete shock as word of it rippled through the community.

At the heart of it all stood a red-brick police station with a worn façade. It was a prominent centerpiece among the modest buildings lining Main Street. Perhaps a silent reminder of the law in a town where everyone knew each other's business.

Behind the station, hidden from the solitary road, Deputy Frank and Vic Porter leaned against a rough wall as they spoke.

Their voices were low, cautious, their eyes darting around as if the shadows were listening. The exchange wasn't idle chatter—it was information Vic had brought, the kind that could change everything depending on who heard it.

Frank's expression was tense, his eyes narrowed as he listened to Vic's account.

"That right?" Frank said, processing the news. He rubbed his chin, a habit he'd picked up from years of dealing with the unsavory side of life in these parts.

"I was wondering whether she would run back up there." His voice trailed off as he considered the implications.

"Not gonna be easy with 'em all runnin' round," he added.

Vic nodded, his gaze darting past the edge of the building.

"Wasn't even sure she was there till she came wanderin' outside. But Ol' Lady Johnson was quick to rush her back in," Vic said, louder than he should have.

The crunch of footsteps on gravel made both men freeze.

Sheriff Ronell appeared around the corner, a handful of freshly plucked weeds in his hand. His sharp eyes took in the scene, noting how both Frank and Vic straightened up at his arrival, trying to mask their conversation.

"Ya talkin' about that Primm girl up at the Reed Estate?" Sheriff Ronell's voice was casual, but there was a probing edge to it that neither man could miss.

Vic, surprised, stammered, "How… how'd ya know about that?"

The sheriff didn't answer right away. Instead, he tossed the weeds into a nearby trash can, the metallic clang echoing in the quiet. He turned back to the men, smiling calmly, though his eyes stayed sharp.

"I didn't until just now," Sheriff Ronell said.

Frank shot Vic a glare, cursing his loose lips.

The last thing they needed was for Sheriff Ronell to start poking around where he didn't belong.

Feeling the need to cover his tracks, Vic said, "Rusty and I were up there fishin', just thought we'd run by the place."

Frank nodded, hoping to steer the conversation in his direction.

"I can run up there, ask her 'bout Clive and all."

But Sheriff Ronell shook his head, dismissing the idea with a wave of his hand.

"Nah, she ain't goin' nowhere."

Frank's heart skipped a beat, wondering just how much the sheriff knew.

"Think she offed Clive?" he asked, testing the waters.

Sheriff Ronell let out a low, rumbling laugh, shaking his head at the notion.

"Frank, yer mother is more of a suspect than that girl. No… she ain't no murderer."

The sheriff's voice was firm, his confidence unsettling. He patted Frank on the shoulder, a gesture that felt more like a warning than reassurance.

"Good job, Frank," he said, his voice taking on a dismissive tone now. "But we got some other priorities."

Without saying a word, the sheriff turned and started walking back toward the front of the building. Frank hesitated for a moment before falling in step behind him, leaving Vic standing alone.

As they rounded the corner to the station, coming up on Main Street, Frank couldn't keep his curiosity in check any longer.

"Which way ya gonna head with this, Marty?" he asked, trying to gauge the sheriff's intentions.

Sheriff Ronell paused, pulling a set of keys from his pocket as he considered the question.

"Ya know, Clive had way too much liquor in the back of his car. Too much for his own personal consumption."

Frank's stomach tightened. He'd been trying all morning to turn the talk away from Clive's suspicious dealings, but now it was circling back.

"Aw, come on, ya don't think he was runnin' it, do ya?" he said.

The sheriff's expression darkened, his eyes narrowing as he looked at Frank.

"Who the hell do you think Granny Primm was sellin' it to? God, Frank, use your brain once in a while—I swear."

His words worried Frank.

While Marty Ronell wasn't a bad lawman, he often was distracted, and Frank had grown accustomed to this behavior. It had made it too easy for Frank to turn a blind eye, taking a cut from the bootleggers when it suited him. But ever since the Alcohol Tax Unit started breathing down the sheriff's neck, Ronell had picked up his pace, and that left Frank uneasy.

Before he could respond, Sheriff Ronell was already heading toward his patrol car, keys in hand.

"Where we goin'?" Frank asked as he climbed into the passenger seat, trying to keep his voice steady.

Sheriff Ronell slid into the driver's seat, his face betraying nothing as he started the engine.

"Figure we might take a look-see at Preacher Clive's house."

Frank sat stiffly as they pulled out of the station and onto the road. The silence between them only fueled his frustration. He had wanted time to search Clive's home and the chapel thoroughly— had already planned his next steps. But now the sheriff was coming along, messing up everything Frank had in mind.

Sheriff Ronell kept his eyes on the road, his thoughts hidden behind a stern, unreadable expression.

As they neared Clive's house, the familiar building came into view. The place felt eerily quiet, almost as if it was holding its breath, waiting for a storm to erupt.

Sheriff Ronell parked the car and stepped out, his gaze sweeping over the house with a sharp, assessing eye. Frank trailed close behind, trying to mask the nervous energy building inside him.

The front door creaked as Sheriff Ronell pushed it open, the sound echoing through the silent space. The interior was dim, with light filtering weakly through the grime-covered windows, casting faint shadows across the floor. Sheriff Ronell moved with purpose, his boots thudding on the wooden floor as he ventured deeper into the home.

Frank followed, his eyes darting around, trying to predict what the sheriff might uncover. As they moved through the narrow, dim hallway, the tension between them grew.

When they reached Clive's bedroom, Sheriff Ronell paused at the doorway, taking in the scene in front of him.

The room was a mess—clothes were strewn about, the bed unmade, and personal items scattered across the floor. It looked as though someone had left in a hurry, or perhaps had been living in chaos for some time.

Sheriff Ronell's eyes narrowed as he stepped into the room, his gaze lingering on the bed.

"Frank… ya knew Clive. Did you know this place only had one bedroom?"

Frank shook his head, his voice a bit shaky as he replied, "I don't think so."

"And why do ya suppose that bed looks like two people been layin' in it?" the sheriff asked, his tone shifting from calm to enraged.

Frank fumbled for a response.

"Well, I don't know… I'm sure Clive most likely slept on his sofa."

Sheriff Ronell's gaze shifted to the pair of neatly placed male slippers beside the bed.

"Does that look like he's been sleepin' on the sofa?"

He pointed to the scattered clothing, including women's undergarments, which were tossed carelessly on the floor.

"And what woman, crazy or not, would leave her unmentionables all a mess in front of an unfamiliar man?" he added.

The sheriff slammed his hand on the dresser, making a loud thump.

He was angry.

The sudden outburst startled Frank, who took a step back.

"Damn it to hell!" Sheriff Ronell swore, shaking his head as though grappling with an unsettling guilt.

"Frank, we brought that girl down here to him. Crazy thing is, I knew she didn't want to come. Now I'm understandin' just why."

Frank's heart raced as he tried to keep his cool. He needed to move the sheriff away from any more discoveries. But how?

"She didn't look so miserable to me the last time I saw her," Frank offered, working to throw the sheriff off the scent.

"Just maybe what yer thinkin' is turned the other way around," he added.

Sheriff Ronell pivoted hard to face Frank, his eyes dark, his hands on his hips.

"Ever see the way Pearl Primm treated her granddaughter? Or her daughter Annie, for that matter? She kept 'em locked up on that hill as long as she could, hidin' them out like she was keepin' them safe. Doesn't sound like no temptin' Delilah in training, now does it?"

Frank swallowed hard, wiping at his brow as the sheriff continued.

"Oh, but Clive… Clive sure been surprisin' me."

Fumbling through various objects on a nearby table, Frank tried to appear casual, unbothered.

"Frank," Sheriff Ronell said in a commanding voice. "I want you to run over to the church and see if anything looks suspicious to ya."

"Like what, Marty? Little flasks hidden in the hymnals?" Frank said with a grin, thinking he was being witty.

The sheriff didn't appear amused. If anything, he looked more annoyed.

"Stop wastin' my time. And it ain't like moonshine runners keep everythin' on their front porch. If Clive's been in business, where's he runnin' it from?"

Frank forced himself to shrug, trying to appear nonchalant.

"Marty, I think yer wastin' yer own time. We don't really know if he was into that kind of trouble. Lots of folks 'round here stock up. Hell, if we searched every pantry in Larkin, half of 'em would be full. And I ain't never seen you arrest no one for takin' a sip now and then," Frank said as he started to turn to go.

Sheriff Ronell's eyes focused sharply as he pointed to the disheveled bed.

"I think I've got a mighty good suspicion about Preacher Clive Jones and his character. Mighty good."

With no other choice, Frank disappeared down the hallway, mumbling again about how they were barking up the wrong tree.

Sheriff Ronell continued his search, his trained eyes scanning every corner of the room. Something wasn't right, and he could feel it in his bones.

As he turned to leave, his eyes narrowed on a small, worn book lying on the floor, half-hidden beneath the bed, as though it had been forgotten or deliberately tucked away.

He bent down and picked it up, flipping it open. Inside, he found something that made him pause.

Between the pages were carefully drawn sketches, delicate and intricate, that captured the perfect likenesses of various people and things around nature. He turned to a page where the face of a man stared back at him—a face he recognized. It was Ian Huggler.

The sheriff's brow furrowed as he studied the drawing. Esther had talent, that was clear. But why had she left this behind? And how long had she been up at the Old Reed Estate?

Slipping the hymn book into his pocket, Sheriff Ronell quickly searched the rest of the house before making his way out.

A flurry of thoughts stormed his mind, desperately seeking clarity.

The ATU was gearing up to come clean out hotspots near Larkin. And the Primms had only been a drop in the bucket—literally. He'd often wondered who was running things in his county, but it had never crossed his mind that the good ol' preacher with the slick smile was involved. Yet Clive's trunk had been full of what anyone would call a solid load of high-quality likker.

But now Clive was dead, and his death wasn't an accident. Somebody had made sure of that.

Oh, he'd learned an awful lot about Clive Jones today. First, Clive was most likely a middleman, maybe even a bootlegger—hell, the former seemed to suit him better. And second, the man made his gut turn. Clive had taken his own innocent cousin and forced her to be his mistress, if that was what you could call it—something the sheriff was certain wasn't voluntary. Days like this made Marty want to retire, hand the job over to Frank, and be done with it all.

As he stepped out the front door, his eyes caught Frank coming back from the direction of the church, shaking his head as if a man already done with the day.

"Find anything?" The sheriff asked, still reeling from the discoveries inside the house.

"Nothin' out of the ordinary, Marty. Even checked the pews," Frank said with a slight smile. "C'mon, ya know there wouldn't be anythin' over there in a house of God. No fella's that evil—Lord might strike him down."

The sheriff gave a slow nod.

"Well, he just might have, Frank. He just might have," Sheriff Ronell said, turning toward his cruiser.

But he stopped, as if pulled back toward Clive's house. He lingered, staring at it for a long moment before his voice cut the air with a warning.

"This ain't over… not by a long shot."

Chapter 29: Broken Souls

The late evening air grew crisp, a strong breeze winding its way through the Blue Hollows. Overhead, the sky lay heavy and inky, brushed with the fading hues of dusk as it surrendered to night.

Inside the old house, the hearth crackled with a hearty fire. But Esther felt untouched by the heat. There was a chill inside her that no mere flame could reach.

Even the supper table, with its warmth and laughter, felt a step removed, as though she were only half-present.

It had been quiet, except for the lively bursts from Benjamin and Rebecca, their chatter coloring the room the best it could. They had been eager to fill Esther in on everything she'd missed.

With her usual sweet charm, Rebecca turned to Esther, teasing though perhaps a little serious, "Ya been gone way too long." The words stung, though Esther knew she hadn't meant them that way.

Rebecca made her promise never to leave again, and when Esther agreed, it wasn't enough. She insisted on a formal agreement, holding out her little finger for a pinky swear. It was such a simple thing, but in Rebecca's mind, it sealed the deal. It lightened the mood in the room and distracted everyone for the moment.

But it didn't last, as Esther's thoughts felt caught up in the shadow of Clive again, despite her efforts to cast him out. She couldn't shake the feeling that it was her fault—that his blood was on her hands.

Beyond the grave, Clive's reach still stretched for her, much as Gran's and Pawdad's once had, pulling her back into his grasp. His face lingered—twisted and cruel—more terrifying than the darkest visions her mind could summon.

Her eyes had drifted to Ian throughout the meal, searching his face for something—anything—that might ease the fear. His smiles came, faint and fleeting, disappearing almost as quickly as they appeared. He tried, but it was as if he had nothing to give, nothing that could reach her across the table. His gaze drifted, unfocused, his troubles somewhere distant, in a place she couldn't follow.

At one point, he reached out, resting his hand on hers, the warmth of his skin a faint connection.

Perhaps it was meant to reassure her or to create a sense of closeness, but the touch felt empty. His fingers tightened in one last squeeze before slipping away, leaving only the coldness behind.

And then, just like that, Ian cut the evening short. His voice was sharp as he told Benjamin and Rebecca they needed to head home, finish their studies, and get to bed. The abruptness caught her off guard. It wasn't like him—so far from his usual calm demeanor.

A knot tightened inside her. Had she made a mistake by coming back?

Had she dragged her troubles into this house once again, casting a darkness over the people she cared so deeply for? The thought wormed its way into her mind, poisoning everything.

Maybe it would be better if she didn't stay, leaving before her troubles rained down on them, just as Abram had warned.

But even through her own fears, she could see Ian was carrying something just as burdensome. His mind churned, his face shifting with expressions she couldn't quite read, as if he were wrestling with an animal without a face.

They had spoken little since she returned, and the distance between them felt just like it had before—before the intimacy of the previous night.

At one point, Esther saw Ian in the kitchen with Clarissa, standing close, their quiet conversation drawing them together. There was a weariness on his face, a vulnerability he let slip only with the older woman.

When Clarissa wrapped her arms around him, rubbing his back in that mothering way of hers, it bothered Esther more than she cared to admit. Clarissa's hand on his back unearthed something in her—a strange mix of envy and fear, as if she were witnessing a part of Ian she longed to reach but never could.

He had never leaned on her like that. He had always been such a rock, but seeing him turn to someone else unsettled her.

Esther couldn't help but feel like an outsider—someone Ian might always keep at a distance. She wished he would open up to her, that he could lay his burdens down with her. But that part of him, the one he showed to Clarissa, remained locked inside, a door she had no key for.

And when he'd said goodnight, it felt rushed, unfinished.

The world felt like it was on fire, and she had no one to share it with.

She wished it could be him.

If not for the promise she'd made to Rebecca, Esther might've run—overwhelmed by that creeping sense of doom.

Her legs ached, the urge to flee like a wildfire spreading through her veins, every instinct screaming at her to flee.

Now, as she sought the comfort of her room, that hunger in her soul demanded something more.

She was always alone.

Even here, in the place she longed to be, she felt as if she might as well be sitting in a forest, dark trees closing in around her.

All she could do was sit at the edge of her bed, staring at the blank wall as shadows danced.

Clive's ghost hovered around her, whispering the things she had wished had died with him, tormenting her.

Esther stood at the final precipice, muttering that she couldn't take it any longer.

She needed to see Ian.

She wanted to see his face, to tell him she was sorry—that he didn't have to fix this. That she wasn't fragile, that she could share the yoke.

So, instead of running from a confrontation, she would face it head-on, demanding he show her what was behind that door.

With a jolt of determination, she pushed past the confines of her room and the house, the cool air rushing over her as she stepped outside.

Barefoot on the dirt, she walked along the narrow path leading to Ian's house. It was as though her feet were guiding her there on their own, the hush of the night wrapping around her, the usual sounds of the evening strangely absent.

The small home sat before her, its dark windows offering no sign of life. Esther stood there for a moment, her courage faltering. The house was silent, an impenetrable fortress of unspoken words.

Ian's door wasn't just shut—it felt closed off in every sense.

But she didn't want to give up. She thought about banging on the door with her fists, but worried he might not answer. It would tear her apart if he didn't. She was too scared to face that rejection again.

Perhaps this was an omen—that it was never meant to be. Only the dream of a lonely girl, a movie she could watch but never step into. His new affection felt fleeting, a kindness without root.

If that was the case, tomorrow she'd ask Ian to take her down to town, drop her off at Clive's—breaking her promise to Rebecca. As much as Esther desired to be here, she couldn't go back to the way it had been before. She was different now, asking for more, wanting more.

She wanted Ian—not just a small part of him.

Abruptly, she turned to leave, but a faint light caught her eyes in the distance. It seeped out from behind the closed wooden door of the barn. The soft glow was enough to pull her back.

Maybe, in his hurry, Ian had left a lantern burning—a dangerous thing.

As she made her way toward the building, a strong gust of wind swept past her. Her heart quickened at it, beating wildly in her chest.

She could feel him. He was in there.

She didn't even need to see his face—his presence mesmerized her, flooding through her like a possession. Her feet seemed to glide above the earth, as if she were weightless. She didn't know what state she would find him in—flesh and bone or drifting in some other realm—but she knew she didn't want to turn back now.

A faint creak rose from the hinges, soft and almost undetectable, as she eased the door open and stepped inside. The space was dim, lit only by a lone lantern hung from a post. The air was rich with the scent of hay and wood, aged by rain.

Closing her eyes, Esther tried to feel where he was in the darkness, the shadows hiding him. She began calling to him from the girl she used to be, speaking words that didn't leave her mouth.

For a brief moment, she wondered if she was lost in a delusion of her own making, something she had conjured up from pure desire.

Just as she was about to lose hope, thinking herself foolish, a voice emerged from the shadows.

"Are you looking for me?" The voice was deep, dressed in bitterness and exhaustion.

Esther turned toward the sound, her eyes straining to see his form in the dark, until the shadows revealed him.

He sat on a crate, leaning against the wall in the corner of the barn where the light didn't reach.

She stepped slowly toward him, trying to draw him out.

Slouched, he had a bottle of some dark spirit dangling loosely from his hand.

"Ian," she said. "I saw the lantern, was just wonderin' where ya were." Her voice carried an almost apologetic tone, though it wasn't the response she had meant to convey.

He let out a dry laugh, hollow and devoid of humor, before taking another swig from the bottle and setting it in his lap.

"Well… here I am," he said. "For how long… who knows?"

Esther had never seen Ian drunk before—he rarely drank. And the tension in his body and voice was palpable. She almost feared what she might find if she ventured closer.

"Why did you come out here tonight?" he asked, cutting through the polite conversation with a knife.

What was she supposed to say?

That she was going crazy, thinking he was a ghost, haunting her ever since she first saw him leaning on that fence?

"What ya mean?" she asked, careful not to stir the tempest she sensed brewing in him.

He stood, his movements controlled as he picked up the bottle and closed the distance between them.

His strides were even, despite the alcohol coursing through him as his gaze locked onto hers.

She didn't move, even when his eyes tried to push her back. It felt as though Ian was trying to make her flee and stay at the same time.

He stopped just a few feet away, cocking his head as a small smile found its way to his lips. He couldn't help it—even now, in the dim light, he found her achingly beautiful.

And there was a look on her face—concern, yes, but layered with something deeper. She wanted to know what was really bothering him, and he could see it in her eyes. She had come out looking for answers.

So, he would lay it all out—everything that had been eating at him since the men brought news of Clive's death. Everything that had kept him from truly enjoying her company at dinner, despite desperately longing to.

He felt bad about how he'd left in such haste—no private moment. Had the day not unfolded as it had, he was certain he would have kissed her on Clarissa's porch.

Ignoring pleasantries, he exhaled sharply, then drew in a deep breath.

"How long… do you think it's going to take… before they figure out I was the last one to run into Clive?"

Ian's words landed like a blow, and Esther's breath stalled. The directness of the question pressed in a reality she hadn't fully considered.

"I ain't gonna say nothin' to anyone 'bout that," she said, as if it were only logical. Why would she? They never had to know.

"I know you wouldn't," he said. "But that storekeeper and his wife… they saw the altercation between your cousin and me in Jasper."

He glanced down, voice tightening.

"Now he's dead."

"It doesn't take much to put a German man away in this country." Ian shook his head, his eyes meeting hers. "You wouldn't know that."

Esther's heart sank as she absorbed the depth of his fear. She had heard the comments in town—rumors of distrust toward Germans because of the war—but had never thought about his concern before.

"Margie Mae wouldn't say a thing," she said, her voice desperate. "She's always been so good to me."

Ian's eyes softened for a moment, touched by her naive belief in the goodness of others. He reached out, stroking her cheek, the roughness of his hand a distinct contrast to the tenderness of the gesture.

"And ya ain't done nothin' wrong," Esther said, her voice trembling. "If anyone's to blame… it's me."

She paused, swallowing hard before she continued.

"I beat on Clive 'til he crashed his car. Left 'im there, knowin' he was hurt real bad."

Her eyes flickered with desperation.

"I'll tell the sheriff the whole truth if he comes out here lookin' fer ya. I'll tell him I done killed Clive by accident," she said, her voice breaking.

Ian's hands moved to her chin, cupping it as he looked into her eyes.

"No. No, you won't," he said firmly.

She searched his face, seeking some reassurance, some sign that everything would be alright.

But all she saw was the same uncertainty that mirrored her own.

"Esther..." he whispered. "I told you I passed Clive on the road last night."

He hesitated, his jaw tightening as the words lingered in him.

"But what I didn't tell you... is that I stopped?"

Pulling his hands away, Ian rubbed the back of his neck.

"He said some god-awful lies about you, and... I hit him. Hard... harder than I've ever hit any man," His voice was laced with regret. "I wanted to make sure he'd never hurt you again."

His voice dropped low.

"But... I never saw him get up."

The admission sat there, unmoving.

He exhaled, a long and slow release, the confession seeming to drain him, his shoulders sagging under its weight.

"I think I killed a man," he said, his voice cracking as the reality of what he had done played again.

Esther watched as his composure crumbled—the strong and unyielding man breaking down before her eyes.

"Who will take care of my children when I am gone?" he asked.

His practical question was fragile and real.

"Clarissa is an old woman," he said as he paused. His failure bore down on him, and he closed his eyes, as if trying to steady himself.

"I made a promise to my wife." His voice broke. "I would raise them… doing my very best, even without her."

The desperation in his words—alive.

For the first time, Esther felt as if she could truly see Ian—not the facade of the man, but a soul who pained as much as hers. She couldn't bear to see him trying to carry the strain of a fate that threatened in the distance.

"No…no, they can't take ya away from us," she said, her voice firm despite the tears welling up in her eyes. She reached for his hand and squeezed it tightly. "Yer a good man, and…"

"When I came to America," he went on, "I thought I would have a better life." His voice turned bitter. "Now I'm going to lose everything—and make my children pay for it."

She couldn't watch him give in to the despair anymore.

Stepping closer to him, she leaned up, took his face in her hands, and made him look at her.

"I'll take care of 'em, if anythin' happens," she vowed with solid determination.

He looked at her, his hesitation visible. His eyes, though grateful, held something else—doubt.

"That's good of you, but…" His voice softened, the uncertainty spilling out even if he didn't mean it to.

Her eyes narrowed—his dismissal, his doubtful tone had stabbed at something painful within her, as if it had been driven through her entire core.

Instead of crying, it made her mad. Because she knew he was wrong.

"What!" she shouted, the word cracking out like a slap.

She took a forceful step back, shaking her head from side to side as if to push away his judgment.

"Ya think I CAN'T?" Her voice cut through the air, sharp and defensive, daring him to challenge her. The edge in her tone made it undeniable—his distrust had struck deep, and she refused to let it slide.

Ian stood there, silent, his stillness only stoking the flames inside her.

His lack of response or correction only fueled her anger.

In an instant, it was hot and wild. She didn't hold it back—pushing forward—she tried to shove him, her hands against his chest, but he didn't move even an inch.

He blinked, taken aback by the fierceness in her voice and actions. He hadn't expected such fire from her, and it left him momentarily speechless. He hadn't intended to upset her, but he couldn't fix it—not with his mind clouded by a liquored haze.

"Esther," he said, his voice low, tired. "I can't do this right now."

She could feel the anger burning inside her, just as it had the previous night. It was rising, pushing up from the ground beneath her.

Why couldn't Ian see her as anything more than a helpless girl? She had fought the devil himself and ripped her soul back from his fingers.

Life with Clive hadn't been easy—in fact, her entire life had never been easy, not even a little. Living at the estate had been a breeze compared to everything else.

And the love she had for his children was a powerful and deep maternal urge.

Hadn't she already proven she was just as capable as any other woman?

All she wanted was for him to see it—to see her—for once, as more than just some sad thing he needed to protect or fix.

It was insulting, and she was angry, really angry!

Esther's eyes flicked to the bottle, still hanging loose in Ian's grip, swaying—a silent dare.

Before he could react, her fingers snatched it, quick as a thief in the night.

The bottle was hers now, and with one fluid motion, she brought it to her lips, tipping it high as though she had nothing left to lose.

She didn't sip. She swallowed the fire whole, letting it burn a trail down to her gut, daring it to do its worst. Her throat caught flame, but she didn't flinch. If she could, she'd drain the whole damn thing—let it scorch away the pieces of herself she didn't want to carry anymore.

Ian froze, eyes wide, the shock hitting him too late. He'd never seen a woman—let alone Esther—drink with such reckless abandon. Not like this.

His chest tightened as he lunged forward, snatching the bottle from her grip and flinging it at the barn wall. The glass clattered, lost in the darkness, but it was too late. The damage was done.

"What the hell, Esther? What are you trying to do?" he said, his voice cracking with surprise as his fingers still shook from the shock of it.

There was a disbelief carved into his face—he couldn't quite reckon with the woman standing in front of him.

She took a step closer, eyes blazing.

"Afraid it's gonna break me?" she spat, her voice tight as she jabbed her finger toward him, daring him to contradict her.

"Ya forget, Ian, I grew up a moonshiner." She moved closer, her breath hot against his chest, her eyes wild. "And how the hell do ya think I numbed his touch?"

Her words stung, each one landing with the force of unearthed pain.

His hand faltered at his side, unsure if he should reach for her or back away.

She had sewn his lips shut with thick thread, and he was frustrated she'd done something so reckless despite his own transgression.

Tears moved to her eyes, unbidden.

"Nothing can break me. Not Clive! Not my Gran! Not you!" she cried, the words spilling out of her.

The intensity—the raw emotion that poured out of her with the force of molten lava—took Ian aback. His throat tightened as he struggled for words, unprepared for the fury she had unleashed.

"Those things Clive said." Her voice faltered, a bitter, broken smile twisting on her lips. "Maybe they're true."

Ian lowered his head, then glanced up, his heart breaking at the sight of what he now recognized as pain.

"Esther… I don't…"

"Know?" she interrupted, sarcasm barely concealing the sadness underneath as she continued.

"Ya don't know how many times I fought Clive off me… or that he pinned me down in a cornfield when I was just thirteen."

Her voice cracked slightly, but she straightened, lifting her chin.

"But I got myself up after."

Ian's arms instinctively reached out for her, but she pulled away, stepping back sharply, as if his touch might burn her.

He hadn't meant to make her confess her darkest hurts. All he wanted was to comfort her, but she pushed him back each time he tried, her palms firm against his chest, refusing to let him quell her Vesuvius purge.

"I am… so, so sorry…," he said slowly, his voice a careful whisper, the weight of her words making his shoulders sag.

Tears had already stained her cheeks, but she stubbornly fought against the next wave, refusing to let them fall.

"Think I can't love a child like my own? That I never loved a little one?" she said as her body swayed, the sheer force of her emotions threatening to knock her off balance.

Ian's hands hovered in the space between them, unsure whether to reach for her again or let her speak.

"I never told no one," she whispered.

Ian heard every word, his chest tightening as she went on.

"I had me a baby once…."

Her breath caught as her eyes drifted down, the ground ready to swallow her whole as memories rushed up to meet her.

At that moment, a slow silence drifted in from the Blue Hollows, releasing a sad truth…

finally set free. It soared up…

into the rafters of the old barn, before escaping...
to the night sky, where it had always belonged.
It had been her secret and for too long...

Esther took a much-needed pause, her hands still clenched into fists as she continued, her knuckles white against the force of her confession.

"When my baby wanted out... I spent all night hidin' out in the woods. I'd seen animals give birth... but never figured it'd hurt quite so bad."

Her lips trembled, and she clenched her jaw, determined not to let it break her.

"I tried not to scream 'cause I was strong. I knew I could do it."

Her eyes darted to Ian's. The pain in them was so visceral, it stole the air from his lungs—a pain of loss... one he recognized in his own soul.

"I wanted him... even if I was just a young'un myself. I really wanted him. I loved him... I felt him kickin' me, hidin', waitin' to be born."

She struggled to get the words out, pacing herself, each one fragile.

"But he never even took a breath... despite my pleadin'."

"So little... he fit right in my hands," she said, lost in the memory, her hands lifting, cradling the tiny, fragile life she had lost—a vision as vivid and real as that night.

Like a bird fallen too soon from its nest.

Her nest.

"The moon was bright that night... and I just stared at how sweet and perfect he looked," she continued.

"Felt so wrong... puttin' his little body in the cold ground."

Esther looked down at her hands, as if they still carried the weight of that unbearable task.

"Had him tucked up in a sock... though it didn't matter much."

"When I finally got up the nerve to go back home… it was nearly mornin', and Gran was good and mad. She beat me for a good long while… but ya wanna know somethin'? Every time she laid into me… it made the hurt inside not feel so bad. Nothin' could ever feel that bad."

And just as suddenly as Esther had started, she stopped. It was as if the wake of the eruption had settled.

The old barn became completely still, the silence drawn into its walls, as if the building itself had absorbed it.

Ian watched her, his eyes wet, struggling to breathe through the ache.

He'd seen pain before, but not like this. Never like this.

The quiet girl he had once thought was fragile was, in fact, anything but.

She had always been strong, silently carrying a sadness for years, never unburdening herself to anyone. It was a heaviness, an unimaginable thing, hidden beneath a pretty smile and bright eyes.

Now that sadness lay bare, raw and exposed, he could only stand there, feeling it as if it were his own.

All he could think about was holding her… taking away the sorrow she carried.

He wanted to give her so much.

To give her everything she needed.

Without a word, he stepped closer, moving slowly until he was standing right in front of her.

He reached for her, pausing when she didn't pull away, then drew her into his arms. As he did, she leaned into him, letting go of a part of herself she had long been tethered to.

Esther's body trembled as her fingers dug into his back, holding on as though he were the only thing keeping her from falling apart.

Ian tightened his hold on her, resting his chin on the top of her head. In that moment, he felt his own pent-up angst unravel, the warmth between them offering a bittersweet solace, the kind only two weary souls can share.

Standing there, holding each other, time felt irrelevant. It was much like the night before, but now in the warmth of shelter.

And though it was a calming balm, it wasn't enough—not for her.

She didn't want to be held just for comfort—she wanted to be held with a stronger purpose, one with more meaning, with desire.

"Can't ya see me?" she said, her voice filled with desperate longing.

With a sudden, cautious movement, she pulled away from his embrace, just far enough to lock eyes with him. Her fingers gripped his shirt, shaking with a mix of emotion as her gaze bore deep into his. Trying to reach his soul.

"Can't ya just love me? I ain't 'fraid of you," she said, her tone trembling and urgent.

She needed to see him there with her—truly with her— standing in the fire.

Ian tried to speak again, but the words stuck in his throat, almost as if he kept them at bay on purpose.

Nothing he could say would be enough to satisfy how he felt, and he didn't want to hear the words his own mind might speak.

So, instead of words, his body moved. This time, when he pulled her in, his embrace was fierce, unyielding, and stronger than before. His entire being shook, like a dam on the verge of destruction.

His heartbeat pounded in her ears as his breath came heavy and ragged, rolling through his torso, deep into his gut. His whole body was breathing for him.

And he couldn't deny the heat of her body against his, the way her form pressed close, igniting a consuming urge.

Esther had never been held like this before.

What had first felt like comfort was evolving, morphing into something new. The barn was spinning around them.

She found her own heart matching his, like a reflection in the water. Every nerve in her body was alive, hyperaware of him.

The musky scent of his skin filled her senses, intoxicating her more than any liquor ever could.

His rough beard brushed against her temple, sending shivers down her spine.

The dreams she'd kept hidden for so long—of touching him, being this close to Ian Huggler—were slipping into reality.

Last year, she'd spent hours, days even, watching him from afar, her want growing with each glance. Now, he was here, his arms wrapped tightly around her, his body melding into hers.

Swept up in a deep wave of desire, she couldn't hold herself back any longer.

Risking rejection, she didn't care.

She wanted to kiss his salty skin, to feel his body against her lips.

Without hesitation or regret, she leaned up and pressed her mouth to his neck. Her lips were soft, her breath hot as it grazed his skin.

Ian's body stiffened for a moment, his eyes closing as he surrendered to it.

The girl he had once kept at arm's length now felt so close, her body real.

Her scent, sweet and distinctly feminine, enveloped him.

The strands of her freshly washed hair tangled in the rough stubble of his chin as she kissed on him. He inhaled deeply, drawing in the mix of her soap and the faint hint of whiskey on her breath.

The alcohol had given them both permission to abandon any remaining reservations or caution.

But it was more than the liquid courage—there was a pull, drawing them together. The tension that had simmered between them for so long now flared, fueling a hunger. If the world was burning, Ian wanted her beside him.

He needed this—he needed her.

At that moment, He decided he wouldn't stop her. In fact, he would encourage her.

His hands slid to her hips, gripping hard as he drew her deeper into his frame, wanting her to feel his desire for her fully. He held her there, firm, his breath heavy and ragged against her.

As expected, it only fueled her determination more.

She looked up at him with wild eyes, an expression that made Ian hold his breath. He wasn't sure if she would devour him, but the look she gave sent a surge of electricity coursing through his body, like a flash of summer lightning.

He had never had a woman look at him this way before—there was something almost feral in Esther's nature that had always excited him. Teased him.

With that, he grabbed her face with his hands, perhaps with more force than he should have, but she didn't seem to mind.

He looked into her sultry eyes, preparing her with his gaze. His anticipation meeting hers.

Then, with urgency, he leaned down and met her open lips.

Her mouth felt even better than he had envisioned—soft, warm, and utterly inviting. The moment their lips met, a surge of heat rushed through him, her taste more irresistible than he could have imagined.

In a moment, they were swept into a vortex.

He didn't hold back, kissing her hard, pouring all the longing in his body into that kiss.

Esther accepted his mouth as if it had quenched a thirst she had carried forever.

Right or wrong no longer mattered—it simply was.

His tongue moved slowly at first, then dove deep, each movement casting its spell, weaving her body to respond to him. She moved in time with him now, following as though he had ultimate control over her. The deeper he went, the more she danced, trembling at the conquest.

Not wanting to let the momentum of their kiss break, Ian turned with her, pressing her body against the support post of the barn, his mouth never leaving hers.

He moved up and down against her slowly, teasing, tempting her with the promise his body held.

A premonition. Emulating what was inevitable.

But when Esther pushed her hips back against him, the wanting in him almost peaked.

Their bodies danced with perfect rhythm and breathless kisses, his mouth meeting hers over and over again.

Ian's body gave his hands permission to roam her torso, feeling the feminine curves of her body under them.

She responded in kind, her hands moving to the back of his shirt, pulling it up, needing to feel his skin against hers.

He changed his footing and quickly proceeded to unbutton and remove his shirt, dropping it to the ground in haste.

For a moment, he hesitated. The last call of his conscience tugging him back, even as his body pushed him forward with a force he couldn't reckon with—desire warred with guilt, worried that he might be taking advantage of her vulnerability.

"I… I… shouldn't be doing this to you," he murmured, his voice not even convincing himself.

Esther, however, was resolute. She looked into his face, her heavy dark lashes fanning her eyes, pulling him toward her with a magnetic and powerful allure.

The spell he thought he had woven over her had shifted, gaining with a power he couldn't resist, as if she had turned it back on him with mastery he hadn't expected.

She reached out, her fingers brushing against his chest, exploring him as though she had studied him from afar. Her hands moved with purpose, tracing the lines of his muscles, claiming him inch by inch.

She clearly had a natural instinct for seduction.

It wasn't fair, Ian thought briefly—who was taking advantage of whom? The notion flickered and vanished as he smiled at her.

Almost as if in a tug-of-war, he pulled the power from her effortlessly again, kissing her firmly on the mouth, letting his hands grip and pull her body to his will.

He felt her knees go weak with desire, like he had taken her to the brink, holding her there for too long.

Her eyes were glazed with passion and whiskey.

Esther's beauty consumed him.

He replayed in his mind how she had smiled at him in the theater the night before—how she had even smiled at the other man, giving away what he now felt belonged to him.

Ian wanted her to know that smile was his, and he refused to share it with anyone.

In a dreamy haze, the alcohol finally catching up to him, Ian's gaze softened as it landed on a patch of loose straw, faintly illuminated by the glow of the old lantern.

Taking her by the hand, his intention unmistakable and deliberate, he led her to the spot. With a careful pull, he lowered her beside him. Her body nestled into the softness of the loose bedding.

In one gentle movement, he drew her closer. Their bodies now rested horizontally on the ground, warmth slowly radiating between them.

His muscular hands moved, fingers tracing the peaks of her figure, as though rediscovering what his eyes had seen the year before.

He could still picture her standing in the kitchen, the wet nightgown clinging to her skin. He had seen every bit of her that stormy summer night. She might as well have been standing there naked.

The warmth of her skin seeped through the fabric. The dim light around them was irrelevant. He could feel the delicate lace slip beneath her clothes—the same one he had glimpsed the night before, when she unknowingly shed her dress and collapsed into bed.

The thought of that thin lace resting against her breasts had interrupted his sleep. The image stubbornly returned to him, even in the quiet hours of the morning.

Ian thought about telling her he didn't want to hurt her, didn't want her thinking he was too rough. But as she lay beside him, here in the moment, he felt her body calling to him, like a sailor to the sea—promising horizons he had yet to explore.

All his thoughts were consumed with finishing what they had started. Maybe it was the way her pretty fingers brushed his cheek, tracing along his jaw, her lips parting in a silent invitation, that told him he didn't need to say a single word.

She was there, her eyes locked on his, her body responding to every touch—willing, clearly wanting, and encouraging him closer. For once, it felt good to be selfish, not worrying about the consequences.

He lay next to her, almost on top of her.

Slowly, he pulled her dress up over her bare thighs. His hand traced a slow path along the soft skin until he reached her undergarments, feeling the cool, glossy fabric glide beneath his fingers.

Emboldened, he slipped his hand inside, pausing as he reached her hidden, secret spot. He savored the feel of it beneath his fingers—touching her in places he had only dreamed of.

Esther couldn't even keep her eyes open. She felt like an instrument being played, music rising from her body.

Her wild nature made her more expressive, less ladylike, and perhaps even a bit too loud. She moved restlessly between groans and biting her own lip.

While he had been trying to excite her, her reaction only excited him further.

Now, more determined than ever, an urgency raced through him at a rapid speed. Despite knowing he should have been more patient—allowing her more time—he could no longer wait, fully aware she wouldn't be able to catch up to him.

And so... like orchestrating the final ballad of a symphony, despite the years of celibacy, Ian called on his experience—his movements confident and practiced—as he set his intention into action.

A smile tugged at his lips as he leaned closer to her, his mouth brushing against her neck, his hot breath leaving a trail of warmth as he slowly worked his way down.

His mouth lingered at her sternum, lips grazing the sensitive skin between her breasts, his tongue tracing delicate lines, tickling her skin.

His hands moved with intent—caressing the curve of her waist, then reaching into the top of her dress. His fingers grazed her nipple, exploring every inch of her form with deliberate precision.

It was a tender distraction from what was to come next, ensuring the power of his seduction had consumed her, waiting until her back arched in rhythm with his touch, her breath heavy.

Seizing the opportunity, he moved to his knees. Once there, he lifted her skirt completely up and, in one smooth motion, slipped her satin panties down, pulling them over her bare feet.

Esther felt a flutter of surprise, a brief flicker of embarrassment, but she tried not to show it. Instead, she offered him a soft smile, which he could barely make out in the dark.

Still on his knees, he unbuttoned the fly of his trousers, pulling his pants and boxers down, the shadows only showing the outline of his full and hard form.

He traced the softness of her inner thigh with his hand as he spread her legs apart.

Esther's body waited for him—an invitation between her legs.

Ian smiled as he shuffled the excess straw out of his way with his free hand, then lowered himself over her beautiful, beckoning body, bracing himself on one arm.

He pulled her body beneath him, guiding her into position as well as himself.

A slight hesitation came over Esther as she suddenly felt her body go stiff. She had wanted this, longed for it, envisioned it, but suddenly it was all becoming too real.

This was going to happen—right now, right then. Scared, she wrapped her hands around his waist, trying to allow it, almost closing her eyes.

She had never consented to sex before, so choosing felt different, as it pulled her from the feelings he had excited in her. But she wasn't going to go back—she didn't want to.

She wanted him, this man, and she had made her decision. With that, she pulled at his torso, trying to make it happen quicker.

Despite being intoxicated, he felt her indecision, which he surmised was nerves, as she nudged him to continue. Beyond that, his brain couldn't reason, as the drive in his body needed to be released.

So… hidden in the deep corner of the old barn, Ian joined her body, and they became one.

His hand gripped her hip, anchoring her as his movements fell into her rhythm, each thrust strong yet controlled. His arm trembled slightly as he supported himself, but he moved with purpose—a fire born from years of longing.

Once connected, truly connected, he lowered himself onto both elbows so he could kiss her.

He found Esther's lips in the shadows, kissing her as he had before, but this time his body danced on hers with a fire.

Every motion carried the weight of everything he had buried— the desire that had been built for her, the long nights in New York wanting to hold a woman, and the loss of his wife—letting her memory rest.

The sadness that had lingered as a shadow over him, always wondering if he could feel this way again.

His body surged with instinct, emotion, passion, and grief intertwined in every powerful stroke.

His breath was hot against her skin as he picked up the pace. A deep moan escaped Esther's lips, though she tried to suppress it.

That sound became his goal—wanting to hear it again, to have her relinquish her hunger to him.

In that moment, it all spilled forth, building like a crescendo—an orchestra of two tangled bodies. His movements were driven, each thrust charged with the need to fill the emptiness within her. He felt his body rise and fall against hers, the primal man within whispering to him, instructing him to bury his seed deep inside her and give her what she had lost.

Eve's form… calling it forth since the beginning of time… a voice no man of Adam could resist.

Esther felt the urgency in his movements—his full presence moving, muscles contracting with a directed purpose. His broad shoulders towered over her, sweat building on his skin, droplets dripping down his neck and chest. The musk of his underarms was heady—it smelled of him, raw and familiar.

Everything about him was perfect. The motion of his body against hers left her questioning reality. Yes, this was what she had wanted, what she had asked of him last summer.

She tried to close her eyes again, but she couldn't. She wanted to watch him, even in the darkness, to watch herself, painting a memory in her mind. A man and a woman—together in an ancient, timeless act.

She had given herself to him, her body melting into his.

It was as though every trace of Clive had been washed from her, erased by Ian's mere presence.

In that moment, she felt claimed, desired, by the man she had wanted for so long—her body and soul awakened, alive, and free.

It built and broke, all in the same heartbeat. Ian's grip tightened around her as he groaned, deep and loud in her ear, with the last of his powerful thrusts. His breath caught before he exhaled, releasing all the tension that had built up inside him.

His body lingered against hers, still and heavy, almost pushing the breath from her. There was a stillness in him as he tried to recover. Then he rolled off her body, trying not to crush her.

He lay back on the soft straw with a deep, contented sigh, his arms raised above his head, staring up at the ceiling of the overhead loft. He licked his lips as he tried to catch his breath.

His breath still heavy, he looked over at Esther—her body still caught in the remnants of their passion, her legs shaking, her own breath hitching.

In that moment, the old Ian returned as concern flickered across his face, realizing he may have placed too much weight on her delicate frame.

"I'm sorry," he said, his voice still winded. "Did I hurt you?"

She shook her head, offering him a small smile, feeling self-conscious as she closed her legs.

She hadn't wanted it to end, but she could already sense Ian retreating back into reality, the weight of what they had just done settling over him.

He pulled himself up, grunting as though he didn't have the usual physical power driving him. He lifted his trousers and boxers, buttoning them up as he eyed the door of the barn, now noting how easily they could have been seen.

He wiped the sweat from his brow and walked over to a nearby bucket of water used to fill the trough. Pulling a handkerchief from his pocket, he soaked it, dabbing at his face before plunging it back into the water.

Then he walked back to Esther and, leaning down, handed it to her. Courteous on the surface, it made her feel painfully awkward.

Was she supposed to just clean up in front of him? Ian, seeing her hesitation, casually turned away, the silence between them filled with unspoken thoughts.

Their passion had ignited and burned like wildfire, leaving him visibly drained. He leaned against a wooden railing in the center of the barn, his arms bracing most of his weight.

The rise and fall of his chest was even now, but the fatigue in his eyes was unmistakable. It was obvious to Esther that he was waiting for her to stand, ever the gentleman.

But it left her feeling rushed, as if she needed to get up sooner than she had planned.

Reluctantly, she moved, signaling she was ready. Ian slowly walked over, reaching down to help.

Unsure of what to do next, Esther brushed her skirt down, trying to shake the straw from her body, pulling a few pieces from her tangled hair.

Catching a glimpse of something white on the ground, Ian walked over and picked up her discarded panties. Smiling, he held them out, waiting until she snatched them from his fingers, cheeks burning. Embarrassed, she wanted to yell, *God, Ian, can you just stop bein' a gentleman for a damn second?* But she didn't.

It wasn't easy seeing it from his perspective, though she knew he was tired, his strength spent in their indiscretion.

But the abruptness of it all left her feeling resentful. She wanted to spend more time with him—to lie next to him in the barn, to be held, not jump up and move on as though it hadn't happened. Ian was already beginning to sober up, perhaps due to exertion, but she could still feel the hum of the whiskey.

"Esther," he began, his voice low with a practical tone. But he didn't finish his thought—he didn't know how to or what he had exactly planned on saying.

How could he put into words the jumble of thoughts flooding back—the worry over Clive's death, the fear that he wouldn't be there to take care of his children, the overwhelming need to protect her, maybe even from himself? To hold on to her despite what he had just done, hoping that what he had done wouldn't jeopardize it. Not wanting to let her go, wishing he could just invite her to his bed to go to sleep.

But she wasn't his wife, and they needed to be discreet. He knew himself well enough to realize he would regret his behavior the next morning. Ian had thought maybe they would kiss a few times today, not that he would bed her in the barn.

The voice of responsibility was always his ghost.

And why had he thought taking a bottle of whiskey to the barn was a good idea? Hell if he knew. The comfortable numbness that had blanketed him earlier was fading too quickly, leaving his mind racing and regret creeping in. The undeniable truth loomed—what had just happened between them, as powerful and passionate as it was, had crossed a line that could never be uncrossed.

Sensing his hesitation, Esther walked toward the barn door, her footsteps soft against the hay-covered ground. She wasn't sure what to do after such an intimate moment, and the quiet between them felt like a rising wall.

Ian's withdrawal—a push-off—left her feeling exposed and discarded. Summoning her courage, she broke the tension, offering him a way out.

"Ya best get to bed," she said, her voice carrying a note of understanding, even though her heart ached for more.

He sighed, relieved he didn't have to say anything more, didn't have to explain himself. With a nod, he turned off the lantern and walked her out, placing a hand on the small of her back as he did.

Once outside, the cool air hit them, and Esther shivered. Her legs felt unsteady beneath her, her mind still reeling from the intimate act, as she waited for Ian to brace the door shut.

It was in that moment, panties in hand, she decided—if he were quick to dismiss her tonight, she wouldn't give him the satisfaction of thinking he'd done right by her.

Maybe she would rattle him the way he had unsettled her.

Perhaps it was the alcohol fueling her sudden desire to be a little mean, or maybe it was just the sting of being pushed aside. She wasn't sure, but she was certain of one thing—she wouldn't do what he expected. She wasn't the same needy girl who cried in the courtyard last year.

Not now. She knew her worth, at least. Knew other men found her attractive.

Even though he was physically and mentally spent, Ian still planned on walking Esther to the back door, wanting to give her a goodnight kiss—maybe restore some sense of propriety after what had just happened. He tried to cling to the idea of being a gentleman, even now.

But when he turned around after locking up, she caught him off guard. She was already a good twenty feet ahead, dashing toward the house, her footsteps fast against the dirt, not even looking back.

"Esther… wait," he called out, his voice soft, hoping she wouldn't make him jog to catch up.

"Night, Ian. I've gotta get to bed," she said, flicking her wrist in a dismissive wave, her back still to him, not sparing even a glance over her shoulder.

He stood there, shifting his weight as he watched her figure retreat into the shadows of the house.

"Alright," he muttered, more to himself than anyone, unsure if she was upset or just as tired as he was.

"Goodnight. Sleep well," he added, loud enough for her to hear but quiet enough not to wake Clarissa, hoping Esther could feel the sincerity in his words.

Everything about her left him feeling puzzled.

He ran a hand through his hair as he watched her disappear inside, the door shutting behind her. With a deep exhale, he began to attempt to unravel the whirlwind she had just stirred in him.

As he made his way home, he thought of last year, of when Esther had propositioned him. She had asked him, plain and simple, if he wanted to "lay" with her.

Well, he'd gone and done it now. And now, he could only hope she wouldn't hate him for it in the morning. A knot tightened in his chest as he replayed her quick exit, wondering if she already regretted it.

Chapter 30: Unearthed

It was an unusually hot spring day, the afternoon sun beating down mercilessly on the Old Reed Estate orchard, where the land stood as a silent witness to the day's toil.

Ian stood knee-deep in a pit, the remains of an ancient tree stump defying his every effort to unearth it. His muscles burned with exertion, his shirt clinging to his back, soaked through with sweat.

The rhythmic sound of his shovel digging into the earth was a steady, almost meditative beat, but peace eluded him entirely. His thoughts were a tangled mess of regret, guilt, and worry. The events of the previous night, what he could remember, replayed in his mind in a continuous loop, each scene more vivid than the last.

He had wanted it to happen—every moment of it—but the magnitude of what he had done bore down on him like the very earth he was trying to break through. A God-fearing man, Ian had always believed in doing what was right, but now, he wasn't sure he could even recognize what right was.

Was it wrong that he'd killed an evil man by accident—if that's what you could call it?

He had forgotten the power of his own rage and strong fists—trouble he'd known too well as a young man, though it had always been for a righteous cause. The image of Clive crumpling to the ground, the dull thud of his body hitting the dirt, echoed in his mind.

At first, Ian had been torn up over it, believing he'd committed an unforgivable act.

But after Esther's confession in the barn, the guilt started to fade, leaving behind only the nagging uncertainty about what came next. And if he could do it over again, he wasn't sure he'd stop himself. Hell, he was almost certain he wouldn't. Clive was the kind of man who didn't deserve to breathe. Death was too kind a punishment for what he'd done to that young, innocent girl—sweet Esther.

The more he dwelt on it, the more rage bubbled up inside him. He wished he could go back to that day when Clive had been holding Esther under his thumb at Paulson's Mercantile. Knowing what he knew now, he'd drag that fat old bastard out onto the street and tear him limb from limb, leaving him for the dogs.

Hearing a clanking sound, Ian stopped, realizing he had been hitting his shovel against a huge rock—probably for the last five minutes.

"Dammit," he muttered.

He decided it was best to let God deal with Clive now—chain his soul in hell, or whatever He does. Then a darker thought crept in—what if he ran into Clive there someday, for the very act of killing him? Without speaking, but loudly in his mind, Ian said, *God, you better put me in a different fiery pit.*

Leaning over to take a drink of cool water from his canteen, Ian let himself drift back to a more pleasant, though equally troubling, problem.

Beautiful Esther, with her long, shapely legs. Taller than most women—slender as a willow, with curves in just the right places. Her fingers, delicate with pointed tips—he'd noticed them when she touched his chest in the barn.

The memory of that touch, the warmth of her body, the taste of her mouth—it filled him with a conflicting sense of longing and shame. He hadn't understood how much he desired her until last night, but in his drunken state, he'd gone too far.

She deserved more. To be courted, treated like a lady—not someone thrown onto rough straw. She should have been kissed on the porch, their hands entwined during long walks. They had moved far past that, and he worried she would resent not having experienced the slow buildup to love.

Ian couldn't help but think about the other man at the theater, the one Esther had flirted with—he might have known how to do it right. Not rushing it, he might've talked softly to her, bought her flowers, and when it came to the kiss, he'd likely have been scared to do it, but eventually worked up the nerve, making it soft and sweet.

But then again, that poor fella probably couldn't handle a wildcat such as Esther. The thought tugged a brief smile from Ian's lips, though it didn't last long. His conscience quickly reminded him that he hadn't exactly done much better. Maybe no one could, really—not with the way she was.

It was just as well her Pawdad wasn't here—if he was, Ian figured he'd be knocking on his door, gun in hand, ready to settle things. And, truth be told, the old man would've been right—he had no defense.

He hadn't even tried to use an ounce of restraint—he had compromised her completely. As a man, he hadn't been careful, not considering the reality that she could get pregnant. It had seemed right in the heat of the moment, driven by the desire to replace what she had lost—perhaps even to bind her to him in a selfish way. He didn't blame the whiskey entirely, but he knew how easily it could plant reckless thoughts in one's head.

And, of course, if it came to that, he would marry her. They were clearly heading in that direction—at least in his opinion—but now it felt like a car barreling down a hill with no brakes.

For God's sake, she was Clarissa's niece. What if she ever found out? The thought of her disappointment in him—well, he didn't know if he could handle it.

Ian grunted, throwing the shovel into the ground with all his might, kicking it down with the sole of his boot. The dirt around the root resisted, mocking him for the effort. He cursed under his breath again.

Abram watched as he struggled, their dispute from the previous day already forgotten, as if it was yesterday's news. They were like brothers, working the land together. Ian was his trusted friend, and Abram could see something was eating at him, but getting it out of him would take time. So, Abram would wait. Ian always came around, eventually, with a little patience.

With a pick slung over his shoulder, Abram studied the problem before speaking, his voice tinged with concern.

"Ya know, this might be a bit easier if I had me somethin' to eat. Haven't eaten for a good six hours or so," Abram grumbled, his stomach growling audibly.

Ian glanced out of the corner of his eye, wiping the sweat from his brow with the back of his hand.

"Go on in, then."

Abram hesitated, sensing something was off.

"Well, ain't ya hungry?"

"Nah," Ian replied, his voice clipped. He stabbed the shovel into the ground again. "Go on."

Abram lingered, studying Ian's tense posture, the tightness in his voice.

"Ya really hate that stump, don't ya?" he said, a smile playing on his lips.

For a brief moment, Ian considered confiding in Abram, letting the words on the tip of his tongue spill out.

But just as quickly, he swallowed them back down, burying them as deep as the roots of the stubborn tree he was trying to remove.

What could he say? That he might have killed a man? That he had done more than just lift the skirt of Clarissa's niece, and now his head was pounding from drinking too much?

He admitted he was angry, though the frustration was aimed squarely at himself.

Waiting for the other shoe to drop was wearing thin on him, and the work wasn't providing the distraction he'd hoped for. His frustration simmered beneath the surface, unyielding, much the same as that cursed stump—stubbornly trying to grow back, sending up green shoots despite being thought dead. They needed this area cleared for more peach saplings, but the old oak appeared determined to reclaim the land.

And… as if his problems weren't bad enough… Esther was walking toward him from the house, looking all dolled up, like nothing in the world could touch her. Her dress caught the light… and the way she moved, calm and graceful, made it seem as though she belonged to a world altogether different.

Her eyes, though, remained on him… while her face gave nothing away.

It left him even more uneasy… worried about what she might say. Maybe she was upset… as she had every right to be.

Seeing her, Ian doubled down on his work, avoiding Abram's questioning eyes. Abram just shook his head, a small sigh escaping his lips as he turned to leave.

"Hope ya know what yer gettin' yerself into," Abram muttered under his breath.

Ian's hands clenched around the shovel handle, his forearms taut. He heard Abram's footsteps fade as he walked back toward the house, leaving him alone with his thoughts—and now Esther.

Esther passed Abram on his way back, offering him a small nod as he said, "Good luck," with a quick glance back at Ian.

Her attention, though, stayed fixed on Ian, knee-deep in the hole he'd dug, both literally and figuratively. She approached cautiously, her steps deliberate, as if measuring the distance between them not just in feet, but in his mood.

She waited for him to meet her gaze, but he kept his focus on the task. Deciding she couldn't wait any longer, she spoke up.

"Ya hidin' out here? Ain't seen ya all day," she said.

Ian didn't look up, his movements becoming more mechanical as he continued to dig.

"No… just got a lot to do," he mumbled, the words almost lost in the sound of his shovel hitting the earth.

She watched him for a moment, sensing the tension in his body, the way he forced himself to focus on the task at hand. The silence between them was heavy.

He was brooding, irritated, and most definitely avoiding her.

"Well, alright then," she said, not wanting to push him, trying not to get scorched by the fire building inside him.

But she didn't leave—standing there, lingering, as if giving him the chance to say something, anything. To be honest, Esther wasn't even sure why she had come out or what she was looking for. She longed to see him, to see the face that had held her the night before. She needed to see Ian, to know if he was still a man or had turned into a ghost.

Despite what had happened in the barn, it hadn't been enough. She hadn't gotten her fill, and he'd haunted her sleep—awake and dreaming.

His scent clung to her dress, and the memory of how it felt to have his body's complete attention left her craving more. So, she dressed herself up all pretty.

She wasn't going to wear shame on her face.

No, sir. She'd put some lipstick over it.

Her reasoning felt sound—for all the bad that had been done to her, God owed her a balance, she thought. He'd have to wait patiently for her to feel bad about what she had done with him. After everything, she had earned the right to feel something good, even if just for a little while.

She wasn't even going to let herself fear what consequences Clive's death might bring. If the sheriff came asking, Ian would not take the blame, and she sure as hell wouldn't let him.

Her mind was made up—she'd tell the sheriff that she had killed Clive. Not by accident, but with purpose. She'd say Ian was lying, that he was trying to protect her, and that she had told him to say those things.

If he confessed, she'd confess more—lie if necessary. Esther would do whatever it took to keep Ian where he belonged.

This life here was his, more than hers.

If these were to be her last days of freedom, she'd spend them happy—surrounded by the people she cared about. Loving Ian's children, baking with Clarissa, and Ian… well, if he would just stop digging that damn hole and come back to her.

Ian's frustration still smoldered beneath the surface. He knew he should say something, but the words felt like lead in his mouth, too heavy to speak. And there she was, just standing there, waiting—quietly.

She didn't seem angry, far from it, which was an enormous relief. Perhaps she was being polite—nice when she shouldn't be.

Esther shifted her weight—she could tell he wasn't in the talkin' mood. She thought she would give him one last chance before heading over to see his children.

"Want me to leave?" she said nonchalantly.

He paused, resting his arm on the tall tree stump, finally looking up at her. His face was tired, his eyes squinting against the sun, clouded with the turmoil he'd been trying to suppress all day.

"I just have a lot to do here… and… I drank way too much last night." His voice was strained, each word pulled from him with visible effort.

"Think I might have lost my good judgment."

As soon as Ian opened his mouth, Esther decided she wasn't in the mood to listen. He was neither man nor ghost—just something caught in between, and she didn't have time for it.

His voice carried the edge of a lecture that hadn't yet begun, a warning wrapped in words she didn't care to hear—refused to listen. She wasn't about to waste what little time she had getting scolded like a child.

No, she had better things to do than stand there and listen to the weight of his guilt—or whatever else clawed at him.

Let him stew. She'd save her ears for something worth hearing.

"Well, I ain't gonna bother ya no more then," she said, her voice a little too bright.

And with that, she turned, her dress swaying as she walked off with a confidence that felt forced, as if she needed to convince herself that this, too, didn't matter. But it did, more than she'd ever admit.

Ian hesitated, his grip tightening on the shovel. Irritation flashed in his eyes. He wasn't done talking, wasn't finished struggling to get his feelings out—feelings he had finally worked to the surface.

But she was already dismissing him, as if none of it really mattered, which only aggravated him further.

He watched her walk away, her steps light, with too much swing, as if she carried nothing on her shoulders at all.

This new Esther really baffled him—this was the second time in two days she'd just walked off.

Ian had wanted to tell her they'd done a bad thing, needing to share the burden of shame, but she didn't seem to care one lick—not even a glance back. It was as if the unsanctioned act they had performed wasn't a big deal.

And she didn't even let him apologize for being a brute. He felt he might have been too rough, too forceful in his actions. Maybe she would've been just fine with a few kisses, but he'd been the one to pull her into the corner of the barn.

The more he thought about it, the more it ate at him. She'd walked off as though nothing had changed.

Was what they'd shared meaningless? Maybe it hadn't been that great in her mind. He was rusty, and he'd only ever been with a few women in his life. Adeline had seemed to like it well enough, but perhaps Esther expected something more.

"Stop thinking about this," he commanded himself, but in truth, he wanted to hash it out, to make sense of the mess between them. Instead, she'd left him standing alone in the orchard with only his thoughts to work through.

As Esther disappeared from view, Ian exhaled sharply, his frustration mixing with something deeper, something just out of reach.

She had looked breathtaking—her hair curled and pinned back like a movie star, but prettier. Those painted red lips suited her so well, and he knew that if he ever took her to the city, he'd have to get used to the longing eyes of other men. Though he thought it, he hadn't complimented her, which he knew was a grievous error, especially when a woman had put effort into her appearance.

Now it was just one more thing to be mad at himself for. He turned back to the stump, letting the tree have it again.

With every shovelful of dirt, Ian prayed—for redemption, for forgiveness, but mainly for the strength to face whatever was coming for him, and that included Esther.

Chapter 31: Home

Ian's home, a cozy cottage companion to the large and stately Reed Estate House, held its own quaint and endearing charm.

Twilight had descended over the countryside, sweeping away the day's warmth. The frosted windows glowed softly, the warm light spilling out into the cool evening. Inside, the warm scent of burning wood filled the room.

Remodeled over the years, the place still reflected the personal touches of dear Adeline's careful hand. Delicate doilies rested beneath lamps, softening the room's edges, while knick-knacks, figurines, and keepsakes stood neatly arranged on shelves—untouched since her death.

Handcrafted wooden beams hung overhead, accentuated by well-worn furniture. The room spoke of time and care lovingly invested, a place built for a family, where children could thrive beneath its roof.

Adeline's presence lingered, woven into all the small details, never forgotten.

Esther only hoped Ian's late wife wouldn't mind that she now sat there, enjoying the fruits of her labor. More than anything, she prayed that wherever Adeline was, she wouldn't be upset about what had happened between her and her husband.

And that Ian didn't deserve to be lonely—Esther could at least give him that.

Though few words had passed between them that day, and despite the tension he'd shown, Esther couldn't help but be drawn to the inviting comfort of Ian's home.

Lingering in her mind, their brief exchange was hard to brush off. And he had kept his distance—not just from her, but from his children, too. He usually returned for supper, always eager to see them, which made his absence all the more surprising. Even Benjamin had remarked on it, sensing something was off.

But Esther didn't mind staying with them, as she loved his children with a fierceness and didn't want to waste any more precious time. Her desire to be close, to care for them, outweighed Ian's foul mood. She wished only to be a source of comfort for both of them—and for Ian, if he'd let her.

She wondered if he'd ever managed to dig out that stubborn tree stump, the one he'd spent hours battling. It wasn't really hurting the land, just sitting there with its gnarled roots deep in the earth. But it clearly bothered him.

The thought of him out there, pick and shovel in hand, struggling for hours, made her question whether his efforts were truly worth it.

She hoped that, as the calm of evening wrapped around them, the distance between them would fade with the lingering light.

Sitting in the front room, Esther's hands struggled to braid Rebecca's hair into a neat row, while the little girl sat on the floor, doing her best to stay still. Benjamin played happily nearby, pushing his wooden toys through an imaginary land. The room was filled with the quiet sounds of home—the crackling fire, Rebecca's sweet murmurs, and the soft hum of vehicles from Benjamin.

With a loud creak, the front door slowly swung open, and a physically exhausted Ian stepped inside, pausing as his eyes adjusted to the light.

He blinked, moved by the scene that played out before him. Esther tending lovingly to his children—her presence bringing an unexpected feeling of calm.

After the day he'd had, the cozy atmosphere eased the remaining tension he'd been holding onto.

He took it all in, finding it idyllic—like something out of an old painting. His children adored her, and she gave them something he couldn't—something softer, more nurturing.

And Ian had been wrong about her, and could admit that, even if only to himself. Clarissa had been right all along—Esther had a natural way about her, as if being a mother was grown deep in her character and soul. He gazed at Rebecca and Benjamin, sitting so contentedly beside her. They reminded him of little pups, finding comfort in her presence.

"Hi, Papa." Rebecca greeted him with a bright smile, her excitement bubbling over as she wiggled in Esther's hands.

Ian set his jacket and a bowl down on the table, offering a weary smile in return.

"Clarissa sent some soup over."

"We already ate," Benjamin piped up from the floor. "Esther made us cheese on toast."

Rebecca nodded enthusiastically. "They were kinda burnt, but we scraped 'em real good with a knife, and they were like new." She turned to Esther with an apologetic look. "Sorry."

"Thank you, Esther. I appreciate that," he said sincerely, his gaze holding a warmth that went beyond gratitude.

Rebecca, still full of energy, fidgeted with her braid.

"If you've been fed, Rebecca, it's time for you to wash up for bed," Ian said gently.

Rebecca pouted, her small face scrunching up in defiance.

"Firefly," she corrected him, her voice taking on a serious tone. "Told ya my name was Firefly, and Pa, Esther ain't done doin' my hair yet."

Esther smiled at their exchange as her fingers gently worked through Rebecca's hair.

"I'll be done soon," she assured.

He nodded in agreement as he collapsed into a chair beside Benjamin, who had left his toys in favor of his father's attention. Ian was exhausted, the weariness showing in the way his shoulders slumped.

But as he watched Esther with his daughter, a smile crept across his face.

Esther was so undeniably beautiful, and it took his breath away. For a moment, he could picture what life with her here might look like. The children, despite having missed her, had slipped right back into their rhythm, as if she had always been a part of their world. Ian admitted to himself, silently, that tonight his little house truly felt like a home.

And he liked it. No, he loved it.

Today, Esther had picked up where he had faltered, not even missing a beat.

He had been out of sorts for a good portion of the day, and she had navigated it seamlessly—though he knew that wasn't something to take for granted.

He quietly acknowledged her many admirable qualities, knowing that any sane man would be lucky to have her. She might not know the great authors, but she knew the common names of every plant and their purposes, having used some last year when his children had fallen sick.

Though you wouldn't know it by looking at her, her body was built for work with the forged will of a frontier woman. She had an impenetrable resolve, one that only grew more impressive the longer he knew her. She was a quick learner, and Ian knew she'd take to reading just as easily, given the right opportunity.

And if he bungled things between them, he knew it would haunt him for the rest of his life.

Foolishly, Ian had played the Devil's Advocate in his mind today. At one point, he thought he should tell Esther that maybe she ought to find someone closer to her age, thinking twelve years might be a bit much. But Esther didn't seem to mind, despite the wear and tear he carried. Perhaps her hard life wouldn't be so easily understood by a younger man, either. She had lived a lot of life, though it didn't show in her pretty smile.

And that ludicrous idea was quickly tossed on the fire he'd burned in the orchard, along with the old stump. The second any man pulled up in Clarissa's drive, he'd be stepping out, ready to go toe-to-toe. Nope, it would have to be him because he was first in line.

He had also wrestled with the guilt of feeling like he had taken advantage of her in the barn. But the way she smiled at him across the room didn't look like someone who had taken offense to his actions. In fact, he was pretty sure she had liked it and wanted more.

And he wanted to give her more, knowing he had no earthly idea how he was supposed to keep his hands off her now, after having tasted the sweetness she offered.

He figured that if this thing with Clive blew over, he'd wait a month or so and drive her over to Jasper, make an honest woman of her. God would have to see his good intentions and realize he was just an imperfect man. If Esther wasn't racked with guilt or regret, he'd follow her lead. God help him.

Ian had spent some time in Clarissa's kitchen that evening before heading home. She had helped him feel more hopeful with her optimistic outlook. He had kept Esther's secret, but Clarissa, with her natural ability to read a face, had already known that Clive wasn't a savory character—easily seeing the expression Esther wore the first night.

It was one she was all too familiar with.

In her younger years, Clarissa had her own run-ins with an evil man before Obadiah. Though she hadn't shared that with Ian, she implied that perhaps Ian had been God's hand of justice when none could be found in a land that didn't punish men for such crimes, often finding fault with the victim.

Deciding not to dwell on it any longer, Ian took a deep sigh and leaned down, unlacing his dirty boots and kicking them off with a soft thud beside the chair. His socked feet glided over the freshly cleaned floor, and as he shifted back, he caught sight of Esther.

She glanced at him, her brow slightly furrowed, giving him a look that was almost like a wife's—mildly disapproving, as if silently scolding him for messing up the spotless floor.

Now that he thought about it, the floor wasn't just clean. It had been scrubbed until it shone. And it wasn't just the floor. Esther had cleaned everything, even putting away the clutter—something Ian had been meaning to do ever since he returned home from New York.

For some reason, it made him sheepishly smile as he shifted forward in his chair once again, the worn fabric of the old armchair creaking slightly under his weight.

Bending down, he swept the dirt into a small pile with his fingers. Leaning over his knees, he scooped the dirt into his hands and carefully poured it into his boot, giving it a little shake to settle the dust.

He looked up, hoping for some sign of approval from Esther, but instead found her eyebrows raised, her lips curled in playful confusion and disbelief.

Settling back into his chair with a satisfied grin, Ian leaned comfortably against the backrest, stretching out his legs as if his work was done. He winked at her, as if to say his odd method was the best he could offer.

Distracted by his antics, Esther tugged a little too hard on Rebecca's hair, making the girl wince.

"Ouch, yer pullin'," Rebecca complained, surprise coloring her voice.

"I'm so sorry," Esther said quickly, leaning down to plant a kiss on Rebecca's forehead. The girl's annoyance faded into a forgiving smile.

"Hope I ain't just puttin' knots in it," Esther said, trying to mask the uncertainty she felt about her braiding skills.

"That's okay if ya do," Rebecca responded with a shrug. "Benji is real good at undoin' them. He fixed my shoes this mornin'."

As she continued her work, Benjamin grabbed a book from a nearby shelf and brought it over to his father, plopping down on the floor with an expectant look.

"Just a little," Benjamin pleaded, his eyes flicking between his father and Esther.

"Ya should hear Pa read. It's like listenin' to the radio, and Swiss Family Robinson is our favorite."

The excitement in his eyes had been too much for Ian to resist. And he wanted the magic of the evening to continue a while longer.

"Just a few chapters," Ian said, giving in.

Truth be told, Esther was more than a little curious. The children had mentioned it several times, always bringing it up when they tried to convince her to help build a treehouse.

Throwing another log on the fire, Ian leaned toward the light and began reading. His voice was smooth, never faltering on the words. His tone shifted depending on which character spoke, much to the children's delight. Esther was captivated. This was way better than the Bible, she thought, wondering if God could take a few lessons from the fella that wrote it.

The evening passed quickly, and the fire had burned down to glowing embers, casting a dim, warm light that made the room feel snug. Rebecca, now fast asleep in Esther's arms, breathed steadily, nestled against her chest.

Ian, noticing the children had dozed off, gently closed the book and placed it on a small side table, the soft thud barely breaking the quiet. His voice had softened, low and soothing, so as not to wake them.

Curled up on the floor at his father's feet, Benjamin clutched a rabbit's foot tightly in his hand.

With a gentle smile, Ian bent down, carefully lifting his son from the floor. The boy stirred just slightly, mumbling something about wanting to ride a zebra.

"We'll find you one tomorrow," Ian whispered, stifling a laugh as he shifted Benjamin's weight in his arms. He glanced over at Esther, who was biting her lip, trying to suppress the giggle rising in her chest. Ian joined in, unable to hold back as he carried his son toward his bedroom.

After tucking the boy in, he returned. Still holding Rebecca, Esther adjusted the sleeping girl in her arms as Rebecca let out a loud, snort-like sound.

Ian playfully rolled his eyes and whispered, "She's a lot like me."

Picking up his small daughter, he cradled her against his chest as she made a tiny whimper.

"Shh… It's all right, little Firefly," he said with a tender voice as he carried her off to bed.

Esther watched him, her heart swelling at the care he took with his children. It was one of the first things she had noticed about him. She couldn't imagine Ian ever raising a belt or stick like Pawdad and Gran had. Even when Benjamin tested his patience, as he often did, Ian always responded with thoughtful control.

Just as Clarissa had said more than once, he really was the best man she knew—and now, Esther realized, the best man she knew, as well.

There was no denying how utterly attractive Ian looked tonight—though he hardly needed any more help in that regard. Everything about him drew her in. His voice, so rich and smooth, utterly mesmerized her. It wasn't just the words, but the way he'd glance up over the book, watching to see if she was listening. It made her heart race, warming her from the inside out.

But a voice crept into her mind, urging caution, reminding her of his words earlier that day about feeling regret—words she hadn't wanted to hear.

Wanting to avoid an uncomfortable conversation Ian might have been holding back on, Esther thought it best to prepare to leave.

Quietly, she made her way to the door, her hand resting on the handle as she glanced over her shoulder. She wanted to capture the memory of the night, holding it in her mind.

Ian returned to find her there.

"Well, ya have yerself a nice night," she said, unsure what else to say.

Swallowing hard, he quickly moved to where she stood, stopping just a few feet away.

"You're leaving?" he asked, squinting slightly, a hint of disappointment in his voice.

She paused, her hand still on the door.

"Better hurry up," she teased with a playful smile. "'Twas real hard sneakin' in last night. Aunt Clarissa sleeps mighty light."

Ian's lips curved into a smile, his expression inviting as he stared directly into her eyes. Not saying a word, he wavered, leaning in as though he didn't want her to leave.

Filling the silence, she offered, "I liked yer readin'."

She watched as he delighted in her compliment, his smile deepening.

"It's a real nice story and all," she added.

Encouraged, Ian took a step closer.

"I can read you more, if you like," he said, his chest heaving uncontrollably.

Esther's hand stayed stuck to the door handle, letting it rattle under her grip.

"I don't know," she said, her eyes narrowing as she searched his face for answers.

What was he really asking?

Did he want to read, or was he imagining them writing their own kind of story?

That moment of hesitation was all Ian needed to see, prompting him to push in closer, his shadow nearly brushing hers.

Slowly, he reached around her and pulled the door from her grasp, closing it behind her. His breath was warm against her hair and neck as he leaned in, lingering just long enough to breathe in her scent. He paused, waiting for her to respond, his closeness carrying an unspoken request.

Esther's body gave a slight shudder, her breath hitching.

Ian reached out and touched her arm, his fingers trailing along her skin. He exhaled, his energy shifting—this felt like the man from the night before, but different.

More controlled. More deliberate.

"I don't want you to leave," he whispered, his voice deep and earnest. "I don't want to be alone."

She frowned slightly, testing his words, uncertain of her own instincts.

"Ya not alone—ya got yer kids, Aunt Clarissa," she said.

"Esther—you know that's not what I mean," he replied, pulling back to meet her eyes. His tone was gentle yet firm, ensuring she understood.

She smiled, a teasing expression playing on her lips—the one she wore when she already knew the answer.

God, he loved it when she did that.

He let out a small, playful grunt in response.

Feeling more confident, he brushed her hair off her shoulder, revealing the pale skin of her neck. He leaned down, inhaling her scent again, his voice low and thick with longing.

"You smell nice… so nice," he said.

The words sent a shiver down Esther's spine as Ian's lips hovered near her ear.

"I want to kiss you again," he murmured softly with persuasion. "I want to kiss you like last night… but I want to remember it better."

Esther's mind raced, trying to reconcile his earlier words with this moment and what was moving through her body.

"Gonna be mad at me again? Not talkin' to me tomorrow?" she asked, her voice tinged with uncertainty.

He chuckled, the sound warm and reassuring as he gently turned her to face him.

"Ah, I can be a stubborn ass sometimes," he admitted, his eyes twinkling with sincerity. "You might have to get used to that… but I usually come to my senses, eventually."

Esther couldn't help but smile at his words, her worry easing at the honesty in his eyes.

He took that as his cue, leaning down to kiss her. The kiss was delicate, like a feather falling through still air. He had just wanted to feel the shape of her lips against his, a soft, fleeting connection. When he pulled back, she gave him a small sigh—one that only deepened his desire.

He studied her mouth—the slight curl at the corners, the fullness of her upper lip, naturally dark pink and perfectly placed on her face.

It captivated him. So, he kissed her again, and this time, the kiss grew more fervent, filled with passion and something more magical.

Without the whiskey dulling his senses, as it had the night before, everything felt sharper, more vivid.

It felt real. Sincere. Far sweeter.

This was the side of himself he wanted to show her—the softer part, the part that wasn't just a brute.

He'd spent the day in his head, forming a plan to slow things down, to be careful, maybe even keep some distance.

But standing there with her, that plan vanished like smoke the instant he looked into her ember-lit eyes. Ian knew it wasn't only their attraction driving this forward—it was a powerful current, like the ocean, with their connection surging beyond anything they could control.

Now, in this moment, he no longer wanted to pace it. He didn't just want to kiss her—he wanted to give in to her plea from the night before—to truly see her.

Esther had let him kiss her. How could she not?

The way he had been standoffish earlier that day had run sharp warning bells, which she'd tried to ignore.

But here he was—so handsome, his accent seducing her with every word, as if he meant to do it. In her heart, she knew that all Ian had to do was ask, and she would stay.

She looked up into his eyes, trying to read him like one of the books he understood so easily, but Ian wasn't so simple.

He smiled, seeing her hesitation, then leaned in to kiss the tip of her nose—a gesture that felt tender, enduring.

There was a strange pleading, maybe yearning, in his face, and though he had been tired earlier, he seemed fully awake, completely present.

Cupping her face gently with his hands, he leaned in slowly again to kiss her. But just before their lips met, he softly whispered, "Esther, you know we're going to have to try to be quiet."

Chapter 32: Keys

A single bulb hung overhead, its metal casing dulled and worn. It flickered sporadically, casting faint shadows that darted across the dingy walls of the small, weathered police station. On the wall, a clock ticked with a steady rhythm, a reminder of time slowly slipping away.

Sheriff Ronell sat at a large, cluttered metal desk, shifting in a chair that seemed too snug for his body. The springs groaned in protest as he moved, his fingers absentmindedly drumming on Esther's hymn book.

Every so often, he'd thumb through a few pages, pausing to look at the drawings before plopping the hymnal down again. His mind was preoccupied, thoughts churning beneath his heavy brow.

Pulling his attention away, he heard the mumble of chatter.

He looked out of a small window, narrowing his eyes at the two figures walking along the sidewalk. Clearly headed in his direction, there was a sense of urgency in their stride.

Ralph and Margie Mae Paulson. Familiar faces in Larkin and pillars of the community. Known for their polite and cheerful expressions, tonight their faces appeared tense and drawn tight. The sheriff shifted uncomfortably in his seat, preparing for a difficult conversation, knowing they'd been fond of their pastor. And it didn't help that the sheriff was still reeling from what he'd seen at the man's home, either.

The station's front door creaked open, its hinges protesting with age, as a gust of warm air rushed inside, stirring the papers on his desk.

Ralph stepped in first, his shoes thudding on the floor, followed by Margie Mae's quieter steps. Ralph bent down to straighten the scattered papers with an apologetic expression, his eyes meeting Ronell's in a brief, awkward exchange.

"Sheriff Ronell," Margie Mae greeted him, her voice insistent, "we've come to talk."

Unfazed, the sheriff forced a smile, though it was little more than a polite gesture.

"Well, hello, Ralph, Margie Mae," he said. "What can I do fer ya?"

Margie Mae exchanged a concerned glance with her husband, her eyes seeking reassurance before she spoke. Ralph gave a slight nod, signaling her to go ahead.

"I heard some mighty disturbing news yesterday," Margie Mae began, her voice a little shaky. "Couldn't sleep a wink last night."

Sheriff Ronell pushed his chair back, his brow furrowing. He knew where this conversation was headed.

"Does this have anything to do with Preacher Clive?" he asked.

Margie Mae took a deep breath, pausing briefly before she went on.

"Sheriff, Esther Primm is a real good friend of mine."

She stopped, her eyes searching his face, looking for reassurance.

"And I need to know the truth," she said. "I'm so fearful for her safety. Last time I saw her, she was drivin' home with Clive… and then they got in that awful wreck."

Her voice wavered slightly.

"What ya suppose happened to her?"

Sheriff Ronell stood up, his boots scuffing the floor as he walked over to Margie Mae. His expression softened as he placed a reassuring hand on her shoulder.

"Ya say Esther was in Clive's car that night? Ya certain?" he asked.

"Yes," Margie Mae confirmed, her voice firm despite the quiver in her lip. "We searched up and down Miller Highway for a good part of yesterday, but she never came home, and no one's seen her 'round."

The sheriff nodded.

"Well… Don't ya worry—she went up to the Old Reed place."

Ralph, who had been silent until now, exchanged a look with his wife—one that spoke volumes.

"I knew it," Ralph said, his tone carrying a note of self-satisfaction. "Told Margie Mae that's where she must be. See, it's all alright, honey."

"Thank heavens," Margie Mae said, as her face began to relax. "I thought maybe the crash had finished her off, and no one was talkin' 'bout it."

Ralph, not wanting to take up more of the lawman's time, tipped his hat.

"Thank ya kindly, Sheriff, for the good news."

But Sheriff Ronell wasn't done. A nagging suspicion was growing that wouldn't let him rest.

He cleared his throat, his voice taking on a more serious tone.

"Ralph, I was just wonderin'. What were ya doin' that night with Preacher Clive and his cousin? A social visit?"

The question hung in the air uncomfortably.

Margie Mae's eyes darted to her husband, confused. Ralph, too, seemed momentarily taken aback.

"Oh, we all went to see a show in Jasper," Margie Mae interjected.

"Is that right?" The sheriff's tone was casual, but his eyes remained sharp, scrutinizing every nuance of their response.

"Yes, sir, and a very good one indeed," Margie Mae confirmed. A genuine smile touched her lips.

"Anything odd happen that night?" Sheriff Ronell pressed. "Make any strange stops with Clive goin' to and from Jasper?"

Margie Mae hesitated, her eyes flickering to her husband as if seeking guidance. Ralph scratched his head, thinking back to that night.

"Well, no," Ralph began slowly. "Clive picked us up at our house. We drove straight there, watched the film, and drove straight back…." He trailed off, his brow furrowing as if something had just occurred to him. "Well, of course, there was a slight scuffle between Clive and that German man that lives up at the Reed place. What's his name?"

Margie Mae's breath caught in her throat, her voice a whisper. "Ya mean Ian Huggler?"

The sheriff's eyes narrowed, his mind racing as he connected the dots.

"Ya say Clive and he got into an altercation? What ya suppose it was about?"

Ralph chuckled, though the sound was hollow, lacking any genuine humor.

"Nothin' serious. Clive just got protective of his cousin, thought maybe Mr. Huggler had some… bad intentions toward her, I suppose."

Margie Mae glanced at the sheriff, her expression conflicted. She hesitated, wringing her hands as she chose her words carefully.

"I really think Clive overreacted, Sheriff."

Her voice cracked, and she swallowed hard before continuing.

"To tell ya the truth, I know he was our preacher and all, but… sometimes, it felt like he wanted more from Esther than just cousinly affection, if ya know what I mean."

She looked down, her face flushed.

"Margie Mae!" Ralph exclaimed, scandalized. "Ya don't know that. There you go spreading gossip."

Her eyes flashed with something akin to defiance.

"Ralph, you didn't see the look he gave me when I said Esther would have a line of suitors outside their door."

Her voice tightened as she recalled the moment.

"Looked like he'd kill every single last one of them," she added, her tone darkening.

"Matter of fact, he said he'd kill Mr. Huggler if he came near his property... or his cousin."

Ralph shook his head, dismissing the notion.

"He was protectin' her," he said firmly, "as any Southern gentleman would do. Simple misunderstandin' is all."

But Sheriff Ronell knew better. He watched the exchange, his mind piecing together the fragments of what he had just heard. Something didn't sit right with him.

He decided to end the conversation, unwilling to let any more awkward truths surface.

"Well, thank ya," the sheriff said, ushering the couple towards the door. "This discussion has been mighty informative."

"It has?" Margie Mae asked, her eyes lifted in confusion.

"Yes, indeed," Sheriff Ronell replied, a thoughtful expression on his face. "Margie Mae, Ralph, ya suppose Esther could stay with ya for a while? Need a good, safe place fer her."

Margie Mae looked at her husband, who hesitated before giving a reluctant nod.

"Of course," she said. "We'll go and pick her up right now."

But the sheriff had other plans. He placed a firm hand on Ralph's shoulder, stopping him in his tracks.

"No worry, I'm heading up there this evening. Bring her down myself. Thank ya again."

Ralph and Margie Mae exchanged one last look before nodding and leaving the station. The door creaked shut behind them, leaving Sheriff Ronell alone with his thoughts.

He was just about to pick up his jacket from the back of the chair when the door swung open again.

Frank, his deputy, stood in the doorway, glancing down the sidewalk with a grin. Chuckling to himself, he finally closed the door.

"Sheriff," Frank greeted, tipping his hat, clearly amused by something.

"Frank," Sheriff Ronell replied, his thoughts still elsewhere.

"Just passed Margie Mae outside," Frank said with a laugh. "You might need to arrest her for giving Ralph a hard time—she looked mighty cross with him."

The sheriff paused for a moment, then nodded.

"Well, the Paulsons just told me Esther Primm was for certain with Clive out on Miller Highway that night."

Frank's eyebrows shot up in surprise at the sheriff's words.

"That so?"

Sheriff Ronell rubbed his temples, a deep frown settling on his face.

"Frank, we'll talk about it in the mornin'. Sun's settin', and I'm sure my wife is already havin' a fit I ain't home yet. Gotta good drive ahead of me."

"Ya thinkin' she done it, Marty?" Frank asked, his tone laced with curiosity.

Sheriff Ronell didn't respond, letting out a long, weary sigh. Frank knew that sound all too well.

They'd hunted tadpoles and coons together as kids, spent years side by side. He had watched his old friend excel where he fell short, earning the coveted sheriff's job over a decade ago, probably because Marty was the better lawman. That sigh always meant one thing—trouble was brewing.

While Sheriff Ronell was a by-the-books kind of guy, he didn't relish locking people up, especially for minor offenses. He often let things slide, preferring peace over conflict.

And though Frank wasn't entirely sure what the sheriff had planned, it was painfully obvious he wasn't being invited along for the drive to the old estate. The exclusion stung more than he cared to admit.

The sheriff took a moment to rally himself, gathering his thoughts before striding toward the door. Just as his hand reached for the knob, he stopped short. His gaze drifted back to the desk, settling on Esther's book. He had almost forgotten it, but something told him he couldn't leave it behind.

After a second, he turned, picked it up, and tucked it under his arm before heading out.

Pausing in the open door, he turned to Frank.

"Hey, Frank, you ever find those keys?"

Frank shook his head. "No."

"Could ya?" The Sheriff's tone carried an edge of irritation. He didn't wait for an answer, already turning back toward the door.

Frank stood there, hands on his hips, his frustration palpable. He watched silently as Sheriff Ronell disappeared into the night.

Through the window, he saw the sheriff's car pull away, its headlights cutting through the darkness. His eyes tightened as the taillights faded into the distance.

What was Marty Ronell up to, and why did he need the keys to the jail cell?

Chapter 33: Turning Pages

Nocturne had settled over the cottage, a blanket of shadow cloaking its fieldstone walls and cedar shake roof. The moon cast silken strands of light through the windows, illuminating ribbons that weaved softly through the darkness.

Inside, Ian led Esther to his bedroom. Taking a deep breath, he quietly shut the door behind him, sliding a chair under the handle to prevent any small intrusions.

He mapped out his intentions, reminding himself to take it slow and not let the moment rush by as it had the night before. He was determined to control it, not wanting it to end in mere minutes, as skipped chapters often miss the beauty of each page—hoping to turn the last page of the book together.

But it wasn't easy. The moment he had her in the room, standing there, knowing what was about to unfold between them, anticipation surged through him—raw and achingly beautiful, overwhelming.

She was like something out of a myth, a creature so unreal that even the best poets couldn't have fully captured her essence.

His thoughts drifted back to earlier in the day, when she had walked out to try to talk to him. Her allure was enigmatic, striking him in a way that left him distracted for hours. For a man like him, not easily drawn from his work, that feeling was rare.

He remembered how her presence had lingered in his mind, even through the thick of his foul mood. His eyes had followed her as she walked away, watching the sway of her hips—a siren's call—something primal stirring in him, something undeniable.

Any man with an ounce of sense would've chased after her.

But he'd restrained himself, determined to prove he could control those thoughts. Yet every time he got lost in his work, she found her way back to him—possessing him.

Ian felt himself falling, wrapped up in her. It wasn't a new feeling, though. It had been there since last summer, but then, he had known how to bury it. He had kept it underground—deep in the earth, clinging to rocks and soil, hiding from daylight.

Drawn to the sun now, letting go of the comfort of the cold ground, he yearned to truly be alive once more. Not satisfied with merely existing, waiting for life to pass.

No more wasted precious time.

If this broke him, it didn't matter—better to feel pain than to feel nothing at all.

Ian had battled himself as well as the old oak.

The root, like an enemy that wouldn't quit, had taken all his strength to wrest from the earth. When he finally pulled it free, there was no satisfaction in the act—only exhaustion. It was as if the thing had been fighting to live, clinging to the soil like it had a soul of its own. And strangely, he had felt guilty, offering it a quiet apology as he severed the last stubborn taproot.

In the stillness of his bedroom, Ian studied Esther's face, looking at the slight upturn of her nose, her prominent eyes—her most striking feature.

Despite being in her twenties, she carried a youthful appearance, easily passing for sixteen. When Clarissa had told him last year, a month or so after Esther had arrived, that she was older than he thought, it had changed the way he looked at her. Perhaps that had been the beginning of his fascination, as he would have never entertained any thought of a girl that young.

He even clarified it with Clarissa the next day, making sure he hadn't heard wrong. The older woman had looked at him with a twinkle in her eyes. "Yes, Ian, she's not too young," she had said, to which he replied that he had no idea what she was talking about.

Abram had also been suspicious when Ian brought up her age on more than one occasion, asking why he felt the need to mention it so often.

Ian smiled, now realizing they'd both seen through him, noticing what he couldn't. But that was okay—he could admit when he was wrong.

And how wrong he'd been, he thought to himself, as Esther's light sigh pulled him back to the moment.

Feeling enchanted, he met her open mouth, their lips moving slowly against each other as the now-familiar taste of her warmed his taste buds.

The idea that he could deny himself this ever again seemed gone from him for good. And he didn't want to think about how he'd have to send her home that night—worried that he couldn't, as he let his hand slide up to cradle the back of her neck. Softly, he held her hair in his fingers as he drew her into him.

His body instinctively recognized hers, responding to the call of her soul, whispering his name with a silent voice only the quietest of lovers could hear. In that moment, his pulse quickened, matching the steady rhythm of her breath against his chest.

He didn't want to be anywhere else or with anyone else. He just wanted to be with this bewitching girl, to pull her into the warmth of his bed, feel the softness of her skin pressed against him, and lose himself in the intimacy they were creating together.

The sponge bath in the barn had been a good idea, Ian thought, as Esther leaned up to kiss his tan neck and chest. He'd even grabbed cologne from under the seat in his truck, not wanting to smell bad after a long day of sweat.

Esther noticed it, leaning up with a suspicious squint in her eyes.

"Ian… you smell real nice."

"You like it?" he asked, already knowing the answer.

"Yeah, makes me want to eat ya up," she said with a wide smile.

It made him laugh as he wondered if she knew her words had more than one meaning. He intentionally took it the wrong way—wanting to.

"That right?" he said as he tugged her close to him again.

He loved that she sometimes said things that were a little off, perhaps not quite fit for polite company, her Southern drawl unmistakably pronounced. He recalled how she had teased him last year, often using old colloquial terms with hidden meanings.

Once, while he was hand-tilling a long row in the garden, having taken his shirt off, hot from the heat, she called out from another row, "Looks like ya just pitchin' a woo, Ian. Best put your back into it—don't half plow it."

It had taken him a minute to figure out what she actually meant, and Esther just smiled back with a smirk when he did. Even Mitsy, who was also helping, had looked shocked but laughed along with him.

No, Ian wouldn't change a thing about her, he thought to himself. Her untamed nature was part of her charm—it separated her from the herd.

But now, with her standing so near, he could no longer resist the need to be with her completely.

No barriers.

Nothing between them.

He hungered to feel the full sensation of their bodies—two lovers, utterly exposed to one another, skin to skin.

He began undressing, his fingers working on the buttons on his shirt as he watched her, eager to see if she liked what she saw. And she did.

Her eyes stayed fixed on him, her lips parting slightly as each piece of clothing fell away.

When he finally bared himself completely, he saw her eyes trace over him slowly. A hint of blush warmed her cheeks, and her mouth lifted in a subtle, almost tentative smile. Yet he noticed the way her gaze dipped, a flash of shyness at the sight of his complete freedom—a moment that only deepened his desire to close the space between them.

Ian had always been confident about his body, and it wasn't lost on Esther. She had never felt that way about Clive—despising his very physical appearance—turning her stomach.

So, seeing Ian like this—healthy, well-built, completely exposed—was something she wasn't quite prepared for.

Light filtered into the room, casting shadows over the defined lines of his muscles, highlighting his strength in every ripple. She took in the sight of him—raw, uncovered, and vulnerable—leaving her breathless. And what gripped her wasn't fear or discomfort, but the overwhelming effect of his presence.

She couldn't deny how beautiful he was—his physique reminded her of the fine European sculptures she had once seen in one of his books, elegant and powerful.

Esther felt she needed to join him in his liberation—not quite matching his boldness, but making an effort.

She leaned over and slipped off her shoes, then lifted her skirt just high enough to reach the clips of her nylon stockings. Slowly, she rolled each one down, careful not to damage the delicate fabric. She could feel Ian's eyes tracing the length of her legs as she carefully placed each foot on the edge of the bed.

Briefly, she glanced up and smiled, still aware of him watching her every move. Gathering courage, she shimmied her panties down quickly, not trying to make more of it than it was, though he didn't seem to mind her haste. She straightened up, signaling that she was finished—the show was over.

Ian sensed her hesitation to shed her clothes fully, so he beckoned her to the bed instead, his voice gentle and encouraging.

"Come over here," he said.

He pulled himself farther back into the bed, reclining against the pillows with an inviting smile. Unsure if she understood what he was suggesting, he teased with a playful, seductive grin.

"Ride me, kind of like you ride a horse."

Esther laughed instantly, the sound lightening the intensity between them for a moment. The idea of comparing him to a horse seemed absurdly funny to her.

"I'm sorry, I've just never ridden a horse like this before."

"I'll try not to buck you off," he said, smiling as he guided her closer.

She straddled him, her knees pressing into the soft mattress, sinking slightly into the bed.

Their lips met in a deep, consuming kiss, her breath warm against his mouth. Holding her face in his hands, he murmured, "Darling, don't you want to sit on me all the way?"

She had never done it this way before—and being on top was something she had outright refused to do. Why would she have volunteered such a thing? After she had finally submitted to Clive, her role had always been passive, letting him use her without ever truly engaging. And though she understood the basic mechanics, she'd never been an active participant.

This felt drastically different, liberating.

Ian pulled her head closer and whispered in her ear, "Scoot back a little, and I'll help you."

She shyly smiled as she moved back.

"That's a bit too far," he said, nudging her closer into position.

"I don't know how to do it like this, Ian," she admitted.

"That's okay, you'll figure it out," he said as he lifted her hips with his hands, a playful yet determined grin on his face.

And she did, as their bodies quickly aligned—a bridge made of desire, skin against skin.

"See… just like riding a horse," he murmured, urging her down to meet his open mouth, capturing her in a deep, intoxicating kiss. His tongue swam with the same fervor as his hardened length pulsing within her.

Ian could see the pleasure etched across her face—her features softening, then tightening as desire overtook her.

As he moved beneath her, her eyes fluttered closed, then squeezed tightly shut, as if trying to absorb every bit of sensation.

Her teeth sank into her lower lip as her fingers pressed into his chest, the tips digging into his skin as the rhythm of their bodies gradually synchronized, like two tides meeting.

He could feel the sensation starting to claim her when an unconscious moan escaped.

The sound echoed in the room, startling him enough to bring a finger to her mouth and gently cover her lips to muffle the intensity.

She responded with a flash, her eyes opening wide as she playfully nipped at his finger—a seductive mischief on her lips, like she was punishing him for interrupting her.

It almost broke him, sending him past the threshold he was trying so hard to control.

Ian was teetering on the edge—every nerve heightened.

Desperate, he stopped her movement, gripping her hips gently to keep the pressure from overwhelming him.

"Give me just a second," he said in a strained voice as he took a deep, steadying breath, his chest rising and falling beneath her.

His muscles tensed, his fingers momentarily pressing into her skin before loosening.

Esther was perplexed, not understanding the delicate balance he was trying to maintain.

A slight line formed between her brows as she leaned down to kiss him again, her lips brushing against the corner of his mouth.

"Ya alright?" she asked softly, her hand resting on his chest, feeling his heart pounding beneath her palm.

"No, Esther, don't," he pleaded with a smile, his eyes squeezed shut as he worked through deep, deliberate breaths.

"I don't think I can even look at your face right now," he mumbled.

She paused, still feeling confused. "Ya don't like my face?" she asked.

"Oh, I do," he said, his voice thick with restraint.

"I like all of you a little too much right now," he added as his hand absently drifted along her arm, his touch slow, as if he was detached from the moment.

She remained still, straddling him, as the tension in his body slowly ebbed away while he gathered his composure.

She watched him, noticing how his eyes fluttered open only after he seemed to steady his breathing.

"Okay…," he said after what felt like an eternity, his voice calmer. "I think I'm good now."

"Are ya sure? Ya actin' kind of funny," she said, half-teasing, half-serious.

"I'll have to explain it to you later," he promised, his hands moving to rest on her bare thighs.

Ian realized that, despite what Clive had done to her, much of this seemed unfamiliar—a realization that struck him deeply. He wanted to tread carefully, mindful of what she might have endured.

The thought that no kindness or gentleness had been shown to her during those vile acts tore at him, making it all the more important to offer her the choice she hadn't been given before. He wanted her to feel safe, to know that this was as much her decision as his.

And with that, Ian refused to let Clive's shadow linger any longer, casting him out, determined to keep this moment pure— something that existed only for the two of them.

With a gentle touch, he cupped her cheek, savoring the beauty of her skin beneath his fingertips. He gazed softly at her, holding the stare as long as she would allow him. She had asked him to see her, so he would do that—his eyes reaching for hers, as far as he could go, beyond this time and space.

But Esther looked away, as if it was almost too much.

Undeterred, his hand drifted to her neck, then down, caressing her shoulders, slowly working his way to her back. At first, she appeared comfortable, but her expression shifted as his hand reached the curve of her spine, coiling away.

It was apparent she didn't want him touching her there, and he believed he understood why—her vulnerability clear. So, he withdrew, moving back to her face as he tenderly smiled at her.

"Esther… Do you know how incredibly beautiful you are?" he said. "I just want to stare at you. I can't help myself."

Her smile reappeared, her light returning, as if he had called her back to him. She leaned into him, and he felt the warmth of her body reigniting the intimacy.

He drew her down to his lips, kissing her slowly, trying to strengthen that connection. His tongue danced in her mouth, and just as the previous night, she caught the rhythm easily.

Every breath, every movement felt lit with electricity, but Ian kept reminding himself to stay grounded, not to let the overwhelming desire pull him too fast.

This was too important. He needed it to be done with care, offering her the kind of experience her body yearned for—maybe even more than she had expected. He hoped the pleasure would rewrite the painful chapters etched into her memory.

Though he knew it was impossible to erase everything, he wanted to give her a new language, a symbolic vocabulary of sensation and meaning, to transcribe this moment into something different, something healing.

Something written in their shared names.

His strong hands guided her movements with a careful cadence, teaching her the pace with a gentleness that contrasted with the intensity of his desire.

Bathed in a soft, ethereal glow from the faint light filtering through the windows, their bodies raw and beautiful in their union.

Esther felt an urge to unleash her hair, as if the updo had been holding her back. Slowly, she pulled the pins free, each one a deliberate tease under Ian's unwavering gaze. His eyes stayed locked on her, and she savored it, drawing out the moment as her dark hair cascaded down her shoulders in soft waves, a gesture of surrender.

Beneath her, she felt his body shudder, his breath catching as he struggled to control the rising intensity. She enjoyed having his complete and undivided attention.

Pulling her down to him, he leaned into her ear, his voice low and teasing as he murmured, "You're trying to make this hard on me, aren't you?" His hot breath lingered, sending a shiver through her.

As she sat up, he brushed away a loose lock of her hair from her mouth as he said, "Aw… I like it when your hair's down. Looks wild, like when I first saw you."

Her lips curled into a teasing smile as she gathered her hair up, feigning to put it back into place.

"Really? Thought you'd like it all done up," she said.

But Ian wasn't having it as he reached up, pulling her hands away, letting her hair fall once more.

With an urgency, he pulled her down to him, capturing her in a long, breathless kiss—ravenous and consuming. As their lips parted, he whispered low in her ear, his hot breath moving down her neck.

"Move on me."

Esther's movements were slow and artistically deliberate, her body finding its current against him as his lower torso lifted to reach her, meet her. Dancing in perfection.

As their bodies rocked together, his hands slid up her sides, his fingertips grazing her clothed breasts. She moaned, offering no resistance.

Encouraged, his fingers worked to undo the remaining buttons of her dress. But just as he began to peel the fabric away, she placed her hands over his, stopping him.

"Don't you wanna take that off?" he asked, his voice a low rumble.

She glanced around, aware of the room's brightness, the way the moonlight seemed to lay them bare under its gaze.

"It's kinda light in here," she said, her voice tinged with vulnerability.

He moved swiftly, pulling her closer.

"I want to see you, Esther, all of you," he said, his voice heavy, laden with a tender lust.

But Esther couldn't shake the feeling of being exposed. She held the front of her dress together, her fingers curling protectively around the fabric.

"Do you want me to put a blanket over the window?" Ian offered.

"Could ya?" she asked, her voice small, almost shy.

Ian nodded and guided her off him with care, rising in his bare and tall form.

He took a blanket from the bed and started to hang it over the window, but as he did, something outside caught his attention.

He tensed, his eyes narrowing as he peered out into the night.

"I... think someone's coming up the road," he said, his concern noticeable. "I can see headlights."

Esther's heart skipped a beat. "Who is it?" she asked, joining him.

"I don't know," he replied, his tone cautious as he watched the vehicle approach, its lights cutting through the dark.

"Wait here," he said in a firm voice.

Hurrying, he pulled on a pair of pants and slipped into his boots, grabbing his shirt from a nearby chair. As he buttoned it up, he made his way to the front door.

"Whoever it is, they're comin' up the road fast," she said as she leaned out from the doorway of his room.

Ian gave her one last look before heading out to investigate.

"I'll be back," he promised, though the angst in his voice did little to reassure her.

Outside, the night air was crisp, infused with the scent of pine and moss coming from the Blue Hollows, blending with the faint trace of smoke. Above, the sky was a wide, star-studded canopy.

The stillness of the night was disrupted as Sheriff Ronell's vehicle rumbled up the drive. The headlights cut through the darkness, momentarily illuminating the front of Ian's home and casting eerie shadows that stretched across the stones.

Then, as the engine died, the headlights blinked out, plunging the world back into moonlit dark, the silence intensifying as if the night itself were holding its breath.

Ian stepped forward, his footsteps barely audible on the gravel, as he moved to meet the sheriff.

"That you, Mr. Huggler?" Sheriff Ronell called out, his voice carrying a note of authority.

"Yes, sir," Ian responded, stepping closer. "What can I do for you?"

The sheriff didn't answer right away. Instead, his hand rested on the gun holstered at his hip, his eyes sharp as they swept over the area.

"Came up here lookin' for Esther Primm. Ya seen her?"

Ian's heart pounded in his chest. He knew the truth, but something inside him—a deep, instinctual need to protect her—compelled him to lie.

"No, sure haven't," he said, the words leaving his mouth with an edge.

Sheriff Ronell shook his head, disappointment palpable in his tone.

"Now both you and I know that just ain't true. Ya know Vic and Rusty were up here yesterday and saw her. No sense tryin' to hide her out. She ain't in trouble. Just wanna talk with her a bit."

Ian's resolve faltered as he glanced back at his house. The sheriff's gaze followed his, suspicion growing in his eyes.

"She in there?" Sheriff Ronell questioned, his tone leaving little room for denial.

Ian nodded, a tightness in his jaw betraying the calm he was trying to maintain.

His strides toward the house were deliberate, each step laced with unease. What did the sheriff truly want with her? He'd claimed she wasn't in trouble, but Ian couldn't fully trust that. He had to remain in control, not let his rising worry show.

With the sheriff close behind, Ian regretted not preparing Esther for this moment, thinking they had more time.

She emerged from the bedroom—her eyes still clouded with concern as she moved toward the main room just as the front door creaked open. She glanced up, her heart momentarily lifting at the sight of Ian, but her brief relief quickly vanished when she noticed Sheriff Ronell close behind him, his stern expression reigniting the tension.

Esther's hands fumbled with her dress buttons, realizing she hadn't done them up entirely. Her fingers were jittery as she tried to make herself presentable.

The sheriff's gaze settled on her in an instant, his displeasure unmistakable. The look on his face sent a shiver straight through her.

"Well… what do we have here?" he said.

Ian realized how compromising the situation must look, and tried to shift the sheriff's focus.

"He's here to ask you a few questions, that's all," Ian said in a steady voice.

But the sheriff wasn't easily distracted. His eyes shifted, narrowing as he turned his attention to Ian, his voice dropping to a low, accusatory tone.

"First, I gotta few questions fer you, Mr. Huggler. Like what the hell ya doin' here with this girl? Ya taking advantage of her?"

The accusation hung in the air like a dark cloud, thick and suffocating. The sheriff took a step closer to Ian, his posture aggressive.

"Ya think it's right, takin' advantage of her like this? You puttin' her in a difficult situation and all?" he continued.

Before Ian could respond, Esther inched forward, her voice brave despite the fear that raced through her entire body.

"He ain't difficultin' me none," she said.

The sheriff turned his gaze back to her, his expression softening only slightly.

"Girl, I fear ya were born without the good sense to judge that. You don't know when you've been done wrong."

Ian's jaw tightened.

"You don't know a thing about her, Sheriff," Ian said defensively.

The sheriff paused, reassessing the situation. The silence dragged on as the three of them stood locked in a standoff.

Esther wanted to speak, to explain, but the words were stuck in her throat.

Scanning the room, the sheriff's attention snapped to the old shotgun propped against the fireplace mantel.

"What other guns ya got besides that one?" Sheriff Ronell asked, his tone sharper now.

"That's the only one," Ian answered, steady but firm.

"You sure about that?" The sheriff pushed.

"Yes. That's it," Ian said as he exhaled through his nose, his expression tightening.

A beat passed before the sheriff leaned in.

"Alright, then. Suppose ya tell me how long this has been goin' on between you two?"

"Goin' on?" Ian echoed, brow furrowed.

"Good God, don't play dumb. I ain't blind. I saw enough 'fore I walked in. So how long ya been messin' around with her?"

Ian hesitated as frustration and anger welled up inside him. He hated having to say anything at all, but at that moment, he determined it would be best to protect Esther's reputation.

"Nothing happened between us," he said, the lie bitter on his tongue.

Sheriff Ronell sighed in disbelief.

"Everythin' comin' out yer mouth is a damn lie," the sheriff barked.

Ian could see that the lawman wasn't buying his story, but he decided not to respond further, choosing to let his statement stand as it was.

Sheriff Ronell, now growing upset, was clearly not convinced. One thing he couldn't stand was when folks thought him a fool. He had a talent for seeing through people's lies, and this was one of those times.

He reached into his pocket and pulled out a small book—Esther's hymn book.

Esther's eyes widened in recognition.

"That's mine!" she exclaimed as she reached for it.

"Hold on," Sheriff Ronell said, holding the book just out of her reach.

He turned through the pages, stopping on one that caught his attention. He turned the book around, revealing a detailed drawing of Ian's shirtless back, his profile captured with striking accuracy.

Ian's curiosity piqued as he shifted, angling himself better to see what the sheriff was displaying.

"Maybe, Mr. Huggler, you'd like to explain why she's got all these drawin's of ya then? It's filled with pages of ya, more than one without ya clothes on," the sheriff said, his voice dripping with insinuation.

Sheriff Ronell turned the page, revealing another drawn image—this one of Ian, his bare torso sketched with precision. The Sheriff's eyes narrowed as he looked from the drawing to Ian.

"Can't imagine why she'd be drawin' such things lest somethin' be goin' on," Sheriff Ronell added.

He shoved the book toward Ian, who turned through the pages, his eyes widening with each new image.

Esther, her face flushed with embarrassment, tried to reach out, snatch it, but he held it firm.

"That's mine. Give it here—it's mine," she demanded, her voice cracking.

Ian looked at her, his expression one of surprise and wonder.

"I've never seen these before," he admitted. "Is this from the lake last summer?"

He paused, turning another page, his voice gentle but filled with curiosity.

"Esther, you drew these?"

Finally, she pulled the book free from his hands, clutching it to her chest.

Ian's eyes softened as he looked at her, a newfound admiration shining through them.

"You are very talented. They… they are beautiful," he said softly.

It felt as though he had just glimpsed into a hidden chapter of her very soul—a book kept closed and guarded.

He realized now that perhaps she had quietly harbored feelings for him—feelings that had lingered far longer than he had ever imagined.

Sheriff Ronell, however, wasn't impressed.

"Sure surprised me too. All this time she's been keepin' her mouth shut but been makin' these pictures," he said.

Ian paused, a profound and moving realization dawning on him.

He glanced at the sheriff, sensing the misunderstanding and feeling compelled to clear it up.

"It's not what you think," Ian said slowly, his voice clear.

"It's her journal… she drew what she couldn't write."

He looked into Esther's eyes again, his gaze steady and reassuring.

"It's a journal, a beautiful journal," he added, letting her know that it was okay.

All Ian wanted to do was hold her, the vulnerability in her tearing at him.

He could see how exposed it had made her feel.

The sheriff, uncomfortable with the visual intimacy between them, quickly changed the subject. He wasn't easily distracted from the job at hand, and his tone turned cold and businesslike.

"Tell me somethin' else then—were you the one who brought her up here two nights ago?"

Ian nodded, his gaze never leaving Esther's—their eyes locked as he gave himself fully to her, accepting his fate.

"Yes, I did," he said.

"Ya pick her up on Miller Highway?" the sheriff pressed.

Ian nodded again, his attention fixed entirely on her, the warmth in his eyes holding her as he let his confession unfold.

"Get in another fight with Clive on his way home?" the sheriff continued, his voice growing sharper.

Esther's eyes pleaded with Ian to remain silent, but Ian couldn't bring himself to lie anymore—especially when he was looking into her beautiful, spellbinding face.

"Yes, I did," he admitted.

"Ya kill him?" the sheriff demanded, his voice cutting through the silence—a knife.

Esther drew a shaky breath—she couldn't bear it any longer. This wasn't how it was supposed to happen.

She couldn't let Ian take the blame.

Her feet felt heavy, but she forced herself into the sheriff's direct path, her voice breaking as she spoke.

"I did it… I did it," she said with boldness.

Her words sat there, stark and unyielding.

The force of her offering, her sacrifice, crashed over Ian, each wave more overwhelming than the last.

It drowned him in a profound realization, shaking his core.

He loved her.

He loved the girl from the hills… and had loved her for a long time.

And he would do it all in an instant again, just to free her.

The truth stirred deep within him, raw and unshakable, building with a quiet force.

It surged from his chest, strong and with direction, coursing through him until it reached his eyes.

There, the tears threatened, his eyes wet, revealing the depth of ultimate care and devotion he could no longer deny.

He couldn't say it aloud, not here, but the depth of his love and anguish was etched into every glance he gave her.

"No—she didn't." Ian's voice broke, strained as he turned sharply toward the sheriff. His eyes burned with an unshakable resolve.

"Don't you dare listen to her," he demanded.

The sheriff hesitated, almost taken aback, the muscles in his jaw flexing as he absorbed the tall German's words. The silence that followed was charged as Ian stood firm, his body charged.

Sheriff Ronell shifted his weight, his hand once again resting on his holster. He squinted, his patience wearing thin, the lack of straight answers grating on him.

"Why the hell don't you just tell me what really happened?" he snapped.

Not giving up, Esther spoke with a fierce resolve, rushing her words as her emotions dictated the speed.

"I made Clive crash the car," she insisted. "He hit his head real hard, and I…"

Unwilling to let his woman battle for him, Ian's posture stiffened. He wouldn't have let her do it before, and he sure as hell refused to now.

"She ran," he interrupted, his voice laced with an aggressive growl. "She had every right to. She was afraid of him, and she should have been." His protectiveness was palpable—he wouldn't let anyone touch her.

"I did what I had to do," Ian added—words he couldn't take back, words that rang out with truth.

The sheriff gave a somber nod, a reflection of understanding in his eyes.

Ian's confession was what he had been after.

For a brief moment, a sad expression crossed the lawman's face, knowing full well what had to come next.

This was the part of the job Sheriff Ronell hated—the moment where justice had to be served, even when the lines of right and wrong were so blurred. Ian had killed Clive, and though Clive may have deserved it, the law was the law.

The sheriff braced himself, his body tensing as he anticipated resistance. With practiced ease, he flipped the safety snap on his gun holster up, wanting quick access.

"I'm gonna have to take ya in now," he said to Ian, his tone resigned.

"Ya might want to talk to a lawyer 'fore ya tell me anythin' more," Sheriff Ronell added, almost sounding helpful, despite wanting a full confession.

Esther's heart shattered at the sheriff's words as a wave of panic surged through her. Her voice trembled as she rushed forward, pleading.

"Please don't, oh please don't," she begged, her eyes wide with fear. "It's my fault, I made him crash the car—I did it, not Ian."

But despite being moved by her impassioned plea, the sheriff pulled out his handcuffs, his voice firm but not unkind.

"I ain't sayin' Preacher Clive ain't got what he deserved, but that's somethin' the courts gotta figure out."

Ian smiled at her, a quiet attempt to prepare her for the worst, before turning to Sheriff Ronell.

"Do you think they'll really give me a fair shake?" he said. "I'm a German man in a country that has every reason to hate Germany. I think you understand what I'm talking about."

They both knew there was a prejudice that would follow him into the courtroom, casting a long shadow over the jury's judgment.

"Turn around," the sheriff ordered, not addressing his question.

Ian didn't resist, allowing the cold metal of the handcuffs to bite into his wrists. Despite the worry growing inside him, he kept it hidden, masking it to protect Esther.

But she could feel it—her body trembling, a reflection of the unspoken fear they shared.

"Please, take care of Rebecca and Benjamin," Ian pleaded, the sincerity in his voice unmistakable.

She nodded, tears streaming down her face.

"Like they're my own," she whispered.

He smiled softly, taking in her beauty.

Sheriff Ronell, however, had other plans.

"Oh, she's goin' with us, got her a place down with that good Mrs. Paulson," he said.

Esther wasn't having it. Her eyes flashed with a resolve—hard as stone. Her voice carried the strength of someone who had endured too much to back down now.

"I am stayin' here," she declared.

She met the sheriff's gaze head-on, her chin lifted defiantly, making it clear that nothing—and no one—was going to make her leave.

The sheriff, slightly surprised by her proclamation, sighed.

"Oh—come on now... don't make this harder than it has to be. You'll be alright down there," he said, working to persuade her.

But this was a fight she was clearly prepared for—her fortitude apparent in her posture.

"I ain't bein' pushed around no more. I'm stayin' right here, lookin' after these young'uns," she said.

The sheriff, realizing he couldn't change her mind and not wanting to agitate what seemed to be a peaceful surrender, gave a resigned nod.

"Alright then, ya stay here," he said.

"Go tell Clarissa what's going on and where I am," Ian instructed Esther with a plea.

Her eyes brimmed with tears as she nodded.

"Don't worry... I'll watch 'em good," she said, wanting him to know he could count on her.

"I know, I know you will," Ian said, his heart aching as the sheriff led him out the front door.

Esther followed behind them, the cold biting at her bare feet as she walked. Her breath hitched as she watched the sheriff guide Ian toward the back of the police cruiser.

Desperately trying to hold herself together, she kept her head high, but the tremor running through her body betrayed the turmoil wild within.

When the sheriff and Ian reached the car, Esther could no longer hold back. In a burst of emotion, she ran up to Ian, gripping at his shirt as she pressed her lips hard to his.

The sheriff, momentarily caught off guard by her public display of affection, paused, turning his head to give them a moment of privacy.

When their lips parted, Ian smiled down at her, his expression gentle as he whispered, "Go on in now, it's cold."

But Esther broke down as she cried.

"It's my fault, everythin''s my fault, Ian. It wasn't supposed to happen this way."

Her unruly hair whipped around her, the night air stinging her skin as he stared at her with tenderness.

"Go on inside now," he murmured, his smile trying to reassure her. "It's okay. I'll be all right."

With a final glance toward the sheriff, he nodded, signaling that he was ready. The sheriff opened the car door, and Ian was guided inside. Esther's heart broke a little more as the door clanked shut behind him, locking him away from her.

She reached out, placing her hand flat on the cold glass where Ian sat, her fingers shaking as if she could somehow touch him through the barrier.

Seeing her despair, Ian leaned his head against the window, returning the gesture of affection in the only way he could.

The car's engine sputtered to life, the deep rumble reverberating in the quiet night.

The sheriff backed the car slowly down the small drive, his eyes flicking briefly toward Esther as if offering a wordless farewell.

Then, shifting into gear, he drove off, the car's taillights fading into the darkness.

She watched as the patrol vehicle disappeared into the night down the small road.

This time, it wasn't her leaving—it was the tall man with bronzed skin and shoulders that could bear the world.

Chapter 34: Rusted Bars

The rural police station stood quiet, a cold breeze slipping in through a window left cracked earlier in the day. It struggled to drive out the musty smell still clinging to the walls—only stirring a stale odor that made the place less inviting.

Outside, boots thudded across the steps as Sheriff Ronell pushed the door open, guiding Ian in with a hand gripping his shoulder. As he scouted out the dark path from memory, the sheriff muttered, "Where's that damn light? Needa get it wired in."

He swiped at the air until his fingers found the dangling chain. With a hard yank, the overhead bulb flickered to life, buzzing loud enough to fill the room. "Ridiculous," he grumbled.

The sheriff's voice came out gruff, carrying more fatigue than malice.

"Ya stay put," he added, while Ian took in his surroundings.

The space was cluttered—two desks buried in papers, a coat rack sagging in the corner, and boxes stacked high near a row of filing cabinets.

Tucked in the back, hidden from view, an iron-barred jail cell sat like a relic from another time. Its thick, rusting bars cast jagged shadows, and inside, a worn cot with a thin mattress rested on a metal frame, offering little more than a place to endure the night.

Sheriff Ronell gestured toward the caged area.

"Bit cold in here," he said as he led Ian forward. "Let me grab a blanket."

The bulky door groaned as the sheriff pulled it open, and Ian stepped inside without protest—exhaustion tugging at him, worn thin from the long day.

The memories of the evening, though dear, hadn't ended as he had hoped.

Esther's tearful face… the sheriff's resigned words… and then an icy realization settled in—his future was no longer in his hands. He was powerless now, with no say in where his body would rest.

As he sat down on the small cot, the springs squeaked beneath his weight, but he didn't notice.

The sheriff, meanwhile, was muttering to himself as he looked around the room.

"Where are those damn keys?" he barked, irritated. "Goddamnit, Frank!" He straightened up, rolling his eyes in annoyance. "Told him to find them 'fore he left."

His frustration was palpable, and in a flash of temper, Sheriff Ronell grabbed a metal pail from the corner and flung it across the floor, into the cell, with a loud clatter.

Ian glanced up but didn't speak, his face blank, lost in the fog of his thoughts.

"Ain't got modern facilities in here," the sheriff said as he stared at the pail. "Damn thing must've been built a century ago." He turned back to Ian, his irritation fading as quickly as it had come.

"Lie on down and make yerself comfortable," he said with a resigned sigh.

Ian did as he was told, lying down on his side, his body still stiff with tension as the cold from the thin mattress seeped through his clothes.

He forced himself to ignore it, his mind too consumed by the events replaying over and over in his head. His wrists throbbed where the handcuffs dug into his skin, and the double-lock made every small movement into a sharp reminder of his confinement.

Leaning over, Sheriff Ronell unfastened one side of the cuffs and attached the other end to the vertical bars beside the bed. It wasn't much freedom, but Ian felt a small sense of relief as the pressure on his wrists eased just a little.

The sheriff scooted the metal bucket closer to the cot with his boot, a practical necessity. He tossed a rough, scratchy gray wool blanket over Ian, its faded edges fraying—a testament to how many others had spent nights in this same cell.

"Gotta tuck ya in," the sheriff said dryly, a faint trace of humor in his voice as he gestured toward the iron door. "Ain't got a key to the damn thing, and I ain't got time to find it tonight. I'll be back in the mornin'."

Ian watched as the sheriff shut him in with a clang, though without the key, it remained unlocked. Sheriff Ronell didn't seem to mind, knowing Ian wasn't going anywhere.

"Alrighty then," the sheriff said with a tired smile. "Good night."

And with that, Sheriff Ronell turned and walked out, pulling the cord of the light and plunging the room into darkness once more, leaving Ian alone with the silence—an unwelcome companion.

He lay still on the cot, the rough blanket itchy on his skin.

In a calm surrender, an act of self-preservation, he allowed himself to return to the whispers of his mind.

The ones that held the echoes of that pretty brown-haired girl.

He thought of Esther, how she almost appeared angelic, as though she had been born too pure for the ugliness of this world. The darkness she had faced had not broken her. She flew above it, seraphic, with a passion and goodness that manifested in an almost otherworldly manner, as if her spirit belonged to another celestial plane.

Her fierce, beautiful body, marked with hidden scars she didn't want to let him see. Marks he had glimpsed through her wet nightgown in the kitchen, during the rainstorm last year, when she had turned her back to him.

Ian thought of how he wanted to tell her that those scars didn't matter or detract from her beauty. They were only where her wings had been ripped away—taken to keep her from flight.

Nevertheless, she had given herself so freely to him, so completely that it was as if she defied that fate. And her defiant will lingered with him, consuming him entirely.

In that moment, when he knew—inescapably knew—that he loved her, something in him shifted, a truth he could no longer deny.

He became utterly hers, bound in a way that transcended even the word.

But now, staring at the dim cell walls, uncertainty settled over him. He wasn't sure how they could navigate this reckoning when the world outside them was hell-bent on keeping them apart. He sighed, awkwardly adjusting his pillow with his free hand.

Not knowing what kind of punishment awaited him, or how long it might last, he couldn't see how it was fair for her to wait, to give up something she had just gained.

To spend her young years in solitude, tied to a man she might never have again. It saddened him, leaving a bitter ache where hope once stirred.

His long legs dangled over the edge as he shifted uncomfortably on the narrow cot. Pulling them in, he curled up to preserve what little warmth he could find.

His mind circled the questions he didn't want to hear, wondering if that had been the last time he would ever feel Esther's body against him.

The last time he would cradle his young children in his arms?

The thoughts lingered, sharper than the ache in his wrists, as the promise he'd made to Adeline burned in his mind, a vow that had begun to unravel before he could fully make good on it.

He whispered into the dark, "I'm sorry, Addie. I'm sorry."

He knew Adeline, ever selfless, would want him to find love again—especially with someone like Esther, who shared that same generous heart and goodness.

Briefly, he wondered if it was possible that, from the heavenly spires above, she had guided him to Esther, knowing he needed her, that the children needed her.

But just as his thoughts had offered him an escape, reality came crashing back.

He wasn't with Esther in a warm house, lying in a soft bed, her body held close to him.

Instead, he was here, in a jail cell in Larkin.

Alone. Cold. Awaiting the morning, which offered nothing but the uncertainty of a future he had no control over.

His American dream, once so vivid, now seemed to drift further away, carried out to sea by the consequences of a righteous cause, an action he could not regret, even if he dreaded where it had led him.

A silence filled the jail, its stillness amplifying his isolation as the air carried the faint, sour remnants of moonshine. Evidence of those who had once occupied the cell and been sick from overindulgence. The smell lingered, mingling with the stale traces of sweat and despair, making Ian pinch his nose. Outside, thunder rumbled in the distance, the sound faint but growing, like a warning from the horizon.

The only light that filtered in was the moon, washing him in a pale blue hue. It felt cold and heartless, despite being the same light that had once illuminated two bodies making what he now acknowledged as love.

He longed to unburden those words to Esther, confess them as though he'd just discovered a beautiful thing that had always been in plain sight.

He had watched as she fought to sacrifice her freedom for his, to bear the entire blame on her narrow shoulders.

That act had ripped free something deep within him.

It was as if she had flung open a door he hadn't known he'd kept locked, a hidden passage buried beneath the layers of his being.

Ian understood the cost of her courage—the strength it took to offer such a gift on his behalf. That realization stirred a yearning to return that bravery tenfold. To envelop her in the same selfless devotion she had shown him.

He was grateful that the sheriff had at least listened to reason and had not held Esther accountable for the accident. In that, there had been some small grace. Ian didn't want to think about what would have happened if the lawman had taken her at her word.

He also noted that the sheriff didn't appear to have a good opinion of Clive, wondering if the trunk full of moonshine played into that reasoning. Perhaps that would work in his favor in the courtroom.

And for his defense, Ian would never allow Esther's reputation to be dragged through the mud. The thought of her having to testify, to divulge the truth of what her cousin had done to her—well, he refused to let that happen. He couldn't even bear to think of it.

As he closed his eyes again, he tried to still the racing thoughts, but his mind refused. It stubbornly resisted, which only made him angrier. *Give me the reprieve,* he silently demanded of himself.

Esther was out of his reach now—skin and soul. Strangely, it felt as though he had called on her to haunt him, unaware that she had been doing the same—tethered to the same longing.

The wind howled around Ian's small cottage, rattling the windows as the storm pressed closer. The wooden beams creaked and groaned under the pressure, as if an apparition were filling the quiet spaces with eerie sounds.

After speaking with Clarissa, Esther had made her way back to Ian's children, not wanting to leave them alone. She curled up behind Rebecca, her arm protectively wrapped around the little girl. Exhaustion toyed with her mind, but she couldn't give in to sleep.

A bolt of lightning flashed outside, followed by a deafening clap of thunder. Esther flinched, trying to remain still, while the little girl slept soundly beside her. The storm, similar to the one that swelled the river the night Pawdad died—another force that had changed her life forever.

Despite being safe under a roof, a strangeness returned to her legs, like a deer in the brush under a predator's gaze, an urge to run, as if it were whispering, "run, girl."

However, this time, it was different—perplexing, as the current glided up her thigh muscles, moving swiftly through her core before rising and settling just behind her closed eyes.

A shadow of something yet to come. A warning carried on the breath of the storm.

The words seemed to echo in her imagination, spoken by a woman's voice she couldn't place, though somehow it felt familiar.

Esther tugged Rebecca closer, the little girl's steady breaths a comfort, a reminder of light amid the chaos.

"Ian, can ya hear me?" Esther whispered, the words no more than a breath, as her mind reached out to him.

Though his physical form was far from her, removed from her in every way that mattered, she tried to sense him in the space between their shared worlds.

She fought against the earthly distance that held them apart, calling him to be her ghost. Esther longed for him to haunt her again, to hold her in the quiet corners of her thoughts, to be felt in the silence, but...

He had revealed himself, fully, a man in his most vulnerable form.

He had offered a part of himself that Esther once doubted he ever could, not after the loss that had hollowed him.

Tonight, she saw it in his eyes—a challenge, daring her to meet him there.

As though he'd decided he would never turn away from her again. The bittersweetness of it lingered, almost frightening in its reality. He had made a choice, one that neither of them could undo.

Esther cursed herself for failing to convince the sheriff that Clive's death was her fault. She had tried, but Ian's resolve had outmatched hers—a force too great.

"You should be here," Esther whispered.

It should have been her in that car. This was his home, and he had sacrificed it for her, giving up everything he cherished—his family, his future, even his own freedom.

He did it all to break the curse placed on her from birth—a wicked plan by Clive that bound her to a pact she never agreed to. Esther prayed that Clive's power, his dark magic, had been ended by destroying his physical body and sending him into the unknown, which Ian had accomplished.

Esther wished she could break another curse—one she had placed on herself. Unlike Clive's sinister nature, this was something she had shackled herself to.

Returning from Clarissa's, she'd found herself searching Ian's home for some liquid courage, but it was bare. She knew Clarissa had blackberry wine, but the older woman hadn't gone back to bed.

For months, Esther had leaned on the fiery spirits, and more than she should have. Now she feared it had taken hold of her in a way she couldn't fix.

Now home, she could no longer justify her regular consumption. She had tried to stop before, failing because of Clive's ample supply. Sometimes, even taking a swig early in the morning to face the man she hated the very sight of.

As she lay there, Esther could feel the craving building in her body, a beast.

Despite being petrified of what lay ahead, she vowed to stop once and for all. For Ian's children. They needed her, not a portion of her.

She also made a vow to find a way to help Ian, to do everything within her power to repay the sacrifice he had made for her.

To fight for him, no matter the cost, even if it meant risking everything.

Chapter 35: No Rest for the Wicked

The hours that had passed in the small jail cell had not come easily. As the night grew colder, time seemed to come to a standstill, bringing discomfort along with it.

The torrential spring showers had returned, and with renewed fury, the thunderous crashes now echoed through the sleeping town of Larkin.

It shook the brick police station as gumball raindrops pelted down on the roof and windows.

Ian lay curled on the cot, trying to make himself small against the chill that the walls didn't bother to hold back. The rough wool blanket scratched at his skin, and there had been a moment when he debated whether to toss it off onto the floor.

The sagging springs groaned beneath him as he shifted, searching in vain for comfort. His arm was stiff from the awkward position—his wrist still cuffed to the cold iron.

Sleep had eluded him for hours, chased away by the endless plague of uncertainty.

But Ian wasn't alone.

Unbeknownst to him, outside, a shadowy blur moved past the barred window, vanishing into the dark.

The wind howled, a feral whisper carrying the faint rustle of footsteps, masked almost perfectly by the storm's fury.

Someone was there—watching, waiting.

Then, for a moment, the storm seemed to hush, as if the world itself had paused to witness what was to come.

Another sudden flash of lightning tore through the sky, the electric burst illuminating the silhouette against the rain-slicked glass—unmistakable, and looming.

Ian lay with his back to the window, unaware.

Without warning, another sound broke the night—a faint rattling.

Keys.

Ian's breath caught as his body tensed instinctively.

The low creak of a door followed, and his senses sharpened.

He was no longer alone.

Lying still, he listened, his heart quickening as muffled footsteps crossed the wooden floor, quiet but deliberate.

Eyes fixed ahead, Ian's mind raced.

This wasn't right—no light had been turned on.

This wasn't the sheriff, and whoever it was, they were trying to be sly.

Ian could hear quiet whispers, barely audible. But enough to set his instincts on edge.

Two figures. Moving carefully.

His jaw clenched, muscles tightening beneath the blanket, waiting.

"How we gonna do this? Suppose she screams real loud?" a voice murmured, low and rough, the words slithering through the still air.

"We're gonna gag her good first," came the reply, cold. "Just gotta know where Clive kept it. Don't be a fool an' go break her neck while holdin' her down."

Ian's entire body tensed.

They weren't here for him—they were after Esther. It only made sense.

Why her?

And who the fuck were these men trying to get to her?

Ian controlled his breath.

"What about Marty?" the first voice asked, quieter now, almost a hiss.

"I ain't worried 'bout him. And will ya shut the hell up, yer walkin' too loud, floors might squeak."

The footsteps grew softer, shuffling closer, each creak of the floorboards tightening the knot in Ian's gut. He knew he'd be forced to act.

His chest tightened as the cell door creaked open.

One man reached out, prepared to grab the figure under the blanket.

In an instant, Ian reacted.

He reached down next to the cot, his fingers wrapping tightly around the cold metal of the bucket.

Fueled with adrenaline, he swung it up with every ounce of strength he could muster.

The pail collided with the man's head with a sickening thud.

A sharp grunt followed as the man staggered backward, hands flying to his head as he stumbled between the bars and the cot.

Dazed, confusion flashed across his expression.

Even in the dim light, Ian caught a glint of recognition—it was Deputy Frank.

Before Ian could catch his breath, the second man rushed at him, and Ian swung the bucket again. But the handcuff binding him jerked him back.

He swung again, the bucket missed its mark as the man dodged to the side, his dark figure weaving through the narrow cell.

The tension pressed in from all sides, making the small space feel even tighter.

Ian didn't hold back, bracing himself against the cot and adjusting his stance just in time to drive his foot forward.

His boot connected with the man's gut, forcing a sharp gasp as the man staggered backward, clutching his stomach.

The police station was filled with the sound of harsh breathing and the shuffle of boots against the floor.

The second man, whom Ian had now identified as Vic Porter, cursed under his breath, staggering to regain his footing.

His eyes darted to Ian.

"God, Frank, that's not her," Vic bellowed.

Shadows danced wildly around them, flickering in and out in the dim light.

The tension was palpable, every second stretching out as they waited, all three men poised for their next move.

Ian's pulse roared in his ears as he readied himself, knuckles white, his grip firm on the bucket he had claimed.

Frank's hand shot to his holster.

With a practiced motion, the deputy drew his revolver and leveled it straight at Ian's head.

The fight halted abruptly as the German man stared down the cold, steady barrel.

Ian could feel the raw fury radiating from Frank, each breath growing heavier, thick with rage.

For a split second, Ian questioned if this was the end—shot in a small Tennessee jail cell, far from any courthouse or jury.

Frank pushed the gun closer, pressing the cold steel against Ian's brow, the metal a brutal reminder of how quickly life could end.

"Ya can't shoot him," Vic hissed. "How ya gonna explain that to the Sheriff?"

Frank paused as he thought over what he should do next.

Ian, half-kneeling on the cot, could feel the danger coiling inside the man as the gun trembled against his skin. For a second, Ian began making his peace, confident Frank would pull the trigger.

But then, with a growl of frustration, Frank yanked the weapon away and swung it with brutal force.

The butt crashed into the side of Ian's head, his temple.

Pain exploded behind Ian's eyes, his vision swimming as he staggered, barely managing to keep himself upright on the cot.

Before he could steady himself, another blow came—this one harder, more absolute—sending him crashing down onto the bed.

His body slumped as blood seeped from the wound, trickling down his face in warm rivulets.

Fighting to stay conscious, Ian's mind grasped at the edges of awareness, but his strength slipped away.

"Tough bastard," Frank said, rubbing his hand as if trying to shake off the lingering tension from the blows he had dealt. He looked around, his eyes darting through the shadows as if piecing together a mental storyline, searching for a way to salvage the situation.

A sly smile tugged at Frank's mouth, a dangerous gleam flashing on his face.

"He must have hit his head on the bar," Frank said, the words slipping out smoothly as he turned to Vic.

"Ain't no way he can prove we was here. A fella'll say anythin' once he's locked up," Frank added, almost pleased with his plan.

Vic, still rattled and unsure, hesitated before nodding, rubbing the spot on his stomach where Ian's solid kick had landed.

"So… what now?" Vic asked, uncertain. "This ain't the Primm girl."

"I get it." Frank snapped. "Figured Marty was bringin' her in, not this fella."

He paused, a slow grin creeping in, relief settling on his face. "The Sheriff must think… he killed Clive. Hell, that's good news fer us."

"But Frank, that don't fix yer other problem. We've searched high and low at Clive's, and it just ain't there," Vic huffed. "Maybe we oughta just cut our losses and get the hell outta here. The big guns are comin'. Don't reckon I wanna be in the crossfire when the ATU rolls in."

"She was out on the damn highway with him, Vic," Frank growled, his voice low and sharp. "I'd bet money she knows too much—seen it all. There's no way in hell I'm leavin' my life behind for this shit, not without seein' her six feet under, next to that fucking Preacher. As a matter of fact, we're gonna bury all of this."

Vic shifted, rubbing his stomach with a scowl. "That Primm girl… don't talk much," he muttered.

"Might work in our favor, but this whole thing's a God damn disaster," Frank said, his frustration simmering.

Without warning, Frank bent down, grabbed the crumpled blanket, and with a rough toss, threw it over Ian's unconscious body.

Frank's eyes flicked around the shadowy cell, ensuring everything appeared just as it should, even moving the metal pail back into position.

Once satisfied, he dragged the door shut, the iron bars groaning in protest before locking it into place. The key made a soft click as Frank hung it back on the nearby hook, the sound echoing in the stillness.

He cast one last glance at Ian's limp form, his eyes narrowing with cold calculation. With a sharp nod to Vic, he turned toward the door, and the two men slipped into the raging storm outside.

The wind howled, ripping through the trees like a wild animal, as rain hammered the ground.

Inside the old iron jail cage, Ian's body lay still, swallowed by the dark shadows, his breath faint.

Chapter 36: Lost Appetite

A clock ticked slowly, echoing through the kitchen, marking time stretched fragile in the morning light. Scattered across the breakfast table were the remnants of an uneaten meal—cold biscuits, untouched cups of coffee, and barely nibbled toast.

Clarissa stood by the sink, scrubbing at a plate, though her mind was far from the chore. Her eyes flicked over to Esther, who sat slumped at the table, her head buried in her arms.

The soft clink of dishes and the occasional crackle from the stove did nothing to dispel the oppressive silence that seemed to choke the room.

Abram leaned by the window, his face set in a deep frown as he stared out over the orchard, gripping the wooden frame too tightly. His usual calm was broken, his agitation clear in every taut line of his brow.

Mitzy, standing by the stove, nervously set a kettle down, her eyes darting between the others.

The tension was thick. Everyone was waiting—wanting news, answers, or any sign that might offer a little sense of relief.

Rebecca and Benjamin hovered near the door, their small faces painted with confusion. They sensed something was wrong and asked about their father, but no one had the heart to tell them the truth.

Clarissa glanced at them, forcing a smile, but it faltered before it could settle. She tried again as she brushed a strand of hair back in an effort to steady herself.

"Why don't ya both go see the kittens in the barn?" she suggested gently, nudging them toward a distraction. "I saw a cute little tabby runnin' around this mornin'."

Rebecca's brow furrowed as she tugged at the sleeve of her dress.

"We tried to catch 'em before," Rebecca said. "But they wouldn't let us pet 'em. They run real fast and hide in the hay."

Benjamin nodded as he fidgeted with a wooden car in his hands.

I've already tried makin' a trap with a crate, but they slip out between the slats. They're real skinny," he added, shaking his head.

"Well, why don't ya take a saucer of milk out there? Maybe that'll help y'all make friends with them," Clarissa pressed, already moving to the fridge.

Not convinced, Rebecca cocked her head, looking up.

"Auntie… I don't think that's gonna work. They're just too mean, only biting at us. Maybe Esther could grab us one," the little girl said, hopeful.

Lost to the quiet storm brewing in her, Esther didn't respond.

Clarissa, her patience wearing thin, pushed a saucer of milk into Benjamin's hands.

"No, honey, Esther's got her hands full today. Now, ya both go on and try yerselves. We've got some things to discuss here."

Rebecca hesitated, her hands on her hips in defiance.

"I'd rather stay here and hear what ya gotta say about my Pa." She pouted. "He just got back from the city, and now he's gone again."

Clarissa's smile tightened as she sighed.

"Listen here, y'all go on out now, just fer a little while. Go on, catch ya one of them kittens. I'll call ya back in a bit."

Giving a reluctant nod, Rebecca glanced at her brother as he held the dish carefully. With one last look at the adults, the children slipped out the back, their footsteps pattering as they headed toward the barn.

The screen door clicked shut, and once again, silence fell over the kitchen. This time, it felt heavier, like a suffocating blanket of worry.

Clarissa turned to the stove, her hands unsteady as she reached for a dishcloth to wipe them. She cleared her throat before speaking, her voice low and taut.

"Abram, I want ya to take a drive down to the Sheriff's today. See if you can find out what they're plannin' on doin' with Ian… where he's goin'. If need be, we'll head over to Jasper and get him a lawyer."

Abram's jaw clenched as he turned to look at her.

"Miss Clarissa, those lawyers cost a fortune. Ya ain't got that kind of money. Them city folk'll bleed ya dry before they even lift a finger," he said.

"God willin', I'll sell whatever I need to." Clarissa's voice hardened with resolve. "We've got Obadiah's old car, or maybe the tractor, it's still got some life in it."

Abram let out a sharp grunt, then moved away from the window and crossed the room in a few steps. At the table, he slammed his hands down with a heavy thud.

His eyes locked onto Esther.

"I'm still tryin' to figure out how they plan on pinnin' this on him," Abram said, his outrage spilling over. "He's only ever done right by you, and now look what's happened. They're gonna lock him away for life, or worse."

Esther flinched at his words as she sat up straighter.

"I told 'im I'd take his place," she choked out.

Clarissa drew in an uneasy breath as she moved to Esther's side, resting a steadying hand on her shoulder.

"Hush now," Clarissa said. "Ain't nobody done nothin' wrong here. Abram, why don't ya go feed the animals and warm up the truck."

But before Abram could respond, Esther shot up from her seat, her chair clattering to the floor as she bolted from the room.

Her feet pounded up the stairs, and moments later, the slam of a door rattled through the house.

The sound left everyone stunned, with Abram just shaking his head in disbelief.

Clarissa dropped her eyes, her heart torn between her own angst and the guilt she sensed Esther was carrying.

"She cares for him somethin' fierce, Abram," Clarissa muttered as she reached down to pick up the chair. "Maybe even more than you ever could. Can't ya see that?"

Abram, his frustration still bubbling over, stormed out the kitchen door, the wood creaking under the force.

Mitzy rolled her eyes as she rocked her cranky toddler, Jeremiah.

"Sorry, Miss Clarissa," she said apologetically. "He always thinks he's right, even when he ain't. Maybe he just don't wanna share Ian with nobody else."

"I gotta remind him sometimes, he's got a wife," she added with a playful smile.

"I sure do love ya, Mitzy," Clarissa said as she gave a firm hug to the young mother.

"Guess I should go see about our girl upstairs," Clarissa added, glancing at the staircase.

"It's all gonna work out, Miss Clarissa. Don't ya worry," Mitzy insisted.

"I pray it does, honey. I pray it does," Clarissa answered back.

Outside, Abram walked toward the chicken coop as Clarissa's words replayed in his mind.

It all bothered him more than he wanted to admit. He had never been blind to the attraction Ian held for Esther—he'd seen how Ian had eyed her all last summer, lowering his tone whenever she was near. During the harvest, it was almost comical how much attention he'd paid to her, as if she might wilt under the sun.

But Abram hadn't said anything then, thinking it was just a passing fancy.

The tall German man was as much of a brother as one could be without sharing the same blood.

And it wasn't as if Abram disliked Esther—he simply couldn't shake the feeling that trouble seemed to follow her everywhere.

Inescapable as iron drawn to a magnet.

Chapter 37: Ghosts

Esther sat slumped beside the bathtub, clutching a bucket to her chest as she retched violently into it. Her body trembled with each heave, the sickness twisting her stomach into tight knots.

She barely noticed the creak of the bathroom door before Clarissa knelt beside her. She could feel the older woman's hand, soft and gentle, stroking her hair away from her clammy forehead.

Clarissa's touch carried the warmth and steadiness of someone who had spent years tending to the sick—a healer's gift that offered comfort even amid the misery.

When the waves subsided, Esther let out a weak groan and leaned her head back against the cold side of the tub. Her eyes closed as she tried to steady her breathing.

The older woman handed her a damp washcloth, which she accepted and pressed to her flushed face.

"Must've caught somethin'," Esther mumbled in a raspy voice as she wiped at her mouth.

Clarissa rose, walking to the vanity, and retrieved a hairbrush. Returning, she sat down on the rim of the tub and began gently brushing the strands of dark hair from Esther's forehead. Her fingers moved gently with motherly care, untangling the girl's dark locks.

Though her movements were calm, her eyes betrayed the worry lurking just beneath them.

"Honey," Clarissa said, her voice gentle, "I worried ya might done caught yerself a nine-month flu." Her words were tender, like a lullaby, offering comfort even as they nudged Esther toward a reality that couldn't be easily dismissed.

Clarissa let out a soft sigh, her breath a blend of resignation and concern, as she continued to brush Esther's hair with slow, deliberate strokes.

"I've been wonderin'," she went on. "Ever since ya got back, I noticed ya looked a bit fuller in the bosom, and ya ain't been eatin' much."

Her voice held a tenderness, a strange certainty.

Desperate to reject the thought, Esther shook her head, as if shaking off the words could somehow erase their meaning.

Yet, deep down, she was terrified that Clarissa might be right.

Esther hadn't noticed any changes in her body, but she had been distracted—perhaps willfully so. And she hadn't been able to keep down her food for a while, hoping it would pass. Now, faced with the possibility, the very thought of it churned in her stomach, making her feel ill again.

Clarissa set the hairbrush down and leaned in close, her voice lowering.

"My darlin' girl," she began, as if treading on delicate ground. "I'm prayin' it ain't so… but if ya are… did yer cousin do this?" She reached out and rested her hand on her niece's arm, holding her steady as the uncomfortable question landed.

Esther felt a chill run through her at the mere possibility. It filled her with a sense of foreboding, tearing apart an already fragile state.

She mumbled, "Oh, God, Clarissa," trembling with fear as she fought to control herself.

Esther had done everything she could think of to keep something like this from happening. Even begging Clive not to touch her, warning him that this very thing was a possibility. But he hadn't seemed worried, dismissing her concerns by saying he knew of a doctor who could "take care of it."

Luckily, over the last couple of months, Clive had his own issues—particularly when he was liquored up—ones that often prevented him from acting on his desires.

He'd lost his ability to perform, and it infuriated him, often blaming her. Perhaps some of it was her fault. Esther knew he struggled whenever he drank too much. So, she drank with him, pushing him to drink more, hoping he'd be left powerless.

But it had its own consequences—there were times she blacked out, unable to remember a blessed thing, and that frightened her even more.

On occasion, Clive would invite guests to his home—mostly men. One night, well past midnight, one of them stumbled into the bedroom and collapsed onto the mattress next to her.

Frightened and unsure where Clive was, she'd gone out on the front porch, waiting almost until sunrise before he finally showed up. Jealous, he accused her of entertaining the man, though she hadn't—or at least didn't recall.

Esther pressed the damp washcloth to her face again, the coolness of the fabric offering little relief against the heat of her shame.

She closed her eyes tightly, wishing the thin cloth could somehow block out everything she wasn't prepared to face.

"I don't know if I can think 'bout it," she murmured, her voice small.

Clarissa took the washcloth from her and went to the sink. The pipes groaned as the water sputtered out. Without saying anything, she wrung the cloth under the cool stream.

"Honey, these things don't just disappear." Clarissa began again, her tone filled with wisdom born of years of watching life unfold in all its messy ways. She twisted the washcloth once more, wringing out the excess water before turning to glance over her shoulder at her niece.

"They've got a way of comin' to light, whether we're ready for 'em or not," she added.

Then Clarissa laid the cloth to dry, bracing herself against the basin as if weighing words in her mind before walking back. Leaning over Esther, she rested a hand on her niece's knee.

"When's the last time ya had a monthly?" Clarissa asked.

Esther swallowed hard, her eyes shifting. "I… I don't remember," she confessed. It had been weeks, maybe months. The passage of time had blurred amid the chaos.

Clarissa stood up and reached for Esther's hand, helping her to her feet.

"Let me feel yer belly," Clarissa instructed as she pressed her palm against Esther's lower abdomen, gently probing for any signs. After a few moments, she stepped back, her face easing into a small, relieved smile.

"Oh, honey," she said with a touch of warmth in her words, "If ya are, ya ain't far along at all. Yer baby only be no bigger than a bitty bean." She reached for Esther's hand and gave it a reassuring squeeze. "That there is mighty good news."

Esther's voice wavered, uncertain, struggling to grasp Clarissa's words.

"Good news? What ya mean?"

Dread circled her quickly, like wolves closing in on prey.

She had tried to let Ian slip away over the last six months, convinced she had no other choice—but now, everything surged back, raw and consuming.

With him locked away and the possibility of a secret growing inside her, everything felt ready to vanish into nothing.

Her mind sank into darkness again, the same old fear gripping her tightly. A sharp, unforgiving voice whispered that she had already lost the game, and there were no more pieces left to play.

How could Ian ever want her after this?

With a strange look on Clarissa's face, she walked to the door and cracked it open, glancing down the hallway to make sure they were alone. The old hinges squeaked as she closed the door, sealing them inside.

She paused for a moment, taking a deep, cleansing breath, her brow furrowed as if she were working through her thoughts, turning back to face Esther. Her voice dropped low, sharing words only meant to be heard between the two of them.

"I saw ya headin' in from the barn," Clarissa said, her tone gentle but knowing. "'Twas late… nearly the middle of the night. Were ya with Ian? Ya know… in the way only a woman can be?" Her gaze was soft but probing.

Esther's cheeks burned crimson, the heat rising to her face as if her very skin betrayed the secret she was trying hard to hide.

What possible answer was there to such a damning question—shame's teeth bit at her tongue.

She worried Clarissa might believe she'd seduced him or that he was merely another man she would take to her bed. And Ian's reputation was sacred at the Old Reed Estate, and Clarissa held him in such high esteem, like family, dear and beloved.

The truth was, it had happened.

But this wasn't a conversation Esther wanted to have—certain she could hear Ian telling her not to say anything, knowing he'd be mortified as well.

She feared Clarissa would see her as a common hussy, unworthy of the trust between them. She searched desperately for an explanation, but when she met Clarissa's gaze, she knew there wasn't one.

So, with a trembling nod, Esther acknowledged the deed, her eyes dropping to the floor.

Unsurprised, Clarissa's expression remained calm, almost as if they were discussing something as ordinary as the weather or planting seeds in the garden.

"Did he get ya good?" Clarissa asked, feeling the need to clarify, in case Esther didn't fully understand her meaning. "Did he leave his seed in ya?" Her voice was direct, tinged with the importance of the question.

Esther nodded again, her shoulders slouching as if she could somehow shrink away from what her aunt had asked, hiding her face with her hands.

Noticing her distress, Clarissa reached out and rubbed her arm. There wasn't an ounce of judgment in her eyes as her hand lingered for a moment. Her presence was a steady rock amidst Esther's inner turmoil.

"Ain't no place for shame here right now, and I ain't throwin' stones at ya young'uns," Clarissa added as she gently brushed a strand of hair from Esther's face. "What happens between a man and a woman sometimes just can't be helped. Two folks bein' kept from each other, well, what ya expect?"

She paused, her eyes searching Esther's for a moment before continuing. "But honey, I'm gonna tell ya somethin' important now. Listen close."

Clarissa leaned in even closer.

"Ya gonna pick the better man to be the papa of this baby. Ya hear me?"

Esther blinked, trying to process the implications of her words, unsure if she had interpreted them correctly.

"I… I don't know," Esther mumbled. Her heart clenched at the thought.

How could she live with the knowledge that she had deceived him? It felt utterly wrong. But the alternative didn't seem any better as she wondered why she was always put in a position where she felt she had no choice.

"Lots of babies come early," Clarissa continued. "Ian won't question ya about it, not even fer a second, even if he might secretly suspect otherwise. I know him. He ain't gonna say a word 'bout it. Couldn't shy away from responsibility if he tried—just the possibility that he's the papa is enough."

Clarissa smiled. "Girl, he's got it bad fer ya. Told me as much yesterday. Askin' if I was good with him courtin' ya. Kinda sweet like he was askin' my permission. Told him it was about time."

Esther smiled, but it quickly gave way to a surge of panic.

"But Aunt Clarissa… ya sure he won't be angry with me? What if I'm askin' him to take on trouble that ain't his? I couldn't stand him hatin' me."

With a warm and confident smile, Clarissa cupped her face.

"He's a good man, and he won't hate ya, honey. It's a baby, and babies are precious blessings, gifts from heaven," Clarissa said. "You may not realize it, but you were a blessin' to yer momma."

Those words struck hard at the heart's marrow—the softest part of Esther's being.

Her eyes welled with tears, and she shook her head.

"My ma left me," she whispered. "Don't see how I was ever a blessin' to her."

Clarissa's face softened, her eyes swimming with emotion.

"Oh—honey, you've always been a blessin'… and I've been waitin' on tellin' ya somethin'. Somethin' that's been sittin' with me fer a long time—years. Thinkin' I should have told ya sooner."

Confusion etched on Esther's face.

Taking a deep breath, Clarissa's eyes were filled with an old sadness—one that had lingered and had never quite found the right moment to escape.

Esther, still reeling from everything that had already been said, held her gaze.

The old woman shifted as though she were searching for the right place to begin. This wasn't a story she told often—maybe not at all—and it was with the truth of things long buried.

She began slowly, her voice low and steady, every word weighed with years of holding them back.

"Baby, I knew yer mama, Annie Primm, quite well," Clarissa said, her tone almost reverent as she spoke the name.

"Matter of fact, I delivered you right here in this very house, in the same bed you've been sleepin' on."

Esther blinked as she shook her head ever so slightly. How could that be possible? This house—this life—had always been so far removed from what she knew.

Clarissa's eyes held Esther's, unwavering, as she continued.

"Annie was a real sweet thing. Looked a lot like ya, maybe a little more red in her hair, but she had that same fire. Mighty stubborn too—just like you. Ya see, you were surely difficult about comin' on out when it was your time."

Clarissa chuckled, though there was a heaviness in her voice.

Esther's mind raced as she opened her mouth to say something, but she couldn't.

Clarissa pressed on, filling the silence with her gentle storytelling.

"It was a sad thing. See, yer grandmother had Annie up on that hill for three days, tryin' to get ya out on her own. She didn't wanna call the doctor—nobody in town knew nothin' 'bout ya. She was ashamed of her daughter. Fer the state she was in."

Clarissa's weary eyes creased at the corners as she remembered the fear that had wrapped around young Annie like a chokehold.

"But with God's grace, somehow, your little momma made her way down that hill to my back porch, kinda like how ya did last spring. She was scared, weak, but mighty determined. Once I got her down on the bed, there ya were. All slippery and wet. Yer cord had kept ya all tied up, but that long walk must have done some good—it worked ya right out."

Esther's face appeared frozen, like the truth had pulled her into a trance.

When she finally allowed herself to truly hear Clarissa's words, her heart began to pound wildly in her chest—a fast, frantic beating, like that of a newborn. So fast it left her struggling to catch her breath.

This woman, her Aunt Clarissa, had been the one to welcome her into the world.

The surrounding walls, the air Esther breathed—they were all part of a past she hadn't known.

Wiping a tear from the corner of her eye, Clarissa continued, her voice trembling.

"I kept you and yer mama hid here for a couple of weeks. But Annie was so scared yer Gran and Pawdad would find her. So, I found her a ride to Jasper and gave her some money for wherever she was plannin' on goin'. She wanted to get away… start over. But, honey, at the last minute, she decided it was best not to take ya." Clarissa swallowed hard. "Annie asked me if I'd give ya a home, love ya like my own… and I said yes. Annie knew I was barren, knew my arms ached for more children, so she kindly passed her lil' blessin' on to me."

"You, my beautiful girl, stayed here with me fer almost a good year."

All Esther could do was gaze into Clarissa's sweet, warm eyes.

It wasn't just the house, it was the woman on the front porch, the one with the long braid.

She had spent the first part of her life looking up at that loving face.

All those feelings— an unexplainable tethering, strange dreams—they were real.

It wasn't just a child longing for something more.

It was the small memories held in a baby's heart.

Esther's chest tightened with emotions too big to process all at once.

Clarissa went on, her voice filled with warmth and love as she spoke of those days.

"Aww, we loved ya so. Adeline—she'd never had a sister, ya know—so to her, you were a dream come true. She wouldn't let ya cry for a second in your cradle before she was pullin' ya out to rock ya. She played games with ya before you could even understand, hidin' behind a chair when you were crawlin' around, lookin' fer her."

Clarissa smiled softly at the memory.

"Even my Obadiah, Lord rest him, had a soft spot fer ya. Always singin' to ya, bouncin' yer little body on his knee to make ya happy."

Clarissa let out a long sigh.

"Though… the poor man was worried—worried 'bout the local law findin' out that a group of Black folks were raisin' a white baby that didn't belong to them."

Her voice lowered as the next words escaped her.

"There was always that fear… hangin' over us. And we tried the best we could to keep ya safe."

Esther's breath hitched.

She had never known any of this—never known about Adeline's love, about Clarissa's care, about Obadiah's worries.

The ground beneath her seemed to shift, pulling her into a past she didn't remember but somehow felt grown in her bones.

"Not sure how yer Gran or Pawdad found out," Clarissa continued. "But they did."

She paused, the memory painting her mind.

"They brought the old, mean sheriff… and he wouldn't even hear us out. Didn't matter what we said or how I begged. I guess they had a right to ya. Threatened to put us in jail fer stealin' ya."

Hesitating, Clarissa's eyes clouded with pain as she continued, slower now, her voice tight with grief.

"He pulled ya from my arms… my baby… and changed yer name."

Clarissa drew in a deep, steadying breath as tears streamed down her cheeks.

"Ya may be Esther to them… but to us, you'll always be our little ray of sunshine—Rebecca."

"Rebecca?" Esther asked.

The name—a name she had spoken so many times before. The name of Ian's beautiful daughter, the one she loved so dearly.

Clarissa nodded, her smile tinged with sadness.

"Adeline missed her little sister, you darlin', so very much. Even as a grown woman. So, she named her daughter after ya—Rebecca, after the little baby we loved so much… and lost."

Esther's heart burst under the weight of the revelation.

Suddenly, a vivid memory flashed, making her gasp.

It was Adeline standing by the fence, watching as she passed with Gran when she was just a child.

The girl had been the spitting image of Rebecca.

Why had she hidden this memory from herself?

She questioned if, as a child, she had played with that very girl in the woods. It felt distant—something lost in a dream—as she wondered if it had been real.

Through streams of tears, Esther said, "I think I might remember Adeline."

"Yes," Clarissa said. "When Adeline was 'bout fifteen, we caught her sneakin' up the hill to see ya. She'd been disappearin' for hours at a time. Ya couldn't have been more'n four or five, but she said she just needed to be with her little sister. To see that you were alright."

"It tore us up to forbid her from goin' up there, worried yer Pawdad or Gran would hurt her for trespassin'. Obadiah had to put his foot down," Clarissa added.

It hadn't been a dream, Esther whispered to herself.

It had been real. Everything had been real.

She had been loved. She had been cared for.

But that love had been torn away without her knowing, replaced by the coldness of Gran's cruel hands.

Tears fell like a river that could no longer be held back as Clarissa drew Esther into a tight embrace.

Struggling to find her voice between sobs, Esther finally asked the question that had been haunting her from the beginning, fearing it would hurt her Aunt Clarissa.

"But if I was a blessin'… why didn't my mama never want me?"

"Oh—honey, it don't always work out that way," Clarissa murmured. "Yer mama… she was just a little girl, scared and lost."

The old woman paused, letting the words settle before continuing.

"What ya don't understand is that you… You were the one who got her out of that darkness yer Pawdad and Gran kept her livin' in. Ya helped set her free, Esther."

"She'd never have left for any other reason but her baby," Clarissa said with conviction.

The words sank into Esther's heart, and for the first time, she felt an understanding. Maybe her mother hadn't abandoned her—not in the way she'd always believed. Maybe, just maybe, her mother had been doing the only thing she knew how to do—survive.

Clarissa's voice grew tender, heavy with years of prayer and hope.

"Let me tell ya somethin' else, child. Since the day your Gran took you… I've been prayin' fer another miracle. I've been prayin' for so many years… hopin' God would bring ya back to me."

Clarissa's smile returned—this time brighter, more hopeful.

"I watched every day fer ya… only seein' ya in passing. But I kept prayin'. Took a long while, but God finally heard me. He found a way to bring ya back… though it's taken Him a good couple of tries to get it just right."

Esther leaned into Clarissa's embrace.

The room stilled, soft and glowing with the warmth of a long-awaited reunion. It felt as though the very air cradled them in its stillness.

This moment had been written in the stars, its threads woven long before Esther knew it was meant for her.

Clarissa's arms wrapped tightly around her, grounding her in a way Esther had never known. There was a feeling of being held fast—not just to the woman in the room, but to the past she thought had abandoned her.

That love had never left her—it had been waiting, patient and steadfast, through the years.

She had been part of a family that had fought to keep her, a family that had never stopped praying for her return.

Chapter 38: Roads

The old truck idled beside the barn, its engine sputtering as if it hadn't shaken off sleep, groaning under the years it had endured.

Abram sat behind the wheel, the morning air thick and humid from the night's showers, clinging to his skin, only feeding his growing frustration. The truck needed time to wake up, just like him, before it could tackle the long road to Larkin.

A knock on the window cut through Abram's thoughts. Mitzy stood there, her eyes sharp. He rolled down the glass, bracing for what she had to say, though he wasn't particularly inclined to listen.

"Ya didn't eat this mornin', did ya?" she asked, already knowing the answer.

"I ain't hungry," Abram muttered, his gaze shifting away.

Mitzy sighed, leaning on the window frame as she handed him a sandwich wrapped in a white kitchen towel.

"You're headin' to see the sheriff, and we both know yer already riled up. Don't go makin' things worse for Ian."

Abram's jaw tightened as he laid the food down on the seat beside him. He didn't need reminding about what lay ahead.

"Ain't right, what they're doin' to him," he said.

"No, it ain't," Mitzy shot back. "But stormin' in there with your blood hot won't fix nothin'."

Abram's mind flashed back to Clive, the preacher who strutted around like he owned the town. Clive had played up the God-fearin' act, but folks like Abram saw through him—especially the people he avoided unless it suited him. Clive had been a slick talker, always cheating folks whenever he thought he could. Now Ian was tangled in his mess—and Abram's blood boiled. He tightened his grip on the steering wheel.

"It ain't fair what you said to Esther in there," Mitzy said sharply. "Ya think she wanted this? She didn't ask for none of it."

"She brought it on herself," Abram grumbled back. "Ridin' 'round with Clive in that shiny car, actin' like she's better than the rest of us—now Ian's payin' fer it."

Mitzy let the silence hang for a bit, then said, "Ya ain't got the whole of it, Abram. Folks don't tell ya nothin' 'cause you're too quick to judge and run ya mouth. Esther's cousin done her wrong, and Ian tried to put a stop to it."

Abram clenched his teeth.

"Woman, he didn't kill anyone!" he barked, louder than he meant to.

Mitzy, trying to be patient, nudged him again.

"Will ya just eat the food, Abram? You yellin' at me ain't gonna help."

"Not gonna lie, my blood's boilin'," Abram admitted, tapping his head on the steering wheel.

"I know Ian—if he laid a hand on that preacher, it was 'cause the man had it comin'. But Ian would've never dealt the final blow. Ain't in him. And why in the hell is Clarissa makin' me take Esther into Larkin?" Abram added, not happy about it.

In his eyes, Esther hadn't earned the right to ask for anything, not after the trouble she'd dragged them into. But Clarissa had insisted, and Abram wouldn't dare go against her. He pulled back his hands from the wheel, stretching out his knuckles, glancing at the kitchen screen door with frustration.

"She's only gonna make things worse," he said, shaking his head.

It should've been a simple trip—check on Ian, find out if the sheriff planned to transfer or charge him, and ensure the situation hadn't spiraled further. But now, as Clarissa came out of the house, Abram could feel the day growing more complicated with every step she took toward him.

Clarissa's sharp eyes locked on him, and with a firm wave of her hand, she signaled for him to wait. Abram sighed.

"Ya best not leave without takin' Esther," Clarissa said, her voice firm, making it clear she wouldn't tolerate any disagreement.

For a fleeting moment, Abram thought about easing the truck into gear and driving off before Esther came out of the house, resting his hand on the stick shift.

But Mitzy caught the glint in his eye.

"Don't ya dare, ya fool," she muttered under her breath. "We don't need Miss Clarissa in jail for killin' ya too."

He quickly pushed that thought aside, catching the displeased look on his wife's face.

And Mitzy was right—he'd never hear the end of it, not from Clarissa. She had a way of making her displeasure known, and Abram didn't care to be on the receiving end of that. No matter how he felt about Esther, he respected Clarissa too much to cross her.

But it didn't stop Abram's jaw from clenching. He didn't like the idea one bit.

What business did Esther have going to Larkin? What could she do besides stir more trouble? She had a way of attracting danger, and he didn't want to be caught in the crossfire.

"I know," Abram said, finally acknowledging Clarissa.

Just then, Esther stepped outside, her hair neatly styled and her clothes more polished than usual. Determination was clear on her face as she walked straight to Clarissa, pulling her aunt into a firm, wordless hug. It was as if they had concocted a plan, leaving Abram in the dark.

He watched them closely, suspicion flickering in his eyes. His gaze narrowed as Esther pulled away from Clarissa and climbed into the truck.

"Let's get this over with," Abram grumbled, shifting the vehicle into gear as they set off toward town. The old engine roared to life, groaning as it navigated the bumpy road.

The truck rattled along, splashing through puddles of mud as they passed through the countryside. Abram focused on the road, but his thoughts repeatedly drifted back to Ian. He was more worried about his friend than he let on, not sure how the estate would hold up without him. Abram knew the work, but Ian was the one who could make deals, bring in extra money, and keep things running smoothly. Ian worked like two men, rarely ever sitting down.

And then there was the draft, looming over Abram—a dark cloud. Thirty-one, strong, and with his knowledge of machinery, he knew he was a prime candidate for the war. The thought of leaving Mitzy, especially after she'd confided just weeks ago that she might be carrying another baby, gnawed at him. All of it sat heavy in his mind, and without realizing it, he found himself driving slower than usual.

Beside him, Esther sat quietly, staring out the window as though deep in thought. Her hands were folded in her lap, but there was an intensity about her silence that made Abram wary. She wasn't just tagging along—her quiet resolve hinted at something she hadn't shared.

As they neared Larkin, the muddy road gave way to the small cluster of shops and houses that made up the town. The sheriff's office loomed ahead, its faded sign swinging in the morning breeze. Abram steered the truck toward it, his gaze focused on the building.

But just as they were about to pull up in front of the sheriff's office, Esther spoke up.

"Abram, I need ya to drop me off somewhere first," she said, her voice cutting through the tense silence.

Abram didn't answer right away, his fingers tightening on the wheel. He could feel the day spiraling further out of control with each passing minute.

"We ain't got time for that," he said, the frustration plain in his voice. "We're here to check on Ian, not run yer errands."

"Please," she said, her tone edged with urgency. "I need to grab a few belongin's from Cousin Clive's house."

Abram shot her a sideways glance, his expression a mixture of annoyance and confusion.

"Why are ya always complicatin' things?" he muttered under his breath, but something in the way she looked at him gave him pause. There was a sharpness in her eyes, a determination he hadn't noticed before.

"Everything that's mine is still there," Esther added, her gaze steady but her voice trembling ever so slightly.

Abram let out a sigh, shaking his head.

"Oh, hell… fine," he said, veering the truck onto a side road that led away from the sheriff's office and toward Clive's place.

They rode in silence again as the road narrowed, leading them to a gravel road near Clive's property.

Esther's hands tightened around the seat, her pulse quickening as they approached the familiar sight of the old church and her cousin's house just beyond it.

Abram pulled the truck to a stop, the engine still idling as he glanced at her.

"Ya sure 'bout this?"

Esther nodded, already pushing the door open.

"I'll meet ya back in Larkin, don't leave without me," she said, her voice quick and breathless as she stepped out of the truck.

Before Abram could say another word, she was gone, slipping around the back of the old church, her feet moving swiftly across the worn grass.

He watched her vanish into the shadows as unease grew in his gut. He couldn't shake the feeling that something wasn't right, but now wasn't the time to dwell on it. With a growl of frustration, he shifted the truck into gear and pulled away, the old engine rumbling as it carried him back toward Larkin. The road ahead stretched into the unknown, with each mile bringing him closer to what awaited.

Chapter 39: Birthday

The main street of Larkin was unusually busy for a Tuesday, with cars honking and drivers waving as they passed each other.

Sheriff Ronell was in a good mood when he pulled up to the small police station, parking next to the old wooden porch. He stepped out of his car, a chocolate cake precariously balanced in his hands, with a soft smile on his face—lighter than his usual stern expression.

The town felt upbeat today—fitting for his birthday, he thought. A nice, cheerful day to go with the cake he hadn't even asked for.

The sound of an approaching vehicle caught his attention, just as he stepped onto the sidewalk. Frank's cruiser rattled up beside him. Vic was slouched in the passenger seat, staring at the sheriff with a tired, unreadable expression.

"Ya just gettin' here?" Frank asked, stepping out of the car with a familiar grin, his rough boots crunching against the gravel, wearing his hat low on his head.

Sheriff Ronell shrugged. "'Twas a slow mornin'. My wife insisted on makin' me a big breakfast. Somethin' 'bout it being my birthday."

Frank chuckled. "That right? Well, happy birthday, Marty." His voice carried an easy cheer as he leaned back against his vehicle, the familiar scent of motor oil mingling with the damp air.

Sheriff Ronell glanced at Frank's vehicle once more, noting Vic's presence again. The peculiar man had his hand resting over his face, shadowing his expression.

"Ya boys goin' somewhere?" the sheriff asked.

"Oh, we headin' out to grab a nice suit for Clive's body," Frank replied nonchalantly. "Folks puttin' on a wake for him today."

The sheriff nodded, his eyes staying on Vic a bit longer before he looked back at Frank.

"Alright then. Hey, when ya get back, come grab a piece of this cake. Afraid I might just eat the whole damn thing myself," he said.

"Sure thing, Marty," Frank said with a wink before climbing into his vehicle. He gunned the engine, and within moments, he and Vic disappeared down the road.

The sheriff walked toward the station door, carefully carrying the chocolate cake. Once inside, the cool air of the office greeted him, a sharp contrast to the blazing sun outside. He carefully set the confection on his desk, running a finger through the frosting, then popping it into his mouth with a satisfied hum.

But his quiet moment didn't last.

The door creaked open with a long, echoing groan that made Abram feel as if his presence had already been announced.

Sheriff Ronell looked up from his cake, his pocketknife hovering in mid-air. Abram's broad frame filled the doorway, his usual calm demeanor clouded with tension. His shoulders were stiff, his hat pulled low over his brow. With each step toward the desk, his boots thudded on the wooden floor, betraying the worry he carried with him.

Sheriff Ronell raised an eyebrow, his good mood fading as he read the seriousness in Abram's expression.

Of course, it wasn't a friendly visit—Abram was here for answers, and he wasn't leaving without them.

"Hello, Sir," Abram said, respectfully removing his hat. "I came on account of Miss Clarissa. She wants to inquire 'bout her employee, Mr. Huggler." Abram's rough, calloused hands twisted the hat, as though pacing himself with the familiar, worn fabric.

Sheriff Ronell paused, looking serious for a moment.

"Everybody knows he married that dark-skinned niece of hers. That makes him a family member, not no employee," he said, his voice matter-of-fact.

Abram cleared his throat but stood his ground.

"Well, sir, might I inquire about him as a member of her family?"

A note of surprise was evident on Abram's face at the sheriff's observation. The man had actually recognized Ian's marriage, despite it being illegal in the state and widely frowned upon by most.

Sheriff Ronell leaned back in his chair, sighing with a slight grin.

"Honestly, I can't tell ya a thing right now," he said, licking another bit of frosting from his finger. "Brought 'im in last night, haven't had a chance to talk with him this mornin'."

Abram's eyes flicked down to the chocolate cake sitting in the center of the sheriff's desk. The smell of sugar and cocoa wafted through the small office.

The sheriff noticed Abram's gaze and smirked.

"What, ya want a slice?" He flipped out a few coins from his pocket and placed them on the desk. "Tell ya what, go grab me a quart of milk and I'll give ya one."

Abram hesitated, the tension in the room thickening. He didn't want to fetch milk like some errand boy, but the sheriff's smile was slowly fading into an impatient scowl.

"Well, I'll just grab it myself then," Sheriff Ronell said with a huff, rising from his chair. "Now don't eat it while I'm gone."

With that, the sheriff headed out the door, leaving Abram alone.

Abram shifted in place as he stood near the front of the station, the dark room unsettling him and stirring a restless feeling deep in his gut. He didn't belong here. Neither did Ian.

His eyes drifted to the birthday cake on the sheriff's desk—a jarring symbol of the man's unsettlingly casual demeanor amid the tension of the situation.

As he scanned the room, Abram's gaze shifted to the jail cell tucked in the corner.

He hadn't noticed it at first, hidden behind an overstuffed coat rack and boxes stacked almost to the ceiling. The clutter and shadows had concealed the bars in plain sight. Abram's heart lurched as he realized Ian was lying there, just feet away.

Curled up on the small, uncomfortable cot, Ian's back was turned to the room. The sight made a knot form in Abram's chest. Even though he'd suspected his friend was still in Larkin, seeing him caged like an animal brought a wave of frustration and rage.

This just wasn't right, and though Sheriff Ronell was most times an approachable, reasonable man, it aggravated Abram that he took Ian's captivity so lightly. Thinking the lawman seemed more worried about eating his damn cake.

On impulse, Abram poked a hole in the top of the cake out of frustration, as if enacting some secret punishment. Regretting it quickly, he rubbed at the frosting with his thumb, trying to camouflage the damage, but it only made it worse. He cursed under his breath, licking away the evidence.

"Well, that ain't good," he muttered, eyeing the uneven spot as his gaze flicked to the door. The last thing he needed was for the sheriff to notice. He thought about Mitzy's words, how she had reminded him not to make things worse.

Abram pushed the thought aside, shoving his hand in his pocket as he made his way toward Ian, trying to forget about the mess he left behind.

Chapter 40: Tithing

Esther had vowed never to set foot in this place again, yet here she was, racing toward the old white church. Her pulse hammered in her ears as she wove the narrow path at the back, shoving through the tangled shrubbery.

The building, which had felt like part of Clive's prison grounds just days earlier, now almost appeared helpless—as though it was his victim, too. Its weathered walls, bleached by the sun and battered by years of neglect, slumped in quiet defeat, burdened by what it had witnessed.

Esther had one goal—and she moved swiftly, worried others might be searching too.

The hinges creaked as she slipped through the unlocked back door. It was still inside. The temperature was cool as the scent of dust and old wood filled her lungs.

She made a beeline for the pulpit. Once there, she paused, feeling the strange power from where she stood, overlooking the empty rows of benches.

This spot, this podium, had been one of Clive's drugs of choice, an aphrodisiac he couldn't resist.

It gave her a sense of satisfaction, knowing Clive would never take his place there again, twisting scripture for his own designs.

She imagined even the Almighty had to close His eyes when Clive was standing here, preaching his poison.

Maybe now this place could be filled with a kind God more like Clarissa's, she thought.

Aware of the need to hurry, she knelt behind the glossy wooden pulpit, her hands shaking as she pried away the small panel at the base.

The wood was rough under her touch, splintering slightly as she worked it loose, wishing she had brought a tool to help.

As she held her breath, she removed the panel and reached down into the secret compartment.

Her fingers fumbled in the darkness, feeling their way around.

Then, her hand brushed against something familiar—the worn cover of an old Bible, hidden there for who knows how long.

Beneath it, just as she remembered, was a small leather pouch with a zipper. She lifted it up, unzipping it, and inside was a row of neatly stacked large bills, hidden away under the very gaze of God.

But beneath that money satchel lay Clive's true power.

He had known the weaknesses of men and bent them to his will—liquoring them up, taking them to a brothel in a nearby county, and capturing their shame in compromising photos. It had always been easier for Clive to hold something over someone's head than to pay them.

He had taken pleasure in watching "so-called good men" fall.

Esther lifted the small box out and opened it. Beneath the cardboard lid was a stack of sins printed on photo paper.

As she thumbed through the snapshots, her breath caught with each one.

Familiar faces stared back at her—Frank and Vic, laughing with lewd women or posing beside crates of moonshine. She hadn't come for these, but there was no avoiding them.

And there it was—the one that made her stomach churn, the one she wanted destroyed more than anything. It felt like she was bound by a contract she had signed with Clive, a deal that cost her soul.

The photo between her fingertips filled her with anger, tears biting at her eyes. She had never seen it until now, but she remembered him taking it in a drunken haze, her mind desperate to numb the pain. Clive had forcefully stripped her, camera in hand.

She paused, looking at the photo, really seeing it.

Just a girl, young, her long, dark, wavy hair pulled to the side. Her thin, bare back—exposed—bared only to humiliate her. Uneven ridges, raised and pale, ran up and down that back. Clive had taken such delight in those scars as any devil would.

But that girl—it was her. And she'd never be again.

She would burn those pictures—all of them—and set everyone free. That was her plan.

Esther's pulse quickened, and she no longer wanted to linger or look at the rest of the photos. She snatched them all up, stuffing them into the pouch.

After zipping it up, she placed it securely in her tight, longline brassiere. With a quick pass of her hand, she made sure it lay flat against her body, concealed beneath her loose dress.

Being mindful, she returned the box and replaced the panel, her fingers shaking.

Her mind flashed back to the day she'd accidentally discovered his hidden lair—his source of power. She had seen Clive here, hiding bills inside. He hadn't noticed her—she'd been too quiet, slipping away before he could turn and catch her spying.

Once, she had considered taking the money and running, even opening the secret space and looking at its contents.

However, Clive's threats of putting her in a pine box had done their job. He would have broken her neck in a second if he'd found her.

Last winter, someone from his congregation had told her about a place called New Mexico. It sounded nice, and she briefly considered escaping there. But the plan wasn't realistic. She knew she'd never be able to leave the state—Clive would send his goons to Jasper to get her before she even had time to make her getaway.

But now… now things were different.

Ian needed a smart lawyer if he was going to have a chance at all, and she had no means of helping him—until now. Taking Clive's ill-gotten gains felt like some twisted form of tithing, a small measure of justice. He'd hurt her, her very body paying the price. Now, his dirty money might help set a good man free.

A defiant satisfaction burned in her chest as she rose to her feet, clutching the bundle tightly against her.

But that feeling was short-lived. Esther's pulse quickened—she was wasting precious time. She had to get back to Abram before anyone caught sight of her here. Still, one more place remained to check—Clive's camera was missing from his stash, and she wasn't sure if it held undeveloped film.

She hurried out of the chapel and made her way around to the cellar doors. The rusted handle resisted her grip, but with a firm yank, she managed to pry it open.

A cool rush of damp air greeted her, carrying with it the earthy smell of mildew and rot. The darkness below felt thick, almost suffocating. Her footsteps landed softly against the dirt floor—the sound swallowed by the eerie stillness.

She hurried, her hands sweeping over the cold ground, feeling her way around the crawl space where Clive hid things. Desperation set the pace as she searched for his instrument of control, knowing it wasn't in the house.

She was terrified that, in one of her moonshine-fueled blackouts, he had taken more photos.

The thought of someone finding his camera and developing the images made her pace quicken. Her reputation in Larkin would be forever destroyed, and even Ian, despite his understanding, would struggle to look beyond it, Esther was certain.

Strange, familiar memories of Gran surfaced as she recalled the cellar's layout—the crevices and corners where Clive might have stashed something. It was pitch black, but she knew this place just as well as the woods in the Blue Hollows.

Esther grunted in frustration as she pushed the table back in front of the small crawl space hidden in the dark recess of the cellar. The wood scraped along the dirt floor, the noise echoing off the cold, damp walls.

She wiped the sweat from her brow, her breath coming in shallow bursts.

The secret stash was empty. Completely cleared out.

As if Clive's sins had vanished with him.

And then… just as the night before, her legs began to throb, a deep ache settling in her bones.

Dread crept up her spine, tightening around her like a warning.

She shouldn't have come down here—not to Lucifer's dungeon.

A voice screamed in her mind, a woman's voice.

It yelled with an urgency Esther had never felt before.

The words rose in pitch and volume, running over and over in her ears.

"RUN, GIRL, RUN!"

Esther heeded it immediately, knowing she had to depart without delay.

As she turned to leave, with the instinct of prey sensing a predator—everything stilled.

The air shifted.

Her breath caught as her eyes fell on a pair of brown, worn boots resting on the cellar steps.

Deputy Frank descended, his figure looming, dark and menacing, against the dim light filtering down the stairs.

His boots scuffed each step, every footfall slow and deliberate—savoring the tension that thickened with every movement.

Esther froze. Her mind scrambled for an excuse, but Frank's cold, calculating gaze had already locked onto her.

"What ya doin' down here, girl?" Frank's voice cut through the silence, low and thick with suspicion.

She swallowed hard, forcing a shaky smile as she struggled to keep herself steady.

"Oh, ya startled me, that's all. I was just… I was just lookin' for somethin'."

Frank stepped closer, his shadow swallowing her as his eyes bore into her, searching for a crack in her story.

"What ya lookin' for, then?" His tone was sharper now.

Esther's pulse quickened. She shook her head, trying to brush off his question.

"Nothin', really… just somethin' I left down here a while back."

Frank's gaze hardened, his patience thinning.

"Ya forget, huh? Bein' so dumb, I bet ya forget plenty. Or… maybe ya don't."

"I was just lookin' for an ol' family Bible," she said, her voice wavering despite her best efforts to sound calm.

She glanced down, praying he wouldn't notice the terror surging through her veins.

Frank took another step closer, his presence suffocating, his voice dropping to a dangerous low.

"Ya keep yer books in a goddamn cellar?"

Before she could answer, his hand shot out, fisting her hair and yanking her forward. She gasped in pain as he bent her over, his grip tightening like a vise.

"Show me where it is," he said. His breath was hot against her ear. "Now!"

"It ain't here no more," Esther said, her heart hammering in her chest.

Frank's laugh was dark as he threw her to the ground as if she meant nothing. She hit the dirt hard, palms scraping against the cold, unforgiving dirt.

"Ya ain't lookin' for no damn family Bible," he said, towering over her. "Everybody knows ya too dumb to read… or anythin' else, 'cept what Clive kept ya 'round fer."

As she lay on the ground, another shadow appeared at the cellar door.

Vic, his scrawny form casting a long silhouette, leaned against the frame, taking in the scene with a twisted smirk.

"Well, look at that," he drawled. "She's already here. Ain't even gotta nab the bitch."

Frank straightened, a wicked grin spreading across his face.

"Yep, a bitch followin' her master's orders," he said. He paused, his eyes narrowing as he noticed the confusion flicker across Esther's face. It stopped him—perplexed him, even.

"Or… maybe she just got greedy. Came lookin' fer it her damn self, savin' me the trouble," Frank added.

Frank crouched down, glaring into Esther's eyes, tilting his head slightly, scrutinizing her as though he were sizing her up.

"Ya think you were gonna come at me, try to own me too, little girl?" He laughed. "Like you ever could. I guarantee you ain't ever gonna get the chance, darlin'. Yer gonna be dead by nightfall."

Vic scratched his chin, his gaze roaming the dark cellar. "Ya reckon Clive hid it here?"

Frank's grin widened as his eyes gleamed with mocking disbelief. "Why in the hell do ya think she's down here, Vic? I swear, sometimes you're just as God-damned stupid as she is."

He petted Esther's hair softly, mocking her frightened state. Her body trembled as he grabbed her chin, forcing her to meet his eyes.

"Now listen here," he said, his breath hot and heavy with threat. "I ain't Clive. I ain't gonna sweet-talk ya or buy ya nice things."

"If ya want a chance," he growled. "Even a tiny chance at stayin' alive, yer gonna show me. You know what I'm lookin' fer, and ya know where it is."

Esther swallowed hard as fear tightened in her chest. There was no escape. Slowly, she nodded, trying to think of a plan—anything—as she stood, her knees weak. She knew exactly what they wanted, and if they found Clive's photos hidden on her body, it would be the end.

Frank's eyes wore a soulless expression, and she was sure he'd murder her without an ounce of regret. At least with Clive, she had held some value. But Frank only saw her as a loose end.

"It's… over there," she said. "Clive kept his stuff over there."

She looked over her shoulder, pointing to the dark, cave-like space, her finger trembling as it aimed at the old drop-leaf table.

"It's behind that," she said, indicating the black void beyond. "It's in there."

Vic moved the obstacle aside and crouched, peering into the crawl space. After a few seconds, he pulled back, frowning.

"I can't see a damn thing," he said.

Frank's glare shifted to Esther, his patience thinning.

"Ya got a candle or somethin'?"

Esther shook her head, her breath catching in her throat.

"No… but there's one in the house."

Frank let out a frustrated sigh, his eyes narrowing.

"Alright then. We'll be right back."

Without warning, he grabbed her arm roughly, yanking her toward the stairs, his fingers digging into her flesh.

"We gonna take us a little stroll," he said, his grip as unyielding as iron.

Frank dragged Esther out of the cellar, the afternoon sun blinding as they crossed the yard toward Clive's house. The humid air clung to her skin, but the heat was nothing compared to the icy panic in her gut.

As they walked, Frank spoke.

"Tell me somethin', what ya see out on Miller Highway last Saturday night?"

Esther's pulse quickened as she struggled to understand what he was implying.

"I don't know what ya talkin' 'bout," she replied.

Frank stopped abruptly, yanking her around to look at him as his eyes bore into her.

"You see anyone out there?" he pressed.

Esther shook her head.

"I swear, I ain't seen a soul out there."

His face tightened, but he didn't say anything more. Instead, he pushed her forward, urging her toward the back steps of Clive's house. The door was locked, and Frank, too impatient to go around to the front, kicked it open with a quick boot, shoving Esther inside.

"Be quick about it," he instructed.

She nodded, pointing to a high cupboard.

"Candles up there," she said.

With a suspicious eye, Frank pulled out a kitchen chair and placed it under the cabinet.

"Go on then," he ordered, his eyes never leaving her.

Esther climbed onto the chair, her heart pounding. She stretched upward and opened the door. Reaching inside, her fingers brushed against the smooth surface of a large baking dish on the shelf as a shiver ran through her.

She needed courage.

Once again, a voice echoed in her head, the same one—now clearer—saying something new.

"DO IT! Be brave!"

"Then you need to RUN! Hear me? Run!"

Frightened, but without a second thought, Esther gripped the dish firmly.

She swung it down with all the strength she could muster, smashing the ceramic against the side of Frank's head.

He yelled out in a roar of pain, stumbling back as blood trickled down his temple.

"Ya fuckin' whore!" he spat, clutching his head. "Ya filthy fuckin' whore!"

But Esther didn't wait to hear more.

She jumped down from the chair and bolted for the open door, her feet pounding against the floor as she fled.

She leaped down the back steps in a single bound, sprinting hard across the yard, her heart drumming wildly with fear.

The freshly plowed fields stretched out before her as she hopped the fence in one fell swoop. Kicking off her shoes, she bolted barefoot across the soft earth.

All the while, the voice shouted in her head, "RUN!"

Behind her, she heard Frank cursing as he stumbled out of the house, trying to follow.

He tripped over the fence, landing face-first in the dirt, but scrambled to his feet, letting out a furious shout that echoed across the field.

"Vic! Vic! Get out here!"

Vic appeared quickly in the yard, his eyes wide with shock as he took in the scene.

"What the hell happened?" he asked.

Frank wiped the sweat and blood from his brow as he squinted against the bright sun. He pointed at Esther, a distant figure fleeing across the open land toward town.

"I gotta go get her," he growled. "She clocked me good… God damn girl runs like a deer."

His chest heaved with frustration as the sweltering heat radiated around him.

"Vic," he said, turning to his accomplice, "you stay here and get a good look at what's in there. And I warn ya—don't cross me too. I'll kill you flat, and ya know it."

Vic shifted with an uneasy nod. His eyes whipped back to the girl, now running with determined speed, her body a blur in the shimmering distance.

"Well, ya best go get her, then," he said, kicking at the dirt beneath his feet. "She's high-tailin' it and fixin' to outrun ya to Larkin."

Frank clenched his jaw as he took a staggering step toward his car.

"I know that! I got eyes," he snapped.

Frank gave one last glance at Esther's figure shrinking toward the horizon. He knew if he didn't catch her soon, everything would unravel.

She knew too much—he was certain.

Chapter 41: Foxes in the Hen House

Abram's voice boomed as he shook the iron bars of the small-town jail cell, his words ringing out in desperation. "Wake up! Ian, wake the hell up!"

He reached out, stretching his arm through the bars, grabbing Ian's boot, and shaking it forcefully.

"Ian! You hear me?" he yelled.

Ian, always the first to rise back at home—the one to catch even the faintest sounds in the night, like foxes in the henhouse— was now locked in a bizarre slumber, frozen beneath a thick sheet of ice.

It was unlike him and unsettling.

The sight of his friend so still, so unresponsive, sent a chill through Abram, making him question if Ian was even alive.

But then, Ian groaned—a low, pained sound—as he stirred beneath the scratchy blanket. He threw the cover aside, wincing as he sat up. His hand instinctively moved to the side of his head, where a large, angry welt marred his skin. Dried blood streaked across his forehead and cheek.

"Ah… hold on," he muttered, his voice thick with exhaustion and pain.

Abram's eyes narrowed, assessing his friend's injury.

"That damn sheriff rough ya up?" he asked, a note of accusation in his tone as he glanced toward the empty desk at the front of the room.

Ian shook his head, blinking as he tried to shake off the lingering fog from the night before.

"No…" he began, but his words trailed off as a sudden flash of memory slammed into him.

His eyes widened in alarm. He lunged toward the bars, as far as he could, his arm stretched out. His fingers gripped Abram's wrist with desperate intensity.

"Where's Esther?"

"She's fine," Abram assured him. "Saw her not that long ago."

Ian's grip on Abram's arm tightened for a moment before he released him, leaning back against the cold metal bars.

"You gotta get her somewhere safe," Ian said, his voice low, desperate. "You've got to hide her, Abram! Frank and Vic…"

The front door of the station swung open abruptly, the sound reverberating through the small room as the brass handle slammed against the wall.

Sheriff Ronell strolled in, the clinking of his boots muted by the worn wooden floors, a full quart of cold milk in his hand, fresh from his errand. He looked almost casual, his demeanor at ease.

But the moment his eyes fell on Abram next to the jail cell and Ian half-sitting on his bunk, Sheriff Ronell's gaze sharpened.

The dried blood smeared across Ian's forehead, dark against his tan skin, caught his attention. His brow furrowed as he took in the scene, his mood shifting from calm to concern in an instant.

"What the hell ya do to yourself?" the sheriff asked, frowning as he set the milk down on his desk and moved closer to the cell.

He reached for the door, but when he pulled the handle, it didn't budge. His brow furrowed in confusion as he looked down at the lock before turning to Abram and Ian with a puzzled expression.

"Who locked this door?"

Sheriff Ronell's eyes darted to the set of keys hanging on the wall, and he muttered to himself.

"Now, Goddamnit, I know I didn't lock ya up last night… 'less'n I'm goin' crazy," he said.

His gaze snapped back to Ian, suspicion painting his features. "Frank come by last night?"

Ian hesitated, unsure whether to trust the sheriff, but the memory of the previous night burned in his mind. He let out a slow breath and nodded.

"Sure did. Knocked me on the head too."

The sheriff's frown deepened.

"Why'd he do a thing like that?" he asked.

Sheriff Ronell stood there for a moment, rubbing the back of his neck, perplexed. He hadn't anticipated any of this when he stepped into his office this morning.

Still, he grabbed the keys hanging on the wall and moved toward the cell door with slow, deliberate steps. The clang of the keys echoed in the room as he unlocked it, his eyes narrowing.

"Were ya tryin' to get out or somethin'?" the sheriff asked, casting a skeptical glance toward Ian, as if assessing the situation.

"I came in willingly last night," Ian responded, frustration lacing his tone. "And how the hell would I exactly escape?"

He jerked his hand up, the cuff clanking loudly against the bar as his eyes fixed on the sheriff.

"Your deputy and that fella Vic Porter—they tried sneaking up on me in the dead of night," Ian added.

Sheriff Ronell blinked, the lines on his forehead deepening as the weight of Ian's words settled on him.

"You said Vic was with him? Why the hell did he bring Vic in here?" The sheriff had a sharp edge to his voice.

It didn't sit right with him, seeing Vic Porter so often by Frank's side lately. Vic was running errands for him, even riding in his patrol vehicle. As a matter of fact, he had planned on having a conversation with Frank later that day about that very thing.

That morning, as Vic sat in Frank's car, a strange feeling had drifted over the sheriff as if those fellas were up to no good.

And why hadn't Frank mentioned the incident with Ian? Not a single word about it out front, like he was deliberately hiding something.

The sheriff had been noticing odd behavior from Frank for a while now. Maybe it started as restlessness—common enough when a man's nearing his mid-forties—but over the last several months, it had gone beyond that. Frank had been changing, and not for the better.

He'd noticed Frank was drinking more, despite living in a dry county, and spending time with less desirable folk—people who didn't reflect well on someone in his position, especially in a place like Larkin.

It was his deputy's duty to be here by 8 AM—not to roll up whenever he wanted. And since when would Frank visit the station in the middle of the night, in a rainstorm no less, just to hang up keys?

Something stunk.

It wasn't right.

It was a weekday. Frank should have been home with his wife, not out doing God knows what with Vic.

The sheriff paused.

His gaze turned distant as he replayed past events in his head. His lips pressed into a tight line, and his eyes drew tight in thought.

"Ya know," he began slowly, his words deliberate, as though working through a puzzle that had been bothering him for too long.

"I've been wonderin' how Vic ever found that Primm still up there on the hill last year. It was covered so damn good, ya coulda walked right over it and never even seen it." The sheriff's words lingered for a moment before he muttered quietly, almost to himself, "Damn good cover."

Sheriff Ronell continued pacing back and forth, his boots thudding against the floor. His mind was racing as he pieced together what Ian had said.

"Frank say anythin' to ya last night?" he asked, turning his attention back to Ian, his eyes scanning the man's bruised and battered face for any clue.

Ian shook his head.

"He wasn't after me," Ian said, his voice low but strained. "I'm pretty sure he was looking for Esther. Somehow, he thought she'd be here."

The sheriff's brow furrowed further, his confusion growing.

"Why? She didn't shoot Clive—you did. Why in God's name would I lock her up?" he snapped.

Abram cut in, his voice cautious but quick.

"Hold on—did ya say he got shot?"

Sheriff Ronell nodded, his voice growing quieter, almost detached, as he recalled the details.

"Shot with a pistol. Right in the head. Left his body on the side of the road."

Ian tensed and instinctively tried to rise, but his wrist remained shackled to the bar.

"I didn't kill Clive!" he shouted, his voice a mix of anger and relief. "I've never shot anyone! Yeah, I hit him really good a few times, but I left him by his car. I didn't know he'd been shot."

Abram stepped forward, his tone unwavering. "Ian doesn't even have a pistol, Sheriff. Ask anyone."

The more Sheriff Ronell thought about it, the more Frank's behavior troubled him.

More so than Vic, Frank had grown close to Clive over the last couple of years—far too close for comfort. Clive had been running liquor right under everyone's nose, and it was hard to believe that Frank, with all his proximity and supposed friendship, didn't know.

No, Frank had known.

That realization burned in Sheriff Ronell's gut like a bad drink.

It was Frank, after all, who had pushed the idea of bringing Esther down to Clive.

He had defended Clive when suspicions were raised, always making excuses for him.

As if laying out the pieces on a table, Sheriff Ronell's mind whirled as he tried to put it all together. Though he didn't want to believe what was becoming painfully clear, Frank had a sidearm.

But it wasn't just that—Frank had also been the one to find Clive conveniently dead on the highway.

He had even offered to bring the body in himself, but Ronell insisted on seeing it firsthand.

Now, it all made sense—why Frank hadn't mentioned the strong smell of liquor or the busted bottles spilling from Clive's trunk until after the sheriff arrived on the scene.

And why the hell had Frank taken it upon himself to send Vic to check on Esther's whereabouts?

That strange exchange behind the station had felt wrong, and there had been an air of secrecy, of something more than casual talk.

Why were Frank and Vic so fixated on finding Esther? Did she know something that could implicate them? Had there been a fallout between Clive and Frank that she knew about?

The sheriff felt a strange reluctance the night before when thinking about bringing Frank up to the Old Reed Estate.

And now, thinking back, that conversation felt all wrong. It could've easily been taken as though he was planning to arrest Esther.

The sheriff had never mentioned Ian as a suspect in Clive's murder, even if jealousy might have been a motive.

He'd held that back, knowing Frank might get hot-headed, too passionate about someone murdering his friend. He wanted to feel out the situation first, be sure before stirring up trouble.

But Frank had acted too fast, too sure. All he'd known last night was that the sheriff had asked for the cell key and mentioned Esther being spotted out on Miller Highway. Somehow, Frank had pieced it together too perfectly.

It wasn't until now that Sheriff Ronell realized—Frank wasn't trying to solve a murder.

He was covering up one.

Sheriff Ronell stopped pacing abruptly, the gravity of it all crashing down on him. His face darkened as the realization hit, a sudden blow to the gut.

"Frank has a revolver," he said, his voice tight, simmering with barely contained rage. "I'm thinkin' he's the one that pulled that trigger."

The sheriff's fists clenched at his sides, knuckles turning white with the intensity of his anger. The burn of betrayal rose in his throat like bile. His eyes flickered with a dangerous heat as they moved to Ian and Abram, though the fury wasn't directed at them.

Frank's fatal error was not admitting that he had been there after sneaking in during the middle of the night. In his panic, he had locked the cell door and hung up the keys, leaving behind undeniable proof of his presence and stripping away any chance of denying involvement if Ian accused him.

Frank had gotten sloppy.

"Son of a bitch!" Sheriff Ronell exploded, his voice filling the room with a raw fury that echoed off the walls. "That bastard's been playin' me the whole damn time! Thinkin' I was his fool!"

Without hesitation, the sheriff stormed into the cell and quickly unlocked Ian's handcuffs, his face still flushed. The cuffs clattered against the iron bars as they fell.

"Why don't ya boys run up and make sure Esther's alright," Sheriff Ronell ordered urgently. "Don't let no one pick her up, whatever they tell ya."

Ian tried to stand, but his head spun, forcing him to sit back down as the dizziness subsided.

"No need," Abram said. "She's down in town."

Ian's heart skipped a beat.

"Where?" he asked.

"Just needed a few of her things from her cousin's place," Abram explained, his voice low, tinged with uncertainty.

"You left her there?" Ian said, his eyes widening as anger flashed across his face.

Sheriff Ronell froze mid-step. He turned back toward them—his face twisted in horror.

"She's out at the preacher's?" the sheriff asked, his voice rising, thick with alarm. "Damn it, that's where Frank was headed!"

In an instant, Sheriff Ronell bolted for the door, his boots hitting against the wooden floor with a force that reverberated through the station.

His hand instinctively reached for the gun holster on his belt, fingers grazing the cool metal of the handle to reassure himself it was there, ready.

The gravity of the situation bore down on him—there wasn't a second to lose.

Ian and Abram exchanged a tense, urgent glance.

Without hesitation, Abram rushed to Ian's side, grabbing his arm and hauling him up.

Ian grimaced, the pounding in his head sharp, but he pushed through the pain, already knowing they had to move.

The transition from the dimly lit station to the glaring daylight was jarring. The sun beat down on them with almost blinding intensity, worsening the ache in Ian's head. He squinted against the light.

As Sheriff Ronell dashed to his car, he barked over his shoulder, "Take the other route! There's two ways to Clive's!" He pointed his finger in the opposite direction of the street to show which way he wanted them to go.

His voice carried as he quickly redirected his gesture toward Ian.

"And for God's sake, don't let that man drive!"

Without wasting another second, the sheriff jumped into his car, slamming the door hard.

The tires screeched as he gunned the engine, spinning the car into reverse before peeling out onto the street.

His police cruiser, built to chase bootleggers, tore away, weaving through the slower traffic as he sped off, leaving a trail of dust in his wake.

Once behind the wheel of the old Ford, Abram floored the gas pedal, the truck lurching forward.

He muttered under his breath, "I'm sorry, I shouldn't have left her there."

Beside him, Ian winced, his hand brushing the gash on his forehead. His breath came out in short, ragged bursts, and his eyes, usually sharp and steady, flickered with raw emotion.

"God, Abram… I love her. I can't lose someone again." His voice cracked, his eyes briefly squeezing shut as if the weight of that admission was almost too much to bear.

Abram glanced over, reading his friend's posture.

Ian's jaw was clenched tight, his shoulders rigid, but his eyes told a different story—worn and desperate. They burned with a fierce determination—the vulnerability was unmistakable.

In that instant, something clicked in Abram's head. He hadn't fully understood Ian's feelings for Esther until now, but it all made sense. And why would Ian give up his freedom to protect her? She wasn't just some girl at the Old Reed Estate. She was his… girl.

And just like Abram would do for Mitzy if need be, Ian had done for Esther. There was no talking him out of it now, either— his German friend was already devoted to the girl from the hills. Once Ian made up his mind, it was set in stone.

Abram tightened his grip on the wheel, the truck speeding down the rough dirt road. The engine roared as they bounced over the uneven terrain, every second feeling weighted, time even holding its breath.

He pushed the old Ford harder, its frame rattling as they barreled through the bends, dust rising in their trail.

Ian, seething with anger and resolve, silently prayed the sheriff—driving the faster vehicle—would make it there before them.

Because this time… he WOULD kill a man. Maybe two.

Chapter 42: The River

Esther's legs burned as she tore across the fields, chasing the distant silhouette of the rural town. Her mind scrambled as her feet fought for balance. She leaped—stumbled—hit hard, the earth rushing up to meet her. Still, she rose, driving forward, her body moving on instinct, cutting through the heat.

The freshly plowed soil was unforgiving, jagged furrows threatening to trip her with every step. Ditches of cold, rushing water sliced through the earth, glistening under the midday sun.

Her one goal—make it to Larkin. She thought about the raging river she had once swum through, fighting the current to save her life. Well, this time, all she had to do was swim through these open fields and reach the other side, she told herself.

Her chest pounded—echoing in her ears. Each breath came sharp and desperate, burning her lungs. Pain tore through her sides, every inhale a fresh stab of agony.

But Esther shoved the pain aside. She couldn't stop. Not now. Not when everything was teetering on the edge of the worst.

Her mind spun in a thousand directions, yet all her thoughts kept circling back to Ian—imprisoned.

Frank had been out on Miller Highway.

And he had plenty of reasons to kill Clive. Their friendship had recently soured, most likely due to the devious power Clive held over him—power that now rested in her brassiere.

She pressed her hand against it, ensuring it was safe—the only chance for Ian's freedom.

She couldn't afford to lose it now—couldn't let this slip through her fingers.

Esther wasn't just running—

She was running for Ian, for the life he chased across an ocean.

Running for Rebecca and Benjamin's father, the man who carved out dreams with calloused hands.

She ran for Clarissa's best man-she knew, the one who stood by in silence when words fell short.

She ran for the sister she hadn't remembered, for sweet Adeline's husband, a man left with only grief.

And, she ran for Annie, who crossed down that mountain, to save the life of her unborn baby.

She ran for Gran, who'd never bind her feet to the hills again—no invisible chains, no heavy words left to hold her down.

But most of all, Esther ran for herself.

She ran to feel the wind, to feel the earth pulse beneath her, to claim the life she'd kept just out of reach—because, more than anything,

Esther wanted to be *alive*.

And Frank wouldn't take it from her now. She refused.

She could hear his car not far behind.

The tires ground and skidded through the deep ruts of the field.

He was getting closer, but the deep grooves of the earth slowed his progress, jarring the car with every bump and dip.

It bought her time.

"Damn you, girl!" Frank yelled.

Esther glanced back briefly, her eyes widening in terror.

She saw Frank's car lurching up and down through the field, closing the distance between them.

He was swerving recklessly, the patrol vehicle's wheels slipping as the moist soil clung to the tires, threatening to pull him deeper into the earth.

But he was still gaining on her.

Panic surged through her veins, and she pushed her aching legs even harder.

She had to cross the road ahead and reach the next field. That was her only chance.

Beyond that, the fields would open up, leading to the outskirts of Larkin, where she might reach help.

Abram, Margie Mae—anyone.

With one final burst of speed, Esther reached the edge of the road and leaped over the fence that bordered it.

Her feet hit the hard-packed earth, sending a shock up her legs.

But she kept going, sprinting toward the field.

She was almost there.

Frank's car surged forward as he pressed the accelerator down, picking up speed. The tires dug into the uneven ground as he aimed straight ahead. With a heavy thud, the front bumper slammed into the fence.

Esther didn't look back this time. She forced herself forward, her muscles screaming for relief as her body reached its limits.

She was halfway across the road when Frank's car broke free of the wooden barrier, the roar of the engine cutting through the air like a predator's growl.

The sound made her heart lurch in terror, an icy wave of dread crashing over her.

He was closing in.

He was going to catch her. He was going to kill her.

Her legs pumped harder, her breath ragged in her throat, but no matter how fast she ran, the sound of the engine drew closer.

Just ahead, the open ground stretched wide—one final leap over another fence, and she'd have one last field to cross. She could almost make out the buildings in the distance, a faint glimmer of hope on the horizon.

But Frank was so close. Esther could feel it—the engine's warm breath on her neck.

Suddenly, the sound of another car reached her ears—a louder, deeper rumble that cut through the air.

Sheriff Ronell's car came barreling down the rural road, his eyes narrowing as he spotted Esther up ahead. She was running, her figure small against the sprawling fields, but what caught his attention was Frank's car tearing after her, gaining speed with every second.

Ronell swerved violently, narrowly missing Esther as she darted across the road and into the following field.

He slammed on the brakes, tires kicking up dust as the cruiser screeched to a stop.

"God damn it!" Sheriff Ronell muttered under his breath as he whipped the steering wheel around, preparing to follow them.

But before he could complete the turn, Frank's car shot out in front of him, blocking his path.

The sheriff's hand slammed onto the horn, blaring a warning.

Frank ignored him. His eyes were locked on Esther, just starting to cross the final stretch of land.

Frank's car smashed through the fence, the wood splintering beneath the tires as he gunned the engine. He would not let her get away—not now.

Sheriff Ronell cursed under his breath and floored the gas pedal, his car tearing into the dirt in Frank's wake.

There was no time to waste. This wasn't just about saving Esther—it was about stopping Frank.

Far on the other side of a pasture, Ian and Abram sped down a different road. The old truck rattled and groaned under the strain, its engine not built for speed.

Ian had one goal in mind—he had to get to Esther before it was too late. But then, it hit them—a sinking realization. They were nowhere near the heart of the fight.

A wide canal blocked their path, with no immediate access. Going the long way around would take too much time—by the time they got there, it could all be over.

"We're on the wrong damn side, Abram!" Ian shouted.

Abram made a quick judgment call, slamming the brakes hard. The truck slid as he turned it around, dirt flying.

"We've got to go back the other way!" Abram said.

The men were visibly upset, but as they glanced across the distance, they saw Sheriff Ronell had almost made it to the chase.

Frank's car was closing in on Esther, and a knot tightened in Ian's gut as fear surged through him.

The uneven ground did little to slow Frank down, his cruiser bouncing but gaining.

Ian watched as Frank inched closer, veering sharply to cut her off, just a few feet behind.

"Damn it, Abram, he's gonna hit her!" Ian shouted, his hands clenching the dashboard of the truck, knuckles white as Frank's car drew nearer to Esther.

Esther barely had time to react.

She leaped to the side, her foot catching in the deep grooves of the plowed earth. She stumbled, nearly falling into an irrigation furrow, but caught herself at the last second.

Frank swerved to avoid the ditch, his automobile bouncing violently as he fought to regain control.

He slammed on the brakes, the tires digging into the soft earth. The car lurched to a stop.

The wheels spun uselessly in the mud, sinking deeper and deeper into the wet soil.

Esther kept running. She didn't dare look back. She could hear the engine struggling behind her, but she wouldn't stop—not now, not when she was so close.

Frank threw open the car door, his face twisted in rage as he jumped out.

His hand shot to the Colt .45 at his hip.

He raised the gun, his eyes narrowing as he took aim at her fleeing figure.

"I'm gonna shoot ya if ya don't stop!" Frank yelled.

Esther didn't stop. She kept running, her breath coming in ragged gasps as she pushed herself harder, willing her legs to keep moving.

The shot rang out, echoing across the field.

Esther flinched but kept going.

The bullet whizzed past her, kicking up dirt a few feet to her right.

Behind Frank, Sheriff Ronell skidded to a stop about ten yards away.

A cloud of dirt swirled in the still air as he killed the engine and yanked the emergency brake. His heart pounded against his ribs—adrenaline surging through his veins.

Without hesitation, the sheriff jumped out of the vehicle, his boots sinking into the soft earth. Pulling his gun from his holster.

He took a breath as he positioned himself behind the car door, bracing his arm against the top for support.

His eyes locked onto Frank.

Frank stood just ahead, his back to the sheriff—menacing in the open field, gun drawn. His pistol barrel gleamed cold under the harsh daylight.

Frank aimed it squarely at Esther, his hand steady.

Sheriff Ronell squinted as the sun bounced off the metal bumper of Frank's car, momentarily blinding him. His grip tightened on his own gun, a deep dread settling in his gut.

Time was running out.

The sheriff's shot rang out, hitting Frank in the leg with brutal precision.

Frank staggered forward, a scream of pain tearing from his throat. Clutching at the wound, his face twisted in shock as blood soaked through his pants, darkening the fabric.

Despite the searing pain, Frank's anger continued to flare.

He spun on his heel, twisting to face Sheriff Ronell.

His eyes were wild—filled with disbelief.

"Ya dun shot me!" Frank bellowed, his voice cracking under the strain.

Frank's gun, now trembling in his hand, swung toward the sheriff, the barrel quivering as he tried to maintain his grip.

The shock in his voice was palpable, as though Frank could hardly fathom that the man he once trusted had pulled the trigger on him.

"Put the damn gun down, Frank!" Sheriff Ronell ordered.

Frank's eyes darted between the sheriff and the trail where Esther had vanished.

The gash in his leg bled heavily, but the urgency of the situation forced him to ignore it.

Everything had fallen apart so quickly—Clive's betrayal, the dark money, Esther knowing too much—leaving only pure desperation.

"She's getting away!" Frank shouted.

"I know ya killed the Preacher, Frank!" Sheriff Ronell shot back, his eyes locked on Frank's every move.

Frank's gaze flicked back to the sheriff, his face pale from blood loss.

His grip on the gun tightened as he raised it once more, aiming it high as if to fire.

"Ya gonna pick her over me, Marty?" Frank asked.

"Don't do it, Frank," Sheriff Ronell warned, his voice low and filled with a sadness that came from years of friendship now torn apart by deception.

A single gunshot shattered the silence.

Its sharp crack echoed across the field, like the toll of a distant bell—final and inescapable.

It carried the weight of absolution.

The inevitable consequence of a wrong too great to be undone. In that fleeting moment, the balance had shifted—a life for a life.

Sheriff Ronell had shot his lifelong friend. The man with whom he'd once shared carefree childhood days. The man who had sat at his dinner table, laughing over shared meals.

An anguish was visible in Marty's eyes as Frank stumbled backward. The force of the shot knocked him to the ground with a dull thud.

The soft dirt embraced Frank's body as he fell, as though the earth itself had been waiting to claim him.

His hand, once gripping the weapon with fierce determination, slackened. The gun slipped from his fingers, falling to the ground.

Frank had been part of his life for so long, and Sheriff Ronell could never have pulled the trigger if he hadn't seen the madness in his friend's eyes—the wild, raging determination aimed straight at him.

It was a shot born of necessity, not a choice. And it left behind a gaping void in the sheriff's heart, knowing there was no going back from this.

The bullet had struck Frank clean in the center of his body. Dark, purple-tinged blood oozed quickly from the hole, staining his uniform and dripping steadily to the ground.

Sheriff Ronell looked down at his old friend, the gravity of what he'd been forced to do sinking in, twisting his usually tough gut.

"Ah, Frank, ya fool," he muttered, his voice thick with sorrow. "Why'd ya make me do that? It didn't have to turn out this way. You were like a second son to my momma."

Frank let out a bitter, rasping laugh. The irony of the situation wasn't lost on him. Blood bubbled up from his mouth as he coughed, the sound wet and painful. He could feel his strength slipping away, but his stubbornness kept him clinging to consciousness.

"She's gonna be mighty mad at ya for shootin' me, Marty," he spat, his voice growing weaker with each word. The defiance in his eyes dimmed as the life drained out of him.

The sheriff stood still, watching as the fight left his old friend.

"Yes… she will be," Sheriff Ronell replied, his voice tinged with sadness.

He watched as Frank's eyes held traces of both regret and acceptance, the realization of his fate dawning on him.

Frank's voice faltered, and he let out a long, labored breath. "I'm gonna die, ain't I?"

Sheriff Ronell nodded as Frank's body began to fail. Blood pooled beneath him, the dark soil slowly absorbing it.

"Sorry, Marty… got caught up… somethin' bad," Frank whispered hoarsely. "I made you shoot me…" His breath hitched, a wet cough rattling in his chest, blood speckling his lips.

"You… would've never picked me… over Annie's girl… yer girl."

Frank tried to laugh, but it came out as a weak gurgle, the life quickly draining from him now.

"Annie was a sweetheart of yers… should've known better," Frank added.

The lawman gave another solemn nod, grief deepening the lines on his face as he placed a hand on Frank's shoulder. There was no anger left in him, only regret. He had never wanted this.

Sheriff Marty Ronell had never told a single soul the truth about Esther, but maybe his actions had finally given him away.

It was true. Esther was his and Annie's—born from a love that had been innocent and pure, between two young people who had promised themselves to each other. Back then, they were full of hope, dreaming of a future together.

That all changed when Pearl Primm got wind of their secret. She had been furious, locking Annie away up on the Blue Hollow Hills. Her father had stood armed and ready, always there to chase Marty off whenever he tried to see her. And he had tried. Oh, how he had tried—coming up that narrow road, only to be turned back at the barrel of a shotgun.

He hadn't known Annie was with child. He only knew she was being kept from him, hidden away from the gossipin' folk.

Eventually, Marty had to give up. He couldn't break through the iron grip of the Primm family, and he had no choice but to accept that Annie had slipped away from him.

Time passed, and he heard whispers that she'd made her way to Jasper, running from the life she'd been trapped in. Marty moved on, trying to bury the ache that had gnawed at him for so long.

It wasn't until years later that he learned the truth—Annie had given birth to a little girl. Their little girl. Esther.

By then, it had been too late. Esther was being raised by the Primms, hidden away just as Annie had been. Marty had told himself that maybe it was for the best, that she would have a stable life.

But deep down, he knew it wasn't true. He knew the life Pearl Primm had carved out for her daughter and granddaughter—one filled with secrets and hardship. Still, who was he to interfere? What right did he have to take her from the only people she had ever known?

Now, though, maybe his actions had betrayed him. Maybe, in trying to protect Esther, the truth he had buried for so long had surfaced.

"Ya want me to tell yer wife somethin'?" the sheriff asked, tryin' to offer what little comfort he could in these last moments.

Frank coughed again, trying to form words, but his strength had left him. His breath grew shallow, his eyes unfocused.

With one last strained gasp, his eyes rolled back, and his body went still.

Marty now stood there, alone in the field.

The wind, the only witness to the truth of his silent nod.

Chapter 43: Larkin

Esther stumbled onto the small-town road of Larkin—her breath in labored gasps. Dark, brown mud clung to her legs, splattered high to her knees, thick and heavy.

Each step felt as though the ground was trying to pull her back down, her dress trailing behind, stained. Her limbs trembled under the strain, barely holding her upright, each muscle quivering, frayed threads ready to snap.

Her skin glistened under the late morning sun, beads of sweat rolling down her flushed face.

Townspeople stood outside their homes and shops, drawn by the gunshots that had echoed in the distance just moments before. They watched her curiously, as though she were an apparition—barefoot and frantic.

Her gaze flickered from face to face, but she could barely make sense of her surroundings. She felt their stares, whispers rippling through the crowd, sweeping over her in waves, but she pushed herself onward.

Esther had made it to Larkin, but she was convinced that her fight wasn't over yet.

Her eyes darted around, searching desperately for Abram, for Ian's old blue truck. That vehicle was her only hope of salvation.

Determined, she forced herself to keep moving, her heart hammering against her ribs as she scanned the street, passing Paulson's Mercantile. Her vision blurred with exhaustion, the figures on the sidewalk reduced to mere shapes.

Margie Mae's voice called out to her from across the road, but Esther didn't register it and didn't reply.

As Esther's knees buckled beneath her, she collapsed against the rough wooden siding of a nearby building. Her hands clung to the edge of the wall as her fingers struggled to steady her.

A fleeting thought crossed her mind of how they must be gossiping about her. *Look at that poor girl. So, she's a hillbilly after all?*

But honestly, Esther didn't give a damn. They could all go to hell. All that mattered was doing what she'd set out to do. A renewed resolve surged within her.

The sheriff's station was in her line of sight, just down the road. She squinted at the empty parking spaces in front of it, her stomach twisting with a sense of dread.

She couldn't see Abram or the truck anywhere.

A shiver ran through her as she wondered where Abram had gone.

Why had he left without her?

Worry built as she thought about the sheriff. She wasn't sure she could trust him after everything that had happened, despite his concern for her the night before.

She was even more confused about why he had intervened on her behalf with Frank, something she hadn't known until she had cleared the field, then briefly turned to see the two men.

Not waiting to see what followed, gunshots rang out behind her.

Even if Ian was in the station, it wasn't as simple as handing over the leather pouch. The photos inside—she needed to get rid of them.

"Where the hell are ya, Abram?" she said, her head spinning in every direction.

Her knees threatened to give out beneath her again as she stood there. After losing her breakfast, there was nothing left to draw on.

The lingering stares didn't go unnoticed as two men walked past, one tipping his hat with a strange look and asking, "Miss, ya alright?" She felt too exposed, too vulnerable.

What if Frank was still coming for her? Fear returned to her once again. He could show up at any moment. Not sure if he'd risk trying anything with witnesses around, she refused to take any chances.

She needed to think, to come up with a plan, but her body begged for rest.

Then, through the haze of fatigue and uncertainty, she heard it—the familiar sound of Ian's old Ford.

That low, steady rumble was unmistakable, like the sweetest music to her ears. Oh, how she loved that truck!

Esther's heart skipped a beat as she pushed herself off the wall, her body moving before her mind could catch up.

She squinted down the road, and there it was—the blue vehicle she'd been searching for, coming toward her, an answered prayer.

With every ounce of strength she had left, Esther stumbled forward—her eyes fixed on the truck.

Each thrum of its engine reverberated in her chest—syncing with her pulse.

As it drew closer, confusion flickered in her mind—there were two people inside.

For a brief moment, she couldn't believe what she was seeing. It felt like a mirage, a trick of the eye, a ghostly image of what she longed for most.

Could it really be him? Could it really be her Ian?

Her legs shook. She just needed to hold on for a few more seconds.

The truck screeched to a stop about twenty feet away as gravel kicked up beneath its tires.

Before she could even blink, Ian had flung the door open with a force that nearly tore it off the hinges.

He was out in an instant as his long strides ate up the distance between them. His boots thudded on the ground, his broad shoulders tense with a mix of panic and frenzy. His eyes locked on her, as if she were the only thing in his world.

By the time Ian reached her, his chest was heaving. His eyes, wild with emotion, searched her face, as if checking to see if she was real, if she was safe.

Without a word, he scooped her up into his arms. His grip was firm, desperate, lifting her off the ground—he needed to feel her weight to believe she was there.

A sigh escaped Ian as his arms tightened around her, holding her close—almost too tight, as if he feared she might slip away. His body trembled from the surge of electricity coursing through him, as if lightning had found its mark.

After what felt like forever, he finally set her down, though his hands never left her. His grip shifted to her shoulders, fingers clutching her skin. His gaze, fierce with worry, swept over her—frantic, scanning every inch for any sign of harm or injury. He needed to make sure she was whole.

"Are you all right? Did you get shot?" Ian asked, his voice tight.

Esther shook her head, words tangled in her throat, breath still too shallow to free them. Her eyes caught the dried stream of blood from the gash on his forehead as her trembling fingers reached for him. She traced the wound as if it might anchor him to her.

Ian's blue eyes pierced through the haze, locking onto hers. Sharp, clear, and full of relief. There was no room left for pain.

After they had circled back, he and Abram had heard two more gunshots echo across the valley. Each jarring ring sent a wave of terror directly into his heart.

A dense grove of green trees had held the truth hostage, hiding the fields from their view as they sped along the road. The truck jerked and skidded, but it hadn't felt fast enough. It felt as though something was slipping away from him.

In those agonizing seconds, Ian's mind conjured its cruelest vision—*Esther's beautiful body, broken and still, lying lifeless in the freshly plowed spring fields.* The soft earth turned up around her, as though the land itself sought to steal her from him.

She was gone. Lost to him forever.

But then, cutting across Larkin, she appeared—like a resurrection, coming back to life. Her fawn-like frame was trembling but upright.

Wild hair spilling loose from its pins, dancing in the thick, humid air in the aftermath of a storm. She stood there—her body shaking. Heart beating. Breath still in her chest.

Painfully real.

Beautifully alive.

"I'm okay," Ian said, his voice soft but steady.

He pulled her closer again, his arms tightening around her, as if afraid she might vanish.

"Esther…" His voice broke, raw with emotion. "I was scared I wouldn't get to you in time. I've never been so damn scared in my life."

His breath was shaky as he rested his head on hers.

"I can't ever lose you. I don't know what I'd do. Please… don't ever leave me. Not again," he said.

She tilted her head up, slowly. Her gaze met his—eyes filled with adoration and relief.

She paused, taking a breath as she let it settle over her.

But then, a small smile crept across her pink lips.

"Did ya break out of jail?" she asked, her voice hoarse.

Ian grinned, shaking his head. "No. You don't need to worry. The sheriff let me out."

Esther pressed her head against Ian's chest, feeling the steady rhythm of his breath—the tide rising and falling beneath her cheek. His arms, solid and sure, wrapped around her—her protector in a world that wasn't safe.

Yet, in Ian's eyes, there was something different. A quiet certainty, as if he'd already seen the edge of the storm and no longer feared the dark clouds gathering. Whatever truth he held, it steadied him, made him unshaken.

She clung to him, still chasing the calm he carried so effortlessly.

He would do anything to quell the storm inside her.

To give her that elusive reprieve.

The grace of peace she so desperately needed after everything they had weathered.

They would no longer face storms alone.

Here, she would rest in the shelter of his arms.

His body would take the wind, bearing the brunt of it for her.

He would shield her, standing between her and the fury, offering the sanctuary she had longed for. This was his promise to her.

Chapter 44: Missing Pages, 1943

Over a year had slipped away, like pages turning softly in a forgotten book. The seasons swept over the Tennessee hills in their slow, deliberate dance, each one carving new pathways in their stories, stitching together moments of hardship and the quiet embrace of grace.

A gentle peace had finally settled upon their lives, a peace forged in the fires of adversity—delicate, as a spider's web, yet resilient.

The sun hovered lazily above the horizon, casting a soft, golden light over the small, wooded lake. In 1943, even as the world burned with war, this place remained serene—a sanctuary cradled by the rolling hills of Blue Hollow.

Wild sunflowers swayed at its edge, their tall, bright yellow heads nodding in the breeze. Birds chirped softly from emerald canopies, their melodies blending with the distant sound of laughter drifting across the water.

Esther sat on a blanket spread across the grassy shore with her baby lying beside her. Golden wisps of hair, like threads spun from sunlight, fluttered against the baby's cheeks as soft rolls of flesh peeked out from a ruffled sundress.

Esther's gaze softened as she watched her daughter, a small soul adrift in peaceful slumber, tiny lips parted as if the heavens had whispered her into being.

Since a young age, Esther had sought to capture fleeting moments, her pencil ever at the ready. Now, nothing had changed— only the subject. With delicate care, she sketched the child she had once carried within her.

Her canvas—a gift from Ian—was a bound book, its crisp pages wrapped in soft leather. Her pencil glided lightly, capturing the gentle curve of her daughter's nose, the roundness of her cheeks, and the faint lines that crisscrossed her tiny palms, as though a map of a life just beginning.

Sketching her felt like capturing a fragment of bliss itself, as if through the lines and strokes, Esther could hold on to something fleeting yet infinite. This child had come to symbolize all the goodness that had emerged from a year of trials—proof that life, despite its struggles, could blossom from frozen ground.

With an armful of wildflowers, Clarissa approached. She lowered herself gently beside the infant, the stems slipping from her hands into her lap as she began to fan the baby's rosy cheeks. Clarissa's weathered hands moved with tenderness, her eyes filled with quiet wonder.

The older woman had been Esther's rock through it all, a tireless pillar of strength always. And it felt fitting, being here with her in this moment, together.

"She's a little ray of sunshine, like her mama," Clarissa said.

Esther raised an eyebrow, a playful grin tugging at her lips.

"Ya sure 'bout that? Ain't always felt like sunshine in me," Esther said.

Clarissa chuckled softly, her gaze drifting from the baby to the water where Ian was splashing around with Benjamin and Rebecca. The children's laughter filled the air, echoing across the lake.

"Honey, why don't ya go join 'em in the water?"

"I'm kinda hot sittin' here," Esther admitted.

"I'll keep an eye on her," Clarissa offered. "She'll be fine." And Esther knew she was right.

Placing her sketchbook on the blanket, Esther tucked her pencil inside to mark her place. With a deep breath, she stood and cast one last glance at her daughter, still sleeping soundly.

As she walked toward the lake, a shirtless Ian met her halfway. Fresh out of the water and breathless, his damp hair clung to his forehead as water dripped from his skin.

A mischievous grin danced on his face as the children called out to Esther.

"You're comin' in, right?" Ian teased.

Esther's mouth curled, her eyes narrowing.

"As long as ya promise not to dunk me," she said, half-serious.

He chuckled, taking her hand.

"I won't, I swear."

"Wait, I don't believe ya," she laughed, resisting as he pulled her closer to the water. "I don't wanna lose my good hairpins."

He stopped, raising a brow in playful challenge.

"Best take them out then," he said.

With a quick smile, Esther let her hair down, the dark waves spilling over her shoulders. She placed her pins carefully on a nearby tree stump before turning back to Ian, who waited patiently, his grin growing into a full smile.

He grasped her fingers again, guiding her into the water. His body moved ahead, scouting the best path as he led her into the lake.

Once they were waist-deep, he pulled her close, his muscular arms wrapping around her. The coolness offered a welcome relief from the heat, and she sighed.

With a protective look, Ian glanced over her shoulder. His expression softened as his gaze settled on the grassy bank where Clarissa sat fanning the baby.

"Is my little Annie-girl still asleep?" he asked.

Esther nodded, resting her head against his chest.

"She is," she said softly.

As the cool water swirled around their legs, Ian held her close—the girl from the hills.

"Esther?" he said, his voice threading through the feeling.

"Hm?" she replied, wrinkling her brow with playful suspicion.

"I really like it when you wear your hair down."

Her eyes sparkled as she smiled back. "I know," she said.

He gave her a playful grunt as he leaned his forehead to hers. And for a moment, the world stilled. The air between them felt electric, the quiet intimacy holding them both suspended.

Ian breathed in her presence, then whispered in her ear, "I want to kiss you. A lot."

She looked up, her blue eyes reflecting the sky.

He took it as his cue, and their lips met in a soft, perfect kiss. They held it, savoring the feeling. When their mouths finally parted, they lingered in the warmth.

He leaned closer again, his warm breath brushing her ear.

"Kids are going to bed early tonight," he whispered, his voice slow, teasing.

Esther's heart fluttered as she understood exactly what he meant.

But before either of them could say more, a splash of cold water interrupted them.

Rebecca and Benjamin laughed, launching a surprise attack as they delighted in their triumph. Water droplets glittered in the golden sunlight, shimmering as they flew through the air.

Ian turned toward his children, a playful gleam in his eyes as he began his swift pursuit. Looking back at Esther, he mouthed, "Now I have a good reason."

"Don't let 'im catch me!" Rebecca squealed, swimming through the water as he chased her. Benjamin followed close behind, trying to send waves of water at his father.

Lively chaos erupted, and Esther found herself caught in the middle as Ian, despite his bulky frame, ducked behind her. He gripped her shoulders playfully, using her as a human shield as he hid from the splashes. Her willowy frame offered little cover as she shrieked in mock protest, a giggle betraying her.

"I only promised I wouldn't dunk you," he said, dodging the sprays as he moved her body back and forth to take the brunt of it.

"Ahh, no! Don't get me all wet!" she cried.

Benjamin smiled with satisfaction.

"Ya know the family rules—don't come to the lake if ya don't wanna get wet!" he hollered as he launched another round.

Rebecca, seeing Esther being teamed up on, came to her defense.

"Pa, no fair! Ya can't hide behind my ma, that's cheatin'!" she said, trying to pull Esther free from his grip with determination.

Esther gave a hearty laugh as she was pulled back and forth.

"Y'all gangin' up on me?" she said as her voice mixed with the sound of splashing.

Pausing, Ian gave Esther a warm kiss on the head before releasing her. It took her breath away.

He loved her, she thought, letting the feeling wash over her.

Drawn back into the water fight, she moved to take her playful revenge.

Life felt perfect, happiness shimmering across the water in the warm glow of the afternoon.

It was one of those rare moments—the kind that washed away past worries, leaving only the pure joy of being together.

A family.

Their hearts light as a breeze made its way down from the Blue Hollow Hills. It rippled across the lake like a song, now written in their love and devotion.

From the shore, Clarissa watched with a contented smile. Little Annie stirred, her tiny hand twitching before settling again as the old woman softly rubbed her tummy.

Reflecting on the souls around her, Clarissa felt a deep, grateful peace. With a soft whisper, she offered a prayer to the wind that stirred through the trees.

"Thank you, dear Lord, for hearing me…"

Epilogue: Tennessee, 2023

The evening sun poured through the tall windows of the Old Reed Estate, casting a warmth over the room. Dust motes floated lazily in the amber beams, creating halos that gave the space a dreamlike quality.

The house, having withstood the passage of years, was like a vessel that had absorbed a lifetime of memories. It had borne witness to love and loss, joy and sorrow.

But today, the air held a unique feeling—one of jubilation.

Through the open window, the hum of voices mingled with the rustle of trees. In the distance, children's laughter echoed, weaving into the fabric of the day.

Inside, seated at the same grand desk, sat Marissa's grandmother. Her hands, still graceful despite the passage of time, cradled the beautifully bound book. *Hymns of Blue Hollow.*

This memoir—this sacred piece of family history—had arrived just that afternoon, delivered into her hands by her sweet great-granddaughter, Marissa, in a moment that seemed to connect generations with a single, unbroken thread of time.

The old woman rose from her seat as she made her way to a nearby bookshelf. Among the many cherished volumes sat a delicate, flower-printed box, its edges worn. She carried it back to the desk, sitting down with a thoughtful sigh.

As she lifted the lid, her fingers brushed against the old hymn book inside. Time had taken its toll on the fragile pages—brittle now, its cover bearing the marks of countless hands and many years.

It had once belonged to Esther—a testament to a life lived through trial and love, hardship and redemption—a relic she had discovered tucked away after her mother's passing.

The book was filled with the songs of a young girl, born in the hills, reflecting her fight to carve out a life she didn't know she was worthy of.

It told of a journey back to the family she had lost, and the home that had been waiting for her.

Setting it down gently, her fingers returned to the newly bound volume resting on her desk. She opened it, turning to the first page, where, in elegant script, the words were written—*To my mother, Esther, my best friend.*

The woman smiled softly to herself as she gazed at the dedication. The memories of her mother, the Old Reed Estate, and the many days spent learning about the land and its people flooded her heart.

She had lived with those stories painted in her mind all her life, but seeing them bound in this book—her mother's story preserved for generations to come—filled her with a deep and overwhelming gratitude.

Turning the newly printed book over in her hands, she felt the leather smooth under her touch. On the back, inside the cover, was a photograph—one of herself. Beneath the image, the name read *Rebecca "Bitty" Huggler-Dubois.*

Standing slowly, she hugged the book to her chest, allowing herself a moment of stillness. The lines around her eyes told stories of laughter, while the softness in her gaze reflected the love she'd been gifted for a lifetime.

Rebecca made her way down the stairs toward the back door. Her footsteps echoed softly as she moved through the old kitchen, almost expecting to see her Aunt Clarissa there, cooking at the stove. Her eyes drifted to the old table, worn smooth from decades of meals and hands.

She paused at the threshold, her hand resting on the weathered doorframe, remembering how her father's broad shoulders once filled it—the smile he wore as he greeted everyone after a long day.

The air outside was warm and fragrant, carrying with it the scent of wildflowers, the kind she liked to pick as a child, filling her with memories of warm months.

As Rebecca stepped out, she was greeted by the sight of her family—a large, joyful group, gathered together with loving faces, all mingling as one.

The estate's sprawling backyard was alive with the sounds of laughter and conversation, the clinking of glasses, and the rustling of leaves in the late summer breeze.

Children played where part of the orchard had once stood, now covered in grass, their happiness echoing. The adults gathered around long wooden tables, sharing stories and memories.

It was a scene of harmony, a testament to the strength of bonds forged over the years.

Rebecca's presence didn't go unnoticed. As she walked across the lawn, a crowd quieted, their eyes turning toward her with a mixture of awe and affection.

She was the matriarch now, the keeper of the family's history, and they all looked to her for guidance and strength.

With a proud, almost triumphant gesture, Rebecca raised the book high above her head. Her voice rang out, clear and strong.

"It's here!" she declared, her eyes shining with emotion.

"She's finally here!"

A cheer went up from the crowd, a collective outpouring of joy and celebration. They knew what this book meant—what it represented. It was more than just a collection of photos and stories; it was a symbol of their family's journey, of the struggles they had overcome, and the love that had sustained them through it all.

Rebecca lowered the book and held it close to her chest once more. She glanced around at all the faces—this story, the land, it lived in all of them.

Like a hymn sung softly in the stillness of a Sunday morning, the legacy of the Old Reed Estate had been passed down through the generations.

As the sun dipped lower in the sky, casting a warm golden glow over the gathering, Rebecca felt a deep sense of peace settle over her. She had lived a long and full life. And though it had not been without its hardships, she knew now that it had all been worth it. That the past, with all its pain and triumphs, had brought them to this moment—a moment of unity, of love, of family.

Rebecca closed her eyes for a brief moment, letting the sounds wash over her like a soothing melody.

And in that moment, she felt her mother, Esther, standing beside her—watching over them all with a smile, her long hair softly moving in the breeze.

Author's Note

Thank you for reading.

If you enjoyed *Hymns of Blue Hollow*, I would be so grateful if you took a moment to leave a review on **Amazon, Goodreads**, or **BookBub**. Your words help more than you know and allow more readers to discover Esther and Ian's story. From the bottom of my heart, I appreciate each and every one.

—

The story doesn't end here—
Book 2: *Where the River Settles*
Book 3: *Held in the Rising Smoke*
Book 4: *Forged by Wind and Song*
Book 5: *Lost Beneath the Stone & Sky*

To stay updated on this ongoing saga and be the first to learn about new releases, exclusive content, and behind-the-scenes updates, you can find me here:

Website: HymnsofBlueHollow.com
Facebook: Hymns of Blue Hollow
TikTok: @kemma_indie_author
Instagram: @KemmaMarShall
YouTube: @HymnsofBlueHollowBookTrailer

Thank you for being part of this journey, for making the Blue Hollow Hills your home, and for hearing its call.